GOING BEYOND THE CALL OF DUTY...

"Stop," she said. "I don't want to hear anymore." As she stared at him, her mind raced with questions. Yes, she had been the one to suggest he go out with other women, didn't mean she wanted to hear the details. "If it was that easy to do, then why didn't you go on and sleep with her?" As she asked this question, a cold lump formed in the pit of her stomach.

Clayton studied Vi, her sharp tone giving him pause. Looking heavenward, he swiped a hand down his face, warring with telling her the truth. "Because I didn't want to make love to her..." The words hung in the air between them. "When my hand covered her small breast, my mind imagined another, more of a handful, much softer," he finally said.

Pinning her with a penetrating gaze, he moved closer. "In my arms, her small frame made me conjure up softer, much fuller curves. I imagined a fuller mouth too, one you could nibble on and sink your teeth into." He paused as if gathering his thoughts. "Everything about her was wrong because... all I could think of was you," he said in a strangled tone.

Closing the distance separating them, Clay suddenly reached for her. Before she knew what was happening, Vi found herself hauled up against him, locked in his embrace. Her hands were trapped between their bodies, the fingers splayed out on his chest as she stared up into his smoldering eyes.

"Clayton... wh...what are you doing?" His nearness robbed her of the ability to move. She stood in his arms, watching his descent as he lowered his head and kissed her. It was a very tender kiss, totally at odds with the tension she felt in the bunched muscles of the arms holding her. Vi didn't have time to respond, it was over in seconds and he lifted his head.

"Mmmmm...this was missing, this softness," he whispered close to her ear. "She wasn't soft like this Vi...like you, and I knew immediately, I couldn't sleep with her."

1

To Clayton, my soul-mate and two of the greatest young men, Marques and Branden- thanks for all your love and support. Thanks to Marcia and Jim for taking me on an editorial journey, it wasn't easy but we did it. Dante-many thanks. Lastly, I need to thank my Lord and Savior, Jesus Christ.

ISBN: 978-0-6152-1267-8

To Love & Protect

Copyright © 2007 by Lynn McCall

Landmarq Management, Inc.

Printed in the United States of America

If you enjoyed reading this book I would love to hear from you. Write to me at – lynnmccall08@earthlink.net or landmarqgroup@earthlink.net

Be blessed,

Lynn McCall

To Love & Protect

By Lynn McCall

CHAPTER

ONE

Craig's watch lay on the table near her bed. Reaching over, he picked it up and saw it was just a few minutes past ten. Although he had a lot to do today, it was still early and those things could wait. Deciding to linger a bit longer, Craig turned over and got more comfortable. It was very warm and incredibly soft there, so he nestled in close behind her. Like a spoon, he molded his long, muscular frame around her softness. Her breathing changed, and she stirred in her sleep when his large hand slid over the shapely rise of her hip.

Not wanting to wake her, Craig's hand stilled. Waiting, he propped his head in the palm of his hand and studied her profile. She resembled an angel – a very flushed and sexually satisfied angel – but an angel nonetheless. As his eyes rolled over her perfect form, he wondered if angels made love like she did. Did they moan and climax so hard it made a man want to weep? When he was certain she was asleep again, his hand resumed its delicate dance across her flesh. Breathing in her scent, his fingers swept lightly over her rounded belly until they reached the underside of her warm, soft breast. More than a handful, he cupped its weight in his hand and instantly his mind played out the way she'd arched against him just a few hours ago, whimpering as he'd taken that tiny swollen crest deep inside his mouth. With that thought, other images danced through his mind. Images of their bodies entwined, straining against one another, until they reached that place where nothing mattered but the two of them—nothing mattered except that moment.

These wayward thoughts caused his body to harden and it wasn't long before his light caress became more insistent. Aroused by his touch, Casey awoke and let out a deep sigh. Stretching her limbs, she rolled over to face him and planted a light kiss on his mouth. Like a flower in search of rain, his body sprang to life as she smiled at him. In the next instant he watched her close her eyes again and unceremoniously throw her leg and one slender arm across his body. Draped freely across his chest, her soft blond hair tickled his chin where her head lay close to his heart.

Craig gathered her close and thought about the reason he'd stopped by this morning. Although this was as good a time as any to discuss it, he hesitated because when he'd brought it up in the past it led to an argument. Not eager to bring it up just yet, he looked around her small apartment very slowly, diverting his thoughts. A slight smile curved his lips as Craig thought about how many times they both joked about her apartment being so small that a person couldn't even change his mind. A frown creased his brow as he thought about the countless times he'd asked Casey to move in with him. Finding a bigger place for the two of them, Craig assured her, would be no problem. She had refused him each time, patiently explaining that she wanted to stay independent, having suffered several failed relationships in the past. Thinking about those past relationships, Craig's mind wandered to the first time they'd met over four months ago. It was a Saturday night...

When his shift ended that night, Craig had decided to stick around to finish up some paperwork. Casey had been a victim of domestic abuse, and came to the police station that night to file charges against some asshole boyfriend who had roughed her up pretty badly. Normally women in her situation looked defeated and scared when, and if, they came to the police. But, not this woman. While she sat in the squad room waiting for someone to take her complaint, Craig noted her expressive eyes, soft-looking full lips and the slight lift of her small, proud chin. Her light, mocha skin tone was in direct contrast to the midnight blue of her eyes, set nicely in a classic face surrounded by a mass of long, honey gold curls. He figured she was either a very, tanned white woman or a mix of something else, although he couldn't be sure. Somehow Craig found himself mesmerized by her. Glancing around the squad room, Craig noticed the other officers on duty were either on the phone or busy with someone else. Even though he was officially off the clock, Craig decided to take her statement and made his way over to the desk where she sat. With quiet resolve in her eyes, she looked up at him as he sat down and prepared to question her. Beyond the black eye and bruising, her beauty and vulnerability struck a cord deep within him.

Before she left the squad room that day, Casey asked him if she would receive police protection from the guy who beat her up. He didn't want to come right out and tell her that all they could do was follow-up on the leads she'd given them and try to track the guy down. For some odd reason, Craig found himself drawn to her and since that night began checking in on her every other day. Their relationship started off innocently enough and, after a while, they started spending a little time together, just talking. They soon decided to stop fighting the mutual attraction that had flared between them almost from the beginning. Giving up the pretense of trying to be friends had led to some very intense sexual encounters, which had eventually led to this... and this was nice.

Lying here now, he realized it wasn't just about the sex anymore because lately he found himself beginning to want more—much more. The wanting made the words tumble from his lips and, before he knew it, Craig blurted out what had been troubling him. "Casey, I want you to come for dinner this Sunday and meet my family," he said flatly.

He felt her stiffen in his arms and the delicate fingers threading through the dense hair on his chest stilled. Casey let out a long sigh, trying to figure out how best to respond. "Craig, you know I can't." She rose from the bed, taking her warmth with her, striding naked toward her tiny bathroom. "We've been over this before," she added in an off-handed manner. "Why don't we talk about it later?"

As she started to leave the room, her plan to postpone this discussion dissipated with Craig's next words. "I'm tired of keeping our relationship a secret," he told her.

She turned to him; her expression shuttered and she replied in a measured tone. "Baby, you said you had a lot to do today, I promise you we'll discuss this later." Then she closed the bathroom door, cutting off any further discussion.

When Casey was safely inside the bathroom, she stood with her back braced against the door, knowing she'd just dodged a huge argument. It had been such a beautiful morning and Casey didn't relish spoiling it. But when Craig got something in his head, he went after it with a single- minded purpose. She knew the more insistent he became, the more resistant she would become. Leaving the room was the only way she could be sure they wouldn't end up fighting again.

Turning on the tap water, she gingerly stepped into the shower and stood under the warm spray. For some reason her mind drifted back to the first time she'd seen Craig...

She'd been scared shitless. Raul would be furious if he knew where she was and what she was about to do. It was bad enough he'd done this twice now and she'd let him get away with it. The first time he'd hit her was right after he moved to town. After a few weeks of unemployment, Raul had gotten drunk one night. Casey remembered that when she tried to take the bottle away, he'd smacked her clear across the room. She'd been a fool to let him stay with her in the first place and now here she was, sitting in this police station wanting to put his sorry ass away.

Taking a deep cleansing breath, Casey closed her eyes and started counting. She thought that if one of these cops didn't come over here by the time she counted to ten, she would just get up and leave. Then she opened her eyes and saw him. He introduced himself as Officer Craig Simpson. Unable to concentrate on what the man said after that, Casey's jaw dropped as she stared at him. The man before her was extremely tall, well built and handsome beyond belief. He had a wide, sensuous mouth with very dark eyes that matched his equally dark, milk chocolate skin. When he flashed it briefly at her, his smile made her heart leap.

Whoa – down girl! Mentally admonishing herself, Casey tried to clear her mind. It wasn't like she'd never seen a good-looking man before. Sure, this guy was clearly not hard on the eyes, but she wasn't here for this. Suddenly, she remembered she was sitting in a police station—with a black eye and bruises—waiting to press charges against the jackass who'd done this.

Ohmigod! She thought. She had bruises and a black eye. Slowly, it dawned on her that while she was salivating over this cop, he was probably repulsed by what he saw. Now self conscious about the condition of her battered face, she bent her head and tried to reign in the wayward thoughts racing through her mind. Trying hard to focus, she realized he was saying something to her. Unfortunately, she'd been so self-absorbed with her own thoughts that she didn't hear what he said. Luckily, his appealing mouth twisted into a warm smile that set her stomach fluttering and repeated his question.

"Ma'am, I need to know who did this to you."

She noticed he had very kind eyes and Casey immediately felt like she could trust him. That one question started the tidal wave of tears she'd been holding back and it brought out all the bad feelings and regrets she had about her past relationships. And so, she told this man, this officer, this stranger everything. She told him who'd beaten her up and all the things that had led up to it. It felt good to tell someone, to finally let it all out. When she finished her story, he smiled at her and briefly covered her hand with his. He hadn't judged her and, in that moment, she felt like she'd found a friend.

Standing under the water, she shut her eyes against the memories and immediately felt ashamed. Craig was everything she had ever wanted in a man. He was wonderful and kind and, lately, it seemed all she ever did was hurt him. He knew how to make her laugh and he definitely knew how to make her burn. Above all, he made her feel whole and hadn't cared about her past and or what other people might think. She wanted nothing more than to feel like he did, but she couldn't. They needed more time, she reasoned. Their relationship was too new and she wanted to savor these wonderful feelings just a bit longer, before they had to end. The fear of his family rejecting her and the very real fear that she might lose him if he had to choose between his family and her, terrified Casey. What if he had to chose, what would he do? What would she do? She couldn't bear to think about it.

The water grew hotter, steaming up the mirror and tiles. As it cascaded over her skin, she thought about losing him. She knew if she turned him down again, it would only hurt him. Although his request seemed so simple, it really wasn't. But Casey knew she couldn't put him off forever. Eventually she would have to deal with all of this. Whatever the outcome, she feared it would not be in her favor. The salt of her tears mixed with the warm spray beating down on her as she laid her head against the shower wall and cried.

In the bedroom, Craig lay staring at the ceiling. Although she'd refused him every other time in the past, her response today angered him. At first he didn't mind keeping their relationship a secret. He respected how she felt and realized she was afraid his family would think she wasn't good enough for him. In all honesty, he thought, she was probably right about how they would react. But dammit, he was a grown man. He didn't have to answer to anyone about anything. What he did and whom he did it with was none of anyone's business. He cared about Casey, and he was certain she cared about him too. He had no idea how or when it happened—because he certainly didn't go looking for it—but somehow loving her had snuck up on him.

He had to admit that he like to at least tell his mother. He was sure she would be cool with this. Since his father's death, Craig and his mother had grown very close. Comfortable around one another, he and his mom talked openly about everything and it just didn't feel right not telling her about Casey. Subsequently, he talked to his mom a lot less these days for fear that he would let something slip. Folding his arms behind his head, he continued staring at the ceiling, feeling the anger that rose in him moments ago slowly drain away. She just needed more time, he reasoned, and eventually she would come around. Deciding not to push the matter further, Craig heaved a sigh of resignation and got out of bed.

The shower was running so she didn't hear him enter the bathroom. As soon as he opened the door he heard Casey crying. He swore viciously. She cried at the drop of a hat lately, but this time she was crying for a reason, and the reason was him. Feeling like crap, he slowly pulled back the shower curtain and joined her under the warm spray of water. Pulling her close, he wrapped his arms tight around her and captured her lips in a tender kiss.

After a time, Craig got out and dried himself off. Padding barefoot into her small kitchen, he opened the refrigerator and surveyed its contents. He had all the ingredients to make omelets, except eggs and milk. She was washing her hair when he re-opened the bathroom door, so he raised his voice a little so she could hear him over the running water.

"Babe, you're all out of milk and eggs. I'm going out to get some provisions. Be back in a flash." She muffled something he couldn't hear over the noise of the shower.

Walking to the corner grocery, Craig made a mental list of a few more things he thought Casey might need. He would have liked to spend the entire day with her, but he'd promised his mom he'd stop by this morning and he had plans to hang out with the guys this afternoon. Oh, well, he thought, after breakfast he'd better get moving.

There were three or four more customers in the market when he walked in. Craig picked up eggs, milk and juice and then wandered toward the back of the store to grab some bacon. He couldn't remember if she liked turkey bacon or beef. As he pondered what type of bacon to buy, he felt something hard jab him in the side. When he tried to look behind him to see who the fuck had rolled up on him like this, Craig felt the barrel of a gun poke him hard in the ribs. As he glanced down, there was no mistaking the gun was real. His mind raced trying to figure a way out of this.

"Hey man, you don't want to do this. Take my money or whatever you want and leave," he said, as the items in his hands fell to the floor.

"Shut the fuck up, yah' hear. Just shut the fuck up."

"Hey man, I don't know you, but listen you don't want to do this," Craig's voice trailed off as his mind searched for some way to reason with this asshole.

"I know who you are, you bastard."

In the store a small crowd had gathered and some of the patrons turned a curious gaze on the men at the back of the store. The barrel of the weapon poking him was jammed harder into his side. Somehow he had angered this man and Craig wasn't exactly sure why.

"Listen," he started again, but was instantly cut off.

"Shut up you bastard. I know you been bangin' her. She thought she could get rid of me, well she ain't gettin' rid of me that easy."

"Listen, you don't know what you're doing here, I'm a cop," Craig said, trying desperately to reign in his own mounting anger and fear.

"Yeah, I know who you are. I'm gonna' fix it so both of you won't be doing nobody anymore, let alone each other."

Sweat accumulated on his upper lip and under his armpits, as Craig realized this was probably the asshole that beat Casey up several months ago. The police investigation at the time hadn't found a trace of the guy. Eventually, Craig had chalked the whole thing up to a punk boyfriend who beat up his girl when he was drunk, then split town when he finally sobered up. His mind turned the situation over and over frantically. How long had this scumbag been watching them? Using all the force within him to wrestle this piece of shit to the floor, Craig twisted slightly and grabbed for the gun. Both he and the gunman rolled around on the floor several times, each with their hands locked around the gun before Craig was able to land a left hook to the side of his face. Craig felt he was going to gain the advantage when the gunman tried to crawl away. He grabbed his ankle, pulling him back. With a powerful lunge, Craig landed on top of the gunman, at the precise moment an elderly woman came down the aisle. The woman screamed when she saw the two men fighting on the floor. Suddenly, the gun went off.

For Clayton Marshall, life couldn't get any sweeter. He had the day off, it was payday and he couldn't wait to pick up his brand new Ford F150. It was an awesome piece of machinery, boasting power windows, locks, doors, seats, a moon roof and a state-of-the art Bose sound system. Outside, it was the ultimate man's truck with 16 liters of powerful V8 under her hood, aluminum rims and enough chrome to choke a horse. Yeah, it was quite a beauty and he couldn't wait to pick her up. All he needed now was his paycheck.

He opened the door to his old Buick and a blast of sweltering heat hit him square in the face—*reality check*. Oh well, he thought, this would be his last day driving in this old bucket of bolts, with its rusted paint job and busted air conditioning. Fortunately there was nothing wrong with the radio. Turning it on, he slid behind the wheel. Beyonce blasted through the speakers, singing about being a "Survivor." Making his way to the station, Clay put the car in gear and shook his head to the music, keeping time with the beat. Traffic on Route 110 was light at this time of morning and he made it to the station in less than ten minutes. Pulling into the rear parking lot of the Amityville Police Station, Clay backed his old clunker in between two black and white squad cars.

Cutting the engine, Clay donned a pair of dark, regulation issue sunglasses and got out of the car, whistling. God, it really was a perfect day, the sun sat high in a cloudless blue sky and its intensity at this hour of the morning was indicative of how the temperature would probably soar by noontime. He and the guys had made plans to meet at Amity Beach this afternoon. Smaller and less crowded than Jones Beach, Amity Beach was the perfect place for an outing. Craig was picking up the beer, Joe was bringing his Jet ski and Jake had the use of his parent's speed boat for the day. Everyone else had been assigned to bring something, so they would have plenty of hot dogs, soda, chips and beer.

Using his access card, Clay entered through the rear door of the station. Still whistling, he ambled over to the mail slots and noticed Stokes and Piterrelli standing over a desk watching something on the monitor. Whatever they were staring at must be pretty serious, he thought, because they didn't look up when he came in.

"What's up guys?" he asked of no one in particular as he surveyed the squad room.

Both officers looked up from what they were doing, but did not reply. Stopping at the mail area, he poked his hand into his slot and came up with a white envelope. Sliding his index finger into the folds, he ripped an envelope open and announced. "Finally...payday couldn't get here fast enough!"

Reading his check and scanning the inserts that came along with it, Clay swung around and rested a lean hip against a nearby desk. "That's it guys, its official now. In the next half hour I'll be picking up my new ride and sending my old bucket of bolts to its final resting place," he said. "Gentlemen, get ready to stand in line to say your final goodbyes."

Suddenly, it struck him that neither Stokes nor Piterrelli had moved, or said a word since he came in. Two more uniformed officers came out of the break room at that moment. They too had nothing to say.

"Newt, Captain Jackson," Clay's greeting died on his lips. Both of them looked as solemn as Stokes and Piterrelli. Warily, he looked around the squad room. Recognizing the silence and the somberness of the room all too well, he thought this can't be good.

"Hey guys, com'on what's the deal?"

His Captain, Mike Jackson, grudgingly spoke up. "It's bad news Clay. An officer went down; it just came in on the wire."

Clayton's stomach suddenly lurched up then dropped down in fear. "Who?" The grave silence that followed his question seemed to last a hundred seconds. "Who?" Clay repeated, his fear mounting, as the seconds ticked by.

In an almost inaudible voice, Jackson replied quietly, "Craig."

"Craig?" Clayton's features twisted in pain and disbelief. No, they couldn't be talking about his roommate, his partner, his best friend, he thought. "That can't be. Somebody's made a terrible mistake."

Approaching him, Captain Jackson placed an understanding hand on his shoulder. Rejecting it, Clayton pushed away from the desk he'd been leaning on, and stood, inadvertently shaking Jackson's hand off his shoulder.

"No, you're all wrong. He's not even on duty today. He told me he was stopping by his mom's this morning and running some errands before joining us later at the beach."

"He wasn't on duty Clay. Craig walked in on a robbery in progress at a convenience store on Chestnut. He was gone by the time the paramedics arrived."

As the certainty of those words raced through Clay's nerve endings, his knees felt weak and his heart sped up, pounding violently against his chest wall.

"Oh shit," he whispered. Moving backwards blindly, he encountered the edge of the desk he'd been leaning against just moments ago. He sagged against it for support, lifted both hands and covered his face.

"No, no way," he said in disbelief. "This can't be happening."

Jackson spoke again. "We think the gunman panicked when Craig walked in and...."

Captain Jackson's voice faded as the shock hit Clay like a blow to the gut. Outwardly he schooled his features into hard, grim lines. But inwardly, it felt like his insides were being ripped apart. How? How could this have happened? He dealt with tragedy on a daily basis. Death, after all, was part of the job. This was different; he'd never dealt with death striking this close to home. Struggling with the conflicting emotions gripping his insides, he drew on the investigative training and methodical thinking of a trained peace officer. This training allowed him to gain a measure of control and, when he spoke again, his demeanor was seemingly calm and his voice appeared steady.

"Was he wearing his vest?" He asked, even though he knew the answer.

"No, he wasn't. He wasn't carrying his service revolver either, not that he would have had a chance to use it, before..." Jackson paused to clear his throat, precluding the need for further details.

Clayton's throat closed up on him, his chest tightened painfully and his knees began to shake. But he held his ground, operating on auto pilot and asked the questions he would normally ask as if Craig were no more than another crime victim.

"Who responded to the call?"

"Piterrelli."

Clayton turned to look at the young officer. His head was down and he was noticeably shaken.

"Piterrelli?"

Piterrelli was silent. His eyes were red as if he'd been crying and his lips were pulled into a grim line.

"Come on, man. Tell me," he urged.

"I'm sorry Clay, Craig was dead by the time I got there and the perp was long gone."

Blinding anger crashed down on Clay, making him want to strike out at something, anything. Startling everyone, he grabbed a nearby chair and flung it forcefully across the room.

Overcome with rage, he shouted, "Dammit, why didn't he wait for me. I offered to drop him off at his mother's this morning, and help him with whatever he had to do. If only he'd let me help him, maybe…" His voice trailed off as a thought suddenly occurred to him.

What the hell was Craig doing over on Chestnut anyway?"

Piterrelli reached out to comfort him, but Clayton shrugged away from his touch.

"Don't! Just, just leave me alone. I need…I just need a minute." Turning, Clayton walked several feet away and planted his hands on his hips.

"Jesus, motherfuckin' Christ!" he shouted. Panic gripped him as a surge of adrenaline shot through him, simultaneously making his limbs quiver and shake, and turning his body hot and cold.

Clayton knew people acted this way in these situations, but had not fully understood them until now. Being a cop, he had seen grief take many forms. When told a loved one was dead, most people would break down hysterically. Occasionally, their grief took the form of anger and some people lost it entirely. Suddenly, he realized it was happening to him. He was losing it. This all- consuming rage coursed through him, making him ready to do battle with anything and everything around him instead of doing what he desperately wanted to do, which was cry for the loss of a best friend. That realization caused the anger to drain away, and left him feeling weak and sick to his stomach. Then the tears finally came. They were big, hot stinging tears that blurred his vision and clogged his throat so badly he thought he would choke.

"Aw, Craig," he was able to get past the lump in his throat. This time he didn't shrink away from the comfort being offered by his fellow officers, as they came up behind and stood beside him, gripping his shoulders and touching his back. With emotion strangling their voices, it was hard to tell exactly who was comforting whom. Clay turned slightly, and suddenly found Captain Jackson's big, burly arms around him, clasping him hard like a father would comfort his son.

Standing in the Captain's strong embrace, Clayton heard random comments from his fellow officers.

"He was a good man, a good cop."

"Damn, he was only twenty four years old. Hell, he'd hardly even lived."

"I'm sure gonna' miss him."

Straightening, Clayton fought and won a measure of control. Studying him, to make certain he was going to be alright, Captain Jackson thumped him on the back and released him. Clayton slumped into a nearby chair and covered his face with both his hands. Vivid pictures flashed behind his closed lids as he replayed the past four hours in his mind...

When he heard the front door open, Clay rolled out of bed. Scratching his chest, he ambled down the hall and almost ran smack into Craig.

"Whatup boy?" Craig said to him in greeting, as he raced past him. "I gotta' piss like a racehorse," he told Clay as he dashed past him in the hallway on his way to the bathroom. A moment later, Clay heard the bathroom door slam in Craig's room. Shaking his head, Clay went into their small kitchen to make some coffee. When Craig came in about fifteen minutes later, Clay offered him a cup.

"Nah," he said and opened the refrigerator. Rummaging around in there for quite a while, Craig finally came out with an open carton of orange juice.

"So, what time are you picking up the new ride?" he asked Clay.

Clay noticed Craig had taken a shower and changed into khaki shorts and a faded Mets T-shirt. His keys were in his hand, and he was obviously on his way out again. That was nothing unusual. He knew how hard it was to work all night then come right in and go to sleep.

"This afternoon, before I head to the beach; you still gonna' meet up with us later?" Clay asked.

Craig stood by the refrigerator, gulping down OJ. He burped loudly, showing his appreciation of Florida's finest, before answering.

"Yeah man, I'm there. But first, I gotta' stop by my mom's," he'd said. "The mower's on the fritz and I promised I'd take a look at it before she went out and brought a new one."

That was just like him, Clay thought, remembering how good Craig was to his mother.

Craig's mom!

Oh, Jesus, Craig's poor mom. Alarm raced through him, thinking about her. His mom had been through enough already, she didn't need this. He couldn't let some stranger knock on her door, and deliver bad news like this.

Swiping a hand across his eyes, he stood and faced Captain Jackson.

"Has anyone informed his family, Sir?"

"Not yet," Jackson replied. "That task would be mine or Rev. Winters."

Clayton knew Rev. Winters. He'd been police chaplain for as long as Clay had been on the force.

"I'd like to do it sir, if it's alright with you."

"You sure you're up for that?"

"I know his family, sir. It might be somewhat easier coming from someone they know."

Captain Jackson paused a moment before saying, "You don't look so good Marshall. Sit down."

He took the chair the Captain motioned him into, trying to come to grips with this but also knowing he couldn't let anyone else tell Craig's family. After a few seconds, he looked up at his superior and pressed Jackson for an answer.

"Well, Captain?"

Considering the younger man's request, Captain Jackson agreed it might be best if Clay were the one to break the news.

"Ok, if you feel up to it, go ahead."

Relieved, but still visibly shaken, Clayton muttered. "It's still so hard to believe." Clasping his hands together, he bent at the waist and rested his elbows on his knees. "A couple of hours ago he was standing in the kitchen, eating cereal!"

"I know. Just yesterday he invited me to the beach with you guys after my shift ended today," Piterrelli added.

Looking closely at the younger officer, Clayton saw pain etched in his features. Piterrelli was built like a wide receiver with a full head of gray hair, even though he was only in his thirties. Just last month he'd invited the entire squad to his sister's wedding in Little Italy. It didn't matter that Clay and Craig were black and Piterrelli was white. The officers in his department were close knit and looked out for each other like brothers. You never knew what situation you might walk into being a cop. It helped to know you had a brother, someone you could trust, to watch your back. This brotherhood went beyond race, religion and all color lines. To these guys, the only important color—the only color that mattered—was blue.

"Hell, Mike, I'm sorry man. You're the one who responded to the call and here I am falling apart over here, when you must have gotten the biggest shock."

"Yeah…" unable to say more Piterrelli, turned away to dry his eyes.

It was Clay's turn to do the comforting. He rose and draped an arm across Piterrelli's shoulder, giving his thick shoulders a squeeze.

"Where is he?"

"He's at the morgue Clay, but don't go over there and don't let his mother go man. He was pretty messed up."

Clay gave his shoulder one last squeeze then dropped his right hand to his side.

"This is going to kill his mom."

"Yeah."

Whatever Piterrelli was going to say was cut short when the front door opened, and Reverend Winters strode in. In his sixties with slightly graying hair, Reverend Winters had kind eyes behind thick, corrective lenses.

"We've lost a good man," he said to the entire room. The calm, subdued quality of the reverend's voice reached each officer in the room.

"The last time I talked to Craig he told me that he couldn't understand why people stayed at a job they hated. 'How do they get up every morning? I love my job,' he said. 'I love getting up every morning knowing I can help people."

Reverend Winters knew everyone grieved differently. Some of these officers would work through it by themselves and others may need to talk with someone to come to terms with their grief.

"Maybe you'll all feel a little better if you remember that. Craig was a great policeman, he was a good man and most importantly, Craig Simpson was a happy man," he added. "I believe we could all use a prayer right now." Grasping the hand of the officer nearest him, Reverend Winters addressed the room. "Let's join hands."

Clay barely heard the reverend's words. His mind was filled with concern for Craig's family, especially his mother. She'd already lost a husband, now he had to tell her she'd lost a son. Craig also had a younger brother, Tony, who was only fourteen, and sister, Janae who was twenty one. While Mrs. Simpson had two other kids, Craig was the oldest and the one she relied on most since her husband passed away eight years ago.

The prayer ended, pulling Clayton back to the present and Reverend Winters walked over to where he stood.

"Captain Jackson said you wanted to inform the family, is that right son?

"Yes sir, that's right."

"Son, if you feel you must, by all means, do so. But, are you sure you can handle it?"

"I'll be fine."

Reverend Winters studied him. Satisfied, he nodded his agreement. "Okay son. Come and see me later if you need to talk, alright?

CHAPTER
THREE

Cynthia Edwards parked her car in back of the salon, entering through the back door of Nu U and turned on the lights and air conditioning. Although she only worked in the shop three days a week for a few hours, Cynthia liked to come in early, finding that was the time of day when she got the most done. During the workday, when the shop was in full swing, there were too many distractions. The Nu U staff normally got in around ten and they were a lively bunch. After they arrived and the shop opened, piped in music would play on overhead speakers and a steady flow of customers came in throughout the day.

Cynthia did not have to work; her husband's business did quite well, but these few hours a week were just what she needed at this point in her life. When Vi asked her to come and work at Nu U a few years back, Cynthia had been surprised. After all, she had been dead set against Vi opening up this beauty shop in the first place. As she turned the coffeemaker on, she thought about that time. It had been a difficult time for both of them.

"Vi, you can't be serious. I mean, opening a beauty parlor at your age. What do you know about running a business?"

"It's not a beauty parlor, it's going to be a salon/day spa and for your information I plan to take management courses."

Cynthia could tell Vi was upset, but then so was she. She was, after all, the older, more responsible one and she couldn't stand by and let Vi squander her dead husband's life insurance money on a whim.

"Vi, don't be foolish. It's ridiculous for you to think about going back to school at this stage of your life, much less trying to start a business."

Unable to hold her temper any longer, Vi told her sister, "Thanks for the support Cyn. I don't know why I'm even discussing this with you. I'm a grown woman and I don't need your permission."

"What you need to do is leave that money in the bank and work on finding a husband and father for your kids," Cynthia shot back.

"Oh, like the last jackass you set me up with? No thanks."

After that, their discussion deteriorated into a shouting match. Afterwards, Vi didn't speak to Cynthia for over two months. Although Cynthia still felt strongly about the choices Vi was making, she did start to miss spending time with the family. Cynthia and her husband had no children. Because of this she treated Vi's children like her own, showering a multitude of affection on them since they were babies.

Within the first few weeks after their argument, Cynthia started feeling badly, but no amount of coaxing would make Vi come for Sunday dinner or talk to her on the phone. Vi made a point to only spoke to Cynthia out of necessity. Fortunately, Cynthia was able to keep up with things through her nephew, Craig. She began calling Vi's house when she knew Vi would not be home and knew Craig would pick up the phone. It was through Craig that Cynthia found out Vi did, in fact, enroll in those business courses at night. He also told her Vi found a part-time job that made it possible for her to be home when the kids got home from school. What she didn't know was that during those tough times, Vi used the insurance money to pay the bills and take up the slack, while she finished her night classes. Then she did something that some people only dream about all their lives. Vi used what was left of the insurance money and opened her business. Her sole reason for starting the business, she'd told Cynthia later on, was to provide a decent living for her family. As it turned out, the business became much more than that.

When Craig proudly announced to his aunt just how well his mom's shop was doing, Cynthia was more than a little surprised. It appeared Vi had showed them all. Apparently she possessed a business savvy and a natural flair for style that the family didn't know about. Her salon seemed to fill a need in the neighborhood and catered to everyone. Nu U was not just a salon—it was an oasis, where women received pampering from head to toe. Not only did the staff style hair, Craig told his aunt, but they did things Cynthia had never heard of, like body wraps and seaweed treatments. At the time it was the only salon of its kind, and had gained a steady and loyal clientele. After a while Craig got tired of being the middle man, as his mother and aunt's silent feud dragged on several months. Trying to get the two women together again, he decided to tell his mother that Cynthia called him just about every afternoon. At first, Vi was upset. The nerve of Cynthia, she thought, trying to ply her son for information. But even though Cynthia had always been a bossy and stubborn woman, she was still her sister so she needed to be the one to break the ice this time around.

Although, Cynthia wasn't sure why Vi asked her to join her business and do the books, she didn't hesitate to jump at the offer. By mutual agreement, the two sisters never talked about Cynthia's initial lack of support, or just how well Nu U was doing, in spite of her family's initial criticism.

Just then, the bell over the front door chimed, bringing Cynthia back to the present. Andre and Nicole walked in laughing and talking. Seeing Cynthia at the front desk pouring over the books, they greeted her in unison.   These two, Cynthia knew, were Vi's best stylists.   About Vi's age, Nicole wore dread locks and jeans to work every day.   She was a hardworking, single mother of two while Andre seemed to be searching for a new lover just about every other month.   Although a bit talkative, Cynthia thought Nicole was nice enough.   On the other hand, she and Andre seemed to butt heads on a weekly basis.   It wasn't his flamboyant style or the alternative lifestyle he led that annoyed Cynthia so much.   It was his lack of discretion and the obvious delight he took in making sure everyone knew he was gay.   That got on her nerves more times than none, like today.   With obvious distaste, Cynthia eyed Andre's too-tight jeans, shiny pink shirt and the bright yellow highlights in his afro.

While Cynthia Edwards was starting her normal workday, Clayton Marshall left the station feeling anything but normal.   Outside the sun dazzled bright against pristine, white clouds.   The beauty of the day was a mockery.   Putting on his sunglasses to ward off the blazing sun, he walked across the parking lot to his car.   Ignoring the sweltering heat inside his car, Clay got in it, rolled down his driver side window and started the engine. The heat inside the car didn't register as he sat there with the car running, completely forgetting exactly what came next. *Oh yeah, put the car in gear*, he thought and in the next instant he was assailed again by the weight of his grief.   It was so overbearing that it choked him, suffocating him where the heat inside the car had failed to penetrate his senses.   He fought for control, put the car in gear and drove down Route 110 toward the Long Island Expressway.

Clay thought about what he was going to say when he reached her house. Craig and his mom were really close—Clay had never heard anyone praise their mother the way Craig praised his mom.   Their relationship was a level above just love between a mother and son.   They not only loved each other, they respected and admired each other.   It always amazed him how Craig and his mom could talk about anything – money, relationships, sports and politics.   If you didn't know them, you might get the impression they were like a modern day June and Beaver Cleaver.   But, they weren't.   They had their share of disagreements, but the nice thing was they never stayed angry at each other for very long.

Whatever was going on, and there was plenty, she and Craig discussed it. And later Clayton would hear all about it from Craig.   He knew a lot about Mrs. Simpson.   Whenever he spoke about her, the admiration and love in Craig's voice made a hard knot of envy form in the pit of Clayton's stomach. She was an ideal mother—hardworking, capable and compassionate—and over time Clay acquired a deep admiration and respect for her that he'd never known for his own mother.

Out of nowhere, something he thought about earlier came back to him. *What the hell was Craig doing on Chestnut this morning?*

Chestnut was clear across town. It was also the poorest section of town, and as far as Clay knew, Craig had no friends over there. Craig told him this morning he had to stop by his mother's and then run some errands. There were dozens of supermarkets and convenience stores to stop at on this side of town, and Chestnut was no where near his mother's house or on the way to the beach.

A car horn blasted loudly, penetrating Clay's thoughts. His mind registered that he was sitting at a stop sign and apparently holding up traffic. If the line of cars behind him was any indication, he must have been sitting there for a while.

Silently reprimanding himself, Clayton forced his mind to focus on his driving. He needed to get himself together before he reached Mrs. Simpson's house. This was going to be hard enough on her, without him falling apart. Craig had told him once she was one of the strongest women he knew. But, even the strongest people broke down, he thought.

Clay spent the entire drive to her house, lost in thought. As he neared her street, he turned right onto Ronald Drive. It was a nice neighborhood with tree-lined streets, and houses with matching shutters and trim that only added to its quiet charm. It was one of those neighborhoods where everyone knew each other. Her house was up ahead on the right. It was a large colonial with bright green shutters and a white picket fence surrounding the front yard. The front door was painted the same green and flanked on either side by big terracotta pots filled with leafy plants and colorful impatiens. A huge magnolia tree dominated the front lawn, its blossoms hung heavy and full on outstretched limbs. The grass had just been cut and looked healthy and green except for one yellowed spot near the curb. An oscillating sprinkler sat near that yellowed patch, pushing water through in a sweeping, fan motion. Its movement was quiet, monotonous and detached as it threw water across Clayton's passenger side window when he pulled into her driveway.

Clay put the car in park, took the keys out of the ignition, but made no movement to get out. He sat in his hot car looking around at everything and at nothing. Craig's mom had a two car detached garage. Both garage doors stood open because it was broad daylight, so the interior was visible to anyone walking on the street. One side was vacant and in the next stall her car was parked, a late model Japanese import, compact but reliable.

As the sprinkler continued its long sweep, it caught him on the arm and wet his front passenger seat. He reached over and rolled the window up slowly as he studied the sprinkler, not realizing why he even bothered. He sat back and stared again into the garage. Inside various gardening tools and equipment sat near an old gas grill. In the back was a workbench that looked like it hadn't been used in quite a while. Tools hung over the bench and two bikes hung from the rafters above.

He leaned his head back against the headrest and pinched the bridge of his nose as a new wave of sorrow assailed him. It cast an invisible, steel band over him and tightened painfully around his chest. He felt tears sting the back of his eyes and willed them away, refusing to cry again. God, how many times had he done that today? Too many, he thought. Letting out a long sigh, he sat up and tried to get it together, vaguely thinking that she shouldn't leave her garage door open like this. Anyone could walk right up and help themselves. He remembered Craig used to warn his mother about this. Every time he did, she would shrug and tell him "We've known every person in this neighborhood for years and everybody does it. But, if someone walking by decides to steal something, let them. That'll be one less thing to clean up or throw out come fall."

Clay was a police officer and he fully agreed with Craig on this particular subject, because he knew it was dangerous to leave unlocked doors, of any kind, on your property. What if someone tried to hide in there until nightfall? They might attack her when she tried to get in her car, or worse, hide inside her car if she happened to leave the car door unlocked. With Craig gone, who would look out for her now? Who would nag her about closing those garage doors? Who would change the oil in her car if she needed it done or repair all the little things that needed doing when you own a home?

While these questions flitted through his mind, something flickered in his peripheral vision. To his right sat the broken mower Craig was supposed to look at. Among the rusty red paint, some of its newer parts stood out and a few silver bolts, nuts and rubber pieces lay near it, twinkling and shiny in the bright afternoon sunlight.

Damn Craig, why didn't you let me go with you this morning? Maybe, if I'd been there I might have been able to help.

He didn't finish that thought, realizing he could sit here all day and do the "What ifs." What good did that do now? Clayton quickly brushed those thoughts aside, got out of the car and walked up to the front porch.

The woman was too trusting by far. Her front door stood wide open and through the screen door he could see straight through the house. From this vantage point he could see down the dimly lit hallway, and beyond that he could see the kitchen. Sliding glass doors stood open to catch the afternoon breeze. His dark glasses warded off the blinding sunlight overhead as he looked heavenward and took in a fortifying breath. Looking down again at his feet, what he was wearing suddenly dawned on him.

"Damn, I should have changed. Changed to what? What does a person wear when delivering bad news like this? Certainly not worn out, beat-up sandals or bright orange and blue swim trucks.

To make matters worse, he was bare-chested under an old denim shirt, which had lost its buttons in the laundry years ago. Well, he thought, it was too late to change any of that now, and pressed the doorbell. When he did this, his left arm brushed against the screen door by accident, and it swung open.

It was open.

Taking off his dark glasses, Clay placed them in his shirt pocket and peered into the darkened house for signs of life. He pressed the doorbell again and tried to push the screen door closed, but it popped open again. In addition to the mower, it appeared the screen door also needed repair. There were a number of small, but important, repairs to be made around this house. Standing there looking around, he wondered who would do them. He mashed the doorbell again, and this time he heard a feminine voice come from somewhere within the house.

"Craig is that you?" he heard her call out. "Come on in honey, I'm just getting ready for work, I'll be down in a minute."

Clay didn't respond. He slowly entered the front entry hall and pulled the screen closed behind him. There was a staircase on the right as you entered the house, leading upstairs. The sound of running water could be heard up there. The living room was directly to his left and beyond that the formal dining room. In front of him, and at the end of the hall, was the kitchen. A kitchen table sat in the middle of the floor and beyond the table, bright yellow curtains framed a window above the sink. The curtains billowed in and out on the afternoon breeze.

As he waited, his body reacted to the unpleasant task he was about to face. A lump the size of a golf ball lodged itself in his throat and his hands shook. Thinking hard, Clayton realized he didn't know how in the world he was going to do this.

CHAPTER
FOUR

Upstairs, Vivian Simpson ran her hands through curly, dark auburn locks. Her no-nonsense hairstyle was shoulder length and required very little attention, which was just the way she liked it. Although she was too busy to fuss with her own hair, Vi took pride in making sure everyone walking into her salon walked out with spectacular hair.

She was an attractive woman with expressive light brown eyes. She also possessed a pretty good figure for having had three kids, working out and keeping fit because it made her feel good, not so much to attract any man. Besides, between work and the kids, she was way too busy to think about men. After applying a small amount of lipstick, Vi smooched her lips together and peered into the mirror. Satisfied with her reflection, she turned off the faucet and wiped her hands on a nearby towel. Blessed with flawless skin, she'd never worn makeup over her coffee with extra, extra cream complexion.

Just before leaving the bathroom, Vi pumped a dollop of hand crème into her palm, switched off the light and walked through her bedroom. As she zipped down the stairs, working the lotion into her hands, she was brought up short. Vi was expecting Craig to be downstairs. He'd promised to look at the lawnmower today, so she wouldn't have to call the landscaper this weekend. When she saw it wasn't Craig, but his roommate and partner, Clayton Marshall, standing in her living room, she was momentarily confused.

"Hello, Mrs. Simpson."

"Oh, hello Clayton I wasn't expecting Craig to drag you over here to help with this chore, but I guess he needed reinforcements. So, where is he anyway?" She inquired and gave him a bright smile. Not waiting for his answer, she turned away from him and picked up her purse from the desk in the hall.

"I'm sorry to cut into your afternoon like this. I know you guys planned to go down to the shore today. I'm just on my way to work, but if Craig wants, he can take a look at it. If it looks like it will be too involved, it'll keep till tomorrow."

Rummaging around in her purse for her car keys, she turned around to face him and continued to have a one-sided conversation. Glancing at him, she noted his appearance. He wore bright floral swim trunks and an open, tattered denim shirt. Dark glasses hung from the front pocket of his shirt. He and Craig were about the same height, she noted, but Clayton was broader in the shoulders, more muscular and mature looking than her son's tall, lanky swimmer's physique. Also, much fairer than Craig, she supposed his clean-shaven head and equally clean-shaven jaw managed to turn many female heads. When Craig moved out and decided to be roommates with this man, who was seven years older than him, Vi thought surely it would not last. However, she'd been dead wrong. Over the past four years, Craig and Clayton had lived together, worked together and become very good friends. Clayton was so much a part of her son's life that everyone knew him and treated him like part of the family at their gatherings.

While all these thoughts ran swiftly through her mind, she glanced at her watch. Absently, she realized, she was probably going to be late for work. Not giving it too much thought, she continued to search for her keys. Her sister, Cynthia, normally got in early and could easily open up. Shortly after Vi opened the salon several years back, she had asked Cynthia to join her. Cynthia was good with figures and handled all the books and financial aspects of the business. Although, she'd gone to school and knew how to run the business end just as well as Cynthia, Vi enjoyed the people side of her business and stayed active ensuring her customers were totally satisfied with each visit. In addition to Cynthia, Vi considered her small staff, Andre, Nicole and Liana, some of the best stylists in the business.

Finally locating the keys in her purse, Vi pulled them out and swung them triumphantly in the air. It wasn't until she was ready to leave that she noticed for the first time that Clayton hadn't spoken a word, since he greeted her and she'd come downstairs. Studying him closely now, she saw that his eyes were red and his mouth was pulled into a tight, grim line.

"Clayton, what is it? Is Craig with you?" she inquired, looking past him now. When she took a step toward him, he swallowed hard, his Adams apple bobbing up and down in his throat.

"Mrs. Simpson," he started and then fell silent. The only noise came from a radio playing faintly somewhere at the back of the house. Vi became instantly concerned, she knew things about this young man that he didn't know she knew. She knew about his awful childhood and how his parents treated him as if they wished he'd never been born. Craig was very quick to tell her Clay was very proud and refused to let his past color his future. It was why her son admired this man so much. His strength and conviction to turn his life around is what made him a good cop, one who was respected by all his fellow officers. Vi welcomed Clayton into her home and invited him to every family gathering they had because she knew he had no one. Just last week when she called Craig's apartment, he was out and Clayton picked up.

Just before she hung up, she automatically invited him to the upcoming Fourth of July BBQ. He'd thanked her and said he'd be there if he didn't have to work. Although, she really didn't know him well, it was obvious something was bothering him. Tentatively, Vi reached out and touched his forearm in concern.

"Clayton," she said, "do you need to talk?"

Clearing his throat twice, Clayton tried to dislodge the lump threatening to close his windpipe. Forcefully, he cleared it on the third try and reached out to capture both her hands within his own. The rose-scented lotion she rubbed on her hands only moments ago teased his nostrils. Instead of feeling slippery, he noted the hands he held were soft and small within his grip.

"Mrs. Simpson, something terrible has happened," he finally said. Searching her face, Clayton quickly decided the only way to get through this was to just say it.

"There was a robbery this morning. Craig was caught in the middle of it and got shot."

"Craig's been shot? How bad is it? Please, Clayton, take me to him." Her eyes registered instant alarm and she tried to dislodge her hands from his and move toward the front door. But, instead of releasing her hands, he gripped them tighter. She looked up at him and the confusion he saw in her eyes made him swear viciously.

Dammit, she didn't understand. After all the thought he put into this, he hadn't explained himself properly!

"Mrs. Simpson, I can't take you to him. He…he's dead."

Two seconds. Three seconds. Five seconds ticked by. She continued to stare at him as if he'd grown three heads.

"I'm so sorry," he whispered.

For the longest time she didn't move, didn't speak. Then, he felt the first tremor when it hit. Her small hands, still clasped in his, began to shake as the shock waves entered her body. Finally, she snatched both her hands out of his grasp and covered her mouth. She stared at him, her eyes filling up, glistening with unshed tears. He watched their light brown, gold-flecked color change to a dark burnished gold, as the tears began to fall.

"Craig?" She uttered in a squeaky whisper of disbelief.

Clay began to ramble, running through what happened as if the hounds of hell were nipping at his heels.

"He was on his way over here, when he stopped off to take care of some errands. We think he walked in on a convenience store robbery. He was off duty, so he didn't have his gun on him, but he never would have had a chance to use it if he did. The gunman must have panicked when he came in."

"Ohmigod."

Her hands dropped slowly to her sides and clutched at the denim skirt she was wearing, bunching the material tightly in her fists. She stared at him wide eyed, before crying out.

"No! Nooooooo! Not Craig! Oh, please not Craig!"

Uncontrollable spasms replaced her normal breathing. Her right hand flew up and she splayed her fingers across her chest, as if that gesture could seal the hole that this mess was ripping through her heart. Suddenly, her body began to jerk and her mouth dropped open, but nothing came out.

Clayton caught her in his arms just as her knees buckled. She fell hard against his chest and he felt his sunglasses scrape painfully across his chest on impact. Yanking them out of his pocket, he flung them across the room and his arms tightened around her, as she slid toward the floor. He held onto her as tightly as any human could hold another person, but her five-foot-five, hundred and thirty pound, slender frame was a dead weight in his arms and he cushioned her fall by dropping to the floor with her.

Her cries were a pitiful sound, as they rose in crescendo along with her mounting grief and terror.

"No! No!...Nooooo!" Squeaky, high keening moans emitted from lips close to Clay's ear and although her eyes were shut tight, tears streamed freely from each corner. The moaning momentarily stopped as she took in a deep shuddering breath, expelled it in a long, rasping rush then burst into a desolate, full-scale weeping that violently racked her slender frame. He held her firm within his arms, feeling her slight weight offer itself into his comfort.

"Not again," she cried. "Lord please, not again." She stopped abruptly, then began again, "He was coming over to fix the mow...mow..." Unable to complete the word mower, she wept uncontrollably.

"I know, I know," he whispered to her softly. She began to tremble violently in his arms and Clayton moved his right hand from her shoulders to guide her head to his chest. Vi drooped against him with her forehead lying near his throat, against his exposed chest where a smattering of dark hair peeked out. Her hot tears flowed everywhere and Clay felt them trail down his chest and wet the front of his shirt. They dripped unchecked onto his fluorescent swimming trunks turning the vivid blue to a dark navy where her tears pooled in spots.

Clayton was aware of all this while he held her, giving her an anchor, something she could hold onto. He felt the cold floor against his bare calves, and the hardness of the paisley printed wall behind him. He sat holding her, not quite a stranger, but certainly not a close friend. He was merely a young man she knew through her son, her dead son. They'd met a handful of times during the course of a year, and talked briefly on the phone when she was trying to reach Craig. Nevertheless, he sat on the floor with this woman, trying his best to comfort her, not sure if he was doing it right. Unable to draw on anything in his past experience, he held on tight, hoping it was the right way for her sake.

He was unsure how long they stayed this way. It was long enough that his entire shirt front was completely soaked, long enough that his back began to ache. She continued to cling to him, quietly weeping and rocking within his embrace. After a while he gently took her shoulders in his two hands and balanced her as best he could against the foyer wall.

"Wait here," he told her looking into her tear-reddened eyes. Her long, dark lashes, spiky from crying so long, clung together and looked like dark crowns over each eye. He got up slowly, every part of his body creaking from being confined in one spot for so long, and went down the hall. Clay stopped in one of the two bedrooms off the hall, which had baseball and football paraphernalia all over the walls, which had to be Tony's room. He foraged under the bathroom sink in there and finally came up with half a box of Kleenex. Grabbing the tissue box, he rushed back down the hall toward Vi. Sitting down again, he put the box on her lap, pulled out several tissues and handed them to her.

She lay against the wall where he'd left her, disjointed and limp as a wet towel, her tears now leaving a darkened trail over the front of her denim skirt. He moved her back away from the wall and gently put his right arm around her shoulders and rested her head against his shoulder once more. Deciding he would give her all the time in the world, if she needed it, Clayton laid his cheek against the top of her head and absently began to stroke her arm. Outside, the noise of cars passing by and the sprinkler reached his ears. In the front yard, the lawn sprinkler continued its monotonous task, saturating the same spot in a long, splattering sweep. After a time, she stirred, took in a ragged breath and sat up. Her face, wet and warm against his shoulder, stuck slightly because of their close contact. He looked at her and asked, "Mrs. Simpson, where are Tony and Janae?"

Vi looked at him, then closed her eyes and whispered, "Oh, God." Janae and Tony didn't know about Craig, she thought. Vi's first instinct was to put off telling them, but she knew she couldn't do that. Ignoring the skirt she wore, Vi pulled her knees into an Indian style sitting position, propped her elbows on each leg and buried her head in her hands.

Gently removing her hands from her face, Clay held them and repeated his question.

"Ja…Janae is in….Florida… with her friend Carol…"

"And Tony?" He pressed her when she would have recovered her face.

"He...he's at the Washington's house for the weekend, over on Maple Street."

"Someone will have to call them," he said, stating the obvious.

Again, she buried her face in her hands, as he made that statement. Clayton didn't know what to do. Should he take charge? His brow furrowed in frustration, it wasn't his place to take charge here. Then, thankfully, he remembered Mrs. Simpson's sister worked at her hair salon. He released her and rose so that he was facing her on bended knee.

"I'm going to call your sister. Is she working today?"

His words caused a wave of momentary trepidation, which she dismissed instantly. Instead of voicing her feelings she simply nodded her head slightly. Kneeling in front of her, he looked down on her bowed head, a neat, curly crop of light auburn hair with copper highlights. "I'm going to call her so she can be here for you, okay?" he told her.

Suddenly raising her head, she looked up at him and began to rise. "It's okay, I'll call her."

Using his strong arms as an anchor, she pulled herself up, swaying a bit. When she took the first step, however, she lost her balance. Luckily, Clayton was nearby and his arms shot out to steady her.

Wanting to give her some privacy, he stood in her kitchen facing the patio door looking out at the backyard. He looked around the kitchen. It was very cheery and everything was clean and neat and in its place. He heard her pick up the phone and punch in a few numbers. After a brief silence he heard the dial tone change to a loud hum, and he turned around. She was bent over the counter, her head drooped between her shoulder blades with the receiver gripped tightly in one hand. Clayton walked over to her and gently pried her fingers from the receiver, loosening her grip on the phone. Looking at the keypad, he found the salon's phone number, which had been programmed into the memory. Pressing the appropriate quick dial number, he waited as the phone rang three times before a female voice came on the line.

"Nu U Salon."

He cradled the phone between his left shoulder and ear, freeing his right hand, which he laid lightly across the back of Mrs. Simpson's neck.

"I need to speak with Cynthia Edwards," he said into the receiver.

Cynthia Edward's voice came through the receiver, very professional with just a hint of confusion.

"This is she, may I help you?"

"Mrs. Edwards are you there by yourself or is someone else in the shop with you?"

The confusion in her voice quickly turned condescending. After a brief pause, she asked impatiently.

"Who is this?"

"I'm sorry, Mrs. Edwards, this is Clayton Marshall. I'm a friend of your nephew, Craig Simpson," he said in explanation. "We met a few months ago at your sister's house. I'm afraid I have some very bad news. Craig was killed earlier this morning in an attempted robbery."

He heard a muffled cry. Picturing Mrs. Edward's reaction, Clayton broke the lengthy silence that followed.

"Mrs. Edwards are you there? Ma'am, please let me speak to whoever is there with you."

He hadn't taken his eyes off Mrs. Simpson during his conversation with her sister. The hand that lay against the back of her neck fell away now, as Vi turned to face him and gently reached for the phone. He listened as she spoke into the phone, alternately crying and trying to console her sister at the same time. When she hung up, Vi turned around to find Clayton standing nearby and went without hesitation into his embrace. As her smooth hands clutched at his shirt front, she whispered to him needlessly, "She's coming."

With his arms around her, the smell of her hand lotion became etched in his mind as they stood in her kitchen. He realized it wasn't a rose scent after all, it was more a naturally fresh scent, with a hint of flowers and very light. As he stood holding her, other memories were stored away in Clay's mind. He memorized the exact angle of the afternoon sun as it spilled through the open patio doors, gently caressing the top of her head, turning her copper highlights to spun gold. The distant hum of a lawn mower, being used just a few houses away, reached his ears. The scent of fresh cut grass was paramount on the afternoon breeze coming through the kitchen window. The refrigerator door was cluttered with numbers and refrigerator magnets. One of those magnets held a handwritten note – *Janae, Delta Flight 104, 2:35 pm.* Another magnet held a picture of Craig smiling broadly and standing next to his brother and sister at a lake.

Unaware that her face had become stuck to the side of his neck, she moved slightly trying to compose herself. His own shirt, which never had much chance to dry from before in the hallway, was totally plastered against his chest. He spoke in hushed tones, trying his best to ease her pain. When there was nothing left to say, he held her in silence, so wrapped up in her grief that his was long forgotten.

   While Clayton and Vi waited for Cynthia to arrive, Casey was across town starting to get worried. She'd been in the shower when Craig popped his head in to say he was leaving. At least that's what she thought he'd said, it was hard to tell with the water running. After reaching his voice mail throughout the day, Casey decided to watch television for a few hours that night. Around ten, she started dozing off and gave up waiting for Craig to stop by. Casey turned off the television and got up to get a glass of milk.

   In the kitchen, which was really part of the living room separated only by a half wall, she poured milk into a glass. Walking back into the living room, she sat down by a small window facing the front of her apartment. As Casey drank her milk, she listened to the steady sound of traffic below on Main Street. Casey tried Craig's cell phone one more time before calling it a night. When she reached his voice mail again, she decided not to leave a message and went to bed.

   A police cruiser patrolling the neighborhood came down Main Street just as Casey went to bed. The squad car passed her apartment window and turned right at the corner of Chestnut. The officer cruising around spotted a parking spot up ahead across the street from the corner market. He slowed down to pull into that spot, and got out to buy a pack of cigarettes. The officer noticed a car with all the windows down parked halfway down the block. Curious, he walked over to this car, finding it odd for anyone in this neighborhood to leave their car windows down at night. He walked around the outside of the car and then peered inside. Checking the glove compartment he found a registration and insurance card. After a quick review of these papers, he walked back to his cruiser and called in the name on the registration. "This is 2141," he said into the hand-held radio connected to his dash. "I need to check on a registration. Craig Simpson, date of birth…"

CHAPTER

FIVE

Clay stood in the background, as the two sisters embraced. While Mrs. Simpson told her sister everything she knew about the shooting, he listened quietly, remembering that everyone in the family called her Vi. Suddenly, Cynthia realized he was in the room and turned to him. He was taken aback when she addressed him.

"Clayton, thank you. Thank you for being here for Vi."

He nodded and, unexpectedly, found himself embraced tightly by this strange woman. He was equally surprised when he found himself returning her embrace with an intensity that stunned him. Usually he was distant with people, radiating to no one, least of all strangers. Yet here he was, totally out of character, comforting Cynthia Edwards, a woman he'd met a handful of times.

When Cynthia asked Vi how she found out, Clayton stepped in, explaining for Mrs. Simpson what happened and sharing all the facts he'd gotten from his Captain about the robbery.

"Our precinct pastor would normally advise the family, but I asked my Captain if I could do it." Clearing his throat he continued, "I hope that was alright."

Vi Simpson immediately sought his large hand, enclosing it within her smaller one.

"You were close to Craig and it must have been hard to come over here," she told him. "I just want you to know I appreciate it."

Clay glanced down at their joined hands and felt the shock waves grab hold of him once more. This time he fought for control of his emotions and won. Suddenly it occurred to him, with all she was going through, Craig's mom seemed to truly care about what he was feeling. The knowledge puzzled and humbled him all at the same time. Turning his hand slightly inside of hers, he linked their fingers together and tried to convey his appreciation.

"Mrs. Simpson, I'm here for you, whatever you need me to do."

She squeezed his hand in response, closing her eyes against his statement, willing the tears to stop. In that moment, he couldn't actually explain why, but he felt an intangible bond form between them.

Watching this exchange, Cynthia interrupted in a somewhat dismissive tone. "Yes, Clayton, thank you for being here today. But I'm here now, so if you must go, well," she paused, trailing off.

Clayton blinked in confusion and the hurt in his voice was evident to Vi when he turned to her and said. "Oh, yeah, okay, I guess I should be going."

Vi shot Cynthia a scathing look, embarrassed beyond belief that her sister would be rude to this man. For the most part, Cynthia was oblivious to the sharp look Vi cast her way. The need to take over every situation, however, was her sister's M.O. Granted, everyone who knew Cynthia knew she was a control freak, except of course, Cynthia. But this was not the time, nor the place to go at it with her sister. Tamping down her anger, Vi turned to Clayton and told him reassuringly.

"No," Vi said forcefully. "No, don't go Clayton. Stay, I want you to, please." And it was true, she was grateful he was here, acknowledging on some level how comforting it was to have a man around at a time like this. Vi wasn't a fool, she knew the days ahead would be difficult and it would be easy to rely on him. If that happened, Vi sensed this young man would probably be very accommodating, but she also knew she wouldn't do it. Although it was nice to have him here right now, she would get through this on her own, just like before. Thinking about some of the things that lay ahead, brought reality crashing back. She had to tell the kids!

"I need to call Janae and Tony," she said.

"I'll call Janae," Cynthia offered and rose from her chair.

"No, Cynthia. Thank you, but she should hear it from me."

Cynthia continued to insist, "Why put yourself through that?"

"No, I'm her mother, I have to do this."

She got up and went into the kitchen, Cynthia and Clay following in her wake.

Cynthia handed her the cordless phone, while Clayton nudged a chair behind her knees, which she gratefully sank into. Guardian angels, she thought, as she steeled herself to the task at hand. The phone rang, and in those short seconds Vi fought for control.

Janae was having a great time. She and Carol spent the entire day at the beach. While Janae could have stayed a bit longer, Carol had insisted they hit the clubs tonight. Then again, since they had arrived, Carol had insisted they hit the clubs every night. Janae was seriously thinking of staying in tonight and getting some sleep, but then she remembered the cute guys they'd met last night. Carol had promised to meet up with them at club Envy again tonight, so they both gathered their things and left the beach early.

Planning to grab a couple of burgers for dinner, they stopped at their hotel just long enough to shower and change. Both girls were dashing around the hotel room getting ready when Janae heard her cell phone ring.

"Janae?"

"Oh, hey mom," Janae answered excitedly. "You almost missed us. We were on our way out."

"Janae, honey, I need you to come home right away. Something terrible has happened to Craig." For a fraction of a second her voice wavered before she forced the words past her lips. "Sweetie, I'm so sorry, I...Craig was sh..shot earlier today." The finality of that statement made Vi shudder. Having to say the words was almost unbearable.

Janae slumped in a chair near the bed, covering her mouth with a delicate hand. The silence stretched out for a time before Vi said again into the receiver.

"Janae, Craig is dead."

"Oh no, nooooo! Oh, mom no... Oh, God...no!"

Feeling her daughter's pain through the phone line, Vi desperately wished she were there by her side, instead of hundreds of miles separating them.

"Janae, I know baby, I know. Please listen Janae, you'll have to get...the f...first flight out and..." it was too much, Vi covered her mouth with the back of her hand to stifle the sob aching to leave her throat. She felt Cynthia arms go around her as Clayton gently took the receiver from her hand.

"Janae, this is Clay Marshall. I'm here with your mother and your Aunt. I'm so very sorry." Talking to Janae was difficult, her words came out disjointed and broken by her weeping. Sometimes she became coherent and asked him questions. Difficult questions that her mother should not have to answer. Keeping his answers short, after a time, Clayton said, "Janae put your friend Carol on the phone please."

Recognizing Janae was too distraught to think clearly, he spoke to her friend Carol about changing her flight arrangements and asked her to call back with those changes so he could pick Janae up when her flight arrived. With those details taken care of, he gave the phone back to Mrs. Simpson and listened to their tearful goodbye. When she hung up, Vi quickly dialed the number to reach Tony and once again her sister offered to help her make the necessary calls. But she stoically refused.

"This is something I have to do myself," she explained. "After I reach Tony I have to call the mortuary, then you can do the rest."

The phone rang several times at the Washington's before the answering machine came on. After leaving a brief message she called information for the mortician's number and waited as the automated voice connected her to the funeral home. She did fine answering the mortician's questions, until they got around to where the body was. Helplessness slammed into Vi, crushing her dwindling resolve.

I can't do this. Her mind screamed as she looked around frantically, repeating what the mortician had asked her.

"Where is he?" She stared at the ceiling, "I don't know…I…"

Immediately, Clayton came over and took the phone, speaking into the receiver with authority.

"This is officer Clayton Marshall of the Amityville Police Department. The deceased was my friend and my partner. Perhaps I can answer your questions." He listened intently and responded to each question the mortician had.

"Brunswick General morgue."

"At 10:00 this morning."

"Gun shot wound."

"Yes."

"Yes, I believe so."

"Yes, the number is 789-1346."

"Hope Missionary Baptist."

"If she doesn't have one, we have one at the police department."

"I believe that will have to wait. I think she needs a little time to make those decisions and we haven't reached all the family members yet."

"Yes, tomorrow at 9:30 would be better. Thank you Mr. Jones."

Writing some information down on a pad by the phone, Clayton hung up and turned to Vi.

"I told him you would meet him tomorrow at 9:30. I hope that was okay. He has enough information for now and he assured me that he would take care of everything," he told Vi.

"I'm sorry. I didn't know they would take him to the morgue so soon," she said looking at him apologetically.

"It's fine. How would you know? Its just police procedure whenever there's a fatality to take the remains there," he trailed off.

Again, it occurred to Vi how good it was to have Clayton Marshall here. If he was still in shock over all of this, he hid it well. On some level, she realized that every time she felt ready to fall apart, he seemed to be right there, stepping in and handling the difficult tasks like a husband or grown son.

Having him with her was like having Craig here and it gave her a measure of comfort. Vi got up from the table where she'd been sitting with Cynthia and went to him. She placed a hand on his shoulder. "Thank you, Clayton, for all you've done today."

"Think nothing of it, really. It's a tough time and I think Craig would have wanted me here to help you. So, if it's okay with you, I'll hang around for a while."

She hugged him hard to show her appreciation for being there. The phone rang as she absently rubbed his back, as if he were her son. Vi listened as Cynthia answered the phone and spoke to Carol.

"Yes, okay Carol. I've got it. Delta flight 74 at 8:49," Cynthia said as she scribbled information on a pad. Before she hung up Cynthia thanked Janae's friend once more and said. "I'm sorry you had to cut your vacation short Carol, but we're so grateful you're coming home with our Janae."

The telephone kept ringing after that and, although she tried the Washington's every half hour, Vi had no luck reaching them or Tony. Cynthia and Clayton took turns making the calls that needed to be made from there. Once, Vi had to take the phone and try to console her mother, who wept uncontrollably. When she finally calmed down, Vi hung up the phone, too drained to speak with anyone else. The house began filling with people after that, each person carrying some kind of dish or casserole. Sitting by herself at the dining room table, Vi wondered. *Why do people bring food at a time like this? Do they think eating will make the families grieving any easier?*

Feeling strangely out of sorts, she was having a hard time grasping the fact this was all actually happening to her. Her wandering thoughts created a dull ache at the base of her skull. Closing her eyes, Vi placed a hand at the back of her neck and began massaging that area to alleviate the pain. It was actually starting to work, when suddenly she opened her eyes and looked up. For one odd moment, an insane urge struck her and Vi realized she'd been about to ask, *Did anyone remember to call Craig?*

She quickly clamped her mouth shut, startled that those words had been on the tip of her tongue. While she silently berated herself, she acknowledged how right it felt to think of him at a time like this. Craig had always been there for her.

Just then, Nicole and Andre walked in and rushed over to where she sat. Nicole, who was her right hand at the salon, hugged her tight. Vi listened as she explained, unnecessarily, her decision to close the salon for the day.

When Vi hired Nicole four years ago, they quickly found out how much they had in common. She was an excellent stylist and, the two of them were very close in age and had a lot in common. Just like Vi had been when her husband died, Nicole was a single mom raising her kids on her own. Having so much in common, the two women had become very good friends quickly and, in some ways, Vi felt closer to Nicole than she did to her own sister. When Nicole released her, Andre moved forward and quickly gathered Vi in a bear hug. It felt more like a baby bear, as his thin arms came around her light as a feather. Because of his alternative lifestyle, Andre, sweet to a fault, fit in well with the women at the salon. And like Nicole, Andre was more than just an employee Vi thought, as she returned his embrace. They were both just like family.

The hours dragged on. Vi's parents arrived a little while later needing more comfort than she was able to give. Rising to the task, Vi tried her best to quiet her mother's piteous weeping, all the while thinking, *I need someone to hold me. I need to cry. When will I have time to cry?*

As that desperate plea swept through her mind, she silently wished that everyone would leave. *Right now! Just get out!*

Just as quickly, she instantly felt ashamed for even thinking such unkind thoughts. Vi ushered her mother to a nearby chair and went down on one knee beside her just as the doorbell rang again. Steeling herself, she rose and prepared to meet whoever it was. As she made her way to the door, Clayton touched her elbow gently.

"Mrs. Simpson, I've got Tony on the line."

Handing her the cordless phone, he kept his hand on her elbow, guiding Vi a short distance away from the gaggle of people in the rest of the house. Leading her down the hall, Clay ushered her into the kitchen. Once there, he stood in the open doorway with his back to her, shielding her from prying eyes in other parts of the house and simultaneously ensuring she had a measure of privacy.

Gripping the phone tight, Vi spoke into the receiver, "Tony?"

"Mom, what's going on? How come Clayton called me? Is everything alright?"

"Tony, Sweetie, listen I have some very bad news to tell you." She sensed the alarm in his voice.

"What is it mom? Is somebody hurt? Did Janae get hurt?"

Pausing to gather her courage, Vi quietly responded, "No, honey, .it's not Janae. It's Craig."

"Craig?" he asked in a whisper.

"Craig was shot today in a holdup and he's dead, baby."

"Dead? Oh, mom, dead? But, but he can't be. He promised we'd go to the Mets game next week."

Several seconds passed before Vi called his name through the receiver. It was hard for Tony to speak, and when he did, it came out cracked and high pitched like it sounded a year ago when his voice was changing.

"Ah, mom."

"I know, honey. I know."

Vi heard him crying softly through the phone line. It broke her heart to hear him crying and not be able to reach out and hold him. Taking a quick, calming breath, Vi spoke to Tony quietly.

"Tony, listen honey, I need for you to come home right away. Put Mrs. Washington on the phone so I can speak with her, okay?"

"Okay."

Trying her best to be strong for him, Vi told Tony before hanging up, "Honey, I'll see you soon. I love you."

Mrs. Washington came on the line, offered her condolences and promised to have Tony home as soon as possible. Vi dried her eyes as she hung up the phone and turned around to find Clayton still shielding her from the rest of the room. He turned around quietly from where he'd been standing and faced her.

"That was tough."

"Yeah," she acknowledged with a slight nod of her head.

"Do you want me to go and get him?"

"No, thank you Clayton, that won't be necessary. The Washington's assured me he'd be home soon."

"Okay, but really it would be no bother. I could leave now and get him for you."

Appreciation flooded her again and she walked over to him and touched his forearm lightly. "I know you would and I really appreciate the offer, but he's not that far and they promised to leave right away. But, if you really meant it earlier, I would truly appreciate you picking Janae up at the airport. I don't want to be gone when Tony gets home."

"I meant it. Don't worry, I'll be waiting for her as soon as her flight gets in."

She turned from him then and sat down in one of the kitchen chairs. Clayton took the chair across from her. After a few seconds passed, he asked her, "Can I get you something? Coffee? Food?"

"No, I couldn't keep anything down, but you go ahead."

"No, I couldn't," Just then, Cynthia came in the kitchen and quietly told Vi, "Clarence is here."

Vi didn't realize she'd been waiting to hear that name, until it was spoken. Clarence Simpson, her father-in-law, was the most beloved man she knew. She walked down the hallway toward him. At seventy, Clarence was very tall and fit for his age. Milk chocolate skin was stretched over his kind face where life left its mark in wrinkles and spots, but the laugh lines around his eyes and mouth revealed he'd found joy along with the pain life brought him. His hair and beard had long since turned gray, but his eyes were still the same warm brown they'd been since the first time she'd met him. Clarence was solid as an anchor and gentle as a lamb. Meeting her halfway, he opened his arms and enfolded Vi in his embrace.

"Vi, honey, I'm so sorry," Clarence told her in his soothing, deep baritone voice. She didn't miss the grief written across his features or the unshed tears in his eyes. "I know this hurts, but we can get through this Vi. We done this before, you and I. God saw us through then and guess what, he'll see us through again dear."

Consoling her parents earlier left Vi feeling drained, but now her spirits lifted a fraction. Listening to Clarence's comforting words was just what she needed right now. If anyone knew what she was feeling right now, it was Clarence. She thought about another day when the two of them had stood just like this, grieving. That was the day she'd lost a husband and Clarence had lost a son. She stood in his strong embrace, feeling closer to this man than her own father, not at all surprised that his thoughts and feelings mirrored her own.

The evening wore on and an endless number of people came and went, bringing more casseroles and desserts. Expressing their condolences, two of her neighbors met Vi at the door, handing her a covered dish. Vi accepted it, thanked them and quickly made her way to the kitchen to put it with the others. On her way to the kitchen, however, she passed the dining room window and glimpsed Clayton standing in the front yard. She watched him walk across the yard and turn off the sprinkler, which had sat forgotten in the same spot, continuously saturating the same area all day long. As he bent to pick up the hose, she saw him swipe a hand across his eyes. Vi made her way to the front of the house and walked out onto the front porch. Sensing her presence, he turned to face her. Vi watched him methodically wind the hose around his bent elbow and open palm.

"You didn't have to bother with that," she started to say.

He broke eye contact and responded quietly, "Yeah, I know. I didn't have anything better to do. Besides, it was getting pretty soggy over here."

Not terribly concerned with the saturated ground near his feet, she continued to watch him. He was obviously upset and doing a very good job of trying to hide it. Vi closed the short distance between them.

"Clayton, why don't you come back inside?"

"No, I'm fine, really," he cut in quickly, not giving her a chance to finish. "I'd better get going anyway if I want to get to the airport on time." And just like that, he dropped the hose in a neatly wrapped pile on the grass, strode across the yard, got in his car and left.

The pilot announced their pending arrival at Kennedy airport just as the seatbelt lights came on. Trays were pushed up and books were quickly put away as everyone buckled up and prepared for landing. Watching the bright lights of the city below her, Janae wondered idly about her mother, and how she was holding up. How was Tony? Were grandma and grandpa alright?

The plane landed safely and everyone rose as the seatbelt light went off. Moving down the aisle, Carol and Janae waited patiently as people reached overhead to pull down their carry-on luggage. Since 9/11, only passengers were allowed beyond the baggage area, so Janae wasn't concerned that no one was waiting at the gate as they got off the plane. Quickly making her way through the airport, Janae assumed her family would be at the baggage area. When she arrived there, she was totally surprised to see Clayton Marshall standing at the Delta baggage turnstile.

"Clayton," Janae cried, dropped her small carry-on bag and rushed toward him.

He opened his arms and gathered her in a huge bear hug. Glad to see him, Janae swayed slightly in his strong embrace, her toes lightly grazed the carpet beneath her feet. Several moments passed as they held onto one another, totally oblivious to the crowd of people rushing by, anxious to be on their way. After a few moments, he placed his large hands on both of her shoulders, setting Janae away from him. He stared down at her and it was obvious she'd spent the entire flight crying.

"Are you okay?"

"I don't know. I mean, I keep thinking this can't be happening."

Lowering her eyes, Janae trailed off, unable to finish her thought. Clayton gathered her in his arms again and Janae clung to him, this time doubling her arms around the back of his neck, as overwhelming grief washed over her. Although this was the first time the two of them had ever really embraced, it felt oddly familiar. Since her brother, Craig, and this man had become roommates four years ago, she'd secretly dreamed of being in Clayton's arms, just like this. It crossed Janae's mind now, how peculiar that it should happen at a time like this. No one knew about the huge crush she'd developed for Clay, except Janae's best friend. Over a zillion times she'd thought about acting on her feelings for him, but something in the way Clay treated her made Janae hesitate. Although he was a bit older—ten years to be exact—Clayton had always treated Janae like a baby sister. Like Craig's baby sister.

She tightened her arms around his neck and lost herself in the moment, completely forgetting where they were until someone brushed against her. Immediately breaking the spell, she turned to see an elderly woman reach for a suitcase as it moved slowly along the turnstile. Suddenly ashamed of herself, Janae released her hold on Clayton and abruptly moved out of his embrace. Remembering why he held her, Janae struggled to compose herself and mentally push her personal feelings aside.

When they separated Clayton shook hands with Janae's friend, Carol. He helped them collect their luggage and carried all four bags with ease as they made their way through the exit doors, walking briskly toward his car. Once there, Clayton put the bags in the trunk, opened the rear door for Carol then helped Janae into the front passenger seat.

No one said a word on the short ride from the airport. Carol sat quietly in the back, while Janae stared out the passenger window, with puffy red eyes. Clayton cleared his throat and opened the windows on his old beater. The lack of air conditioning didn't matter so much at this time of the day, as a gentle breeze blew inside the car. He thought about how he and Craig spent half the day last Saturday trying to fix the air conditioning in this very car. After several hours, Clayton recalled telling Craig it didn't make sense to waste the rest of a perfectly good Saturday on this when his new truck would be arriving soon.

The new truck! With everything that went on today, he'd completely forgotten about it. He'd been so hyped about picking it up earlier today, and for weeks it was all he and Craig had talked about. They'd made plans to rent a couple of dirt bikes, haul them in the back and drive across the country on their next vacation. At a red light up ahead, Clayton quickly checked his incoming calls and saw the dealer had tried to reach him four times today. After everything that happened this afternoon, it would have to wait. Picking up the new vehicle now seemed so insignificant.

Janae was deep in thought, hardly aware of traffic speeding by outside her window. All through high school and even after she went off to college and Craig moved away from home, she and her brother had remained close. She always thought about the two of them married with kids of their own, those kids would be close just like she and her brother had been. Now, for some reason, she felt cheated because Craig would never get married or have kids. Her kids would never play with his. Hot tears rolled down her cheeks, as she realized this was probably the first of many disappointments to come.

She turned away from the window, looked across the front seat at Clayton and voiced some of her inner turmoil.

"Ya' know, Clay, it's so unfair. I mean, I just realized Craig will never get married or have kids. We always talked about the future and how our kids would be really close." She sniffled a bit before continuing, "I feel so cheated and selfish for even thinking about that now and how it's going to affect me."

Taking his eyes off the road briefly, Clayton looked over at her and quietly shared some of his feelings too. "I know how you feel," he said reaching over to stroke the back of her hand that lay flat on the seat between them.

After a time she asked. "How are Tony and my mom holding up?"

"Tony should be home by the time we get there. As for your mom, man, your mom is like a rock. Craig always said she was a strong woman and today I've seen it for myself."

"Oh God, Clayton, it's going to be awful without him."

He closed his hand around hers, holding it tight in silent agreement.

It was late when they reached Janae's house. Luckily Tony had arrived moments before they got there. Clayton stood by and witnessed mother, son and daughter pull together into a grieving trio of sorrow. He watched Janae's aunt, Mrs. Edwards, walk over and hug her friend Carol before leaving to give them a little privacy. With no place to go and nowhere particular in mind, he left the house through the front door and wandered into the backyard.

He sat down on a redwood picnic bench and looked around the backyard, letting his mind drift. Clayton immediately recalled the many barbeques and family gatherings they'd had in this very yard. Functions he'd been invited to where everyone had treated him like one of the family. He remembered distinctly the first time he'd been over here. Everyone clapped him on the back and gave him a warm welcome and a pleasant warning, *"Clayton, around this house, you serve yourself or starve"* Amid loud music and contagious laughter, Clayton had been ushered over to a table laden with food and a cooler stacked full of ice cold beer.

The memory faded as a cool breeze slipped through his open shirt front. He shook slightly and sat at the picnic table taking in his surroundings. It was really quiet out here, he thought. A pleasant fragrance emanated from a well-tended flower bed a short distance away, and tall arbor vitae's sectioned off her backyard from the neighbor's. He wondered idly about this family and how it must feel to have someone to turn to at a time like this, someone who could lessen your pain by just being there. The love displayed in this family was foreign to him. No one had ever said they loved him and he, in turn, had never loved anyone.

The only memories he held of his childhood were bad ones. The stench of two drunken parents, the filthy apartment they lived in, and having to care for his younger sister because his parents were too intoxicated to care. His father had two stages to his drinking. Stage one was drink until he passed out. Stage two was to drink and then beat the hell out of Clay and his mother if she tried to stop him. If he had to compare childhoods, Craig's would have been "Happy Days," while Clayton's was closer to "Nightmare on Elm Street." His parents, Lyle and Mamie, still lived in the seediest part of town over on Chestnut. His nostrils flared as he caught an imaginary whiff of his baby sister's diaper, which his mother hadn't bothered to change all day. When his sister ran away on her fifteenth birthday, Clayton wasn't far behind, leaving home at an early age and never looking back.

He hadn't thought about his sister in years and thinking about her now made him remember how he grew up, fending for the two of them as best he could. He was just a kid himself and not much of a cook, but he did what he could to make sure his little sister had a meal. Unfortunately, what little money his parents had was usually squandered on alcohol, leaving very little for food. He'd taken to stealing sometimes—food items mostly—so he and his sister would have something to eat. One day he got caught stealing produce from the market down the street from their apartment. Instead of calling the cops, the store manager made him work off what he'd stolen by sweeping and cleaning the market after school. It was the first act of decency he'd ever experienced and probably was the first time he felt useful. After a time, the manager started giving him food and vegetables to take home. The store manager claimed the items were stale and ready to be thrown out, but Clayton suspected he knew Clay's family had no food and, thankfully, took the items home. The store manager had been kind to him and Clayton remembered watching him interact with his own family in the store. Their influence made him realize all families were not like his and that there was a better life outside of the way his family lived.

The sound of the glass doors sliding open interrupted his thoughts, and Clay looked up as Mrs. Simpson stepped out onto the back patio. When she walked over to him and asked if he'd like to stay the night in the spare bedroom, Clayton respectfully declined the invitation. Although he didn't relish going home to his empty apartment—where reminders of Craig would be everywhere—he figured he'd probably already overstayed his welcome. He rose from the redwood bench, preparing to leave. "No, thank you. I should go."

"Clayton, I hate to think of you facing that apartment alone."

He wondered again how she could worry about him, or anything else for that matter, at a time like this. "It's okay," he said in a reassuring tone. "I'll have to face it sometime. Oh, I almost forgot, I've been given time off work until after the funeral. So, anything you need, just let me know." Unsure if he was overstepping his bounds again, he plundered ahead. "I mean, I can box up his things for you. Or, if you wanted to do it, I could help out or disappear if you need to be alone. Just say the word."

She smiled in response and thought about pressing the issue of his staying the night. She was certain he was unaware of how drained he looked and she started to say just that when he spoke, cutting her off.

"Don't worry about me, really. You should go back inside, your family needs you and you look real tired." He started walking away, in his colorful shorts and sandals. Reaching the gate that led to the front of the house, he opened it and walked along the path. He had almost made it around the side of the house when she called his name. Clayton turned around to face her again.

Wanting to express her gratitude for all he'd done for her today, Vi struggled with the right words. He'd gone out of his way the entire day; going to the airport, coming over to tell her the sad news and practically lending a strong shoulder for her to lean on all day. Finally, she gave up trying to find the right words and told him what was in her heart. "Clayton, thank you for everything today, I don't know how I would have gotten through today without you."

He nodded slightly, a brief, warm smile curving his lips before he turned to leave again.

"Clayton, wait."

When she called his name again, Clayton turned around once more. He watched her quickly dash back into the house, only to return in a few seconds holding a small dish covered in foil.

"I know you haven't eaten all day. Warm this up and eat something tonight, okay?"

Thanking her, he took the foil covered plate from her outstretched hands, said good night and left.

His apartment complex, like half a dozen others in the neighborhood, was fairly new. Initially, he had planned to live alone and lived in this apartment by himself for five years. Further renovations to the complex, driven by expensive homes coming up in the area, forced his landlord to increase his already exorbitant rent. When that happened he decided to start looking for a roommate. The first thing he did was put a flyer on the bulletin board at work.   There were several officers Clayton knew he could never share quarters with, but Craig appeared to be different.   He was the only candidate who didn't bat an eye when Clay told him about his one rule regarding cleanliness.   In fact, for some reason Clayton didn't examine too closely, Craig had been the *only* candidate.   Later on, after the two men agreed to be roommates, Craig sheepishly admitted that he had taken down Clay's flyer, fearing someone might get to the apartment before he could.   He remembered sizing Craig up and laying out some ground rules from the get go.

"My parents were alcoholic pigs.   I lived that way for so long, I refuse to ever live that way again.   I'm not a fanatic, but I like to keep the place neat and clean.   If you can handle that, then we can get along," he'd told Craig.

Craig looked him square in the eye and responded, "When my father died, my mom had to go out and work.   She would make us do chores, and if they weren't done right, we'd do them all over again until she was satisfied.   I cook, clean, do laundry and windows and I don't have a problem with being clean and keeping it that way."

The two men had summed up each other carefully.   Apparently satisfied after this brief assessment, they shook hands and moved Craig's stuff in the very next day.

When he opened the door, everything looked normal.   Craig's running shoes sat next to the door and his coat still hung in the hall closet.   Clayton walked through the living room and past the kitchen, stopping at Craig's open bedroom door.   Lingering there, the full force of his partner's death suddenly hit him.   Craig's holster lay on top of the dresser and laundry lay on his bed.   The way he left things, it looked like he might walk through the door at any minute.   Moving further into the darkened bedroom, Clayton sat down on Craig's bed and gave into the tears burning the back of his eyes.

When Clarence answered the phone the next morning, he knew Vi was very angry by the tone of her voice.

"Cynthia's really done it this time," she told Clarence in greeting.

Inquiring with a kindhearted sarcasm, Clarence asked, "What has your lovely sister done this time?"

"Clarence, she's gone too far this time. Too far."

While Vi quickly explained to him what the funeral director told her this morning, she could hardly contain her annoyance. "Can you believe her nerve?" Not waiting for Clarence to reply, what Cynthia had done this morning tumbled at break-neck speed from Vi's lips. "Clarence, I have never been so mad in my life. When the funeral director told me Cynthia had already been there and made all the arrangements, I could hardly believe it. She knew I had plans to go over there this morning to make those arrangements."

"Now Vi, don't go getting yourself all upset." The fact Cynthia had done something like this did not surprise Clarence in the least. However, trying to put what happened in perspective. "We all know how Cynthia meddles in everything," he added.

"But, she...."

"Shhhh," the calm in Clarence's voice helped soothe Vi's already frazzled nerves. "Don't waste anymore time on it. What you and I have to do is go down there right now and undo what she did, and then we can fix everything to the way you want."

Vi took a cleansing breath and fought to control her temper. Clarence had unknowingly volunteered for what she planned to ask him when she woke up this morning. "Oh Clarence, I had hoped you would come with me this morning. Thank you."

He stopped any further discussion and told her solemnly, "Sweet girl, you have touched an old man's heart. In fact, I was just on my way over there to catch you before you left, hoping to tag along."

At the mortuary, Clarence's help turned out to be a blessing in disguise. There were many things they needed to decide on, and discussing her ideas with Clarence made quick work of it. There was the choice of casket, what type of flowers to order, and would there be a soloist? The list of questions seemed to go on and on. The last item to decide on turned out to be the easiest—changing the funeral home music to that which Cynthia had chosen. Both she and Clarence decided Craig's favorite music should be piped in, instead of traditionally solemn organ music. Further bucking tradition, Clarence suggested to Vi that they lay Craig out in his favorite Mets jersey instead of a suit. "He wore a suit maybe six times in his whole life. I think he'd like to rest in something comfortable."

Vi agreed with Clarence and promised the director she'd bring Craig's personalized Mets jersey by later in the day. The jersey had been a birthday present from Clarence, and Craig wore it to every home game the Mets played. She remembered Craig joking before each game – *the Mets couldn't win unless he was watching them in his lucky jersey.*

They were just about to leave when the funeral director thought to ask if there would be pallbearers for the procession. Momentarily stumped, Vi looked to Clarence for help. Clarence, bless his heart, didn't let her down. "That nice young man Clayton mentioned yesterday there might be close to a hundred officers at the funeral from the state and county police. It seems they always turn out when someone in their ranks is laid to rest. Maybe, we could ask him about pallbearers, dear?" Clarence suggested in his gentle, baritone voice.

It took nearly two hours to undo the things Cynthia had put in place. They worked to change the funeral arrangements to what she and Clarence felt Craig would want. Feeling calmer now that it was all done, Vi walked out of the mortuary arm in arm with Clarence, the anger she'd felt earlier completely gone. Outside the sun shone bright, positioned high in a cloudless sky. Rush hour was over and only sporadic mid-morning traffic coasted by on Route 110. Across the street a bus was stopped at the corner picking up passengers, most of them elderly citizens and mothers with baby carriages.

"Well, that settles it," she told him as they walked toward Clarence's car, a large Chevy station wagon.

Clarence shot her a questioning look, "What's that?"

Looking to him for confirmation, she told him, "Well, I was going to put off getting Craig's things together, but maybe the sooner I do it the better."

"You sure you're up to that today?"

"Yeah, I'm fine," she continued, "Besides, we need to get his clothes back here by 5:00 today, before the mortuary closes."

"Okay, if you're sure, I'll go over there with you."

As they drove over to Craig's apartment Clarence and Vi talked about Craig, reminiscing on some of the times that stood out in both their minds.

"Remember the time his team won All State Champion in his senior year?"

"Yeah, I remember. I loved going to those games. He was quite a short stop."

"How about the time he paid a scalper $250 for those Luther Vandross tickets because the show was completely sold out?"

"Oh my, do I? I remember nagging him nonstop about blowing his first full paycheck on it even if—as he put it—his date was 'really hot'."

Clarence pulled up to the apartment complex, shut off the engine and turned to face Vi. Reaching for her hand, he enclosed it in his large, age-spotted palm. "Before we go in there, I want you to know that if it gets difficult for you, I'll be there with you and so will Clayton." Pausing to gain control of his own emotions, he eyed her solemnly before continuing. "Vi, we both know it's not easy being a parent, and times like these are some of the hardest. But we need to remember we had Craig for twenty four wonderful years and nothing can take that from us."

Vi reached over and touched his weathered cheek, wondering how it was possible to love this man more than she already did.

Clayton strode to the door, answering it on the second knock. Freshly shaven, he opened the door wearing jeans that hung a bit low on his hips and nothing else.

"Mrs. Simpson," he said in surprise. "I didn't know you'd be stopping by this morning." He grabbed a shirt hanging on the coat tree next to the door and quickly put it on. Not bothering to button it, Clay stepped aside, allowing Clarence and Vi to enter the apartment. Momentarily, her gaze traveled over him, stopping when she reached his eyes. His eyes were tired and red and he looked like he'd had a rough night.

Vi said hello as she crossed the threshold and gave him an affectionate hug. A faint, woodsy aftershave lingered in the air and she noticed the subtle change in him from yesterday. Yesterday he'd seemed strong and solid, but today he looked slightly vulnerable. When they parted, Clayton turned toward Clarence, giving him a strong, firm handshake.

"Clarence, good to see you again," Clay replied.

"Clayton, how are you holding up, young fellow?" Clarence gave Clayton a solid clap on the back in greeting, walked briskly inside and sank down onto the soft, leather sofa. "We're sorry to barge in like this, but Vi forgot her cell phone so we couldn't call you ahead of time. The funeral home needs some of Craig's things and we thought it might be best to try and get some of his things together today, if that's alright with you."

"It's fine with me, I just…" he trailed off, reluctant to finish what he'd been about to say.

Sensing his hesitancy, Vi urged him to speak freely about whatever was on his mind. "No, don't stop, please finish what you were about to say."

"I just thought this would be pretty hard on you and that maybe Tony or Janae would be here to help you."

Hearing the concern in his voice, Vi tried her best to reassure him she was going to be okay. Besides the fact she hadn't actually planned to do this today either, she certainly couldn't have enlisted the kids help this morning. Last night had been a particularly rough night for both of them. Wearing a brave smile, she spoke to him reassuringly. "They were asleep when I left this morning. We all had a pretty rough night. Anyway, Clarence is here.

"Well, I can stick around and help out too," Clayton volunteered.

"Clayton, please don't feel like you have to hang around and help us. I know you must have things to do."

"No, I don't mind helping. Really," he assured Vi, then sat down on the sofa opposite Clarence, facing the older man.

She watched him talk quietly with Clarence, offering to help them in any way he could and deciding which room to tackle first. Thinking about what he'd been about to say made her think of her children. Unable to sleep, Tony and Janae had climbed into her bed during the night. However, out of all of them, she knew this young man probably had the toughest time last night. After all, he'd been closest to Craig for the past four years, sharing an apartment and working together. She imagined it must have been very hard for him to walk into this apartment last night. Not voicing those sentiments, Vi walked over to the sofa. Always the gentlemen, Clayton stood up immediately so she could sit down. Vi shook her head to indicate that she was fine standing. She smiled at him as a sudden thought struck her. "Did you eat my spaghetti last night?"

She watched as he placed a strong hand to his mid-section, where his shirt lay open. Managing a slight smile, he rubbed the long fingers of his left hand against an extremely flat abdomen. "Yes, ma'am, I ate all of it this morning. It was real good, thank you."

Looking away, Vi's eye wandered around the living room until she spied his cordless phone base, sitting on a small glass and chrome end table. When Vi asked to use his phone, Clayton promptly retrieved the cordless phone from the kitchen counter where he'd left it earlier.

After punching in the salon's phone number, Vi was mildly surprised when Cynthia answered on the first ring. Some of the anger she'd felt earlier crept into her voice when she spoke to her sister.

"Cynthia, I'm at Clay's gathering some of Craig's things. I tried you at home this morning, when I found out what you did."

Cynthia heard the suppressed annoyance in Vi's voice right away. Playing for time, she responded slowly, "Vi, what on earth do you mean?"

Losing patience with Cynthia's feigned innocence, Vi lost no time getting right to the point. "Why did you go behind my back and make my son's funeral arrangements?"

"But Vi, I…"

"What gives you the right to do such a thing?" Cutting her off, Vi deliberately lowered her voice, desperately trying to reign in her temper.

"Vi, honey, I'm sorry. I thought I was doing you a favor, what with everything's that's happened."

Vi felt herself losing it all over again. What Cynthia did this morning was typical of what she always did—take charge. No matter whose feet she stepped on, Cynthia always felt it was her right to take charge. Lowering her voice to a firm whisper, she spat out. "You had no right." Then, gaining some of her composure back, Vi told her pointedly. "In any event, we were able to change everything so I guess there was no real harm done."

"Who's 'we'?"

The fact her father-in-law remained close to the family even after Vi's husband had died annoyed Cynthia, and Vi knew this. However, Cynthia's inquiry took Vi by surprise, so she answered honestly, "Clarence and I." There was no reply, so Vi filled the void. "Cynthia, before you leave today, have Nicole call and reschedule everyone for the rest of the week. Then go ahead and close the shop early. In fact, if Nicole is there, let me speak with her."

Cynthia took it upon herself to act as second in charge when Vi wasn't at Nu U Salon and the fact that Vi asked to speak with Nicole directly was not lost on her. Suspecting Vi was still angry with her for making the funeral arrangements, Cynthia handed the phone to Nicole, silently fuming.

In the background, Vi heard Andre yell, "Is that Vi?"

Nicole mumbled something she couldn't hear, then her voice came back clearly in the receiver. "Andre sends his love. How are you and the kids holding up?"

"Oh, as good as the circumstances will allow. We forced ourselves to get up this morning, take a shower and eat. It was more than any of us wanted to do."

"It'll be rough for a spell Vi, but we're all here for you."

Appreciating the genuine concern in Nicole's voice, Vi smiled wryly. More than an employee, over the past few years Nicole had become one of Vi's closest friends. "My kids slept with me last night, Nicole. My kids haven't done that since they were in grade school. They curled up on my bed and we talked about Craig till it was almost daybreak."

"You must be exhausted, girl. Don't worry, I'll handle everything and call you later."

Hanging up the phone, Vi stomach roiled as she walked back into the living room. Hearing the unladylike noise, Clarence and Clayton looked up as she entered the room.

"Sorry guys," she apologized. Vi suddenly realized she hadn't eaten in over 24 hours and got Clarence up so early, he probably didn't have a chance to eat either. In a mildly embarrassed tone, Vi addressed the two men. "Well, I don't know about you guys, but when my stomach makes those noises, it's definitely time to eat."

Clarence smiled in agreement and confirmed that he didn't have time this morning for anything but a cup of coffee. Clayton denied being hungry when Vi asked him, but she quickly insisted that he needed to eat too. Vi decided to run out and pick up breakfast at the bagel place on the corner. Clarence stood up and immediately offered to go with her, suggesting they stop at the supermarket while out there and to pick up some more boxes.

While they were gone, Clay wandered around the apartment. After a few minutes, he ended up in the kitchen. Pulling out a chair, he sat down at the kitchen table and paid a few bills. When that was done, he got up and decided to get a head start boxing up Craig's things. He started in his bathroom.

Big mistake!

Craig's shaver sat on the sink, as if it were waiting for him to amble out of bed and use it just like he'd done hundreds of mornings in the past. His toothbrush still hung in its holder over the bathroom sink. Gripping the sink, Clayton squeezed his eyes shut, fighting the sense of loss that seemed to assail him at the oddest times. This is how Vi found him.

CHAPTER

EIGHT

Using the key Clayton gave her before they left to pick up breakfast, Vi opened the apartment door. While Clarence retrieved the bigger boxes from the car, she'd taken breakfast and a few smaller boxes in her arms. Entering the apartment with her arms full, Vi called out to Clay as she closed the door with her foot. When he didn't answer, she set her burden down on the living room coffee table and walked down the hall looking for him.

"Clayton? They were all out of bagels, so Clarence went over to McDonalds to get breakfast sandwiches and coffee," her words trailed off as she came upon him in the bathroom.

It was a bachelor's bathroom. Masculine colors dominated the walls and the scent of cologne and shaving cream permeated the air. But those things paled in comparison to what she encountered as she got closer to the open bathroom door.

Clayton was in front of the bathroom mirror, slumped over the sink. He was unaware of her presence, and she took in his drooping shoulders and watched as they shook slightly. Vi looked at his reflection in the mirror, his head was down but she could see tears running freely down his face. His solitary sadness touched her deeply. Approaching him from behind, she slipped her arms around his waist and laid her cheek between his shoulder blades, holding him in comfort. He'd never gotten around to buttoning the shirt he donned earlier and her fingers came in contact with his bare chest, where his shirt lay open.

When she touched him, he sucked in a sharp breath and his arms fell to his sides. Clay squeezed his eyes closed as she held him like this, and neither of them said a word. Outside of their breathing, the only other sound in the room was a bird singing outside the bathroom window. Finally, he drew in a fortifying breath, expelling it with a harsh shudder. "You know, I don't think I realized it until yesterday. I loved him like a brother, but I never told him."

"Clayton, he knew it and I know he felt the same way."

"But I never told him, ya' know?"

"You told him in so many countless ways," she told him reassuringly. "I can't count how many times he told me you worked on his car, or covered his shift so he could get away for the weekend." When he didn't respond, she continued to try and convince him. "And how many times did you wash his car just because you were out there in that parking lot washing your own? Believe me, he knew it."

"Yeah, but... but I never told him. I've never been good with these things."

This last statement escaped his throat in a ragged whisper and her mother's heart wrenched at his desolate admission. It was unbearable to think that love had been so absent in his childhood. Removing her arms from around him, she grabbed his shoulders and turned him around to face her. "Think about it. Did he ever say it to you?" When he didn't say anything, she looked into his eyes. Searching his face, she spoke earnestly, trying to ensure he would hear and understand what she was about to say. "Clay, even brothers by blood have a hard time saying they care about one another," she reasoned. "Most men are uncomfortable expressing their feelings—it's normal. Trust me when I say to you, Craig felt the same way about you. I can remember several times he came over for dinner and refused to take leftovers home unless I had enough left for you too."

"Yeah, but..."

"No buts. Since the two of you moved in together, not one holiday celebration went by without Craig making sure you were invited. He'd say, *'Mom, don't forget to invite Clay. If he's not on duty, he'll spend the holiday alone, if we let him.'"* Searching his face to ensure he really understood, "So, stop beating yourself up?" she implored, touching his strong chin with the tip of her fingers.

In that moment, the air in the room seemed to heat up noticeably. Clayton felt as if his nerve endings were tingling from some unseen electrical current in the room. They stared into each other's eyes, for what seemed like forever. Was she aware of this change? This awareness, this shift in the atmosphere? If she was, she quickly hid it behind a nervous smile, chucking him on the chin with her fist playfully.

"Now, do you feel better?" she asked him encouragingly.

He couldn't have uttered a word if he'd wanted to. Suddenly his throat clogged up and every muscle in his body tensed in reaction. When he nodded, she stepped back, giving his shoulders a quick squeeze for good measure before releasing him.

A short time later, they rejoined Clarence and sat at the kitchen table to eat McDonald's and talk about the arrangements made earlier that day.

"Oh, by the way Clayton, the funeral home mentioned we needed pallbearers." Vi searched his face when she said, "We were wondering if you could talk with the officers that were close to Craig at the station, and see if they would be willing."

Clay cut off her inquiry and quickly offered. "Of course, I'd be glad to. I'm sure Stokes and Piterrelli would be more than willing."

"Good. And what about you Clayton, would you also consider being a pallbearer?"

He looked at her seated across from him at his small, oak kitchen table and said. "I'd have been insulted if you hadn't included me Mrs. Simpson. I'd be honored."

She smiled and grasped his hand across the table. Clarence smiled his gratitude also. After they finished eating, Vi cleared the table. Looking around the kitchen, she discovered odd plates and cups from her house that Craig had brought to his apartment. They formed a mismatched table assortment of cups, plates, forks and knives in this kitchen. She did notice that all the dishes, however, were sparkling clean and neatly put away in the cabinet. Circling the cooking area, she ran her hand over the countertop. It was also clean.

She entered the living room where Clayton and Clarence were working together, filling up small boxes and taping them closed. Straightening her shoulders, she announced, "I guess I might as well tackle his room next."

Rising, Clayton moved ahead of her down the hall. He opened the door to Craig's room, then stepped aside to allow her to enter. Vi looked around.

"It's so neat and clean," she said in surprise.

"Yeah, Craig knew I was a bit of a clean freak when he moved in here because of my past. He told me that was not a problem because while he lived at home you ran a tight ship." Clayton smiled faintly before he confided. "He said something about your Saturday morning cleaning requirements before anyone was allowed out with their friends."

She moved over to the dresser where some of her son's personal belongings were laid out. His holster and gun lay in a chair next to the bed. A brush and more bottles of cologne sat on top of the dresser. Moving into the room behind her, Clayton handed her several white envelopes.

"I've paid all the apartment-related bills, but these are personal ones that I thought you should have," he said, handing her the envelopes.

She took the envelopes from him and began looking through them. "This is his credit card account. I guess I'll have to call and cancel these." Sighing heavily, she continued studying the envelopes in her hands until her vision blurred, making the address information waver before her eyes. "Oh, God....oh, God, I'm so tired of crying," she whispered desperately.

Without hesitation Clay moved over to where she stood and took her in his arms. She went willingly, his strong arms lending her a measure of comfort.

Although his eyes were dry now, his heart beat along with hers, chest to chest in their shared misery. Holding her in the security of his arms, it occurred to him how often he'd held this woman in the past 24 hours. Past relationships aside, he'd held her closer and longer than any woman in a very long time. While it made him feel good that she seemed to rely on him, it also felt very foreign to him. Besides the fact that he let very few people get close to him, Clayton didn't quite know how to deal with this type of loss. No one close to him had ever died before.

The closest relationship he'd ever had was with his baby sister, Sabrina. When Sabrina ran away at fifteen, he had no one. He knew from the postcards he received every few years that she had five kids now and the man she'd run away with was incarcerated. Clayton left home soon after Sabrina did, and hadn't had any contact with his parents since. He knew in his heart that if his parents died tomorrow, he would not shed one tear.

Clayton released Vi when Clarence walked into the bedroom, holding Craig's Mets shirt. The gift from his grandfather had Craig's name stitched on the back. Vi shared with Clay their plans to lay Craig to rest in the shirt. He listened intently to her and Clarence explain the funeral arrangement changes they'd made and he seemed to be pleased, much to Vi's surprise.

As the day wore on, the boxes they packed began to pile up in Clayton's living room. Most were marked for Goodwill, but a few had Janae's and Tony's name on them. Vi brushed her hands on the worn jeans she had on and looked over at Clayton as a thought occurred to her.

"Clayton, before you say 'No,' you should know I will not take 'No' for an answer this time." Taping up the last box, he paused and gave her a questioning look. Vi waited until she had his full attention, then she politely informed him. "You're coming back with us tonight. I can make up the spare room or the sofa for you, so go grab a few things."

He was slightly amused by the ring of authority in her voice and deeply touched by her generosity, but he couldn't. When he started to decline, she quickly cut him off. Smiling at him to take some of the bite out of her next words, Vi calmly told him. "Didn't I just say I wasn't taking 'No' for an answer? Besides, what else do you have to do tonight except wander around in this empty apartment?"

"I couldn't." Stalling for time, Clay pounced on the first thing that came to mind. "I have to pick up my new truck before the dealership closes tonight." There, that was at least partially true. The dealership had called all day yesterday when he didn't show up to finalize the paperwork.

Apparently that was only a minor concern to Vivian Simpson. He watched her pick up her handbag and stride over to the front door, calling out instructions to him as she left through the front door. "Then come over as soon as you pick it up. Pack a bag and Clarence and I will see you later, alright?" She turned around right before the closing the door. Her eyes bore into him, willing him to concede.

"Okay," he agreed, out of excuses.

She gave him a satisfied smile, right before the door closed.

CHAPTER

NINE

A short while after Clarence and Vi left his apartment, Clayton drove to the car dealership. Finalizing the paperwork didn't take long and, within the hour, Clayton was leaving the apartment, carrying a small overnight bag in one hand and the keys to his new truck in the other.

It was a quiet evening, normal in everyway, signifying that the world had moved on. The occupants in cars next to him on the freeway were not aware he'd just lost a best friend or knew the degree of turmoil coursing through him. Besides the questions he had surrounding Craig's death, Clay's mind was suddenly preoccupied with thoughts of Vivian Simpson. Trying to block this train of thought, he focused on the details of the shooting, rehashing what they knew, searching for clues. After a time, he gave up trying to concentrate as she crept into his thoughts again and again. Giving his mind free reign to focus on just her, the visions that ran through his mind were troubling, to say the least. They crowded in on him—disturbing thoughts of Vi Simpson in his arms, Vi Simpson standing behind him, holding him close and absently running her hands over his chest. The time they'd spent together over the past few days had been different than any other time they'd spent before.

Without a doubt, Vi was one of the strongest, most admirable women he knew. In this most difficult of times, she still had the strength and stamina to console others. For some unknown reason, he was experiencing something on a much deeper level that made him acknowledge that she also was a very beautiful woman. Soft and shapely, café mocha brown and petite, she was definitely not lacking in the areas that separated the girls from the women. He shook himself slightly in an attempt to shut down the niggling, improper thoughts running through his mind about Mrs. Simpson. But, they lingered. Innocent as it was, her touch had elicited unwanted things from his body. Her cool, slender hands had branded his chest with their gentleness. This morning, something undeniable had shifted between them, at least for him. The memory of her nearness earlier today in that bathroom had made him hot and cold all at once. What passed between them today was something he'd never felt before. What was it? Had she felt it too? Of course not!

Shaking himself harder this time, Clayton finally put a mental choke hold on this useless line of thinking. Unsure of himself and where these feelings had come from, he made a decision; whatever was happening, he damn sure wasn't going to act on it. *It wasn't right. Was it?*

While Clayton drove the rest of the way to Vi's house, deep in thought, Casey was across town feeling too nauseous to get out of bed. After a light dinner, she lay down for a little while, hoping to ease her suffering. Coupled with the fact she hadn't heard from or seen Craig in three days, the constant queasiness persisted. She'd left over half a dozen messages for him. If he was still mad at her, she reasoned, he could have at least called back!

Fine, she thought, *let him be mad.* Casey closed her eyes and turned over in a huff, trying to recall the last time she'd seen him. She remembered he'd left that morning without saying goodbye. Although she knew about the busy day he had planned she didn't question why he had left so abruptly, because of their argument that morning. Opening her eyes, she threw back the covers and swore inwardly. When they argued in the past, it had never lasted this long. Not calling for three days or picking up his cell phone was juvenile. It was inexcusable, childish and thoughtless. Sitting on the edge of her bed pouting, it suddenly occurred to her that acting childish and thoughtless was so unlike Craig.

Walking barefoot across the room, Casey got out of bed and went into the bathroom to take a shower. As she stepped under the warm spray of water, she felt the slight swell of her belly as she thoroughly soaped her body. A heated sensation assailed her and nestled very low in her abdomen. In her mind, Casey recalled the last time she and Craig were together, right here in this very shower. She closed her eyes as an answering throb developed between her thighs standing still under the showerhead. Enjoying the pulsing stream of water cascading over her skin, she smiled as the recollection of their coming together danced behind her eyelids...

Craig had been upset when she slipped out of bed that morning to take a quick shower. To her surprise, as soon as she turned the water on, he slipped inside the stall behind her and joined her under the warm spray. When she turned around, his lips covered hers in a sweet, tender kiss that quickly turned probing and insistent. In her mind's eye, Casey pictured how his arms had slipped around her waist. How big his hands were, as they slid slowly down her soapy body to cup her firmly from behind. Caught up in the feel of his arousal, pressed so intimately against her abdomen, Casey's own hips swayed toward him in liquid invitation. She felt Craig's entire body tense in need, as her seductive movements went straight to his head, causing the muscular arms beneath her fingertips to harden and bunch.

In a flash, his grasp on her backside tightened as he lifted her with ease and pinned her back firmly against the shower wall. She remembered wrapping her arms around his neck, holding on tight while he positioned himself between her thighs. Then he was there, entering her in one powerful, fluid movement.   Her breathing became labored as he took possession of her flesh, driving into her again and again, completely taking her breath away.

Then, the doorbell rang. *The doorbell rang?*

The ringing bell invaded her delicious thoughts and it took Casey a moment before she realized someone was at the door.   When she did her, eyes popped open and the hot memory instantly slipped away, like so much water down the drain.

Thinking it might be Craig, she reached for a towel.   She dried off quickly and threw on a terry cloth robe.   Rushing to see who it was, she felt that hopeful feeling slip away as she opened the door to find J.R. standing there, wearing a huge grin.

Reading her obvious disappointment, the boy couldn't help teasing Casey as he walked inside.   "What? Were you expecting Brad Pitt?"

She smiled slightly as he came in, and gave him a brief hug before closing the door.   Feeling the need to explain she told him, "Very funny. I thought you might be Craig," then a sudden thought struck.   "Is everything alright at home," she asked.   "Are you okay?"

"When has anything ever been alright at home?"   His neutral tone gave nothing away.

Casey walked over to her small sofa and sat down.   Looking at him, she tapped the seat next to her, motioning him to join her.   "So, what's up?"

"We got kicked out of the Center."   His off-base answer and hesitant tone threw her for a moment.   She sat waiting for him to explain and he didn't disappoint her.   "Me and the guys can't play basketball there anymore until my coach gets back to supervise us."

Thinking there had to be more, she prompted him, "So, what else?"

As if on cue, he opened up completely, sharing what was really on his mind.   "She's got another new boyfriend.   This one's into crack."

Casey knew J.R. was speaking about his mother.   Since J.R.'s dad left, it seemed his mom had the misfortune of meeting more than her share of losers.   Casey studied him in silence, her own worries fading as she focused on the boy.   Although they were distant cousins on his mother's side, their families had never been close.   So she was surprised when he started coming around when she moved back in town several months ago.   They started spending a lot of time together and Casey quickly became genuinely fond of J.R.   That's how Casey found out about his situation at home.   Whenever things got out of hand at home, J.R. would normally crash at his coach's apartment.   Her moving back in town, however, meant he had one other place to go when there was trouble at home.

J.R. slumped lower on the sofa, getting comfortable. Without another word, he picked up the remote control, aimed it at the TV and turned to Cartoon Network. "Anyway, I couldn't stand hanging around there anymore, so…" he shrugged his bony shoulders nonchalantly and looked over at her. "Since I couldn't go to the Center, and coach wasn't home, I came here."

"You know you can always crash here, kid. The sofa's a little lumpy but it's all yours."

The assuring tone in her voice made the boy smile, but when she looked away, J.R. noticed the drawn look on her face and dark circles under her eyes. Much wiser than most fourteen-year-old boys his age, J.R. sensed something was bothering Casey and asked her about it.

After a moment's hesitation, she sighed heavily and looked at the boy. "Craig and I had a fight three days ago and I haven't heard from him since."

J.R. knew that his coach's friend and Casey talked sometimes at the few practices she went to. He was not, however, aware that the two of them had hooked up. "So, why don't you call him?"

"I have but his voicemail keeps picking up."

J.R. was certain whatever she was worrying over couldn't be good for the baby she carried. Unsure how to help her, J.R. suggested she call Craig's job.

His job! Casey thought. *Why hadn't she thought of that?* She quickly got up to make the call.

"Amityville Police, Sgt. Piterrelli speaking."

"Hello…I…I'm looking for Craig Simpson."

The bombing voice belonging to officer Piterrelli was silent for so long that Casey thought he hadn't heard what she said. "Hello, are you there?" she asked.

"Yes, ma'am I'm still here. Uh, may I ask who is calling?"

"I…," Casey caught herself, before blurting out her name. Recovering quickly, she continued, "I'm a personal friend of his."

"Hold on a minute please."

Before she could say anything else, classical music came on. Casey held the receiver to her ear so long, she felt sure the man forgot he put her on hold. Then, a new voice came through the receiver.

"Hello, ma'am, this is Captain Jackson. May I ask whom I'm speaking with?

The agitation that crept into Casey's voice turned slightly desperate as she addressed this new person. "I told the other guy I'm a friend and I've been trying for days to get in touch with Craig Simpson." An uneasy feeling washed over her as she tried to explain to this Captain Jackson. "Listen...if he's not there, can I at least leave him a message?" The dead silence that followed her last question lasted much longer than before, making her extremely nervous. When the man who called himself Captain Jackson finally spoke, Casey had no idea how much his next words would change her life forever.

"Ma'am, I'm not quite sure how to tell you this, but Officer Simpson was shot and killed three days ago."

J.R., who was watching television with his back to Casey, turned around when the phone hit the floor with a thud. In a flash, he was scrambling off the sofa as Casey hit the floor, right after the phone fell from her hands.

CHAPTER

TEN

Trying to sleep was hard. Clay lay with his arm bent behind his head, staring up at the ceiling. Although it wasn't his, the sofa he lay on was soft enough. It didn't take a rocket scientist to figure out the reason for his sleeplessness. Coupled with the fact that he'd felt like an intruder all evening, he lay here in her house wanting to kick himself for accepting Vi Simpson's invitation in the first place. He stared up at the ceiling in the semi-darkness, thinking about his arrival earlier in the evening.

When Clay arrived at the Simpson home that night, the house was full of people he didn't know. In the kitchen, Mrs. Simpson was busy fixing plates of food for a group of people seated at her kitchen table. Craig's old girlfriend, some friends from high school and cousins he'd never met before looked up when he entered the room. After Clay was introduced to everyone, they invited him to sit with them and a plate of food was put in front of him. Taking the vacant chair next to his, Janae sat down close beside him. She explained to him everyone had been looking at Craig's old yearbook and some old family photo albums. A melancholy smiled touched her lips when she pushed one of the books his way, inviting him to take a look.

And he did. While he ate fried chicken and potato salad, Clay flipped through several family albums. There were numerous pictures of Craig and his family, smiling and happy at various places they had visited. For some strange reason the conversation around him faded, as he poured over the photos quickly picking out Mrs. Simpson in each one of them. Vi was radiant in all the photos, smiling and sharing happy times with her children and late husband. Looking at the photos made it feel like he was peeking into the windows of happy people, watching them share something he'd never known.

Everyone left around midnight and besides Tony, Janae and Mrs. Simpson, Clayton and her father-in-law were the only ones left. Clayton suddenly began to feel like an intruder. He wasn't part of this family, so what the hell was he doing here? As if reading his thoughts, Janae and Tony wandered into the kitchen to find him. They were both planning to watch a video in the den and asked him to join them. Instead of waiting for his answer, Janae hooked her arm in his and ushered him into the den. Like it or not, he'd ended up on the sofa, sitting in between Vi's kids watching a predictable action hero flick that supposedly made millions in the movies. He glanced over at Mrs. Simpson in the darkened room several times. At one point when he looked her way, it appeared she was sitting in the black recliner by the window crying. However, when the movie ended, she got up and turned the lights back on. If she had been crying, there was no evidence of it now, he noted.

Clayton watched Vi kiss her father-in-law on the cheek before Clarence retired to the guest room. When she came back into the den carrying sheets and a pillow, Vi smiled at him. For the second time that night she thanked him for letting Clarence take the guest room and agreeing to sleep on the sofa. Clarence did not plan to spend the night, but as the evening progressed he realized Mrs. Simpson was worried about his driving home alone so late. He took the bed linens from Vi and assured her the sofa would do just fine. When she left, Clayton put the linens down on the sofa and started emptying out his pockets. Looking for his cell phone, he searched his pants several times before realizing he must have left it in his truck. Clayton walked out of the den and down the hall toward the front door. On his way out the door, he was surprised to hear Janae call him from the top of the stairs.

"Clay, wait, I'll go with you."

Thinking she'd already gone to bed, he stood at the foot of the stairs watching her come down, still wearing the denim skirt and T-shirt she'd had on all evening. Smiling sweetly, Janae slipped on a pair of flip flops sitting near the closet door, then threaded her arms through his and ushered him out the front door. As they walked toward his truck, which was parked a little ways down the street, Clayton noticed she didn't release his arm. Feeling a little apprehensive, Clayton untangled his arm from hers when they reached his truck. Digging inside his pocket, he found the keys and unlocked the driver door. Leaning inside the truck, he rummaged around in the arm rest for a few seconds. After a few moments, he popped his head out the truck and held up the cell phone.

"Got it. I thought I'd left it at..." Clayton's words died on his lips, as he turned around to find Janae standing almost on top of him. She stood so close to him, they were practically toe to toe.

"I see," Janae replied, just a bit too brightly. "I know how you feel. I wouldn't know how to survive without my cell phone."

Although she smiled innocently up at him, what he read in her eyes made him feel a little uneasy. He took a step back, feeling the coolness of the driver's door at his back he put some distance between them. He watched her hook her thumbs inside the small front pockets on the miniskirt she wore. The movement made the tiny skirt shift a little lower, exposing a good amount of her midriff. Clayton's unease increased a notch. Silently wondering what in the world had gotten into her, he shifted a little and started to step around her. "Well, I guess we'd better get back inside. It's getting pretty late," he said. But when he moved to go around her, Janae placed the cool tips of her French manicured fingers on his forearm.

"Clayton, before we go back in, I have something I want to ask you. I know it's not really the best time and all, but…"

Before she could ask or hint at what he thought she had in mind, Clay cut her off. "We can discuss whatever you want inside. It gets a little chilly at night, and you must be a bit cold." As he said this, his eyes wandered over the outfit she wore and his gaze left no mistaking what he was referring to.

"Oh, no, I'm fine really. I just wanted to thank you for being so supportive. I know my mom's grateful and, well, I was thinking maybe after all this is over you could still come over."

At this point Clayton cut her off, deciding it was best to get back inside. "Yeah, sure I like hanging out with you and your family. If your mom continues to cook like she did tonight, I'll be over for dinner a lot more."

Janae studied him in silence for a moment, then quickly recovering, pasted a sweet smile on her face and turned to go back in the house. However, it was Clayton this time who detained her. Suddenly, he reached out and touched her arm, stopping her progress. There was something on his mind that he needed to discuss with her. Now, he decided, was as good a time as any. When she turned around, he quickly dropped his hand to his side.

The light touch of his hand on her shoulder, although brief, gave Janae a small flicker of hope.

"Janae, wait." Knowing he had to say this first to buffer what he had to really tell her. "I told your mom earlier, but I want to tell you also – if there's anything any of you need, I'm just a phone call away."

He hesitated, not sure if what he was about to say was appropriate or if it was even his place to do so. Weighing his words, Clay told her in a quiet tone, "listen, there's something else I'd like to talk to you about."

The hopeful look he saw in Janae's eyes quickly vanished with his next words. "This morning, your mom and grandfather came over to gather some of your brother's things. Your mom's a real tough lady, but I could tell it was rough on her. I kept thinking that it might have been easier for her if you or Tony were there."

He watched her chin lift defensively and tears well up in her eyes as the implication of his words hit her. Feeling lower than the belly of an ant, Clayton reached out to touch her arm again, then thought better of it and dropped his hand. "Janae, please don't cry. I didn't mean to make you cry, really. I just thought that you being the oldest, well, if you were there it might have been easier for her."

Her jaw wobbled when she addressed him in a hushed whisper. "I....I couldn't Clay. I told mom I couldn't. I never thought she'd do it on her own, I thought she would wait."

Realizing she couldn't go on, he watched a tear slip down her cheek and spoke to her in a quiet tone. "I'm sorry. I know this is tough on all of you. It's just that, she and your brother were pretty close and now that I've had a little opportunity to talk with her, really talk with her, I can see why. Your mom is terrific and strong as a brick house, but..."

Finally reaching out, Clay wiped a tear from Janae's cheek with the pad of his thumb, then grasped both her hands. "She's bound to miss Craig a whole lot more after the funeral, I think. So, all I'm saying is stick around her more. You know, be there if you can." When she looked up at him this time, the hurt he'd seen in her eyes before was gone, replaced with quiet understanding.

"I will," Janae promised. "And I'll talk to Tony too."

Clay gave her hand a light squeeze and led the way back to the house. When they walked back inside, Janae turned to him and gave him an affectionate hug. "Good night Clay, see you in the morning," she said simply and walked down the hall toward her bedroom.

Laying here in the dark remembering everything that happened earlier tonight, Clayton knew he couldn't spend another night here. Although he appreciated their hospitality, he knew he didn't belong here and the sooner he got back to his normal routine, the better.

Tired of staring up at the ceiling, Clayton turned over on his makeshift pallet. Although the sofa turned out to be comfortable, the heat in the room made the sheets stick to his bare chest. Normally he slept in nothing at all. But tonight, for modesty sake, he'd donned a pair of lightweight sweatpants. Light traffic could be heard on the street outside and, although he was mentally exhausted, sleep continued to elude him. Swiping at the perspiration on his brow, his mind continued to wander over all the events of the past few days, thinking sleep would never come he closed his eyes.

The sound of a door closing woke him. Disoriented, Clay sat up, unsure at first where he was. Then he remembered that he was sleeping on the sofa at Craig's mother's house. He remembered one minute staring at the ceiling thinking he would never get to sleep, and the next being knocked out cold. Then there was a noise that he wasn't sure he'd dreamed or actually heard that pulled him from a very deep sleep.

He waited patiently for the sound to come again. When it didn't, Clay began to think he'd imagined it. Then, just when he was certain it was nothing, Clay heard the sound again and realized it was coming from the kitchen. While this was a good neighborhood and the likelihood of someone forcing their way into the house was remote, his police instincts made him get up quietly to check things out.

The light over the stove helped his progress as he made his way into the kitchen. Although he'd been certain the noise had come from this room, it appeared no one was in there. Clayton was about to turn around and leave when he caught a movement in his peripheral vision. Walking further into the kitchen, he came to the patio doors and saw her sitting outside.

Clad in a floral satin robe, Vi sat on a chaise lounger with her feet up. The night was comfortable after such a hot day and a warm breeze slid through the screened patio door. Although she sat in the darkness, he made out a bottle and glass sitting beside her on a low table. Sensing she might want to be alone, Clayton turned to leave.

Vi looked up and saw him through the glass doors, just as he turned to go. With a wave of her hand, she beckoned him outside. She motioned him toward the chair that sat next to her as he stepped out onto the patio. Smiling slightly, she looked his way briefly and surprised him with an apology. "Sorry if I woke you," she said softly.

Easing his tall frame into the patio chair next to her, Clayton quickly assured her. "You didn't. My work hours make it hard to fall asleep at this hour."

In response, she picked up her glass and brought it to her lips, saying nothing. When he glanced her way, she appeared to be a million miles away. Just when he thought she wasn't going to say anything else, she surprised him and replied very quietly, "I couldn't sleep either. It felt like the walls were closing in, so I came out for some air." With that said, she abruptly got up and went back into the house. In less than a minute, she was back carrying another beer and glass for him. He hadn't asked for anything, but when she offered him the beer, he took it.

They sat in silence for what seemed like a very long time, drinking and looking up at the stars. The silence was not uncomfortable. On the contrary, it felt nice. She finished her drink and laid the glass down with a sigh.

"You alright?"

"I'm as alright as a person can be at a time like this."

"Mrs. Simpson, please don't take this the wrong way, but I've seen you constantly moving around for days, taking care of everyone else while they're mourning. Maybe you should just stop doing so much and let some of the family take care of you."

"I don't mind taking care of things. Keeping busy takes my mind off things," she said flatly.

Fearing he'd overstepped his bounds, Clayton quickly added. "I'm sorry. I didn't mean to pry, really. But, sometimes no matter how strong we are, we never realize how much we need to lean on someone else every once in a while."

Vi glanced over at him, thinking—not for the first time—how intuitive this young man was. Unknowingly, he'd hit the nail right on the head, because she'd been thinking the very same thing all day. "Clayton, don't apologize, I appreciate your concern. I just needed some downtime to deal with all this, but I'm doing okay."

"If you want to be alone, I can leave, it's no problem," he said and moved to get up and do just that.

She grabbed hold of his arm, stopping him. "No, please don't go. I like your company. Please sit with me a while."

And so they sat, talking and drinking beer. They talked about Craig, but some of what they discussed concerned him and what his plans were. She was curious if he'd need to find a new roommate. What did he think about the change in funeral arrangements? What did he think about the detective handling Craig's case? Talking with her like this about everything and about nothing came very easily. Mildly surprised at that revelation, Clayton felt himself relax for the first time that day. It was four o'clock in the morning by the time Clayton and Vi realized how late it was. Stifling a yawn, Vi rose to her feet. Clayton did the same, gathering their glasses in one hand and sliding the patio door open for her with his other.

Trying not to wake anyone in the house, they walked silently inside. At the last minute, she turned around to face him, quietly joking about seeing him again in a few hours. She thanked him once more for sitting with her. Then, to his surprise, she placed a very warm kiss on his cheek before going to bed.

He watched her leave while putting their glasses in the sink. Walking back into the den, Clayton laid down on his makeshift sofa bed and folded his arms under his head for the second time that night. Staring up at the ceiling, he accepted the fact that sleep would not come so easily this time around.

They made it look like he was sleeping. Wearing his favorite baseball jersey and matching cap, Vi acknowledged that although the person lying there resembled her son, in death he lacked the vitality that Craig had while he was living.

Vi was standing in the mortuary vestibule, taking in the changes she had the funeral director make. Hearing the faint sounds of music piped into the small room, she smiled. Over the past two days, Vi decided to make some changes in the service, doing what she thought Craig would want. The music playing was one of those changes. He loved smooth jazz and Vandross. So, instead of the dreary music customarily played at funerals and wakes, she selected several songs from Craig's personal CD collection. One of those tracks spilled softly through the speakers overhead, as people filtered into the small funeral home chapel.

As they came by to view the body, everyone stopped to give their condolences to the family sitting in the front row. Vi had gotten up just a little while ago to check something with the director. With that detail taken care of, she started to go back inside but lingered in the vestibule a bit longer, reluctant to go back in right away.

Looking toward the front of the chapel, Vi saw her children sitting beside Clarence in the front pew. She was glad they were with her today. Vi had hardly seen them in the past few days, with their friends coming by so often to hang out or go out somewhere. While she was glad they had friends who cared about them and offered a welcome distraction, she also missed having them around her. Lately the house had felt strangely empty in a way it had never felt before. Clay and Clarence had only stayed the one night at her house and, with the kids gone so much, she had been basically alone for the past several days. With no one around and nothing to do, Vi had been left with her thoughts. And, over the past few days, she'd had a lot of time to think and prepare for this, but now it seemed like hardly enough time.

Vi walked slowly up the aisle toward the first pew and sat down beside her family. Sitting there, staring at Craig lying up there in that mahogany box, she tried to come to terms with all that had happened in the past four days. How did one prepare to bury a son? Scratch that absurd question. A mother couldn't possibly prepare for this because a mother was not supposed to bury her son!

People continued to come in through the double doors of the chapel and walk down the aisle. After viewing the body, they stopped at the front row, shaking hands and giving their condolences to Vi, Clarence, Tony and Janae. After shaking three dozen hands, Vi began to wonder idly, why did people always say, *"I'm so sorry."* She guessed it was because they didn't know what else to say. It struck her as odd, counting the number of times she'd heard those three words this week. Vi knew if she had a dollar for each time she would probably have enough money to …

A muffled commotion at the back of the room caught her attention. Turning in her seat, Vi saw her parents and Cynthia and her husband, Tom, standing in the vestibule. From the looks of things, the noise had come from her mother, who looked none too pleased about something. Vi got up and walked down the aisle toward them. "Mom, Dad, is everything alright?"

"What type of music is this to hear at a funeral?" Her mother's disapproving words matched her equally disapproving expression.

Bless his heart, her father, who had always been the voice of reason whenever her mother lost it, said very calmly as he took hold of his wife's arm. "Now, now dear. Vi has enough to deal with—this is no time to discuss music."

Vi watched them go up the aisle, then turned her attention to Cynthia, who was still standing there. As Cynthia began to speak, Vi saw Clayton approach the chapel from outside. He smiled and entered the hallway at the same moment Cynthia rounded on her in a huff. "Have you lost your mind?" Cynthia said, incredulously. "Vi, this is a funeral for God's sake. I knew you changed the arrangements, but this is beyond belief."

Instantly, Vi decided not to give into her rising anger and responded to Cynthia's high-handed attitude in a different manner. She pasted a serene smile on her face and quietly addressed her sister. "I'm sorry the music is upsetting to you Cynthia. But Craig liked this music and I felt it was only fitting that we play his favorite songs today, of all days."

Her calm response seemed to light a flame to Cynthia's already burning indignation. When she puffed up her chest, obviously prepared to spew out a heated retort, Cynthia was surprised to feel her husband's hand on her elbow, quickly ushering her out of the hallway and up the aisle. She favored Vi with a fleeting, irritated look over her shoulder before allowing Tom to lead her away without further protest.

Vi stood watching her sister and brother-in-law make their way down the aisle, too embarrassed to turn around and face Clayton. Obviously, he'd witnessed their heated exchange.

"I like it," Clayton said from behind her. Trying to assure her that she'd made the right decision no matter what other people thought, he continued to make reference to the music. He touched her elbow gently, and Vi turned around to face him. "You made the right choice Vi, and I'm sure Craig is somewhere listening to this song and liking it too." From the brilliant smile she gave him, he knew his words had made her feel better.

Vi hugged Clayton briefly, then watched him go inside. There was nothing like the combined forces of her sister and mother to put a damper on anyone's parade. Knowing how close she'd come to losing her temper a moment ago, Vi lingered in the foyer a moment longer, trying to tamp down her irritation before joining her family again.

When she turned to go back to her seat, she saw Clayton standing at the head of the church viewing Craig's body. He wore a nicely tailored black suit and his hands were in his pockets. She watched as Tony and Janae got up from their front-row seats and walk up to stand on either side of him. Janae quietly slipped her arm through Clay's right arm at the same time he draped his other arm across Tony's shoulders.

Clayton left immediately following the wake. Instead of going back to the Simpson's home with everyone else, he said his goodbyes and left. The only problem was that once he started his truck, the idea of going home was not very appealing.

Instead, he decided to stop by Valcaro's for a beer. The bar was not crowded at this time of day. Even so, several women gave him sidelong glances and a few sat down on the stools next to him. After a time they realized he wasn't interested in any company, as he sat there for hours nursing the same beer, completely lost in thought.

He felt restless and strangely disconnected, but the thought of going back to the Simpson's house with Craig's family had left him feeling uneasy. As much as he wanted to go, he knew he didn't belong there. It wasn't because they made him feel unwelcome. On the contrary, everyone treated him like one of the family. There was just something that bothered him when he was around them and that was one of the reasons he'd left early two days ago. Spending one night with them—a family so warm and caring—unnerved him. A person could get hooked on being around them, he thought and sighed heavily. Finally, chalking his feelings up to his lousy upbringing, Clayton acknowledged the truth. He was uncomfortable with the love in the Simpson family because it was so foreign to him.

Preparing to leave, he took another swallow of his beer just as a petite blond sat down next to him. Although she had a nice figure, the lines around her mouth and eyes spoke of hard living and too much make up. She wound her arm through his and boldly rubbed an ample breast against Clay's bicep. The smell of liquor on her breath assailed his nostrils when she asked him to buy her a drink. Smiling in apology, Clayton told her he had to leave for a meeting. Finishing his beer, he freed his arm from her grasp and rose to leave. Slipping outside into the night air, he reconciled himself to making the trip home. While he didn't relish going home, Clay realized he couldn't hang around Valcaro's all night either.

It was pretty late when he got home. Clayton pulled into his apartment complex fighting the mental fatigue that had gripped him all day. All thoughts of his fatigue vanished, however, as he pulled into his complex and found someone waiting there for him. In the shadowy darkness of the parking lot, he barely made out the figure standing there. When he saw the boy, it immediately clicked in his mind what he'd forgotten about this week.

"Oh shit, J.R.!" Pulling into the spot in front of his apartment, Clay didn't get a chance to get out any explanations.

"Where the hell you been man?" As he walked up to his front door, the boy shouted so loudly at him that Clayton was afraid it would awaken his neighbors.

Visibly upset, J.R.'s slight frame began to shake as he became further annoyed when Clayton didn't say anything right away. "We started practicing without you last night. Then Marcus and Jamal got into a fight and we all got kicked out of the gym."

Shaking his head in disbelief, Clay mentally berated himself as he approached the boy. He'd completely forgotten their weekly basketball practice at the recreation center.

"J.R., I'm sorry," Finally reaching his side, Clay's apology was cut off.

"Forget you man. We don't need, you know. We'll find someone else to coach us."

Clay had had enough. He opened his front door, quickly clamped a hand around the back of J.R.'s neck and ushered the boy inside of his apartment.

"What the fu...?" Surprised, J.R. began to yell louder, "Get your hands off me man. I don't take that shit from my mom's boyfriend and I ain't taking it from you either!"

Clay released the boy and immediately started apologizing again. "Sorry, kid, but you need to chillax—you're waking everybody up. I've been kind of busy the past few days," he said, hesitantly.

"Yeah, yeah, I know. I've heard it all before. Too busy for the likes of little, poor-ass punks like me."

"Stop it, okay?" Raising his voice, Clay took a deep breath, then began again in a much calmer tone. "Just stop it, okay?" Moving deeper into the apartment, Clayton walked over to his sofa and sat down, motioning for J.R. to join him. The boy stubbornly refused to sit down and glared at him, but remained standing. Clayton knew he had to start from the beginning to get the boy to understand. "Listen, you remember my roommate, Craig, who came down sometimes to help me coach?"

A silent nod acknowledged Clay's question.

"Well, he was shot four days ago. He's dead."

J.R. remained silent, but for a much longer time. Then his face registered what Clayton had just told him. "Shit man, that's fucked up. I liked him— he was nice to me. Hey, I'm sorry man." Obviously uncomfortable with all this talk of shooting and death, J.R. sat down beside Clay on his sofa, unsure of what to say or do next.

"Who started the fight? Clay finally asked him.

"What? Oh, Jamal. I tried to tell those assholes to quit it, but they threw us out of the gym anyway. We can't go back without you, or somebody else to supervise."

Silence again.

"This sucks man. Without you or Craig—ain't nobody gonna' give a shit about us now," J.R. spat out with his head down.

Clay cuffed him around the neck again, more gently this time. Looking at J.R., Clay instructed the boy in a calming voice. "Don't say that and stop cussing. I told you about that, didn't I?"

"Oh, yeah. Sorry, my bad."

Clay looked at him earnestly and said, "Listen, you know me, and you should know I'm not going anywhere. I just need a few days before I can get back over there, okay?"

He studied the boy intently, waiting until J.R. nodded in understanding. Satisfied when he did and that everything was cool between them, Clay clapped the boy on his back. Studying the fourteen-year-old boy, Clayton acknowledged he definitely had a tough exterior. But inside he was just a lost young boy, hiding behind this tough act and a vicious tongue. He remembered when his and J.R. paths accidentally crossed several years ago.

J.R. and his buddy had been caught shoplifting. While his friend got away, Clay had tracked J.R. down on foot. He remembered it being one of the longest chases he'd had in a while. Winded, he pushed a little harder and closed the gap between himself and the boy. It wasn't until Clay caught up to him and turned him over that he realized he was only tackling a kid. Back then he was a smelly, skinny, foul-mouthed kid. He had gray eyes and a massive curly afro. When you saw him your first thought was that he must be Hispanic, but later Clay found out his parents were black and white. In the back of his squad car, he remembered the boy spewing profanities at him all the way to the station. Once there, Clayton sat the boy down at a desk in the corner, gave him a Coke and asked where his parents were. But when he asked that question, J.R.'s entire demeanor changed. Right before Clay's eyes, the boy transformed from a tough-as-nails hellion to just a normal, scared boy. He recalled how his bottom lip quivered when J.R. had broken down, crying just like a baby.

In that moment, Clay saw himself in J.R., who was a lot like the young, lost boy he'd been long ago. Although, J.R.'s situation was slightly different from Clay's when he was younger, it was just as awful. It turned out that J.R. lived with his mother, who was addicted to cocaine and she kept various boyfriends around who supplied her with drugs in exchange for her charms. Occasionally, some of these guys roughed J.R. up, but there had been others who tried to violate him sexually. Clay didn't find all this out, however, until about a month after the shoplifting episode. It took that long for J. R. to open up to him. The day he'd chased J.R. down on foot, Clay decided, on a whim, to let the boy go on the shoplifting charges. He also remembered how the kid's jaw dropped clear to the floor when he realized Clay was letting him go with a warning. Although J.R.'s jaw had dropped open when Clayton let him go, he quickly clamped it shut when he heard he was being let go on one condition—that he promised to show up at the park the next day.

Clay sat on a park bench near the basketball court over on Chestnut, half expecting this kid not to show. Surprisingly, he did and he kept on showing up everyday for the next two weeks. They played basketball and Clay started teaching him some of the fundamentals of the game. Even though he came to the park every day acting totally disinterested, the boy was a fast learner. And at the end of their time together, he looked happy to have learned something.

Eventually he started bringing a friend or two with him and, before long, Clay was teaching basketball to J.R. and about ten of his buddies. After their game, his friends would leave but J.R. would always linger. Clayton started taking him to get a burger afterwards, guessing there wasn't much to eat at his house. It was during those meals that J.R. finally opened up to him. Clay, in turn, shared the horrid memories of his own childhood.

After a time Clayton grew fond of the boy and J.R. began to trust him. It was during that time he told J.R. he could depend on him whenever he was in trouble, but that he had to tough it out. Clay knew the boy had a cousin he stayed with when things got out of hand at his place, but he also offered his apartment as refuge whenever J.R. felt he needed to get away for a while. On several occasions over the past two years, J.R. had been forced to stay the night at Clayton's place. Other times, when Clay was on duty and J.R. had to get away from his house, he stayed with his cousin. He'd told Clayton her apartment was very small and he couldn't stay there long, but she never turned him away when he needed a place to sleep.

"When's the funeral?" J.R. asked, bringing Clay back to the present.

"Tomorrow," he replied. Then, as an afterthought, he asked, "Did you eat today, kid?"

"Yeah, I ate."

Eyeing him carefully, Clay asked J.R. pointedly, "When was the last time you ate?"

Looking down at his feet, J.R. fell silent for a moment before admitting, "This morning."

Clay got up from the sofa and headed for the kitchen. "Come on, let's go make you a sandwich."

The funeral was nice. Why did people always say that about funerals, Vi wondered? Or sometimes they would say, *what a nice going-home service so-and-so had.* With her mind a million miles away from where she desperately didn't want to be, Vi wondered how a person could put the words "nice" and "funeral" together.

The law enforcement presence at Craig's funeral was astounding. The sheriff's department, uniformed officers, detectives and chiefs of police from all the neighboring towns showed up. They provided a proud uniformed presence and exemplified a dignified respect for their fallen comrade. In fact, in addition to the pallbearers, more than half the church was filled with law enforcement personnel.

She caught a glimpse of Clay as he walked with the coffin as lead pallbearer. They all looked alike in their law enforcement finery. But somehow he stood out from the rest. Vi had never seen him in formal uniform before and was astonished by how mature he looked in it, standing very tall and fit. Both his hands were encased in white gloves and he wore shiny, black leather shoes. The rigid collar of his dark, brass-buttoned uniform coat fit perfectly, stretching impressively across his impossibly broad shoulders.

Although Vi had seen him many times in regular uniform pants, a shirt and tie, she'd become accustomed to seeing him in civilian clothes. That was nothing compared to the way he looked today. It was hard to pinpoint, something in his bearing made Clayton's maturity and manliness more prevalent than at any other time she'd seen him before.

After the funeral was over, Clayton shook hands with the family and made his way down the line to Vi. When he reached her, their eyes met and held and, in that moment, something passed between them. The silent support they exchanged was filled with an underlying subtle awareness. Although brief, the exchange felt a lot like the awareness that normally passed between a woman and a man.

Back at the house, Vi sat half listening to one of her neighbors, feeling too numb to absorb anything except a deep disbelief that this couldn't possibly be happening to her. The service and group of people clad in black, the eulogy and kind words from some of Craig's closest friends were all a blur. Stoically, she went through the motions. The only thing getting her through this day was the knowledge that Janae and Tony were there by her side. Unfortunately, the day dragged on. After all, whoever heard of people going straight home after a funeral?

As the afternoon wore on, people continued to come over, bringing with them every dish imaginable. Counting the food in her refrigerator with what lay on the table, they now had enough to feed an army. It was completely ridiculous, but the single thought in her mind as she began greeting yet another person, carrying yet another covered dish was, *I don't believe I have enough Saran Wrap.* Vi spent the next two hours having meaningless after-funeral conversations, accepting condolences and telling every other person who asked, *"No I'm not hungry. But please, help yourself."*

After a while, Cynthia and her husband, Tom, took her parents home and Janae and Tony left with their friends. Only a handful of people remained along with her and Clarence. When they arrived earlier, Vi assumed Clayton would join everyone else at her house after the funeral. However, after several hours, it became clear he wasn't coming. Surprisingly, she found it was his company she longed for right now over anyone else.

Feeling very tired, Vi decided to leave the small group she was sitting with downstairs. After a time, she slipped upstairs and retreated to the confines of her bedroom. Immediately she slipped off the black, five-inch heels she'd worn all day and bent over to massage her toes. Smoothing the ache in her foot, she vaguely recognized the discomfort she was feeling was the main reason she rarely wore high heels. Closing her eyes, Vi heard the muffled voices beyond her bedroom door downstairs and started to feel the ache in her feet subside. Squeezing her eyes tighter, she sighed deeply and mentally shed the invisible blanket of strength she'd carried all day. The cloak fell away and the flood gates opened, allowing her tears to fall in the solitude of her darkened room.

CHAPTER
TWELVE

They say time heals all wounds. Unfortunately for Vi, they just didn't say exactly how much time was involved. About a week after the funeral, Vi woke up very early one day. She got out of bed, brushed her teeth and padded barefoot into the kitchen to turn the coffee maker on. While it brewed, she loaded the dishwasher, and then went out front to get the Sunday morning paper.

With the paper tucked under one arm and her coffee in hand, she went out back and sat in the chaise lounger on the patio. Only the birds were out to keep her company this early in the morning. She laid her coffee on the low table nearby and settled deeper into the cushions to read the morning paper. After ten minutes, she put the paper down on her lap, quickly losing interest in the world news.

She looked across the backyard, feeling more than a little annoyed with Tony for not cutting the grass. Lately, he seemed to spend a lot more time with his friends or talking on the phone with somebody named Briana. The other half of his time he spent in his room moping around, eating and sleeping.

Janae, on the other hand, was keeping pretty busy. Although she had a few more days at home before she went back off to school, the plans she made to go back with friends took up much of her time. In fact, one of the friends had a truck and had agreed to haul some of Craig's things back to her dorm room next week.

This morning when Vi woke up, it dawned on her that her family seemed to be drifting apart. She decided they needed to do something—something routine that would bring them all together. Going to church this morning seemed like a good start toward bringing normalcy back into their lives.

The sound of the neighborhood waking up reached her ears. A dog barked, birds chirped in their nests and, in the distance, a car door slammed. The sweet sounds of the morning lulled her, and Vi began to feel tired lying under the sun. With all the trouble she had falling asleep lately, she decided a small nap couldn't hurt. She would just close her eyes for a minute, she thought.

Clay got off work around 6:30 that morning. He'd been meaning to call Mrs. Simpson to discuss a small matter, but due to his hours the past few days, seeing her had been nearly impossible. Turning his vehicle in the direction of her house, he decided to stop by on the outside chance she would be up this early.

He parked his truck and got out, noting one of her garage doors stood open as he walked up the driveway. He decided she was either not home or forgot to close it again. As he got closer to the front door, he saw that her car was still parked in the garage on that side where the garage door had been pulled down.

When he reached out to ring the doorbell, something made him hesitate. The screen and front door were closed. Every other time he'd been here, her front door was always open, unless it was winter time. They were probably still asleep. Deciding it was too early to chance waking everyone, Clay turned to leave. What he had to discuss with her would have to wait until later. As he came down the front porch steps, he noticed the condition of her front yard for the first time. The grass needed cutting and the hedges were in need of a trim too. Walking slowly back down the driveway, he noticed her gardening tools and lawnmower through the open side of the garage.

After working all night, he was normally too wired to go straight home and fall asleep. Usually he stopped for breakfast before going home or watched television until he got tired. This morning was no different. If he went home now, he knew it would be at least two hours before he could shut it down and catch a few "z"s. As an idea struck him, Clayton looked in the garage again. He got back in his truck and turned the ignition on. The engine purred quietly and a welcome blast of air conditioning filtered through the vents. Unaware he was humming, Clayton drove home.

Growing louder, the sound of the lawnmower reached her. Vi was in limbo—that place halfway between sleep and consciousness—when she heard it. Tony must have decided to roll out of bed and cut the grass, she thought vaguely. It was about time. She'd only asked him to cut it a million times this week. Just then the sound of the lawnmower grew even louder, catapulting Vi into wakefulness. She woke up, feeling disoriented and thinking someone was cutting the grass and, her sleepy brain registered, it sounded like they were pretty close to her yard.

Vi came awake slowly, stretching her limbs to alleviate the stiffness of sitting in the chaise lounger. Just as a powerful sense of awareness grabbed hold of her, she realized she must have fallen asleep. But for how long, she wondered? Looking to her left, Vi finally was able to identify where the lawnmower sound was coming from. It was her lawnmower and her grass being cut by a bare-chested sweaty man. She rubbed the sleep from her eyes.

Funny, but she didn't remember calling the landscaper out this week. As Vi became fully awake, rubbing the last bit of sleep from her eyes, she realized the sweaty, bare-chested man wasn't the landscaper after all. To her mortification, the sweaty, bare-chested man cutting her grass was none other than Clayton Marshall.

As if he were rooted to the ground with invisible concrete, Clayton stood behind the mower, unable to take his eyes off her. Blood raced fast and furious through every part of his body when he saw her lying there. Powerless to do more than just stare, he acknowledged that on some level, he probably couldn't have moved from that spot if his life had depended on it.

For the space of a heartbeat, neither of them moved or said a word. Then, reality set in and they both began to move and speak at the same time.

"I'm sorry… I…," he began.

"Clayton, hi… um, what are you…. You startled me."

Nervously, Vi rose from the lounger, fumbling to close the loosened sash on her robe. *My God*, she thought. *What in the world is he doing here? How long had she drifted off?* She wasn't sure. She was sure, however, that she'd been practically half naked in front of him.

Sensing her discomfort, he started again, "I'm sorry, I had no idea. I thought everyone was still asleep."

Her dream returned to her then, where she thought it was Tony mowing the lawn. But in reality it was Clayton. *What a sweet thing for him to do*, she thought. *What an odd thing for him to do.*

He must have read the confusion on her face and hurried to explain. "I wanted to stop by and talk with you about something when I got off this morning. Unfortunately, when I got here, it looked like everyone was still asleep."

Clayton began to realize that the more he explained, the more confused she looked. So he did the only thing he could do—he kept talking. "So, I was going to leave when I noticed the grass was badly in need of a cutting and your mower was just sitting in the garage." When she still didn't respond, he added, "Someone left the garage door open all night I guess."

That statement caused her face to heat up even more than it already was because that "someone" was her. Vi couldn't count the times Craig used to admonish her for leaving those doors open like that. With a guilty look, she finally said, "That someone would be me, I'm afraid. It's a bad habit."

"Well, everyone forgets," he said, very carefully. "But, it's kind of dangerous, you know, leaving it like that. I mean, this is a nice neighborhood and all, but you never know." He trailed off.

"I know," she said, shaking her head, because she knew he was right. "Craig always used to warn me about leaving those doors open."

As the silence fell between them again, Vi couldn't help noticing again he was bare to the waist and covered in perspiration. Well, if someone went around shirtless as much as he did, they had better have muscles and abs like his to pull it off, she thought. She continued to stare at him, taking in the rest of his attire. A worn baseball cap sat backwards on his head, worn faded jeans covered his legs and work boots protected his feet. Obviously, he'd dressed for the task, she thought.

As the silence lengthened between them, Vi colored again, realizing she was staring. Mentally chastising herself, she reluctantly pulled her eyes away from his sweaty body. Speaking awkwardly, she began, "Clayton, really, I don't know what to say." Cinching the belt on her robe tighter, she continued, "You shouldn't have done this, but I'm eternally grateful. I asked Tony about a million times this week to do it. Wait 'till I see that boy," Her stern words were betrayed by the smile playing across her lips.

"It's not a problem, think nothing of it," he said casually. "When I get off work this early, I normally work out or do something to make me tired. This will take the place of my workout this morning."

Vi started to offer him money, but guessed that that would insult him. After all he wasn't a fourteen-year-old boy. Wanting to do something, she said, "How can I repay you? Please let me fix you breakfast."

"Already ate, sorry."

"What can I do then?"

Searching her face, he said, "Some cold water would be nice."

"Sure, come with me. How about a glass of lemonade instead?," she asked him, as she turned and went back into the kitchen through the patio doors.

"Water's fine, but lemonade is better, if it's no trouble," he said, following her.

"I must have fallen asleep out there, which is funny because I haven't been sleeping very well lately," Vi said with her back to him, needing to explain away the fact that she fell asleep outside. "I guess the morning air made me tired."

Clay wiped the sweat from his neck and forehead with the T-shirt he'd taken off earlier, when it got too hot. Tucking one end of it back in his rear pocket, he sat down at the kitchen table and watched her at the sink. She found a pitcher, filled it with water then went to the refrigerator for ice. When she reached up to get lemonade mix from the cabinet, the material of her robe tightened enticingly across her backside. He swallowed hard, his eyes powerless to do anything but watch the material stretch across her body with every movement she made. The silk robe fit like a second skin. Involuntarily, his mind played out how he'd come upon her in the backyard just moments ago.

It had taken him by surprise finding her there. When he finished mowing the front yard and walked to the back yard, he'd never expected anyone to be out there. He faltered, as a short-lived internal battle ensued within him. When he saw her lying there fast asleep, the gentleman in him wanted to turn away, but the licentious male in him wouldn't allow Clay to move a muscle. Hell, if his life had depended on it, he would have been unable to move.

In a New York-minute, his mind cataloged the delicious vision she made lying there. A cup of coffee or tea sat forgotten on a low table beside her chair. His eyes trailed over the tiny blue, green and yellow flowers that covered the silk robe she wore. It lay open from top to bottom, the soft material barely covering her body. In her sleep it must have come loose, because the only thing holding it together was a long red sash tied at her waist. The loosened robe revealed some type of short, pink frilly thing she wore underneath. From his vantage point, the swell of one very ample breast came dangerously close to falling out of the top of this frilly garment and a full length of leg was exposed for all to see. And what a pair of legs they were, he noted. They were long and shapely and she had tiny feet tipped with red painted toenails. Perfect. Mesmerized, he stood very still, taking all this in, while other parts of his body began to twitch and stir.

Whoa, down boy, he was mentally chastising himself at the precise moment her eyes opened. It had been the shock on her face when she woke up that finally made him look away, and instantly made him feel like some kind of pervert.

The sound her delicate voice interrupted his thoughts. "Actually Clayton, I'm glad you woke me when you did, or I might have overslept." She shared with him her thoughts about getting the family back to normal. "I've been thinking how nice it would be to go to church this morning like we used to. I think it will do us all good."

Continuing to watch her as she explained all this with her back to him, Clayton had to wrench his thoughts back to what she was saying. "Why is that?" he asked vaguely, struggling to keep his mind on their conversation and out from under her robe.

"I just had a feeling that Craig would want us to get back to normal." After a moment she continued. "I mean, Janae will be heading back to school soon, Tony will go back to basketball day camp and I need to get back to work full time. It just feels like it's time, you know," she said.

He only nodded and took the glass of lemonade she handed him. It was good. He drank it quickly, handed the glass back to her and rose to leave. "I should be getting back to the yard. I'll be done with it in a little while."

"Clayton, thanks again, you really shouldn't have. Why don't you join us for dinner tonight?"

"You know I never turn down a meal, but I gotta' work tonight. Can I get a rain check?"

"Of course you can. You know you're always welcome." As an afterthought, she asked him, "Oh, hey, what did you want to talk to me about?"

"It can wait," he said, knowing she was on her way to church.

"Are you sure?"

"Yeah, no problem," he said and left the kitchen to finish mowing the lawn.

CHAPTER
THIRTEEN

In his room, Tony was talking on the phone when Janae passed by his doorway.

"Hey Cassanova," she said to her brother. "Why aren't you dressed for church?" she asked him from his doorway.

Tony hung up the phone and gave his sister a long, suffering look. "'Cause mom said I didn't have to go. I'm gonna' stick around and do the hedges and then help Clay finish the yard," he told his sister.

That's how Janae found out Clayton was outside, mowing the lawn, shirtless and sweating in places she'd always dreamed of exploring. Whatever else Tony said after that was lost on Janae as she hurried to her room, checked on her makeup and made her way to the kitchen.

Vi was unloading the dishwasher when Janae entered the kitchen. She grabbed a bottle of water from the refrigerator, as she greeted her mother and walked over to glance out the kitchen window. Clayton was nowhere in sight.

Turning, she looked at her mother. She was a good-looking woman for her age, Janae thought. The fitted pantsuit she wore was tailored to perfection, easily suited for church or any corporate boardroom. It was complemented by a flowing, feminine blouse in vibrant hues that set off the white suit she wore.

"Mom, Tony told me he got yelled at for not cutting the grass. He's still in his pajamas, walking around in a funk."

"I didn't exactly yell at him honey, but I was upset," Vi said in clarification. "Clayton should not have to come over here and cut our grass. I guess I should start using the landscaper again," she said as an afterthought. Tony came into the kitchen and caught the tail end of his mother's last statement.

"No, mom," he pleaded. "Don't call the landscapers, I promise I'll do it next time. I just got caught up in some things. Sorry."

"Sure you don't want to go with us today? We can wait for you to get ready," Vi asked him, again hoping he had changed his mind about going to church.

"I don't really feel like going today," he told his mother apologetically. "Maybe next Sunday, okay?"

"Okay, but eat something and then go help Clayton finish the yard as soon as you're done, alright?"

"Sure thing mom," he said and left the kitchen.

Janae put the bottle of water back in the fridge and went to the sink. She began to fill a thermos with water and ice and then turned around facing her mother. "It's awfully hot out," she told her mother. "I think I'll take this water out to Clayton," she said and left the kitchen by way of the patio doors.

"Good idea," Vi called to Janae's retreating back as she left the kitchen. "Hey, take the keys with you Hon, and start the car. I'll be out in two minutes."

Clayton glanced up and saw Janae walking toward him. He cut the engine on the mower and waited until she reached his side.

"Hey Clay," she said when she reached him. "Mom and I thought you might want some water before we left." Smiling sweetly, Janae handed him the thermos filled with water and let her eyes slide over him before she told him. "It should stay pretty cold for a while in this."

Clay smiled as he took the water she offered. Opening the top, he brought the thermos up to his lips and took a few giant swallows. When he replaced the top and swiped a forearm across his mouth, he noticed that Janae was still standing there, watching him. She nervously looked away when he caught her staring and started studying her shoes as he took another swig of water. When he finished this second pull on the thermos, he caught her staring again. Although she quickly looked away, it was too late. He had enough time to see her eyes wander slowly, over him. She left him suddenly wishing he'd kept that T-shirt on, even if it was over 90 degrees outside. Clay took another pull from the Thermos and continued to stare at the top of her head, as Janae continued to stare at her feet. Her French-manicured toes peeked out of strapless, white sandals. Finally, he broke the silence between them and said, "Well, I guess I'd better get back to work. Thanks for the water."

As he bent down to crank up the mower again, Janae realized she was about to miss her opportunity. She looked up at him, wide eyed and nervously wringing her hands together. "Ah, Clay, I was thinking. I mean, I'm going back to school in a few days, and I thought maybe we could…"

Her words were interrupted, as he quickly spoke up, purposely misunderstanding what he thought she was about to say. "Yeah, I know. Your mom told me. Why don't we all go out to dinner before you leave? I know a great place downtown, it'll be my treat."

For several intense seconds, she continued to stare at him like she wanted to add something, or clarify she'd meant just the two of them getting together.   Apparently, deciding against saying whatever it was she had on her mind, she told him instead, "Yeah, okay. We can all have dinner."

Clay smiled again, turned back to the mower and didn't dare look up until he was sure she'd walked away.

Wow, that was close, he thought. He'd always thought of Janae like a younger sister, Craig's very young sister. That hadn't changed for him, but apparently it had for her. He stood up, watching her walk back toward the house, taking in the sway of her hips as they moved in time with her bouncing pony tail. The pink summer dress she wore fit nicely over her slender figure. He knew any red-blooded male would be very interested in her. He knew she was very interested in him. He also knew with certainty that he was not interested in her, in that way.

About five minutes later, he watched them leave for church. Janae waved at him, started the car and pulled it out of the garage. She got out from behind the wheel and made a very seductive show of easing into the passenger seat.

Then, Mrs. Simpson caught his attention as she came out the house and walked down the driveway.   She wore a well-tailored, soft-looking, white linen pant suit. The thigh-length jacket was open, showing off a floral chiffon blouse.   The blouse draped over the collar of her suit in flowing folds and stood out against the stark whiteness of the jacket she wore. He watched her with pure masculine interest, intrigued by how she managed to look soft and feminine and cool and refined all at the same time. Vi waved to him as she slid behind the wheel, the cuffs of her blouse, which extended beyond the jacket arms, flowed freely on the morning breeze.

Tony was on the phone longer than he'd anticipated. It seemed Briana's best friend told her he was at the movies with another girl last night. Half an hour went by before he realized he still had chores to do before his mom got back from church. He let Briana know he was a bit annoyed with the whole mess and told her he had to go, ending the call.

Tony raced down the hall, out the door and into the garage. He found the hedge trimmers, walked around to front of the house and got busy. Clay found him cutting the hedges a few minutes later when he came around to the front of the house. "Hey, Clay," Tony called out to him.

Clay waved, sat down on the front porch and took a drink from the garden hose he'd turned on earlier. Tony put down the garden shears and walked over to sit with him on the porch. When Clay offered him a drink from the hose, Tony gladly took it.

"Sure is getting pretty hot out here," Tony said, holding the hose up to his mouth to take a swig. After drinking from the hose for several seconds, he wiped his mouth with the back of his hand and told Clay, "Man, thanks for cutting the grass. Mom has been on me to get it done all week."

Clayton looked at him earnestly before asking, "Why didn't you do it, then?"

Not looking at Clay, Tony shrugged his shoulders and said defensively, "I don't know. I was gonna' get it done today. Honest."

Sighing, Clay hung an arm across the boy's shoulder in a reassuring gesture before saying, "Yeah, I believe you, but listen," he paused, making sure he had Tony's attention. "Don't give your mom such a hard time, alright? Don't make her ask you to do something more than twice." Treading very carefully because he didn't want to hurt the boy's feelings but, at the same time, needing to drive his point home, he added, "This is a hard time on everyone and she's depending on you."

He watched Tony closely as he said this, and was glad to see the boy nod his head in understanding. "Good. You're the man of the family now, you know. So you have to step up, okay?"

After their talk, Clay and Tony finished the hedges together, washed up in the kitchen sink and sat down to drink more lemonade. Clay glanced at his watch a while later. Although he wanted to hang around and talk with Vi, it was getting pretty late. He stood up and prepared to leave.

"Listen, I wanted to talk with your mom, but I need to get home and start getting ready for work," he told Tony. "Do you have a pen and paper handy so I can leave her a note?"

"Yeah, sure," Tony said and got up from the table. He walked over to a kitchen drawer next to the stove and pulled out a pad and a pen. He handed it to Clay just as the phone rang. Clay started writing a brief note to Vi, while Tony answered the call.

It was late afternoon when she got home. Janae left immediately after church to hang out with friends, so Vi decided to join her sister for lunch. The afternoon flew by once the two of them started talking about the salon and problems with a back order of supplies they were expecting this week. When Vi got home, she went directly to her bedroom, changed into jeans and a tank top, then headed to the kitchen to start dinner. She didn't notice the envelope with her name on it until the roast was in the oven and the rest of dinner was underway. It lay on the counter propped up against the microwave. Walking over, she picked it up and turned it over. She was just about to open it when the doorbell rang. Vi stuck the envelope in the back pocket of her jeans and hurried to the door.

"Clarence, you're early. Come on in."

"I thought I might come by early to help you cook or gossip over coffee," he told her with a mischievous gleam in his eye.

"Now you know I never gossip," she said with feigned innocence.

As she stood aside to let him enter, he asked her. "Okay, my dear, if you say so. Say, where are my grandchildren?"

"Janae's will be home in time for dinner and Tony's upstairs with the phone glued to his ear again."

"Oh, is that a recent affliction?" he asked.

"Yeah, I think its called phonacitis," she joked. "Come on out back. It's too hot for coffee, but we can have some lemonade out on the patio until dinner's ready."

By the time they finished a pitcher of lemonade, dinner was ready. After eating, Clarence played a game of chess with Tony while Vi lay on the sofa watching a sitcom. The envelope in her pocket was all but forgotten.

CHAPTER

FOURTEEN

She missed him at the station. Vi got up early the next morning, hoping to catch him before he left work. Unfortunately, when she reached Amityville Police Station, she found out Clay was already off duty. Vi got back in her car and drove over to his apartment, hoping to catch him before he went to sleep. When she got there, she hesitated before knocking. What if he was already asleep, she thought? Then, realizing what she had to discuss couldn't wait, Vi knocked on his door and waited. While she waited, she thought about the envelope in her purse. Vi was so tired last night, she'd forgotten all about it. When she gathered clothes this morning to start a load of wash, she found it tucked in her back pants pocket. When Vi sat down to open it over her morning coffee, she nearly fell off her chair when she saw what was inside.

Clay answered the knock on his door, wondering idly who it could be this early in the morning. He was surprised to find Mrs. Simpson on his threshold.

"Mrs. Simpson," Clay said in surprise when he opened the door to let her in.

"Hi Clayton, sorry for stopping by so early, I tried to catch you before you went to sleep," she told him apologetically.

"It's no problem, really. I just got off and haven't been to sleep yet."

"Listen, we need to talk about the envelope you left me yesterday."

"Oh, that. Well, I tried to hang out until you got home from church, but it was getting kinda' close to my shift. I left a note in there explaining…" he trailed off.

"I got the note, but…"

Clayton cut her off, almost forgetting his manners. "Please come in. Can I get you something to drink or eat?"

"No thanks," she said. "I'll pick up something later, while I run my errands." Getting back on track, she told him. "Besides I wanted to talk with you first. Clay, really, I can't take this money."

Leading her to the sofa, Clay motioned for her to sit down. Sighing, he sat down beside her. Studying her intently, he began, "Mrs. Simpson…"

"How many times have I told you to call me Vi?" she said, interrupting him.

"Okay, Vi. Craig and I bought this furniture together. The cashier's check in that envelope is rightfully yours."

"But, $1,100.00?" she questioned.

"That's about half of what we paid for it, unless you think its worth more," he trailed off.

"It more than enough, Clay but...."

"No," he held up a hand to stop any further discussion. "Vi, listen. It was either pay you half, or sell it and split that money with you. But I really didn't want to sell it."

Looking at him, she tried one more time to reason with him, "Clayton, that furniture is yours now I wasn't expecting a penny for it, really."

"I know that, which is why I left a cashier's check. I knew if I'd left you a personal check, you would have just torn it up."

"But..." she started to protest again.

"No, buts, Mrs. Simpson—I mean Vi," he said quickly, correcting himself. "I needed to do this, anything else wouldn't be right." He saw that she was thinking about what he was saying. He noticed that whenever she was deep in thought, she chewed on her bottom lip. His jaw tightened as his eyes were involuntarily drawn to her mouth with that action.

Man, it is getting hot in here. Yanking his thoughts away from the edge of her white teeth nibbling into her full bottom lip, Clayton stood up. Before she could come up with any further excuses, he said. "Look, I was just getting ready to work out. Why don't you join me?" The distraction worked like a charm. Satisfied with himself he watched as her mind quickly changed gears.

"What? Now?" she said, looking down at what she wore. "I'm not dressed for working out. Besides, I still have a few errands to run."

Clay looked her over. She had on one of those lightweight, cotton running suits. It was lavender, with white stripes running down the side of her pant legs. She also wore a tank top and running shoes. Perfect, he thought. "You're dressed just right for what I have in mind," he told her.

"I can't, really, I," she started to say.

"Oh, come on, the errands can keep. I'll even buy you breakfast afterwards." His handsome smile tempted her. Coupled with the charming, lop-sided grin she was coming to know very well, it made it virtually impossible to say no to him.

"I don't know," she started to say again.

Sensing she was wavering, he pushed harder. "Come on Vi, it'll be fun." He watched her front teeth bite down, worrying her lower lip in thought again.

Then, with a deciding look in her eyes, she said to him. "Okay, but I insist on buying breakfast." Vi was instantly rewarded with his hundred-watt smile.

"Great," he said, turning to leave the room. As he made his way down the hall to his bedroom, Clay told her, "Give me three minutes to get dressed!"

Clay was right, she did have fun. He was a member of a popular downtown fitness club. For a health and fitness club, it had everything imaginable. It boasted a hair salon, daycare, restaurant, tennis, swimming pool and yoga classes. It also had a great cardio room and a huge advanced and beginner's weight room.

Every surface was either wood or chrome, and where the walls were not painted white or mirrored, there was glass separating the different areas lending an open, but connected, feeling to each room. They went directly into the weight room and spent about an hour there using free weights. Clayton showed Vi proper form on the machinery in there to target certain muscles. Since Vi didn't have a change of clothes, they bypassed a vigorous cardio workout in the treadmill room.

Leaving the club an hour later, they passed the cardio room and Vi noticed all the equipment had a built-in fan, TV and radio. As they made their way to the parking lot to find Clay's truck, Clay saw Vi smiling. Giving her a quizzical look, he asked, "Care to let me in on the joke?"

Turning his way, she said in a suddenly serious voice, "I was just thinking, with fans, music and TV on all the equipment, your club makes it pretty hard to find an excuse for not exercising."

He laughed at her comment, something he didn't do often, and Vi realized it was a surprisingly nice sound. It was also contagious, and she found herself laughing along with him.

He took hold of her hand and said, "Come on, let me buy you breakfast."

They went to an IHOP restaurant a few blocks away. Breakfast was scrumptious, which probably explained why people kept crowding in when they got there and were still coming in when they finally left. Vi smiled at Clayton as he sat across from her sipping on his second cup of coffee.

"Clayton, I had a wonderful time today. Thank you."

Smiling at Vi from across the table, he told her, "It was my pleasure." The waitress came by at that precise moment and left the check. Vi picked up her handbag and quickly retrieved a few bills from her wallet. Before she could pull out enough money, Clay placed his credit card on top of the check, and slid it over to his side of the table.

Watching his actions, Vi began to protest. "Clayton, let me at least pay half."

"Vi, put your money away," he said, his tone inviting no argument. As their waitress passed by again Clay handed the check and his credit card to her, stopping any further discussion.

"Thank you, but next time breakfast really is on me," she said and reluctantly put the money back in her wallet.

After dropping Vi off to pick up her car, Clayton went home to get some sleep. He thought about the pleasant morning they'd just shared and started making plans to do it again, before drifting off to sleep.

As it turned out, he called her the very next day to see what she was doing. And just like that, over the next few weeks, they fell into a routine and met at the club to work out regularly.

It was a busy Monday at the salon and instead of going out to eat lunch, Vi and Nicole chose to order sub sandwiches and eat out back where a small table and chairs were set up for days just like today. Nicole had shared with her earlier that morning that there had been another blow up in Vi's absence between Andre and Cynthia.

"You're going to have to deal with this eventually, Vi. Your sister can't stand Andre and because he knows she detests his lifestyle, Andre flaunts it even more."

When their order arrived, Vi took their sandwiches outside and sat down at the small wicker table in back. She popped open a can of soda and prepared to enjoy the beautiful weather and pastrami on whole wheat sitting in front of her. Nicole joined her and the two women didn't exchange one word for a full three minutes, as they sank into the best sandwiches in Amityville. Wiping mustard from the corner of her mouth, Nicole looked up at Vi and caught her friend smiling and staring off into space.

"What are you smiling about over there?"

Unaware she'd been smiling; Vi looked over at Nicole, embarrassment creeping up the back of her neck. "Oh, nothing," she replied.

"Sure looked like something to me. Go on, spill it."

There were no secrets between Vi and Nicole. When Nicole had come to work at Nu U, the two women quickly became good friends.

"I was just thinking about something funny that Clayton told me."

"So, share," Nicole prompted before taking a big bite from her club sandwich.

Vi went on to tell Nicole about a domestic violence call Clayton went on. When Nicole pointed out domestic calls were usually pretty dangerous, Vi quickly explained this particular call was far from dangerous and in between laughing, she related the funny story Clay had told her.

When she finished, Nicole spit out a portion of the soda she'd been drinking as the two women broke out in laughter. Nicole had a hard time composing herself and listening to the rest of story until something Vi said caused her to stop laughing.

Realizing her mistake, Vi abruptly fell silent. Somehow she'd forgotten herself and casually let it slip that she and Clayton had discussed all this over dinner last night.

Nicole, who had been in the process of taking another bite from her sandwich, peered curiously over the top of her sunglasses at Vi. "Dinner, huh? So, besides workouts at the gym, you and Clayton seem to be spending a lot of time together."

Mistaking the deliberate tone of her friend's voice as censure, Vi quickly started explaining how she and Clayton happened to be together last night. "It's not what you're thinking. Tony bailed out on me at the last minute for dinner and the movies and Clayton just dropped by." When Nicole didn't say anything in response, Vi continued nervously explaining. "I was in the middle of making dinner and it would have been rude not to invite him in," she said in a reasonable tone. "Anyway, when he asked where Tony was, I told him about our plans to take in a movie that evening, but that Tony forgot and made other plans with his friends."

Nicole was silent for so long that Vi began to feel anxious. She liked spending time with Clayton—they were friends and she and Nicole were friends. If she couldn't tell her best friend about something like this without her tripping, who could she tell? Then to her relief, Nicole's next words alleviated the anxiety Vi was feeling.

"Well, I don't see anything wrong with the two of you spending time together. You're both adults and, let me tell you, if a handsome, younger man wanted to spend time with me and take me out, I wouldn't hesitate for one second."

Vi smiled at her friend and the two women finished their sandwiches discussing other topics before their lunch hour was up. Nicole left the table first to go back inside and call one of her kids, while Vi stayed behind a moment longer, enjoying the beauty of the day. Her mind wandered back to the other night and what a perfect evening she and Clay had shared...

When Vi got home from work last night, Tony had been lying on the couch with one leg hooked over the sofa arm and the phone plastered to his ear. She waved to him when she came through the front door.

"Hey Mom," he called to her as she started to go upstairs.

"Hi sweetie," she said. "Give me ten minutes to change. I figure we can grab a bite, somewhere downtown, before the movie." Vi called out to him before she reached the top landing and closed her bedroom door.

"Ah, Briana I gotta' go. Maybe I'll see you later?" Tony spoke into the receiver in a hopeful voice. Satisfied with her reply, he hung up the phone and raced upstairs after his mother.

Vi answered the knock on her door, and found Tony standing there, shifting nervously from one foot to the other.

"Mom, I'm sorry. I completely forgot we were going to the movies tonight."

She opened the door wider for him to come in, forgetting all about changing out of the jeans and T-shirt she'd worn all day at work. "What's up?" she asked him as he walked further into the bedroom.

"Me and Mike are going to Star Time to hang out. His mom is on her way over here now to pick me up," he told her, apologetically. Star Time was a movie theater, arcade and pizzeria. It was also a popular hangout for kids Tony's age.

"Let me guess, maybe someone named Briana will be there too?" she asked him in a teasing manner.

"No, Mom," he said, way to fast. Then, "I mean, maybe, I don't know. It's really gonna' be just me and the guys."

Vi put up her hand to stop any further explanation, "It's no problem, Hon. You go on and have fun."

"Are you sure Mom?" he asked sincerely. "I'm really sorry."

"Sure, I'm sure. We can do the movies any time."

"Thanks Mom." At that precise moment a car horn blew outside. Tony looked at her and said, "That's Mike's mom, see you later." Then he raced down the stairs and out the door.

"Be home by ten," she yelled after him.

After Tony left, Vi changed into khaki shorts and a white, cotton tank top. The top had a pretty eyelet neckline and lacy straps. Last weekend, before Janae had gone back to school, Vi took her shopping for new jeans. She'd seen this top on display. It was very delicate and feminine and, although Vi didn't own anything like it, she'd bought it for herself on a whim. Besides the comfortable cotton feel of the top, it was perfect for hot, muggy summer nights like tonight.

When Vi finished changing, she went downstairs feeling the stillness of the house surround her. Not in the mood for ordering takeout, or going to the trouble of actually cooking for herself, she decided to make a huge salad and eat it on the back patio. As she pulled the ingredients out of the refrigerator for a Caesar salad, the doorbell rang. When she answered the door, Vi was surprised to see Clay standing there.

"Hello Vi, how are you?"

"Clay. Hi, I'm fine. What are you doing here?" She asked, stepping aside to invite him in.

"Tony called me earlier about picking him up for basketball tomorrow. I was working when I got his voicemail."

"Oh," was all she said.

"I've been trying to reach him for the past hour, but your line has been busy."

"Oh yeah, that would be Tony's new pastime—talking to Briana, leaving Briana a message or talking to his friends about Briana," she told Clay jokingly as she walked down the hall, making her way back to the kitchen. Clayton followed her and sat down at the counter, watching her arrange a head of lettuce on the cutting board and resume cutting it into small sections.

"Could I interest you in joining me for dinner? I was just about to make a chicken Caesar salad, so it's nothing fancy."

Clay gave her a slow, lopsided grin, and got up to wash his hands at the sink. Over his shoulder, he told her, "Now, you know I never turn down a meal." He came over to stand next to her at the countertop, surveying the items she had spread out to make their salads. "What can I help you do?"

They made fast work of chopping up pieces of chicken, cucumbers and lettuce for the salad. Vi set the table for two and put a pitcher of ice tea in the middle along with a loaf of French bread and a bottle of red wine.

They spent a long time over dinner talking and laughing; then Clayton suggested they go ahead and see that movie she and Tony were supposed to see. Vi agreed right away, surprising him and off they went. There were a couple of unexpected gory parts to the movie and, although he was a good sport about it, Vi felt a little foolish when she grabbed his arm each time something scary happened.

Vi had a great time at the movies, although toward the end of it Clayton grew kind of quiet. When she asked him about it, he said he was just a little tired. By the time they got back in his truck she figured he must have gotten a second wind because he asked if she wanted to stop for a latte instead of going straight home. Kind of tired herself, Vi graciously refused.

Vi's nice lunch and even nicer thoughts about last night were abruptly interrupted by a phone call from her supplier. When Nicole yelled out the back door she'd finally gotten the impossible man on the line, Vi knew she had to take the call. Walking back inside, she reluctantly left the pleasant weather and her pleasant thoughts behind.

Across town Clayton was having similar thoughts about last night. He'd slept later than usual, surprising himself when he rolled out of bed to find that the morning had slipped away and it was now closer to one o'clock. When he got up and jumped in the shower, his thoughts immediately turned to the other night.

Surprisingly relaxed around one another, he and Vi had laughed and talked throughout the meal, completely enjoying each other's company. Clay especially liked the sweet tinkle of her laughter and how her eyes lit up each time she heard something funny. He found himself thinking up ways to make her laugh, just so he could see her react that way over and over again.

Recounting his work day and various other topics, he found himself lingering over his third glass of wine, long after the meal was finished. It was a complete turn on the way she'd sat across from him all evening, leaning forward and genuinely intrigued by his stories and listening intently to everything he said. He remembered mentioning the domestic call he'd gotten earlier that day. Recalling the sweet elderly couple, Clayton had taken another sip of wine and smiled faintly across the table at her.

"That sounds like it could be dangerous," she'd said.

"Usually it is, but this call was a little weird. I had to break up a fight between a sweet little eighty-year-old woman and her eighty-year-old husband."

Refilling their wine glasses, Vi cast an uncertain look at him from across the table. "So, what's so weird about that?"

"Well, apparently the couple belonged to a nudist group for seniors out in the Hamptons. The group, I found out, detests clothing so much that they go nude every chance they get—without getting arrested that is."

"Okay," she trailed off, not quite sure what was so weird about his story.

"Well, that's exactly how they answered the door when I got the call—in the nude."

"Ohmigod!" Covering her mouth in astonishment, Vi began laughing hysterically. Between her splayed fingers, she sputtered, "You're kidding, right?"

"No, it's true. They both came to the door as bare as the day they were born," he said, a smile playing across his lips.

"Oh, no. Ohmigod!" she cried again.

Laughingly, he told her, "I've never seen so much flesh hang and sag before in my life." When he said this, Vi lost it completely. She let out a very unladylike snort, and laughed so hard she started to tear up. When her laughter died down, Clay made a suggestion.

"I've got an idea. Why don't we go ahead and see that movie you and Tony planned to see tonight?"

Wiping the tears from her eyes, Vi said trying to compose herself, "Okay, but this time I pay."

Clay gave her his charming, lopsided grin, which she knew loosely translated into, *okay, if you think so.*

On the ride home, Vi sat quietly in the passenger seat of his truck. Gazing at the impressive interior of his truck, she'd looked over at him and suddenly asked.

"Clayton, how is it that I'm the last one to get a ride in your fabulous new truck." Her teasing tone made him smile because she had no idea how many times he thought about taking her for a ride in his truck, but couldn't think up a plausible excuse. Without thinking, he blurted out as much and told her. "I've been meaning to give you a ride for quite a while."

Wow, what an idiot. That hadn't come out right - at all!

Pulling into her driveway, Clayton quickly tried to clarify what he'd just said. "I mean, I only took Tony and J.R. to basketball practice. When they got in here, the sweat alone forced me to air out the truck for several days."

"Oh," she said, "and what about taking Janae to her friend's the other night?"

"I was only helping a damsel in distress."

Vi gave him a questioning look, clearly not looking convinced of whether he was telling her the truth or not. Shrugging his shoulders apologetically, Clay held up his hands in surrender and admitted. "Okay, you caught me. I meant to ask you, but your kids are good at sponging rides." When she folded her arms across her chest in disbelief, he added teasingly, "Okay, would you believe that I was saving the best for last?"

Punching his forearm playfully, her small fist bounced off that hard surface like rubber. Clay laughed as he got out of the truck and walked around to open her door. When he walked her to the door, Vi had given him an affectionate kiss on the cheek before going inside.

He'd driven home last night thinking about what a good time they'd shared, unaware that Vi was having similar thoughts as she took off her shoes and prepared for bed last night.

Little did Vi and Clayton know, besides the two of them, there was one other person thinking about their date too. Janae took a break from studying, recalling her phone conversation with Tony the other night. After what he'd told her, Janae knew she had to find a way to make her move.

When she called home last night, Tony picked up. He'd just gotten home and found mom's note attached to the refrigerator, telling him she and Clay had gone to the movies.

"Hey Squirt," Janae said to her brother in greeting.

"How's it going, Old Maid?" he shot back at her, jokingly.

"What kind of trouble you gettin' into lately?"

"Let's see," he paused, pretending to ponder her question. "I robbed a bank, stabbed a few people. Oh, I almost forgot, Mom's sending me off to a troubled boy's home."

"Yeah, right," she said, knowing Tony was a goody two shoes. "I seriously doubt you even know how to spell the word trouble."

When his laughter died away, she asked him, "Is Mom home? I need to get her credit card number to charge my running shoes for…"

"She's not home. They went to the movies."

"I can't believe she'd keep Grandpa Clarence out this late, its way past his bedtime," she said in a teasing tone, assuming her mother was out with her grandfather. "It must be some movie."

"Mom didn't go with Grandpa. Clay took her," Tony told her nonchalantly.

For a millimeter of a second, Janae was shocked. She recovered quickly and asked Tony. "How did that come about?"

"I forgot we made plans to see a movie tonight, and then something came up and I couldn't go. So, Clay took her."

Visibly relieved by what she heard, Janae said, "Oh, that's nice." Then she added, "So, you're okay with Clay taking Mom out?"

"Yeah, sure Clay's cool. I mean, it's not like it was a real date or anything. He and Mom hang out sometimes," he explained to her in a very blasé manner.

"Really?," Janae inquired.

"With you at school, it's only me and her and I'm not always here. So, Mom's by herself a lot lately."

"Why are you out so much?" Janae asked, changing the subject.

"Just out, you know, hanging with the guys."

"Oh yeah," she continued to drill him. "Does one of the guys go by the name of B-r-i-a-n-a?"

When Tony heard his sister drag out Briana's name, he knew instantly his mother and Janae had been talking. "Man, nobody can keep a secret in this family, can they?" he said in an exasperated tone.

They went on teasing each other for a few more minutes. Then Janae told him her girlfriend was coming home for the weekend and she planned to drive down with her. After hanging up, Janae sat on her bed mentally, chiding herself for having a mini panic attack a minute ago. After all, the idea of Clay being even remotely interested in her mother was ludicrous. Mom and Craig had been real close, and before he died they used to hang out sometimes. It was just like Clay was keeping her mother company now, Janae reasoned. It was nice of Clay, she thought, to fill in now that Craig was no longer with them.

Janae looked around the dorm room she shared with her roommate, Renee. It was comfortable, as far as dorm rooms went. They had a color TV, DVD and matching paisley comforters for their beds. She digested the fact that her being away meant Tony was the only one home now to be with their mother. Yeah, home was nice, but being on her own was even nicer. If Clayton found time to keep her mother company than good for him, she thought.

Janae looked up as her roommate, Renee, came through the door and sat down at the small computer work station they both shared.

"So, did you decide to come with me this weekend?" she asked Janae.

"Yeah, I think I will. I've got some unfinished business at home."

Renee noted the mischievous gleam in her friend's eye right before she inquired. "What are you up to?"

"Remember that really hot guy I told you about last week?"

"You mean the cop with the cute ass?"

"Yeah, that's the one," she replied with a knowing smile.

"Girl, the way you described him, it made me want to go out and commit a crime, just so he could arrest me."

The two girls broke out laughing and began clowning around, fanning themselves dramatically and pretending to fall out in a dead faint.

When she gained her composure, Renee admonished Janae for not telling her she'd managed to hook up with "Cop-o-licious."

"Hey, didn't you say he was much older than you?"

"He's not that much older. Besides, I'm sick of these immature college boys. I want a real man," Janae replied with a touch of indignation. "Anyway, I just found out he has entirely too much free time on his hands."

"So," Renee prompted.

With a determined look in her eye, Janae replied, "I think I'll go home and keep him occupied."

Renee laughed at that statement and turned on the computer to begin working on a report due next week.

CHAPTER

SIXTEEN

It was after midnight when Vi pulled up in front of Nu U. She got out, walked around to the passenger side of her car, and hauled the supply box from the front seat. After opening the front door, she put the heavy box on a nearby counter and switched on the lights.

The Total Woman World Conference was in New York all week. Today alone, it drew more than twenty thousand women to the convention center. With the way Vi's feet hurt, it felt like more than half of those women stopped at Nu U Salon's booth.

All day, she took turns with Andre and Nicole greeting people, talking about what the salon had to offer and giving out complimentary samples. Vi insisted they all dress professionally, but chic, for the event to let their potential patrons know Nu U was not just another beauty salon. She wanted them to know Nu U was a business dedicated to the working-class woman. The ones who worked all day and took care of their families, balanced their life perfectly, and needed some- *me time*- every once in a while. Essentially, Nu U offered these women a temporary oasis from their regular work-a-day life. Nicole's catchy slogan had been plastered onto a banner that stood proudly in front of the Nu U booth. It pretty much summed up her mission—*Nu U Salon--where catering to you is our business.*

Toward the end of the day, Vi typically liked to give complimentary mini facials herself. Today, however, she let Andre do most of them, knowing if she had to stand any longer than necessary in these high heels, she would scream.

Once the conference was over, they packed up everything and prepared for the long drive home. The supplies on display at the show had to be brought back to the salon tonight, before it opened up tomorrow morning. Vi volunteered to do this so Nikki could get home to her kids, and Andre, well Andre could go about doing whatever it was he did on Friday nights. Vi checked the salon voice mail for messages, and then flipped through the mail. Finding nothing that couldn't wait until tomorrow morning, she put the mail back and walked over to the styling area.

Plopping down in one of the high salon chairs, Vi heaved a huge sigh of relief and kicked off her left shoe. Both her legs dangled for a second or two before she raised her left leg, placing her left foot across her right knee. Once her foot was within reach, she began to rub the ache away. Stifling a yawn, she closed her eyes and thought about this morning's events. Vi wasn't sure if her clientele would increase by seventy-five percent like the conference salesman had predicted, but she did know three things for sure. One, the conference had been a huge success. Two, she was bone tired. And three, her feet hurt like hell.

It was a quiet Friday night. Clay clocked a couple of cars on Route 110 going five miles over the speed limit, then decided to sweep through the downtown area, just to check on things. Major crime was not readily associated with Amityville.

It was a quiet town full of people who knew each other and had lived here for years. This made for a peaceful community. Every once in a while they had a major crime or had to help Suffolk County on a car chase coming through their jurisdiction. For the most part, domestic disputes, disturbing the peace, petty assaults, and speeding made up the majority of their work.

As he patrolled the quiet streets a bone-weary exhaustion stole over him as his mind turned to the meeting he'd had earlier that day with homicide. The fact that they had no new leads in Craig's murder investigation was very discouraging. Deep in thought he drove down one street after another, until something made him turn down Main Street and drive by Vi's shop. He saw her clearly through the glass front window of her salon. There was something about this woman that made him feel like a super hero with extrasensory powers, because whenever she was nearby, his entire body tensed and his senses became fully alert.

His spirits lifted as one part of him was pleasantly surprised to see her, while the other part was annoyed with her for being here so late, and obviously alone. All the other businesses along this stretch had closed hours ago, their doors locked and windows darkened. Besides the street lights and neon store signs, the entire block was completely dark. From the street, her place was the only one lit in the darkness and from this vantage point, looking inside the brightly lit salon, was like looking in a fish bowl. He sat in his squad car for a minute watching her.

She wore a tailored red suit, with a short jacket that ended just above her tiny waist. The matching skirt hugged her curves and ended just a few hot inches above her knees. His eyes traveled appreciatively over every inch, slowly perusing her with pure male interest. The provocative turn of her shapely calves drew his eye, encouraging further travel down to her incredibly slender ankles and a pair of extremely delicate feet encased in very high, spiky heels.

Clay parked the squad car across the street from Nu U salon and got out. He continued to watch her as he made his way across the street. Completely unaware her every movement was visible from the street, he watched Vi sit down on one of those high chrome stylist chairs and slowly raise one leg and cross it over her other—*In a classic Sharon Stone move*!

And then it happened. The unexpected movement caused him to miss a step and he nearly landed face down on the pavement. It happened so fast; one minute he'd been crossing the street casually appraising her crossed legs, then the next moment she moved and…

Sweet Jesus, Mary and Joseph! He completely forgot how to breathe.

Clay's steps faltered as he watched Vi uncross her legs and kick off one shoe. Then suddenly her skirt rode up impossibly high on her thigh as she raised her leg again and nonchalantly placed her ankle across one knee and began massaging her foot. For one second all he saw was legs as the skirt seemed to disappear from view. He couldn't be sure if it was her unexpected actions, or the brief glimpse of skimpy white panties that caused his heart to skip a beat. In any event, it floored him. Clay had to take a few seconds to gather his wits. Then realizing he was standing dumbstruck in the middle of the street, he gave himself a mental shake and proceeded toward the salon's front door. In the darkness outside Vi still hadn't seen him approaching, nor he guessed, was she aware of the seductive performance she'd just given him.

Vi sat in the high salon chair, idly rubbing her foot and pouring over the month end supply order, unaware of Clay's approach. When she heard his light knock on the glass door to the salon, it startled her. Surprised, she slid off the chair too quickly and banged her foot painfully against the chrome leg.

"Ouch!" she yelped.

Standing up, Vi winced in pain and pushed her aching foot back into her shoe. Once she had it back on she walked over to unlock the door. Seeing it was Clayton, she opened the door with a smile, ignoring her pain.

"Hey you," she said in greeting and stepped aside to let him in. "You know, I'm really too old for you to be sneaking up on me like this. You almost gave me a heart attack." The smile she gave him cancelled out the stern tone of her voice.

On the other hand, Clay's voice was full of sincere apology when he replied. "Sorry, I didn't mean to startle you. I was on patrol when I saw the lights on in here."

"Well, then I guess I should feel kind of special, having my own personal officer looking out for me," she said in a teasing, light tone. After motioning him inside, she turned and walked a distance away. "Come on in," she called over her shoulder. As he followed her into the room, he couldn't help noticing she seemed to be limping. He let her take two more steps to be certain, and sure enough, she was clearly favoring one foot over the other as she walked.

"What's wrong with your foot?"

"What? Oh…it's nothing."

"Looks like something to me."

Vi stopped walking and turned around to face him. She made a saucy show of planting both hands on her hips before throwing him a sarcastic smile. "Well, let me see. Besides standing on my feet all day, I also banged my foot when you scared me half to death just now."

She turned around again and walked toward the salon chairs and work stations in the middle of the shop.

"Let me see it, does it hurt?"

"Clay I was only teasing. It's nothing, really."

"It might help if you took off the high heels." This comment made her turn around again and face him. Jokingly, Vi twirled a few times in front of him, performing a dramatic runway model turn and flashing him a cheeky smile. "Really, you couldn't possibly expect me to wear flip flops with an outfit like this, do you?" she said raising both hands, palms up, for emphasis.

The teasing light in her eyes, however, began to fade when she locked gazes with him. His eyes held a smoldering heat, as he took in her words and let his eyes travel over everything she emphasized. His intense scrutiny roamed very slowly over her body from head to toe, then, just as slowly back up again. When his eyes met hers once more, Clay said very slowly in an unfamiliar husky tone, "I wouldn't think of asking you to change anything about that outfit."

Vi noticed the hoarse quality of his voice and her own breathing became labored under his heated perusal. Although the answering heat that suffused her body was not unpleasant, it started to make her a little nervous. Lately, this new awareness popped up between them. Whenever they were together, the two of them would always tease one another and joke around. Then suddenly, they reached some type of invisible boundary and the fireworks began. When it happened the air between them would crackle and snap and his eyes would smolder, like they were now, and Vi's stomach would flutter like crazy. Usually they both ignored it until it passed, but trying to hide from this heightened awareness lately was becoming very difficult.

"Well," she said, breaking the tense silence and turning from him, she sat down in one of the stylist chairs. Motioning him to take the chair next to her, Vi said swallowing very slowly, "Have a seat." Taking a second to catch a fortifying breath, she waited for him to sit down.

Clayton ignored the chair next to her and turned around in a small circle, searching the room. Spying a ladder back chair sitting in a far corner, he walked over to get it.

Vi watched him, wondering what he was about. When she saw him pick up the wooden chair and walk toward her with it, she said to him curiously, "Clay, don't sit in that chair, it's not very comfortable."

Clay reached her carrying the chair easily in one hand. With a commanding air he placed the chair right in front of her, sat down and moved to touch her.

"Let me see your foot."

Vi watched in shock, as he reached for her injured ankle. The stylist chair was in its elevated position, making it easy for him to capture her foot. He grasped it lightly in his strong hands and brought it to his lap.

"Clayton," she said with a slight tremor in her voice, "Really, that's not necessary." To add strength to her protest she tried to inch her foot out of his grasp, but he wouldn't budge. When it looked like her actions would dislodge her foot from his hand, Clay closed his long, strong fingers around her ankle. Confidently assertive, he commandeered her ankle and for reasons Vi couldn't fathom, he seemed reluctant to give it back.

"Stop squirming, I said I want to see your foot." The light command in his voice did not brook any further arguments, so Vi let him examine her foot.

"Ah, Clay, I'm fine really. When I saw you at the door, it startled me and I accidentally banged my foot against the chair, it's really fine now."

"Yes it is," he said in a soft whisper.

"What... what did you say?" she asked.

"Nothing, you look tired—long day?" he said, changing the subject.

"Yeah, but today was a huge success. My feet were killing me the whole time, but we made some pretty impressive sales."

"This foot," he asked, holding up the foot cradled in his palm.

"Yes, that foot," Vi told him. Starting to feel a little foolish, she gave a much harder jerk this time and almost got her foot dislodged from his grasp. Clay was too quick for her though, quickly clamping both hands around her ankle again. Then he did what her body had been aching for all day.

"Ohhhh..." she cried out and closed her eyes against the extreme pleasure she felt, as his strong fingers found all the aching spots and began massaging the pain away.

"Feel good?"

Vi didn't hear him; she was too involved with the magic his fingers were creating. As Clay massaged her foot, Vi was in heaven. Her throat worked as his knowing hands smoothed over her arch, stroking across her sensitized skin, hitting all the tired, aching spots she couldn't see to find. He applied slight pressure to her instep, zeroing in on the spot that kept cramping up all day in those torturous heels.

My God! She thought the man definitely had skillful fingers. Forgetting how improper this might seem to anyone idly passing by, or that she'd never in her life had any man massage her feet, Vi sat back for a few moments to try and enjoy this impromptu foot massage. It was torture though, pure torture. As his strong, but gentle, fingers kneaded her receptive foot, a curiously funny tingle ran up her calf, then up her thigh and beyond. As he continued laboring over her foot, she fell into a delicious languor that made it hard to concentrate on what he was saying.

"Wh... what were you saying?" She pushed past the hazy state her brain had developed under his ministrations.

"I asked why you're here so late. You know you shouldn't lock up this late by yourself, it's not safe."

Vi wished to God, he would stop talking, so she could focus in on the delicious tingle his touch was sending throughout every nerve ending she possessed. Somehow her foggy brain registered that his last question required an answer from her. Very slowly, she was able to push her next words past her thickening tongue, "I usually don't. Normally Andre's here with me when it's late."

Clay raised a questioning brow at her, before commenting. "You mean, if he's a hundred pounds soaking wet Andre?"

That made her laugh out loud, "Yes, I mean that Andre."

The sound of laughter tinkling from her throat made Clay's gut clench painfully.

"Besides, I wasn't working tonight," she said, indicating why she was here so late. "We had the women's conference in Manhattan today.

"So," he said very quietly, still concentrating on turning her foot back and forth in his gentle hands, massaging the ache from her feet. "How was it?"

And, just like that, with his asking that one little question, he had her body and mind totally relaxed. With one simple question, all the excitement, enthusiasm and fatigue of the day rolled off her tongue. He always had that effect on her, making whatever she said appear to be the most important thing at that moment. He put her instantly at ease, and did something few men ever did. He asked a question, and then stopped to listen, showing genuine interest in what she had to say.

As he listened to her talk, Clayton continued to run his hands over her injured foot. She closed her eyes when his fingers found a particular spot near her gentle instep. His strong hands touched her calf, as his other hand applied gentle strokes to her heel. Totally absorbed in what he was doing, he smoothed his hands over her arch and ran his thumb over her foot and ankle with intimate familiarity, inching higher to include her calf muscle.

"What are you doing?" Her eyes popped open in inquiry.

"Just making sure you didn't hurt your leg too." His head was still bent over her foot when he responded. "You know if you had, it would be my fault, so there'll be no charge for my services, Ma'am."

The teasing tone in his voice didn't mean he wasn't determined to hang onto her foot. He held on tight as his hands continued to travel over her foot and calf. She watched his bent head, examining her ankle and foot, turning it this way and that and not saying a word. He was still in full uniform, which probably meant he was still on duty. Vi couldn't quite explain it, but lately the sight of him in casual clothes—let alone in uniform—caused her heart do a circus routine against her ribs. This supercharged awareness was a new feeling, and as much as it frightened her, it was also very thrilling. Just then he hit a particularly troublesome spot and Vi closed her eyes again as he worked out the kinks.

Clay smiled at the tiny mewling sounds she made as he ran his fingers up her tender arch, and then kneaded the skin around her toes and heel. The stockings she wore looked like her skin and felt satiny soft against his fingertips. Beneath the thin nylon, he felt the warmth of her body. Although, he'd never given a foot massage to any women he'd ever known before, when he walked in here, and discovered she hurt herself, he'd starting doing it like it was second nature. He had to admit that touching her like this was doing a number on his willpower. His hands felt damp and the warmth working its way through his body quickly made his heartbeat escalate. When the temptation to run his hands further up her leg became too great, his fingers stilled and Clayton reluctantly released her foot. He saw a flash of awareness in her eyes when she opened them and gazed at him.

Vi read the heat she saw in his eyes and, for the briefest of moments, she returned it. It was there one moment, then just as quickly, it vanished and then she plastered a bright smile on her lips and stood up. "God, Clay that felt good. My feet thank you, and I thank you."

"You're welcome," he told her, then eyed the sexy high heels on the floor next to her chair. "Too bad those shoes hurt so much, because they look sensational on you."

Not sure how to respond to that comment, Vi wisely ignored it.

"So what brings you by?" She asked this for lack of anything better to say.

"I was on patrol and spotted your shop all lit up. You know, with the lights on in here, it's like looking into a fishbowl."

Vi glanced at the salon front window and the darkness of the street beyond, before saying, "Yeah, I guess you're right about that."

"So, explain to me again why you're here so late, all by yourself?" His question brought her out of her daydreams, and for a moment she had to think about what he meant.

"Oh, after the women's conference in Manhattan today, someone had to drop some things off for our Saturday rush tomorrow, is all."

"I see," he said very slowly, then. "And, that someone had to be you?"

"It was a very long day, and I let my staff go on home while I dropped this off," she said, indicating the box of supplies on the front counter. "Tony's staying with Clarence tonight, so I didn't have to rush home," she reasoned. "So, I volunteered."

Coupled with the frustration he'd felt earlier the careless note in her voice suddenly annoyed him. Unable to pull them back, his next words revealed some of that anger. "Why do you always go and go? Your not super woman, you know."

Vi's eyes widened at his briskness of his tone and her chin rose defiantly. "I'm not trying to be a super woman, as you put it."

"Yes you are, at work and at home. It's not safe to be here alone at this time of night, a lot of things happen to women alone like this. And another thing, it's not always a good thing to do everything for everyone, they tend to forget to do for themselves." Although he sensed she recognized the truth in his words, she raised her chin defiantly and remained stoically silent. Refusing to acknowledge him she sat in silence, her back rigid in anger. Watching her, Clay realized too late that he'd probably overstepped his bounds. He also realized sharing with her the fact they had zero leads in Craig's murder would serve no purpose. Suddenly angry with himself for allowing his own frustration fuel his words, Clay let out a heavy sigh and grabbed hold of her hand.

"Vi, I'm sorry, I had no right. It's just that I worry about you and I don't think you take as much care with yourself as you do with everyone else." She heard the sincerity in his voice and forgave him even before he said, "I'm sorry, okay?" When she didn't say anything, he added, "Come on, you know you're not really mad at me."

When he reached out and gave Vi a playful right hook to the jaw, she gave him a reluctant smile. Her smile grew as she silently acknowledged, it would be hard to stay angry at this man.

Clayton felt a weight lift when she smiled at him, showing she clearly accepted his apology. True to his law enforcement background, his sincerity was quickly followed with a forceful request.

"Promise me next time that you'll have someone come here with you this late at night. Everything you do in here with the lights on is visible from the street."

The concern in his voice touched Vi and she quickly agreed to this small request, feeling glad someone took the time to look out for her. When Vi got up and started putting items from the box she'd brought in earlier back on her display shelves, Clay got up and walked over to help her. As they worked he didn't say anything, silently handing items to her to place back in their respective spot. When he did speak, what he said took her totally by surprise because it came right out of left field.

"What was he like?"

Clearly confused, she had to ask, "Who?"

He hesitated a second, before saying quietly, "your late husband." She was silent for so long, Clayton thought she didn't want to talk about it, and so, he let it drop. Then, with a faraway look in her eyes, she spoke revealing a lot about how she had felt about this man who had been in her life so many years ago.

"He was a good man, hardworking and a good father."

"Were you happy?"

"Of course we were, we had three kids."

"I didn't ask how many kids you had. I asked were you happy—really happy?" His voice had taken on a quiet, soothing quality.

She thought about what he was asking and why he would want to know. Beyond his intelligence and strength, she had learned in the past few weeks there was more to this complex man than what lay on the surface. She also acknowledged, she would not have gotten the opportunity to know him better if it had not been for her son's passing.

Finally, she looked away and sat down on the stool behind the front desk, near the supply display shelf. "We were happy, in the beginning. In the beginning he didn't work so much, he wasn't so driven by his job. When we were newly married he dreamt about climbing the corporate ladder and then making enough money so we could travel to tropical places on a yacht and buy me designer clothes and flowers for no reason at all. I loved his dreams until they started to eat away at him and our marriage."

He stood near the stool she sat on. Her lowered head was a mass of soft auburn curls. From this vantage point he picked out the copper highlights shooting through each strand and fought the urge to plunge his hands into its softness. "So, did he climb the corporate ladder?"

"Oh yes he did and then some. But, it was never enough. After that he kept working harder toward the next promotion. He pushed himself constantly. Like the day he was killed, I asked him to have someone else make the presentation. But, no he had to do it all himself, always fighting to be the best." She looked at Clayton then, that faraway look in her eyes was gone, when she said.

"I feel strange talking to you about him. I mean, it must sound like I had a bad marriage, but Clay I didn't, honestly. My life was good."

"I believe you," he said reassuringly. "To me, it just sounds like you were both two people who had the same goals but couldn't agree on how to reach them."

Vi studied him and it dawned on her how he was always listening to what she said, listening so intently as if it were the most important thing in the world. Then he picked apart what was said and got to the meat of the issue without effort. After a time he asked her another question that further shocked her.

"So, did you date a lot of people after your husband passed away?" The look she gave him made Clay think he may have crossed the line, so he quickly added, "I mean, I don't remember Craig saying anything about anyone special when he talked about you after his dad passed away."

Vi took a long time to answer this question. When she did, her response didn't leave any room for further discussion. "I don't go out much anymore. I did for a time, but not anymore."

They finished putting the supplies away and Clayton helped her lock up the salon. He saw Vi safely to her car and received a friendly hug goodbye before she got behind the wheel. Right before she pulled away though, she stuck her head out the car window and told him, "Oh, don't forget about Labor Day, and don't forget to bring J.R."

Tuesday after Labor Day, Vi was in her office paying some bills. Nicole walked in a short while later and started the coffee machine. She poured a cup for Vi and herself, then walked over to the empty desk next to Vi's and sat down before the shop got busy.

"How was the holiday?" she asked.

Vi considered her question, it was Nikki that encouraged her to go ahead with her regular Labor Day plans. Initially, Vi was going to cancel it, not sure if everyone was ready for a holiday celebration with Craig's passing only months ago. Nikki had told her she thought the outing was exactly what her family needed. As it turned out, she'd been absolutely right.

"Labor Day was fun. Clayton and Clarence took turns at the grill. Both of them had a special sauce tasting competition."

"Wow, sounds like Clayton is becoming part of the family."

Remembering the holiday events, Vi thought about that for a moment and smiled, recalling Clay and J.R.'s claim that their special sauce was so good, *"It would make you slap your momma."* While Clarence and Tony pretended their special barbeque sauce recipe was so tasty, its contents had to kept under lock and key.

Her family had had their annual football game, which was slightly different this year with Clayton heading up one team and Vi the other. Vi won the coin toss and wasted no time picking J.R., causing Clay to quickly grab Tony when it was his turn. When Vi chose Clarence next, Clay, bless his heart, sauntered over to Vi's mother and unceremoniously threw an arm around her small shoulders, making her his second choice. Her mother, clearly flattered, hugged Clay back and then posed for them all, flexing her non-existent muscles like Hulk Hogan. Vi's next pick was Janae and her Dad went to Clay's team. Cynthia and Tom chose to sit the game out and cheer everyone on. The game was tied when J.R. told Vi to go long. Vi went long to try and make the winning touchdown. She almost had the ball within her grasp when Clay tackled her to the ground. They stayed tangled a bit longer than necessary, however, before he helped her up. When he released her Vi glanced around quickly, luckily, no one seemed to notice.

"Well, family outings are all well and good, but what I want to know is, when are the two of you going out on a real date?" Nicole's question yanked Vi's attention back to the present with a thud.

"What? I told you before, Clay and I are good friends. Besides, you know I don't date anymore."

"Vi, really, that was so long ago. I thought now would be different."

Besides Craig, Nikki was the only person who knew why Vi swore off dating after her last date four years ago. Being recently divorced with children, it seemed Nicole understood some of the things Vi had gone through. So, naturally Vi had shared what happened that horrible night with her friend. Cynthia and Tom had set Vi up with a business colleague they both knew from school. The four of them went out to dinner one evening and, in front of Cynthia and Tom, the guy seemed to be a perfect gentleman. Foolishly, Vi took this man back to her house afterwards, offering him a cup of coffee because she knew he'd drank a bit too much over dinner. The gentleman routine quickly vanished once he got inside her house. To this day she believed if Craig hadn't been upstairs asleep, and thankfully woke up when he heard all the commotion, that so-called "gentleman" would have raped her. Thinking about how badly her last date had gone so long ago, Vi shook her head. "No, Nikki. No dating for me ever again. Clay and I are friends. Very, very good friends and that's all."

Clayton stopped by Nu U early Saturday morning. Figuring he must have just gotten off work because he was still in uniform, she gave him a bright smile when he entered the salon. Glad to see him, she walked toward him. But before she could reach Clay, Andre and six of their customers pounced on him as soon as he walked through the door. One corner of Clay's lip turned up in his cheek and his charming, lopsided grin fell into place as he spoke to his adoring fans.

"Ladies, ladies, please control yourselves—I know I'm irresistible."

Completely ignoring his remarks, the women surrounded him as one of them took the coffee carrier from his hands, while another relieved him of a huge box filled with éclairs, doughnuts and honey buns. Knowing first hand that nothing flowed faster in a hair salon than doughnuts, coffee and gossip, Vi laughed hysterically and watched Clay step out of the way and hold up both his hands in surrender.

Turning an exasperated look in Vi's direction, Clay walked over to her and said, "Wow, I'm hurt! I thought those women were hot for me, when all they really wanted was my buns."

Smiling back at him, Vi took one of the French vanilla lattes he'd brought in before replying. "Unless your name is Krispy Kreme, I don't think so."

Amidst all the commotion, Cynthia walked in. When she said good morning to everyone, the customers ignored her, too busy talking amongst themselves. Nicole and Andre gave only a cursory greeting as she passed them, then quickly went back to their heated debate over the merits of chocolate éclairs versus glazed doughnuts.

"Mornin' Cyn," Vi said, handling her sister a cup of coffee. "Hope you didn't eat yet, Clayton brought us all breakfast."

Cynthia took the latte Vi handed her and turned toward Clayton. "Clayton, this is so nice of you. What brings you by here so early?" she asked him while sipping the hot brew.

"I'm just gettin' off duty. We usually work out at this time, so I figured I'd buy Vi a coffee since she had to work this morning."

"We?" Cynthia inquired, looking from him to Vi for further explanation.

Taken aback by her question, Vi quickly volunteered, "Yeah, I've given up running in the morning in this heat." When Cynthia didn't say anything, Vi felt compelled to explain further. "Clayton was nice enough to get me a guest card at his athletic club. You should see this place Cyn, all the cardio machines and treadmills have fans and TV's. It sure beats running outside," she finished in a rush.

Taking another sip of her coffee, Cynthia eyed Clayton over the top of her cup and suggested, in an offhand manner, "Gee, Clayton that's awfully nice of you. Maybe you can take Janae there sometime. She'll be home this weekend, you know."

Vi studied him over the rim of her coffee cup, while Clayton let Cynthia's none-too-subtle hint hang in the air. "Yeah, sure. I mean, if she has the time. She's probably coming to spend time with her friends and family," he said, hooking his thumbs inside his gun belt.

"Oh, I'm sure she'll make time for you," Cynthia informed him and walked off toward their small office in back of the salon.

When she left, Clay turned to Vi. "So….," Clayton said into the silence that followed. "Are we still on for tomorrow?"

He noticed Vi's hesitation when she replied, "Oh yeah, sure. What time?"

"J.R. and I will pick you and Tony up around four o'clock."

They'd made plans two nights ago to go watch the boy's game at the Youth Center tomorrow. Clayton coached basketball at the Youth Center over on Chestnut a couple of times a week. The boys he coached had all been in trouble at one time or another and most came from troubled homes. Vi knew out of all the boys, J.R. in particular was very special to him. Clayton talked about J.R. all the time, praising how well he was trying to do in school or how good J.R. was at basketball. It was obvious to Vi, he was very fond of the boy. She thought it was wonderful for a kid like J.R. to have Clayton standing behind him, cheering him on when he needed it most.

Right after Clayton brought J.R. with him on Labor Day, J.R. and Tony started talking on the phone from time to time. Tony also became a new member of J.R.'s fan club when he invited Tony to the Youth Center to play basketball with him and his friends. She didn't find out until much later, but it seemed some of the boys teased Tony about his basketball skills, or lack thereof, the first time he went down there. On his own, J.R. had taken Tony under his wing, and shown him the fundamentals of the game. As a result, Tony's game had improved and he and J.R. became fast friends.

"Hey, earth to Vi, earth to Vi," Clayton said, waving his hand in front of her face.

"Oh, sorry. Were you saying something?"

"I'd give more than a penny for your thoughts just now."

"It was nothing really. I just realized I never really thanked you for taking Tony to your basketball camps at the Youth Center. He really enjoys going."

"Not a problem, beside Piterrelli came down last week to help out."

Vi had met Officer Piterrelli a handful of times and knew he was one of the officers Craig had worked with.

"Tony told me Piterrelli helped him with his jump shot," she supplied in a distracted tone.

"I know. It helps to have an assistant down there. Sometimes those kids can be a handful."

"Maybe you can convince him to volunteer permanently," Vi suggested as she sipped her latte.

"I'm trying. He's already blackmailing me about that," Clay told her letting out a short laugh.

"What's he looking for, a winning lottery ticket?" Vi asked him jokingly.

"No. It's nothing that easy. He keeps saying he'll volunteer permanently if I go out with his wife's friend." When he said this, his dismissive tone made Vi wonder about the prospect of Clayton going out with other women. She quickly decided to take this opportunity to discuss something that had been troubling her for some time. Thinking about what Cynthia had said earlier, she had to admit that lately she and Clayton did spend a lot of time together. While she enjoyed hanging out with him, he was a young, attractive single man.   Certain that she had been monopolizing his time lately, Vi carefully broached the subject with him.

"Clay, maybe," she started.   "Maybe you should go out with Mrs. Piterrelli's friend."

The smile on his face vanished and he studied her for a moment, in silence. When he didn't respond, Vi nervously forged ahead. "I mean, you've been so sweet keeping me company. Even though I enjoy hanging out with you, I feel like I'm monopolizing too much of your time."

Clayton went very still after she made this statement. When he spoke again, he asked her very carefully, "So, what are you saying? You want me to go on some blind date?

"No—I mean yes. If you want to, I don't know..." she trailed off.   Vi realized she was rambling. She took a deep breath and tried to gather her thoughts.   From the look on his face, she knew this was coming out all wrong.   "Clay, I enjoy hanging out with you, but I don't want to get in the way."   When he continued standing there, staring at her and not offering any response Vi continued, not knowing the impact her next words would have. "I don't know, maybe Cynthia is right. You could go out with Janae or go on that blind date, or go out with some other girl. I just don't want your spending time with me to stop you from meeting people."

He stood with his hands on his hips, loose legged and, to anyone who didn't know him, he appeared fine. Inside, Clayton was anything but fine. The lines at the corner of his mouth grew more defined with each word she said to him.   Composing himself, he tried to reign in his temper and finally addressed her.

"First of all, I'm a grown-ass man. Secondly, I spend my time the way I choose and with whom I choose. If I didn't want to spend it with you Vi, trust me, I wouldn't."

"Clay, I'm sorry I didn't mean to make you angry. I..."

"I'm not angry," he said quickly, cutting off her apology. "I just assumed we'd become friends, but I guess I was wrong."

"No, Clay that's not true..."

Suddenly his visage cleared and he smiled. She noticed, however, the smile didn't reach his eyes and if she hadn't known him so well, she might have missed that telling sign.

"It's okay. I understand what you're trying to say. Maybe, you're right. Maybe I will go out on that blind date, after all."

He looked around the shop suddenly, as if looking for a quick get away then began walking toward the front door. He spoke to her as he made his way to the door. "Listen, I better get going and let you get back to work. Don't work too hard and I'll see you tomorrow, alright?"

Clayton didn't wait around for her reply.   He said his goodbyes very quickly and strode out the door before she could even formulate a response. Although outwardly he appeared to be okay, she knew he was probably pretty angry. She also knew it probably wasn't such a good idea to continue spending so much time with him.   What she didn't know was why she suddenly felt so lousy.

On the other side of town, Casey was waiting to see the doctor. There were at least a dozen pregnant women like her at the free clinic.   The only difference between Casey and these women was that most of them already had one or two children with them.   Those children, bored with waiting so long at the doctor's office, were all running amuck in the tiny waiting room. Their mothers seemed oblivious to the pandemonium the kids were creating in this drab, cramped waiting area.

A few senior citizens waited in the chairs closer to the back of the room. Casey decided to sit among them for a measure of quiet.   She sat down next to an elderly man who greeted her politely with a nearly toothless smile. Casey smiled back and settled into the hard, green plastic chair to wait her turn.   Resting her elbow on the arm of her chair she massaged her temple and closed her eyes against the dull headache forming there.

The day after she found out Craig was dead was his funeral. While they laid Craig to rest, Casey was confined to a hospital bed, desperately trying not to lose her baby. The spotting she developed after she fell had continued for four days straight. She wasn't allowed to get out of bed, and when she did it was only for a few minutes to use the bathroom.

The only visitor she had while she was there was a social worker, who discussed her options and insurance coverage. It was pretty clear after that meeting that she had no money and with Craig gone, no idea how she would get insurance coverage.   After that meeting, it also became apparent the hospital staff was in an awful hurry to discharge her and it was no surprise when they released her just one day after the spotting stopped.

Her spirits fell, thinking about the money issues she was faced with now. Casey remembered how Craig had insisted on paying for everything when he was alive.   As she looked back now, Casey felt growing sadness thinking about how hard she had fought against him taking care of her.   Thinking about the last time she'd thrown his concern back in his face, caused her a moment of pain.

"Look, I'm not taking no for an answer," Craig's tone brooked no argument. "If you don't care enough about this baby, think about your own health!"

"I won't be taken care of Craig," she'd protested. "I can take care of myself and I sure as hell can take care of this baby."

Realizing he needed to take a different tack with her, Craig sighed heavily. He propped his hands on lean hips and paced the floor in front of her. Looking heavenward, he had taken a deep breath before trying to reason with her again.

"Casey, listen I know you're capable of taking care of yourself and the baby. I'm not trying to say you're not." He sat down across from her and reached for both her hands across the small kitchen table. "I care about you, you know that," he told her earnestly. "If making sure the baby has good medical care will ensure me the woman carrying the baby will be fine, I don't see how you can argue with that."

She remembered looking into his eyes and seeing only sincerity and love shinning there. Immediately she felt bad for ever doubting him and reached for him. Her anger deflated, Casey squeezed his hand tight and said. "I'm sorry. You're right and I'm very lucky to have you."

Craig got up, came around the table, and pulled her to her feet. She came willingly as he gathered her in his arms. "That's my girl," he said planting a kiss on top of her head. "I love you Casey. With me around, you don't have to worry about a thing."

The nurse called out another name and the old man sitting next to Casey got up. She looked around and saw that the waiting room was emptying out, albeit very slowly. She knew for certain at least six of the people remaining were ahead of her. Casey slumped down in her chair, but when she closed her eyes this time, a tear slipped from the corner. Now that Craig was gone, she realized how much she had loved him, how much she'd come to rely on him and how much he had changed her life. She thought about her circumstances now and how everything had changed suddenly. Deep in her heart she realized from this point on, nothing would ever be the same.

When she left the free clinic two hours later, Casey was still deep in thought. Shading her eyes from the blinding sun, she left the drab building housing the Amityville Health Clinic and walked the eight short blocks home. She knew now Craig had been right all along, good healthcare was very important. Craig had been right about a lot of things she hadn't bothered to listen to. Full of regret, she knew if she had the chance to do things differently, she would. Somehow she had to get over the pain and regrets she had about her relationship with Craig and what could have been, and find a way to move on. The most important thing now was taking care of her baby properly. She could do this. Pride aside, she would do this for Craig, for herself and for the baby. With newfound resolve, Casey began to mentally make plans. First, she thought, she needed a job, something light duty and with a good health plan.

Possibilities for the future ran furiously through her mind as she walked home. Totally preoccupied, she was too deep in thought to notice the figure that shadowed her movements. She didn't notice when the man followed her into the park as she took the shortcut home, or as she crossed the street in front of her apartment complex. It wasn't until she slipped her key into the door that she suddenly felt she was being watched. Glancing around, Casey studied the people around her and on the street. Not seeing anything out of the ordinary, she chalked it up to her overactive imagination. Unable to shake the nervous feeling, she quickly entered her apartment and locked the door behind her.

He cancelled the plans they had the next day. When Clay called to cancel his plans with her and Tony, the phone rang several times. Luckily, Tony picked up instead of Vi. J.R. had a big basketball tournament today, and Clayton had taken time off to be there. Wanting to surprise J.R. with a bigger fan club, Clay had invited Vi and Tony to come along. That was before he'd unexpectedly stopped by the salon the other morning, and before she practically told him to stop wasting his time and go out other women.

Vi was in the shower when he called, so he apologized to Tony for the late notice and gave him an excuse that the tournament had been cancelled.

"You want me to have Mom call you back?"

"No," he said, a bit too sharply. "No," he repeated slowly. "I'm gonna' be busy. Just tell her I called, alright?"

"Ok," Tony said and hung up the phone. Tony lay back down on the sofa and began to put his IPOD headphones back on. Right before he adjusted them over his ears, Vi came downstairs.

"Who was that, Honey?" Vi asked, as she came down toweling her hair dry.

"It was Clay – he's not coming."

Vi stopped drying her hair, "Did he say why?"

"He said they cancelled the tournament." Tony picked up his Ipod headphones and was about to put them on again, when he remembered to tell her. "Oh yeah, he said you don't have to call back, he's going to be busy."

Clay wasn't busy, in fact, he was a little bored. He'd taken the day off for the tournament and to spend some time with the boys and Vi, and now he had ample time on his hands. When the tournament ended at around six p.m., he took a very excited J.R. to IHOP for dinner. They had a good meal and Clayton listened intently as J.R. described the game play by play, as if Clayton hadn't been in the crowd watching. It gave him great satisfaction knowing he could provide some nice memories for this kid, something good to mix in with the bad ones when he looked back on this time. Clayton had no one to do that for him when he was J.R.'s age.

Dropping J.R. off around eight o'clock, Clayton had come home and sat down to watch television. After two hours he'd quickly gotten his fill of

Seinfeld, BET and Jerry Springer, and was just about to call it a night when someone knocked on his door.

"Janae," he said in surprise when he opened the front door. "What are you doing here?"

"Hello to you too," she said and placed an index finger to her pursed lips, pretending to ponder his question. "Mmm…let's see… I was in the neighborhood. Will that work?"

The come-hither look in her eyes was his first clue she'd just told him a blatant lie. The second clue came when she sashayed past him and he got a good look at what she was wearing. Clay had never seen Janae dressed quite like this before. She wore a stretchy, skin tight orange dress and very high, spiky heels. Too shocked to respond, Clayton watched her strut across his living room with that dress molded so firmly to her derriere, it looked like someone painted it on. He caught himself staring and quickly shut the door. When she reached the sofa, Janae made quite a show of crossing her legs as she sat down. Following her into the living room, Clayton deliberately took the seat across from her before he asked, "Was there a party I missed tonight?"

Her lips were painted a glossy, wet-looking candy apple red. He saw the whiteness of her teeth as she gave him a slow, seductive smile and a small, bubbly laugh erupted from her throat when she told him knowingly, "The party is just about to start."

The sexual innuendo hung in the air between the two of them and Clayton was perfectly fine with letting it hang there until eternity. He plastered a totally clueless look on his face and tried his best to sidestep whatever this girl had in mind.

"So, are you on your way to a party?" he asked casually, wondering where in the world she'd be going dressed like she was.

Janae heaved a long breath and let it out very slowly. She couldn't decide if he was acting naïve deliberately, or if the real meaning of what she'd just said actually did go right over his head. Trying another approach, she gave him a bright smile and said very sweetly, "No, silly, I'm not going to a party."

Totally confused, or at least trying to be, Clayton stood up and walked toward his small kitchen. Once he got there, he offered her a glass of juice.

"Juice would be nice," Janae sat watching his movements from the sofa. As he bent down to retrieve a container of juice from inside the refrigerator, Janae watched him bend at the waist, peering into the refrigerator.

Yessiree!   His rear was every bit as tight as she remembered, she thought. With a pent up sigh, she watched him straighten, pour juice into a tall glass, then walk back toward her. He handed her the glass and sat back down.

"So, what brings you by?"

Janae sat forward, leaning toward him. The action served up a generous view of her bosom, which appeared in danger of spilling out of her dress. "Clay, I need your help. I dressed up this way and went out with a few friends tonight that I haven't seen in a very long time."

Unsure what all this had to do with him, Clay waited patiently for her to continue.

"Anyway, there's this guy I like and, well, he showed up tonight at the club we went to. I guess I had a little too much to drink, and made a fool of myself trying to get him to notice me."   The blank stare he gave her made Janae hurry through her explanation.   "So, there we were, having a nice time, dancing, drinking wine spritzers and making a ruckus, and this guy, he doesn't even glance my way."

Clayton sat through Janae's rambling, thinking there must be a point somewhere in this story. He decided he had better help her get to it, or they could be here literally all night.

"So, exactly what do you need my help with?" he questioned.

She stood up before him then, with both palms raised in supplication and got right to the point.   "You tell me, you're a man. What's wrong with me?"

"Janae…I," totally caught off guard, Clay really didn't know what to say.

She let her hands drop to her side, and walked over to him very slowly, closing the small distance between them.   "Clayton, look at me. Why wouldn't a man be attracted to me?" she asked, then added as an afterthought, "Are you attracted to me?"

He wasn't certain if her question was rhetorical or not. In any event, his answer obviously didn't matter because what she did next totally stunned him.

"I really don't understand it, maybe you can help me understand," she said as she began to swivel her hips and spin around in a sensuous dance. The tight dress she wore emphasized her suggestive movements each time she spun around, gyrating to a non-existent song.

Stopping directly in front of him, she moved her pelvis seductively in a slow, rhythmic motion, humming softly to a song that existed only in her mind.   "Tell me, if I moved in front of you like this," she did a little spin in front of him, grabbing his full attention, "would it turn you on?"

Too shocked to respond, Clayton left the question unanswered just like all the rest. He was totally speechless. As her hair flew around her shoulders with each seductive turn, his mind raced to find a way to deal with this.

His dilemma was solved in the next instant as Janae, slightly breathless, made one final twirl, then ended up—either by accident or design—on his lap.

"Whew, I guess those spritzer's went straight to my head!" she said in a rush as she wound her arms around his neck and wiggled her bottom against him, getting comfortable.

Bells and whistles went off simultaneously inside Clay's brain and he shot up off his seat like a jack in the box, nearly dumping Janae to the floor in the process. He helped to steady her before she hit the floor and made an effort to deposit her back on the sofa. "Listen, Janae, I don't think I'm the man to help you."

When Clayton tried to unloosen her arms from around his neck, she held on tighter. Smiling up at him sweetly, she hung on tight and her voice came out slightly slurred as she asked him innocently, "Why not?"

"Because…because your like my little sister and…" he didn't get a chance to finish his explanation because Janae pulled his head down with surprising strength and clamped her mouth over his. Clayton was instantly involved in a heated foray, as the force of her very persistent tongue cut off any further protests he might have had. For a split second he was lost; it was too easy to get lost as her persuasive mouth searched out every male nerve ending he possessed with her tongue. Her swirling tongue made him forget who he was, and his body reacted like any man would to a very hot little…*Whoa! Whoa! Whoa!*

Like a cold December rain, reason washed over him. Grasping both her shoulders, Clayton broke the kiss and set Janae away from him.

He immediately grabbed her purse, took her hand and headed straight for the front door. Janae legs wobbled a bit as he half dragged, half carried her to his truck. Clay deposited her into the passenger side front seat, but Janae, clearly not ready to go, made a dash for the door as if she wanted to get back out. When he caught her by the waist, to stop her from getting out of the car, she gave him an alarmed but funny look. He studied her with a doubtful expression for the space of thirty seconds, saw her suddenly smile, then deposit the contents of her stomach, along with half a dozen wine spritzers, all over his front seat.

CHAPTER

NINETEEN

By eight o'clock Vi had Mrs. Randolph under the hair dryer. As a rule she had very few customers. Supervising the shop, the spa treatments and the business end of the salon usually kept her pretty busy. However, she still had several customers who preferred her service over anyone on her staff. Mrs. Randolph was one of those longtime, loyal customers. When Mrs. Randolph was done, Vi put her in a chair and began to curl her hair into a style the older woman had preferred for the past five years.

As the older woman chattered away, Vi's mind wandered to other things. Maybe it was too early in the morning, or maybe she could blame what happened next on her lack of sleep last night. In any event, she was totally unprepared when Andre blurted out, loud enough for the entire shop to hear, "I'm so hungry right now I could eat a cow."

Nicole laughed along with him and asked, "Why didn't you stop for breakfast? Did you oversleep again from partying all night."

"Girl, you know how I do, anyway," Andre said slowly and glanced over in Vi's direction. "Vi, whatever happened to your officer friend? You know, the one with the tight buns who used to bring us breakfast on Saturday. I've been missing his hot, sweet treats," Andre said with a smirk. Then as an afterthought, he added, "Oh yeah, and the doughnuts and coffee he brought with him were good too!"

The amusing sexual innuendo in Andre's statement made the curling iron in Vi's hand slip a notch, and she nearly burned Mrs. Randolph's neck. While Nicole and the customer occupying her work chair broke into uncontrollable laughter, Cynthia gave Andre a horrified look. Before Vi could respond, Cynthia shot Andre a distasteful look and barked.

"In case you haven't realized, this is a place of business," she shouted. "Your gay lifestyle and antics are hardly fit for a professional workplace."

Cynthia gathered all the papers she'd been working on and got up. She passed Vi on her way to the back office and whispered so only Vi could hear, "Vi, you really must do something with that man." Cynthia threw a sharp look in Andre's direction for emphasis, before walking swiftly out of sight.

Andre and Vi stared at Cynthia's retreating back, then at each other, but it was Andre that broke the silence. "Well, looks like somebody has her panties in a bunch," he commented, with amusement in his eyes.

Vi shook her head and told her client to sit tight. After she excused herself, she hooked Andre by the arm and led him a few feet away. When she had him in the break area of the shop, Vi spoke to him in hushed tones. "First of all, if you're referring to Clayton, he's been very busy at work. Second of all," she told him heatedly, "Cynthia is my sister. I don't mind your kidding around, but you've really got to start showing her more respect, Andre."

"Sorry Vi," Andre said earnestly. "My bad, you know I don't mean any harm."

Vi let out a deflated breath and looked at him. "I know you mean no harm. You have to forgive me, I haven't been sleeping too well lately," she explained. "Sorry, if I flew off the handle just now."

"Why don't you take off after you're done with Ms. R. Me and Nikki can handle the flow."

She thought about his offer and decided with only one late afternoon appointment on her calendar, she just might take off early. "I have one more appointment at 3:30 this afternoon," she told him. "Can you handle it?"

Andre assured her they could and after Mrs. Randolph was done, Andre and Nicole sent her on her way. Vi stopped at the mall, the drugstore and then the cleaners. It was Saturday afternoon and folks trying to get out of town or to the beach, clogged the Long Island Expressway. On her ride home, Vi had a lot of time to think about what Andre said earlier.

To tell the truth, she really didn't know if Clayton was busy or not. The last time they'd spoken, he'd been angry when she suggested he go out with other people. That had been close to two weeks ago. Since that time, she hadn't seen him. He stopped calling and dropping by. He called, when he knew she wouldn't be home, and cancelled their workout sessions. She thought about the voicemail messages Clay had left her. For some reason that she didn't want to examine too closely, she did not erase those messages. The sound of his voice, each time she replayed his messages, did strange things to her insides. The feeling was not altogether unpleasant, but definitely disturbing.

Nearing her exit, Vi signaled and merged to the right lane. She got off at exit 32 northbound and drove the rest of the way home, deep in thought. If she wanted to be totally honest with herself, Vi acknowledged, she missed Clayton's company more than she thought possible.

Tony had a sleepover planned for tonight at Mike's house, so Vi ate a light supper and went to bed early that night. Deep in slumber, the sound of the doorbell ringing did not penetrate her sleep. The loud banging on her door that came afterwards, however, certainly did. Vi sat up in bed. For the longest time she rubbed her eyes, squinting at the alarm clock on her bedside table. Who would be knocking on her door at this hour, she thought and swung her legs over the side of the bed.

She wore a short-sleeved night shirt, covered with tiny powder blue flowers and slits up both sides that reached her hip bone. It was a Christmas present from Janae, and Vi wore it a lot because the cotton material made the shirt comfortable to sleep in on hot summer nights. The banging continued downstairs and, not bothering to grab a robe, Vi hurried to the front door in her bare feet, thinking there might be some type of emergency. As she came down the stairs the knocking grew louder.

What in the world? Vi raced to the door, peered through the peephole and quickly opened the door, shocked to see who it was. Standing slightly behind the door, Vi came face to face with Clayton Marshall. He wasn't in uniform; on the contrary, he wore well-fitting black jeans and a rust-colored dress shirt. Standing on her threshold his aftershave—a clean woodsy scent she associated with only him—wafted to her.

Conflicting emotions warred simultaneously within her. While she was glad to see him after so long, she was also annoyed with him for avoiding her in the first place. Momentarily confused by his presence on her doorstep at this hour, Vi was unable to find her voice at first. When she did find it, naturally she asked.

"Clayton, hi… what are you doing here?"

Forgetting for the moment how she was dressed, Vi stepped from behind the door. Clay took in her attire, what little there was of it, and thought absently,

Did the woman always answer the door so scantily clad?

Thinking about that and the last time he'd caught sight of her in similar attire made him remember the reason he'd come over here. His hand came out and gently pushed the door further open. Vi didn't think about the fact she hadn't invited him in. His serious demeanor and sure movements as he came in and closed the door behind him overwhelmed her. She'd never seen him like this before. His serious expression was disquieting and in the face of it, she was unsure what to say. He stood facing her after closing the door, only the street lamps and a full moon for light. His big frame seemed to fill her small foyer as she stood watching him for a minute. When it seemed he wasn't going to say anything, Vi said to him a bit nervously, "I was beginning to think you were avoiding me."

Unsmiling, he didn't bother responding to what she said. Instead he informed her unnecessarily, "Obviously, I woke you," he said quietly. "Sorry about that, but what I had to say couldn't wait."

She didn't know what to say to that. So, she said nothing. He appeared a bit restless and agitated, but after a moment he asked her in an off hand manner, "Do you have any idea where I've been tonight?"

"How would I know?" confused, she stared at him.

"Let me tell you," he interrupted. "I've been on that blind date you thought was such a good idea."

She looked at him closely. The street light coming through the bay window shone brightly but left part of his face in shadow. Watching him closely, Vi struggled with how strange he was acting, then it struck her.

"Clayton have you been drinking?"

He didn't answer her, but instead said very slowly, "Her name was Lisa Lopez, by the way. She was kind of pretty in a malnourished sort of way, newly divorced and very, very friendly." Clay paused here, as if thinking about his next words. "We went to a Latin dance club she knew about and had a pretty good time."

As she listened to him, a lump formed in Vi's throat. She swallowed several times, trying unsuccessfully to dislodge it.

He stood staring at her, watching her eyes grow wide and fill with hurt. When she didn't say anything, he continued to talk, knowing the unease it brought her. "We went to a late dinner afterwards with Piterrelli and his wife. All through dinner, though, she kept brushing up against me."

"Clay...I don't..."

In a hushed tone, he stopped her again. "No," He said with a cruel twist of his lips, not allowing her to interrupt. "I have to tell you. Where was I? Oh, yeah, Ms. Lopez. Every time she laughed about something Vi, Ms. Lopez would run her hand down my arm or thigh. At first, I dismissed it as accidental, until I took her home."

Not wanting to hear more, she blurted out, "Clay I really don't want to hear wh..."

"But, I want you to hear," he said harshly. "After all, you thought this blind date was a good idea, remember?"

She noted the sarcasm in his voice, but made no comment. The urge to run upstairs and hide was almost unbearable.

"Anyway," he went on. "After we left the club and I took Lisa home, that's where things got real interesting."

Vi opened her mouth to speak, but Clayton placed his index finger over her lips to keep her quiet.

"I have to admit, I did make one mistake when I took Lisa home. When I gave her a polite kiss goodnight, she grabbed hold of me with more strength than I would have credited her for. Then she planted her lips on me and gave me her version of a proper kiss goodnight."

Suddenly, Vi's mouth felt very dry inside and she swallowed twice before finding her voice. "Clay I...I can't say that I blame her, you're a good looking man, and...."

"No," he pinned her with a commanding tone. "You don't understand, do you?"

She noticed his voice was quietly controlled and even though he spoke calmly, a muscle ticked in his strong jaw, revealing how close he was to the edge. Not able to grasp that fact, Vi stood too stunned to move, letting his next words shock her into further silence.

"She reached for me Vi, fondling me through my pants while she rubbed all up against me."

Speechless, Vi gave him a mortified look. She didn't want to hear this, didn't want to hear anymore, but she couldn't seem to make him stop.

"I could have had her right there Vi, right up against the door to her apartment and she would've let me take her, Vi. In fact, she would have welcomed it because Ms. Lopez made it pretty clear she wanted something more than a friendly kiss."

His harsh, mocking tone sliced through her. Realizing he was trying to hurt her, Vi struck back, "I don't care what happened," she spat at him. "Why are you telling me this?"

"Because it was your idea, Vi," he replied quietly.

In that instant, she felt an unreasonable hatred towards this faceless, unknown woman. The woman's name, Lisa Lopez, didn't help form a picture of what she looked like. The pictures that did formulate in her mind were unknown female hands, rubbing him in places just as he described. Vi felt suddenly ill and knew there were deeper feelings behind this hatred but her subconscious was unwilling to examine them right now. No, right now she wanted to lash out at Clay, lash out and hurt him the way he'd just hurt her.

"Don't hand me that!" Vi was good and mad now, and her voice rose slightly as she accused him. "If it was that easy then why didn't you do it? Why didn't you go on and sleep with her?" As she asked this question, a cold lump formed in the pit of her stomach.

Clayton studied Vi, her sharp tone giving him pause. Looking heavenward, he swiped a hand down his face, warring with telling her the truth.

"Because I didn't want to make love to her…" The words hung in the air between them and she looked at him, her eyes wide and searching, waiting for him to continue. "When my hand covered her small breast, my mind imagined another, more of a handful, much softer," he finally said.

Pinning her with a penetrating gaze, he forged ahead. "In my arms, Ms. Lopez' small frame made me conjure up softer, much fuller curves. I imagined a fuller mouth too, one you could nibble on and sink your teeth into." He paused as if gathering his thoughts. "Everything about her was wrong."

His words, his heated admissions, caused Vi's heart to race. Heat suffused her body from head to toe and, out of nowhere, she wanted to run and hide but her feet stayed rooted to that spot. Who was he comparing this woman to? Was he referring to her? She quickly dismissed the silly notion. There must be any number of women he knew, who had the attributes he referred to. Satisfied with that rationalization, she said as much to him.

"I don't know what you want me to say," the hurt she felt made her voice a strangled whisper. "I realize there must be plenty of women you know, that you might prefer more, but why come here like this?"

"Because," he shouted. "Because I wanted you to know I could have done it. I almost did, she had me inside her apartment, running her hands inside my shirt and everywhere else, but…."

What he'd begun to say hung suspended in the electrically charged air between them. She held her breath waiting for his next words, but when they came, Vi realized she was totally unprepared for them.

"But, all I could think of was you," he said in a strangled voice. Closing the distance separating them, Clay suddenly reached for her. Before she knew what was happening, Vi found herself hauled up against him, locked in his embrace. Her hands were trapped between their bodies, the fingers splayed out on his chest as she stared up into his eyes.

"Clayton… wh…what are you doing?" His nearness robbed her of the ability to move. She stood in his arms, watching his descent as he lowered his head and kissed her. It was a very tender kiss, totally at odds with the tension she felt in the bunched muscles of the arms holding her. Vi didn't have time to respond, it was over in seconds and he lifted his head.

Finally finding her voice, she looked up at him with widened eyes, and whispered, "You…you must be drunk. What's wrong with you?"

He shot her a smoldering look and instead of responding to her question, he lowered his head once again. This time, however, he didn't kiss her.

Burying his face in the sweet hollow beneath her earlobe, he lingered there. His hot breath on that soft expanse of flesh made her feel hot and cold all at once and weakened her knees.

"Mmmmm...this was missing, this softness. She wasn't soft like this Vi, like you, and I knew immediately, I couldn't sleep with her. I couldn't do it," he whispered close to her ear.

Unable to pull it back, she asked him, "What did you do?"

"I left," was all he said.

When she felt the wall at her back, Vi was surprised. In the midst of all this she hadn't felt her feet move. She felt the heavy beat of his heart, the intensity of its steady rhythm under her fingertips forced reality to sink in. Her hands, which lay trapped and useless between their bodies, now pressed lightly against his chest. He was out of control and certainly strong enough to ignore her slight pressure. For a split second she thought he would, as she felt the muscles bunch and tense in the arms surrounding her. Then he released her and immediately stepped back.

"I think you'd better go," she uttered in a slow raspy voice.

He stared down at her, his eyes smoldering with desire. After a moment, he banked the fire within and, like a curtain, the heat in his eyes disappeared. In its absence they now appeared cold and blank.

"Ok," he said quietly. Giving her one final look, Clay turned around, opened the door, and in the next instant he was gone.

Vi lay across her bed staring at the phone. Chewing on her bottom lip, she fought the urge to pick it up. Pinching the bridge of her nose, she sighed deeply and closed her eyes. Over an hour had passed since she asked Clayton to leave. After he kissed her and left so abruptly, she walked upstairs to her bedroom feeling confused. By the time she reached the top of the stairs, however, Vi was angry.

How dare he come over here and insinuate... He was trying to ruin their friendship, plain and simple, she thought as she lay on her bed staring up at the ceiling. Although she was used to the house being empty, tonight the quiet seemed to close in on her. Alone with nothing but her thoughts, a million questions swirled in her mind and she found sleep hard to come by. After replying the last hour in her head over a hundred times, she kept coming back to,

What in the hell just happened? Vi couldn't figure out what had gotten into him. He had to be drunk, she concluded. The more she thought about it, doubts entered her mind. Had she somehow given off some type of misguided signals? Vi worried her bottom lip, pondering that possibility. No. No, she couldn't come up with any instances where she may have given

him the wrong idea about their friendship.   They were close.   That was all.
Vi sat up straight in bed, as it suddenly occurred to her - *just like she and Craig had been—like mother and son. Only he wasn't Craig and Clay was not her son.*

Oh God! Frantic, Vi wondered what she was going to do. He couldn't possibly have feelings for her. She wanted to believe he had been drunk, but she knew from experience he seldom drank very much because of his past. By the time a painful headache developed at the base of her skull, Vi was exhausted thinking about it.   Well, she concluded, if he wasn't drunk earlier, then he must have lost his mind.

That thought stopped her dead in her tracks. Mentally chiding herself, Vi acknowledged, *if she was going to be totally honest here, she thought, she had to admit she did enjoy his attention just a bit more than she should?*

In retrospect, she had to admit to herself, if it were any other man, and if their ages weren't so far apart, she would definitely be attracted to a man like Clayton. But he wasn't any other man, she thought sighing in defeat, and she was definitely older than him.   Her subconscious piped in, since we are being honest and all, in a taunting voice. *And another thing, you know damn well how you felt when he started talking about having sex with that hussy, what's her face – Lisa- I'm so hot -Lopez.   You were jealous, pure and simple!*

Vi looked over at the phone one more time. This time she actually picked up it up and started to dial his number, before she caught herself and banged the phone down in frustration.

"No, dammit, I won't call him!" She said out loud, mentally kicking herself.   She desperately needed to share these disturbing feelings with a friend. Problem was, Clay was her closest friend and she certainly couldn't discuss any of this with him. It was also too late to call Nicole. Vi was back to being angry with him for ruining their friendship. What the hell was the matter with him for stirring all this up in the first place! Fed up, she snapped off the bedside lamp light, punched the pillow beneath her head and tried to get some sleep.

The sound of the phone ringing roused Vi from a troubled sleep. At first, when she sat up in bed, she wasn't sure if the phone had actually rang, or if she'd imagined it. Thoroughly exhausted, Vi decided it was just a dream and prepared to lay down again. But then it rang once more, jarring her fully awake.

"Hello?"

"Vi?"

"Clay!" Glancing at her bedside clock she saw it was after three in the morning.

"Vi...hi, sorry for calling you so late." When she didn't say anything, Clayton continued, needing to get this off his chest. "Vi, I'm sorry....about earlier, I mean. You were right, I was very drunk."

As soon as he said the words, she felt like an invisible weight had been lifted from her shoulders. Terribly relieved, she tried to tell him.

"Clay, I..."

"No let me finish," he interrupted. "I need for you to know I would never jeopardize our friendship," he told her earnestly. "I hope my little display earlier didn't do that."

Enormously relieved, she found herself apologizing too. "It didn't, really. I'm sorry too for pushing you on that blind date. It's none of my business who you go out with."

Wanting to take full responsibility, Clayton brushed aside her apology. "That's not the issue here. The issue is I had a bad night and...and I was out of line."

"Its okay, really," she assured him. "I can think of plenty of bad days I've had recently that you've helped me through. I owed you that much."

"You don't owe me anything," he said forcefully. Then in a much calmer voice he added, "I guess I kinda' took my frustrations out on you. I'm ashamed to admit that, but I wanted you to know how really sorry I am."

A feeling of warmth and happiness suffused Vi. "Clay, stop apologizing. We're friends right?"

"Are we?" He asked her earnestly. "Are we still friends?"

"Yes we are."

"Good."

"Now, about calling me at this hour, if you plan to call me again this late, I want you to know friendship only goes so far," she said trying to bring some levity into a very serious conversation.

Vi heard him laugh lightly over the telephone line, and it was like music to her ears. "Listen," he said, "I gotta' work tomorrow, but I'll call you and we can go workout or do something soon, alright."

"Okay, that would be nice," she said. "I've been eating pizza with Tony every other night, and getting pretty worried about being able to work off all those calories."

He laughed again, told her goodnight and hung up the phone.

As Vi replaced the receiver, she felt an enormous sense of relief. Satisfied the confusion over his uncharacteristic behavior earlier tonight had been cleared up and their friendship was still intact, she lay down again and settled in for a good nights sleep. As she drifted off, a tiny niggling thought plagued her. It kept trying to reach her consciousness, then flitting away again as sleep beckoned her. It was something she'd touched on earlier. What was it? Something about Clay's drinking habits…

About two weeks later, Vi sat at her desk early one morning going over some invoices. Unable to focus on her task, Vi put down her pen and began chewing on her bottom lip. It had been more than two weeks and in that time, Clayton hadn't called or come by. She thought about the last time they'd spoken. At the time she'd been certain everything was back to normal. Now, however, she wasn't so sure. She was still deep in thought when Cynthia walked in. Unsure why she was in today, Vi asked her sister, "Cyn, what are you doing here, today is your day off?

Cynthia walked over to her desk, sat down and opened her top drawer before answering Vi's question. "Tom is out of town again, so I came in today to catch up on some paperwork."

Cynthia's husband Tom owned a thriving computer software business. When he first started the company, Vi recalled Tom working long hours to put the company on its feet. His business was doing very well now, so she wondered about the trips he'd started taking frequently. But since Cynthia seemed unconcerned, Vi didn't give it much thought. Vi liked Tom. He was mild mannered, tall with kind eyes and one of those thick mustaches that went out of fashion in the 70's. His soft-spoken nature was so at odds with her sister's domineering personality, Vi often wondered how the two of them had stayed married for so many years.

Going back to the invoices she'd been working on, Vi lowered her head once more trying to concentrate. After a moment, she glanced Cynthia's way and found her sister sitting at her desk, staring into space.

"Cynthia, is something wrong?

Cynthia quickly recovered, and pasted a smile on her face.

"Oh, no everything's just fine," Cynthia said, surprised at how easily the lie slipped past her lips. Actually before the other night, everything had been fine, Cynthia rationalized. She was used to Tom working late nights, but something else happened a few nights ago that still had Cynthia puzzled. Recently, Tom had begun to stay at the office later and later and, when he did come home, he was so distant he might as well have not been there at all. Searching her mind, Cynthia tried to pinpoint exactly when the trouble started.

Tom had surprised her by coming home early for dinner the other night. Cynthia recalled what a good mood he'd been in. Cynthia was in the kitchen getting ready to make a sandwich, thinking she would be eating alone again tonight. When he walked in, Tom kissed her on the cheek and started making himself a sandwich with the fixings she'd laid out.

"Tom! I didn't know you'd be home. If I'd known I would have prepared something special for dinner."

"Not to worry, pastrami on rye is my favorite anyway," he said as he heaped a generous portion of pastrami onto a slice of bread. Out of habit, she asked him about his day and was given a brief synopsis of the new account he'd acquired that day. When Tom casually asked Cynthia about her day, Cynthia couldn't help discussing the disgraceful way Andre acted at the Salon earlier that afternoon.

"Tom, I swear I don't know why Vi puts up with that man. He's a disgrace and the way he dresses and talks… well, it's really disgusting."

Tom had grown very quiet, while making a second sandwich and listening to her go on about Andre. Cynthia hardly noticed as she heated up to her topic, "I realize times have changed, but I just don't approve of men having sex with other men."

Tom put down the knife he'd been holding and braced his arms against the counter, listening to Cynthia's small-minded views. Totally caught up in her own world, Cynthia did not try to hide the distaste dripping from her voice.

"Why, just today a woman walked into the shop and accused Andre of sleeping with her husband. I can't even repeat what he said to that poor woman, but I can tell you, whatever it was made her leave the salon in tears."

At some point, during her tirade, Cynthia realized Tom hadn't said one word. She turned to look at him just in time to see him dump his sandwich down the garbage disposal and lick mustard off his middle finger.

"Oh Tom, here let me make that for you," she said moving to make him another sandwich.

"No Cynthia, that won't be necessary. I just remembered I have some unfinished orders that need to get out, so I'll need to go back to the office."

Cynthia walked over to him and picked up a kitchen towel lying on the counter. Absently, she wiped a speck of mustard that clung to his mustache; the man was forever getting food stuck in that thing, she thought idly.

"I thought you finished everything and we could sit down for a nice meal."

"Sorry," he said and strode to the front door. With his briefcase in hand, he called over his shoulder, "I may be late, so don't wait up for me."

The sound of Vi's voice broke through the troubles plaguing Cynthia's thoughts.

"I'm sorry Vi, did you say something?"

Vi was certain now, that something was definitely troubling Cynthia. However, she knew her sister would rather die than confide in anyone.

"I just asked you three times, when Tom would be back from his trip."

Brushing off Vi's question, Cynthia informed her in a dispassionate tone, "In a few days, but I'm not complaining. Tom's business is very demanding. After all, if it weren't for his hard work, we wouldn't be able to live in a big house in one of the most affluent communities around."

Vi watched her sister recognizing this routine. Tall and slender, with classically cut short hair to match her impeccable wardrobe, Vi knew from experience her sister measured everything by the amount of material possessions a person had. If she and Tom were having trouble, Cynthia would consider it a sacrifice that had to be made. She also knew from experience no amount of prodding would force Cynthia to talk about what was bothering her. Even though she stuck her nose in everyone else's business, when it came to personal matters, Cynthia normally kept her own counsel. So, Vi didn't push the issue.

At that precise moment, Nicole walked into the back office. Giving Vi and Cynthia a cheerful greeting, Nicole walked over and poured herself a cup of coffee, pretending she didn't notice Vi was the only one in the room who greeted her in return. Puzzled, Vi shook her head slightly. She knew Cynthia didn't like Andre because of his sexual preferences. Why she disliked Nicole was a mystery Vi had yet to solve.

Abruptly, Cynthia stood up and Vi watched her gather her things and a few ledgers, as if she were leaving.

"Cynthia, are you leaving? You just got here."

"I just remembered an appointment I forgot about. Anyway I can work on these books at home," Cynthia replied and made a hasty retreat.

Nicole shrugged her small shoulders and exchanged a questioning look with Vi. Taking the seat Cynthia had just vacated, she sat down to drink her coffee and said, "Well, she left in a hurry."

"Yeah, that was strange. I think something is bothering her."

"What else is new?" Nicole responded cryptically. When she looked up at Vi over the rim of her cup, she noticed the dark circles under her friend's eyes. "Since we're talking about things that bother people, from the looks of you, it appears something is bothering you too."

"Yeah, well it's nothing really. I just haven't been sleeping too well lately."

"Yes, I can see that. So, how about telling me something I don't know."

Thankful to get it off her chest, Vi did just that. After she finished telling Nikki about Clay's strange behavior the other night, and his apology immediately afterwards, Nikki was silent for so long Vi started to worry.

"Well?" she prompted her friend. "Say something."

"I don't have anything to say. I've been saying all along that man wants you, and I don't mean as a friend."

"No," Vi said in denial, shaking her head adamantly. "He was drunk Nick, and he apologized. I was certain everything was fine when he called later. But now," she hesitated, "I'm not so sure."

"Well, last time I checked the two of you were adults, and if you both like each other, it's no one's business but yours."

"Even if he was interested in me that way, he's way too young and…"

"And what? You're afraid, aren't you? Afraid your sister will have a shit fit, afraid that you just might have feelings for a young, handsome virile man. You are not too old and he's definitely not too young to do what I think the two of you both want."

Having always considered herself as liberal as the next person, Vi was shocked to find her cheeks heat up in the face of Nikki's bold innuendo. Speechless, she stared at her friend, trying to formulate a response.

Wearing a satisfied grin, Nikki was glad to see she'd gotten Vi's attention. Good, she thought, Vi could use a little shaking up. Not missing a beat, Nikki casually added before she got up to leave.

"Yeah, take as much time as you need to think about it. And, when you're through, if you're still convinced the two of you are just friends, go on and pick up the phone and call him."

Vi thought about that, and looked pointedly at the phone. Before she made a decision to call or not call him, Nicole popped her head back into the office and said, "Oh, after you make that call, we need to discuss the time bomb ticking between Andre and Cynthia. Your gonna' have to deal with that headache sooner or later Vi. But first, make that call."

Clay's answering machine picked up when she called his home number and cell phone. As an afterthought, she dialed the number to the station and was surprised when the dispatcher put her through.

"Amityville Police, Officer Marshall speaking."

His familiar deep voice reverberated through the receiver, making her stomach flip flop in response. "Clayton? Hi, sorry to bother you at work…"

He was silent so long, Vi guessed she'd caught him off guard. Filling the void, she began to ramble spilling useless chatter into the deafening silence on the other end of the phone. "I'm surprised you're there. I felt sure they'd put me through to your voice mail."

"I'm sitting in front of a mountain of unfinished paperwork," he said, finding his voice.

"Oh, well that explains it," she replied, glad that he was at least responding now.

"Captain Jackson told me to knock off early and get it all done. Translation—don't go home until you're finished."

"Oh."

Struggling to find something to say, they both fell silent. After a brief period he asked her. "So, Vi, what can I do for you?"

"Oh, I don't know. I kind of got the feeling you were trying to avoid me." When he didn't respond she asked the question, which had been troubling her for days. "I mean, with the other night. We're cool, right?"

"Yeah, we're cool. No worries." She noted the coolness in his voice.

"So," getting down to the reason she called him. "I was wondering what your schedule was like. If I don't start working out again soon, it'll feel like I'm starting all over again."

"I, umm…I switched shifts with Piterrelli for the next few days, so I won't be free in the mornings," he said, explaining a bit too quickly.

"Oh, well, we don't have to go in the morning you know. How about going in the evening?" she suggested. "When's your next day off?

"Tomorrow."

Vi wasn't sure if she imagined the hesitation she heard in his voice before he supplied this information. "Good. With no work tomorrow, tonight would be perfect."

Ohmigod! She thought, rolling her eyes heavenward, *somehow in the past few days she'd become a pushy, forceful, desperate woman.* "I mean, if you want to," she added quickly, then waited several tense seconds before he replied.

"Okay, but I've got a few things to do with J.R. So, it'll have to be late."

"Late is not a problem," she assured him.

"Okay. I'll see you around 9:00 then," he said simply, before hanging up the phone.

Clay didn't want to see her tonight. When she called earlier today, Vi had caught him off guard. Since that call he'd been tempted to cancel their plans for tonight at least a dozen times. After the last time he'd seen her, he wasn't sure if he could handle being near her this soon. His frustration only mounted, every time he thought about the mistake he'd made in going to her house in the first place, and the even bigger mistake he'd made when he kissed her. Adding to his torture of remembering that kiss was the certainty she may have been responding to his frustrated advances the other night, if only for a few seconds. Instinctively he knew even if she had responded, she would never admit to having any feelings for him. On some level he understood her desire to pretend nothing was happening between the two of them. So after apologizing the other night, Clayton decided it might be best to keep his distance for a while. He didn't want to rock the boat again until he had a chance to sort through the feelings he was beginning to have for her. If he acted on those feelings again and guessed wrong about how she felt, Clay realized he could ruin everything.

Picking up the phone, Clay decided it might be better to stay cool, play it safe and cancel this thing while he still could. He punched in her number and the phone rang twice before he noticed Piterrelli walking toward his desk, and hung up.

"Hey man, there was a call for you about ten minutes ago on line one. Did you get it?"

Knowing he hadn't heard his name paged all morning, Clay's temper flared.

"Why is it so hard to get someone to take a message around here?"

Piterrelli eyed Clay cautiously. Everyone in the squad room knew he'd been in a sour mood all day, and it seemed Piterrelli was the only fool brave enough to go near him. After all, Pitt reasoned, they were friends and he was worried about him but he wasn't about to get yelled at for something he didn't do.

"Listen man, don't chew my head off. I would've taken a message but I was taking a call on line four myself."

Clay exhaled slowly and quickly apologized to his friend. "I'm sorry man. I didn't mean to come at you like that. It's been a rough day."

"Welcome to my world," Piterrelli shot back jokingly.

When Clay didn't comment or smile after Piterrelli's poor attempt at humor, he really started to worry. He watched as Clayton silently bent his head over his work and proceeded to ignore him, even though he was still standing there.

"Hey man, what's eating you? I told my wife you'd be pissed after that blind date with Lisa the other night. Listen…"

"No, that's not it. Like I said, I'm having a rough day."

Just then, Clayton's phone rang. When Piterrelli walked away, Clayton immediately picked it up.

"Officer Marshall."

"Hey man," J.R.'s voice came through the receiver.

"Hey kid. You alright, what's up?"

"I just wanted to let you know I'll be at my cousin Casey's for a while."

Clay met J.R.'s cousin Casey a few times at their weekly practice games.

"So, do I pick you up for your game at her place next week?"

"Yeah, Casey's not doing so good so I'm looking out for her."

Listening to J.R., Clayton couldn't help feeling a sense of accomplishment. J.R.'s life at home was very similar to what Clay's life had been like at that age. The fact that he was doing something good and looking out for someone else was a sure sign the kid was on the right track, even if his parents were screw-ups.

"Anyway, she's real scared, man."

Clayton was too busy taking pride in how well J.R. had been doing lately, so he'd only been half listening until J.R. said this.

"What? Who's scared and why?"

"Dammit man, what's wrong with you? Weren't you listening to me?"

"Sorry, I've been a little pre-occupied today." Not wanting to get into his personal problems, Clayton quickly apologized and pressed the boy further.

"So, who's scared and why?"

"Casey, man. She thinks someone's been following her."

"Maybe she's just getting a little paranoid."

"No," J.R. insisted. "Last night someone broke into her apartment."

Clay sat up a little straighter, the police officer in him stepping to the forefront. "Did they take anything? Did she call the police?"

"No man, nothing was missing. It was just like someone was messing with your stuff, but you know you didn't do it."

"Okay, let's back up. Why would someone want to scare her in the first place?"

"Oh shit! I forgot to tell you the most important part."

"For the umpteenth time, stop cussing." Clayton impatiently admonished the boy and quickly urged him to continue. "Now, what do you mean—the most important part of what?"

"Well, you know Casey sometimes came down to the gym."

"Yeah, I know. Go on," Clayton prompted.

"She met Craig there a couple of times when he filled in for you, Dog."

"Okay," Clayton was totally clueless where J.R. was going with all this.

Sensing his confusion, J.R. quickly tried to clue him in.

"You don't get it, do you?"

The foul mood he'd been in all day made it very hard to hide the impatience in his voice. Clayton took a deep breath, before asking J.R.

"Get what?"

"They met before somewhere dude, only I didn't think anything about it until now."

"What in the world are you talking about? Listen, J.R, I've got a pile of work to…"

"Casey told me she and Craig got real tight man."

"So, he was trying to talk to her, so what?"

"No Dog, they were way past talking. They were gettin' busy…you know, knocking boots."

Clay was stunned. Craig had never mentioned any of this to him.

"How do you know all this?"

"Casey told me. He was with her right before he got shot."

"What?" Apparently, Clayton said this a bit too loudly. Seeing that the other officers in the room were glancing in his direction, he quickly lowered his voice.

"J.R., tell me everything you know."

When Clay hung up with J.R. twenty minutes later, he felt a rush of adrenaline wash over him. Here was a clue to Craig's murder no one knew about. It also answered two things that had been bothering him since Craig's death. It explained why Craig had seemed so preoccupied in the weeks before the shooting, and why the hell he'd been over on Chestnut that morning in the first place. He knew he needed to let the homicide detectives handling the case know about this information right away, but something made him hesitate. He and Craig had been more than roommates; they were friends, almost like brothers. While part of him felt a little betrayed that Craig had this whole other secret life he'd never shared with him, he had to wonder why he felt the secrecy was necessary.

Then it dawned on him, Craig obviously hadn't told his family either! Knowing how close Craig had been with his family, Clay was very surprised. No, he decided, he needed to speak with this woman first before anyone else did. J.R. also told him Casey was having a hard time with the baby she was carrying, which opened up another can of worms. Did Craig know Casey was pregnant before he died? And, was the baby she carried Craig's child?

CHAPTER
TWENTY-ONE

Clayton looked up as the glass doors opened to the club, expecting Vi to walk through. Instead a group of young girls entered all chatting happily about a competition they were preparing for. In an effort to minimize the time they had to spend together, he had arranged to meet her here instead of picking her up. While he waited for her, Clay came up with at least fifty reasons to leave before she got there. Unfortunately, all of them meant he had to stand her up when he could have simply cancelled earlier in the day.

Sitting in the lobby, he tried to come to terms with his feelings. On the one hand he definitely wanted to see her again, but on the other he couldn't risk a repeat of what happened last time they'd been together. Recalling that night in her foyer, Clay settled deeper into the lobby chair. Physically and mentally tired, he acknowledged after his meeting earlier today with Casey, he had more than his feelings for Vi to sort through. As a steady stream of people came through the automatic glass doors, Clay mentally cataloged all the information Casey had given him earlier that day.

Her building was depressingly shabby like all the other houses lining Chestnut Street. Beyond the peeling paint and broken blinds, Clayton supposed at one time these were nice homes for new families just starting out. Unfortunately, those folks had left long ago and only the small, untended yards and empty flower boxes remained. When he'd walked up to her building, Clayton pulled the pad from his belt flap to check the apartment number. In the narrow hallway, he had to climb the stairs two at time to the third floor in the stifling heat. When she opened the door, Clay studied the petite, blond woman who greeted him, recognizing her vaguely from some of J.R.'s practices. Her heart-shaped face held expressive green eyes with deep, dark circles beneath them. Her long, curly hair was the color of golden honey, and he imagined that women paid good money for coloring just like it at expensive hair salons.

As she let him in, Clayton glanced around casually, noting her place was little more than a studio, cramped but very clean. He followed her into the living room and immediately removed his hat. Placing it under his arm, Clayton remained standing, having no idea what he would find out. However, by the time he left an hour later, he felt more energized then he'd felt in a long while. After weeks of dried-up leads, he now held new information that could possibly lead to Craig's killer.

"Okay, let me see if I have this right," he'd said, reading over the notes he'd taken during their conversation. "Your boyfriend, Troy, died in a car accident a few months ago. He was driving but somehow his friend Raul, who was a passenger, survived? Then Raul loans you money to move here. You move here, then Raul shows up on your doorstep unexpected." Pausing to look at her, Clayton waited for Casey to acknowledge he'd gotten everything right so far. He watched her nod her head slightly, before continuing. "And, you let him move in with you temporarily because you still owed him money. Then, let me see," he said consulting his pad once more. "After a while, he started to act funny when you went out, checking up on you and who you went out with, right?"

Again, Casey nodded her head slightly, focusing all her attention on both her hands folded in front of her on top of the small kitchen table where she sat. After a second or two, he continued to recap.

"Okay, then one night he goes nuts when you get in late. After accusing you of sleeping around, he tries to force himself on you and…" he trailed off. Recalling her exact words, when she told him what came next had given Clay a sudden chill. Tentatively, she had begun explaining to him.

"Raul seemed alright at first. Besides loaning me money to move here, he called to check on me a few times. I was surprised when he became violent." She got up suddenly and began pacing.

Clayton watched Casey wring her hands in agitation as she related the rest of her story. It was obvious to him she hadn't seen this creep for what he was. Clayton had seen a zillion guys just like Raul in his line of work. They started out friendly, but that behavior usually ended with the women filing restraining orders or assault charges against these so-called male friends.

"Then what happened?" he prompted her.

"I pushed him off me and told him to get the hell out and…"

A muscle began to tick in his jaw as experience told him how these situations usually escalated. "Did he hit you?" he asked pointedly.

"Yes," she responded quietly and lowered her lashes. Casey stopped pacing and sat down again at the table. Her agitation was evident in the way she clenched and unclenched her hands.

"Casey, do you think Raul was involved in Craig's shooting?"

"I don't know who killed Craig. But, I do know someone's been following me since I got out of the hospital."

"Do you think Raul's the person following you?

"I don't know, I think so. When he hit me I filed charges against him, but I haven't seen him since."

Getting back to the business at hand, Clay made some more notes in his pad before asking her, "Did the police find any leads on him back then?"

"No, I don't believe so. At least Craig never told me anything anyway."

"Craig?"

"Oh yeah, when I went down to the police station to file charges against Raul, Craig was the officer who helped me." Mulling this over, Clayton acknowledged this was one more thing Craig hadn't shared with him. Seeing the confusion written in his features, Casey made an attempt to explain.

"You looked shocked. It's ironic that I went in to file charges and met Craig. I didn't know he knew you or J.R. for that matter until later. But," as she said this, Casey touched Clay's forearm lightly, "from the moment I met Craig I swear that my whole life turned around. Craig was everything to me and I want you to know that it wasn't his idea to keep our relationship a secret. I made him do it."

His sole reason for going to see Casey had been to discover what she knew and if there was any connection between that and Craig's shooting. In light of what she'd just said, however, Clayton suddenly had a million questions that had nothing to do with the investigation. Curious about the secrecy, he had to ask. However, as soon as he did, he instantly regretted giving into that curiosity as he watched tears spill from her eyes.

"He did it to please me. Craig didn't want to keep anything from his family or you. We fought about it all the time...," her voice trailed off here before she added. "He was very close to his family and I knew I hurt him every time I refused to meet them. But, I'm not really the type of girl you bring home to meet your mother."

He watched her let out a long sigh, rotate her head on her shoulders to release the tension gathered there. As he watched her, silently digesting what she'd told him, Clayton found himself identifying with some of what she said. Admitting she had came from nothing, and for a very long time feeling like nothing, had plagued her. Growing up as he had, Clayton understood isolation and all the loneliness that went along with it. This woman, for whatever reason, had been left to fend for herself. Clay thought about all the times his parents had gotten drunk and left him and his little sister to fend for each other. Thinking about it, he concluded Craig must have cared deeply for this woman. Why else would he go along with hiding what they shared? He acknowledged with a wry grin that it was not uncommon for a man to do strange things when he was in love.

Clay flipped his pad closed and walked toward the front door. Right before he opened it, he turned around to face her. "Casey, I have to let the homicide guys working Craig's murder case know about what we've discussed."

Following him to the door, Casey assured him, "Okay, but I've told you all I know."

"I know, unfortunately, they'll still probably want to speak with you."

She nodded in understanding and stood by the door waiting for him to leave. Pausing on her threshold, Clayton turned to address her again. "You know, you should have listened to Craig," he said quietly.

"What do you mean?"

"I know Craig's family, they're great people. If you were special to him, I'm very certain they would have welcomed you with open arms."

Deep in thought, Clay didn't notice the automatic doors open when Vi walked into the club. Surprising him, she placed a gentle hand on his shoulder, unnerving him so bad he nearly jumped out of his skin. Muttering a hurried greeting, he stood up, hugged her briefly, then quickly ushered Vi downstairs to the workout areas below.

Vi realized she was a few minutes late, but the way Clayton's two fingers at the small of her back nudged her forward, you would have thought being late was a crime.

This late in the evening, the health club was practically deserted and Vi noted fitness staff personnel cleaning up some of the empty areas. Frequented by young professionals, the gym was at its busiest Monday through Thursday, when most people chose to work out right after work. However, on Friday and Saturday, those same working professionals had no problem giving up their workout for happy hour.

Although they exchanged polite small talk walking inside the gym, it was hard to ignore how tense Clayton seemed tonight. Once they entered the cardio room Clayton had very little to say. Vi, trying to keep up her end of the conversation and his, grew tired and began to follow his lead. She stepped onto the treadmill next to him and began a brisk walk, listening to music through the attached headphones.

After 30 minutes of cardio, they both walked next door to the free weight room. This large room was light and airy, with white walls and mirrors on three sides and a big glass wall facing the front of the club's common areas. Beyond the glass, a large carpeted hallway ran the full length of the room, connecting the weight room to all the other parts of the club. Besides several Cybex machines against the wall, there were black leather benches positioned about the room for free weight lifting. Remembering the first time Clayton brought her there she smiled, thinking about how he'd acted as her personal trainer, showing her how to lift the weights and focus on a particular muscle.

They worked out in silence. Clay immediately sat down on a nearby bench with his back to Vi, and began doing arm curls. Breathing heavily, he began to lift more weight than usual, relishing the strain and working up a sweat.

Besides the two of them, the room was empty and, without the luxury of headphones, the silence between them was more obvious. Again, Vi took his lead and started her workout in a far corner, watching the television overhead. After twenty minutes, however, their workout put them near one another, and Vi tried again several times to engage Clay in conversation. Each time she received only one word responses from him and, for the most part, he kept his head down and worked in silence.

Using the towel hanging around her neck, Vi wiped perspiration from her brow as she finished her last set. Instead of going on to the next machine, she stood with her back braced against the glass wall and studied him. The fact he appeared distracted and more than a little distant tonight bothered her. Taking the bull by the horns, Vi sighed heavily and said into the silence, "You've been awfully quiet tonight Clay. Is something wrong?"

Raising his head, Clay was forced to look at her, which was something he'd been trying to avoid doing for the past two hours. When he did, all the tension he'd felt earlier as she entered the club returned in full force. Against his better judgment, he let his gaze slide over Vi, and a small muscle bunched in his jaw as his eyes took in her negligent position and the outfit she wore. His torturous journey started at the white running shoes she wore, then traveled slowly up over the pink socks pulled low around very delicate ankles. Taking a detour, his eyes settled on her one leg, drawn up and bent at the knee, and braced nonchalantly against the wall behind her. Back on track, his gaze continued at the curve of her thighs, which were sheathed in black Spandex shorts that stopped at the knee and left her calves bare. His quest ended at her top, eyeing with appreciation the way it stretched nicely over her torso and revealed several tantalizing inches of her midriff.

When she suddenly crossed her arms over her chest in annoyance, obviously waiting for some type of response from him, his heart began to race. Desperately trying to gather his thoughts, Clay watched in fascination, knowing she was completely unaware how that small movement exposed a generous amount of cleavage and rendered his tongue inoperable for several heated seconds. Finally finding his voice, he gave her a cursory response, "I just had a really rough day. Nothing's wrong." Thinking that would be end of it, he bent his head once more to continue his workout. Unfortunately, it wasn't.

"You're probably tired from work. Maybe my suggestion we come here tonight wasn't such a good idea."

"It's okay, really," he supplied, and looked away.

Vi watched him methodically lift the weight he held. Over and over he bent his arm at the elbow, the powerful play of muscles in his strong forearms and biceps, flexing and expanding with his every movement. Sweat rolled down his forehead, and perspiration stood out on his exposed limbs. Besides the sneakers and loose shorts he wore, the only other garment covering his body was a gray cotton shirt, which was cut very low leaving his chest exposed and most of his upper torso on either side. Vi's mouth went suddenly dry. Snapping her gaze back to his face, she took a deep breath and spoke again. Like a dog with a bone, she probed further, tryng her best to chew away at what was troubling him. "You know, if you want to talk about whatever is bothering you, I'm right here," she offered. "I mean, what are friends for?"

Friends, he thought. Was she kidding?

Not choosing to reply, Clayton continued bending and straightening his right elbow in silence.

"I have to tell you, I'm really glad we cleared the air between us," Vi continued, trying to pretend she wasn't being ignored and carrying on this one-sided conversation all by herself. She waited a few seconds for a response, but still nothing. Although he kept saying he was fine, it was obvious to her he was anything but. Breathing heavily, she decided to address the invisible elephant in the room head on. "Listen Clay about the last time we saw each other...."

That got his attention. He put the weight down, laced his fingers together and sat, straddling the bench, watching her. Nervous now under his close scrutiny, Vi plunged ahead.

"I want you to know it was no big deal. Everyone drinks a little too much sometimes. Plus, I realize I kind of pushed you to go on that blind date. I'm sorry about that and I promise to butt out next time."

Apology said, Vi waited for him to say something—anything—only he didn't say one word. He just sat there staring at her, making her feel more nervous than she'd been in a long time. The silence stretched uncomfortably as she stared back at him, expecting some type of reaction. After a few moments she gave her shoulders a negligent shrug, deciding to let the matter drop, before adding, "Anyway, I've forgotten all about it and I think you should too. It was no big deal," she said on a final note.

No big deal? The way she made him feel every time he looked at her was a very big deal!

Surprisingly, her last words finally got a reaction out of him, if you could call it that. Vi wasn't sure what it was she'd said to replace the neutral look he'd given her all night to this new, purposeful glare. In the face of it she became a little alarmed. It wasn't so much what he said that made her nervous, because he still wasn't talking. It was steely look he shot her way that made her want to turn tail and run. Then, in a flash of movement, she watched him swing one long leg over the bench and stand up. With lightening speed he ate up the short distance between them, reserving whatever he had to say until he stood toe to toe with her. With only a few scant inches separating them, Vi found herself caught in his penetrating gaze and unable to move as the intensity of his dark eyes bore into her.

"So, you think it was *'No big deal'*?" The mocking question rumbled from his throat and hung in the air, silently daring her to reply. "You're wrong Vi. It was a big deal. I think you're just too scared to admit it."

Glimpsing the challenging light in his eyes and the harsh tone in his voice, Vi was uncertain what to say in the face of his obvious agitation. Towering over her, she felt his hot breath on her cheek and his nearness had a direct effect on her inability to move.

The simmering frustration Clayton had been feeling all day began to boil over and although he didn't want to appear angry, he couldn't help the harsh tone of his voice when he added. "In fact, if you weren't so busy putting all your energy into pretending nothing happened, you'd have more time to think on it and see that I'm right."

Totally speechless, Vi was powerless to do more than stare up at him. She saw his intensely dark eyes fill with indecision, frustration and something else. Was it suppressed longing? Suddenly, he reached out and grabbed both ends of the towel hanging around her neck. Trapped by the towel around her, Vi felt him tug on the ends he held within his grasp and slowly draw her flush against him. The smoldering heat she witnessed deep within his chocolate, brown eyes seared into her, making it impossible to move now, even if she wanted to. And then it happened. The air around them fairly crackled with electric current and tiny sparks began to dance as his head slowly descended toward her right before his lips claimed hers in an extremely wet, toe-curling, bone-melting kiss. When he sought her lips this time, her muddled brain registered on some distant level how different it was from the last time.

The kiss they shared in her foyer a few weeks ago had been a surprise. But this kiss, this kiss was intensely deliberate. This was no subtle meeting of lips, she acknowledged as her knees threatened to give way. The feel of his lips on hers this time was urgent, blatantly sexual and very demanding. Coaxing her to join in, Clay tilted his head to gain better access and ran the tip of his tongue slowly across her lips.

When he traced the thin line that parted her lips, Vi felt herself respond and instinctively, opened her mouth a fraction. His persuading tongue took full advantage of this small invitation and slid quickly into that tiny opening, plunging deep inside. The taste and texture of his swirling tongue made her head spin and Vi trembled within his arms. The dizzying effect of his expert mouth took her breath away as he delved deeper and deeper still, enticing her tongue to come out and play. When she joined in the foray, using her tongue and teeth to reach the farthest recesses of his mouth, Vi felt a moment's triumph when the muscular arms surrounding her bunched and tensed in response. A tiny moan slipped involuntarily past her lips as her arms went around his waist and grabbed onto the sides of his loose shirt. Bunching the material of his shirt in her hands she held on tight, as the onslaught continued.

Slowly his sanity returned and Clay, reluctant to release her, placed tiny sipping kisses on her wet lips. Although his hold on her loosened, he still held onto the ends of the towel around her neck.

Vi tightened her grip on his shirt, disinclined to let him go, when she felt him take a step back. With the material of his shirt still clutched in her fists, she stared up at him with wide eyes, returning the desire written in his penetrating gaze.

When she released his shirt and would have wound her arms around his neck, he took both her hands in his strong grip. Holding her hands a little tighter than necessary, he searched her eyes to see if she fully understood what was happening. Deciding to make it clear, he spoke in a slow, deliberate tone.

"I'm through pretending Vi." The bold statement fell from his lips in a commanding whisper. "I don't want your daughter, or any other woman for that matter, I want you."

He watched as the impact of his words sunk in and her eyes grew wider than before in astonishment. Although he was painfully aware, revealing himself like this effectively ruined any chance of resurrecting the platonic friendship they'd shared previously he refused to pull the words back. Knowing he'd reached the point of no return, Clay plunged forward, holding nothing back. "Vi, you need to recognize what's happening between us—and don't tell me you haven't felt it too." Glad that everything was finally out in the open, gave Clayton the courage to finish it. In a confident measured tone, he told her, "Don't get it twisted—you need to understand that I don't want to replace your son, and I damn sure don't need a mother. I need a woman, Vi. I need you," he said without apology then released her.

After bearing his soul, Clayton couldn't seem to look at her anymore. Retracing his steps, he walked slowly back to his bench and sat down. The thought of picking up the weight, however, and resuming his workout was out of the question. Uncertain what to do now, he laced his fingers together, bracing both elbows on his knees, and bowed his head staring at the floor. Feeling physically exhausted and frustrated beyond belief, Clayton suddenly realized what he'd just done and sat there mentally kicking himself.

You just blew it, Marshall! His mind screamed. Silently calling himself every kind of fool, he sat on that bench coming to grips with the probability tonight might be the last time he would ever see her. Although he'd just given her one helluva ultimatum, for the life of him, he couldn't bring himself to take it back. Deep down he knew if she couldn't honestly face this thing between them, he certainly couldn't continue pretending otherwise.

Unable to do more than stare after him, Vi remained standing like a statute against the glass wall. Her mind raced a mile a minute, as her brain struggled to come to terms with all that he'd said. Then suddenly, it hit her like a freight train. The shock of what just happened, his kiss and everything he'd said slammed into her, galvanizing her into movement.

When it happened, it happened so fast, even Vi didn't see it coming. Like a person having an outer-body experience, one moment she saw herself standing with her back pressed against the glass wall while Clay sat alone on the weight bench across from her. Then, in the next moment, she found herself standing above him. Using both hands, she placed her cool touch to his strong jaw and lifted his face up. When he looked up into her eyes, Vi held his gaze and brought her lips down over his, quickly picking up where they'd left off, just moments ago.

One, two, three seconds ticked by while her lips moved urgently against his. Five, seven, ten more seconds sailed by as they continued to seek each other in blinding need. Like a flower needs rain, she realized she desperately needed this. That need drove her to try and get closer, but when she found she couldn't get close enough what Vi did next surprised her and damn near gave Clay a heart attack. With her lips locked to his, she leaned over him without breaking contact and suddenly threw one slender leg over his lap and sat down - straddling him!

Sweet Jesus! Her unexpected actions triggered an answering desire within him that threatened to consume them both and quickly burn out of control. Instantly tightening his arms around her, he drew Vi flush against him.

Trembling in response, she felt his large hands slide low over her backside, eliciting a soft moan from her lips. Her head swam a little when he deepened the kiss and slid his fingers possessively over that soft expanse, brazenly cupping her from behind, while their mating tongues met and swirled, over and over again. A shiver ran through Vi then...something clicked, making her pull back. Suddenly remembering where they were, and the fact they were in full view of anyone passing by the glass wall, she pushed lightly at his chest. "Clay, someone might come," she whispered and reluctantly tried to pull her mouth away.

He wasn't ready to let go, tightening his hold on her Clay quickly drew her back in.   And Vi, overwhelmed by his sweet mouth and very imaginative hands, let herself be drawn in. When he captured her lower lip again and began to gently nip at that swollen treat, reality began to wash over her again, forcing her to recall why they had to stop.

When she pushed away this time, he reluctantly released her and let out a heavy sigh.   Discovering their racing hearts beat in unison, Clay laid his head in the soft valley between her breasts, nesting against her pillow softness for a few seconds more. Closing his eyes and savoring the feel of her in his arms, he smiled in satisfaction. Surely what they just shared was proof she felt the same way he did. Inwardly he leapt for joy and settled close to her feeling a tremendous sense of relief.

CHAPTER

TWENTY-TW0

Four days passed before he saw her again. It had been four long days and he couldn't seem to reach her by phone or get her to return any of his voice mail messages. Clay's frustration mounted thinking it was only four short days ago when he put everything on the line and thought he'd won hands down. Four days since he'd kissed her so thoroughly that it would have been hard for her to misinterpret his intent. Four days since she'd swung her slender legs over him, settled her sweet bottom in his lap and proceeded to kiss him senseless. As far as Clay was concerned, it had been four days too many, and somehow he intended to do something about it.

Every time he thought about what they did at the club, on that bench, in that glass enclosed weight room, his heart began to race. Clay sat on the sofa in his living room, staring off into space. The television was on, but he ignored, it, his mind full of what he would like to have done on that weight bench if she hadn't pulled back. In the past four days just the thought of her sweet face, or her even sweeter lips, had him walking around in a state of semi-arousal. Frustrated, he quickly stood up, adjusted his package to relieve the ache and strode into the kitchen to grab a beer. He opened it and pitched the top into a nearby garbage can, then slumped down into a kitchen chair. Taking a long pull off the bottle, he swiped the back of his hand across his mouth. No help there, he thought.

Well, if a cold one couldn't quench his thirst and tamp down the desire making his nature rise like a school boy, maybe a shower would. Clayton got up suddenly and made his way to the bathroom, pulling the lightweight shirt he wore over his head as he made his way down the hall. Once in the bathroom he stepped out of the jeans he'd put on as soon as he'd gotten home earlier. He hadn't bothered with underwear earlier, so when his jeans hit the floor the object that desperately needed cooling sprang to life. Turning on the taps, he quickly stepped under the water. Bracing his hands against the tile, Clay closed his eyes and let the water wash over him.

Big mistake! Behind his eyelids Clay's mind conjured up what the next step would have been on that weight bench with Vi, had she not broken their kiss. He could still taste the sweetness of her luscious bottom lip and feel the softness of her backside. His fingers wiggled remembering how they kneaded her soft bottom and drew her closer against his aroused body.

Damn! She was driving him crazy. One minute she was pretending they were nothing but friends, and doing her best to ignore the sparks that flew every time they were in the same room. Then in the next instant, she was literally humping him in front of a glass wall, pressing her full breasts into his chest and thrusting her tongue so far down his throat Clay swore he tasted a bit of heaven.

My God, he desperately wanted this woman. How she could ever have thought of him as a son was beyond him. The numerous things he imagined doing with her didn't exactly inspire any motherly thoughts in him. In fact, some of his thoughts right now, he thought wryly, could get a man arrested. Much to his mortification, when he stepped out of the shower ten minutes later, Clay found himself even harder than when he went in.

What the...? He moved purposefully through his apartment with the smooth limbs of a sleek panther, unmindful of his nakedness. In his bedroom Clay flopped down on his bed and picked up the phone to try her number again. When her voicemail came on, he slammed the phone down and got up, making his way back into the living room. Pulling on the pair of jeans he'd discarded earlier, he thought about what to do next. What he needed to do was sit her down and talk this out, but his schedule since last weekend had been hectic, to say the least. Sitting down again his frustration mounted knowing he was on graveyard shift for the next few days. Sighing heavily, he realized all he'd be able to do, keeping those hours, was continue to try reaching her by phone.

Closing his eyes, he pinched the bridge of his nose and thought about last weekend. He had more than his share of regrets about last Saturday. Still under the delusion they should avoid as much contact as possible, he'd come up with the bright idea to drive separate cars to the club. In retrospect, he'd mentally kicked himself at least a dozen times since Saturday for making those idiotic arrangements. After what happened in the weight room all he'd been able to think about was what he could have done in the close confines of her car, or better yet his truck. Noticeably shaken they walked to her car instead, neither of them sure what to say or do. After exchanging a brief kiss he was left standing in the parking lot. Watching her go, he imagined pulling her out of her car and into his, to work on finishing what they'd started in the weight room. Instead, they'd both gone their separate ways and hadn't spoken since.

Slumping lower on the couch he leaned his head against the sofa back and closed his eyes again in frustration. To his chagrin, the Vi show started up again, behind his eyelids. In living color, wide screen, play-by-play high definition, images of her wrapped around him swirled behind his closed eyelids. When the blood pumping in his body made a mad dash toward his crotch, Clay let out a loud groan and opened his eyes. He sat up as a sudden thought struck him. He couldn't let her avoid this. He knew if he did, she may never come around again. Refusing to believe she wasn't just as affected as he was by all this and angry with the constant state of arousal he was in, he got up and went back into his bedroom. No matter how bad his schedule was tonight, Clayton was determined to see Vi. As he got ready for work, he tossed the situation over in his mind and came up with a plan. He wasn't sure what little Ms. Vi was thinking but, if she thought she could kiss him like she did, then turn tail and run…well, she had another thing coming.

That evening Vi lay on the sofa watching TV and waiting for Tony to get home from the movies. Tony came home around 10:30 and sat with her for awhile eating popcorn, then retreated upstairs to call Briana. Deciding to finish the movie she'd been watching, Vi stayed downstairs by herself. She was still wide awake when the movie went off at 11:45 and began flipping through the channels. When Tony lumbered down stairs a few minutes later, Vi picked up her head. "Hey, sweetie, are you still on the phone?"

"No," Tony answered, panting as he raced down the stairs. "Briana's gonna' call me back in ten minutes, her mom had to make a long distance call."

Vi lay back down to watch Jay Leno a little longer as her son made his way to the foot of the stairs. Just as he rounded the stair case Tony saw a car pull into their driveway. Recognizing the car, he stopped momentarily in front of the open screen door and waited for Clay to get out. When he reached the front porch, Tony unlatched the screen door for him and called over his shoulder, "Hey Mom, Clay's here."

Scrambling to get up, Vi nearly fell off the sofa.

"Hey Tony, I thought you were going to help your mom remember to lock this door at night." The high-five Clay gave the boy when he entered the door took the edge off his words.

"I do Man, but we gotta' keep it open tonight, the air conditioning is busted again. It's so hot we're just to trying our best to catch a breeze," Tony replied, smiling up at him.

Vi heard him ask Tony if she was still up, as he stood in her small foyer. Quickly checking her appearance, Vi went into a panic as she looked down at herself. She wore an old pair of running shorts, a black tank top and nothing on her feet. Oh well, she thought, too late to do anything about that. She did think to run a hand through her hair, frantically finger combing the curls into place, before walking toward the front door.

Greeting him breathlessly, she realized the sight of him after so many days began to do strange things to her insides. "Clay, what are you doing here?"

Just then, the phone rang and Tony raced past them up the stairs to answer it. "Mom, I'll get that in your room," he called down to her before she heard her bedroom door close.

Watching Tony's progress from the foot of the stairs, Vi returned her gaze to Clay when the bedroom door slammed shut. He was watching her and she studied him briefly, trying to figure out what to say. He was still in uniform. As usual, his tie was perfectly knotted and the form-fitting shirt he wore looked freshly starched and clean. Under his shirt, the protective vest he wore added more width to his already wide chest and the twenty pounds of paraphernalia he wore around his waist gave off an air of authority that went along with his job. She noticed he wasn't wearing his hat and his clean-shaven head glistened under the light coming from the living room lamp. Remarkable, she thought, suddenly realizing she could stand here all night and drink in the sight of him. After so many days without seeing him, he was a sight for sore eyes, exuding a robust manliness that made her tiny foyer seem even smaller than it really was.

Totally oblivious to the thoughts running through Vi's mind, Clay didn't bother answering the question she'd asked him. If she didn't know why he was here, she would soon find out. He let his eyes travel slowly over the length of her. She looked so good, it was hard to focus on the reason he had come over here in the first place. Clayton quickly caught himself and squashed the intense heat rising within him. "We need to talk," he said simply.

"I... I know...tomorrow, I promise I'll call you and..." She didn't get a chance to finish before he told her.

"No. We need to talk, right now."

"Aren't you on duty?" Vi asked, stalling for time.

"Piterrelli's covering my calls for an hour, this won't take long."

"Okay," she said and stepped aside motioning him into the living room. "We can talk in here."

"No. I need for you to come for a ride with me for a little while."

She raised a brow at the commanding tone she heard in his voice. At a loss for words, Vi stated the obvious. "Clay, it's after midnight, I can't leave Tony alone."

"Tony will be fine," he said as if what he proposed was so simple. "Go tell him you're going with me for a little while and that you'll be right back."

The determination in his voice and his serious demeanor did not invite any argument. Feeling guilty for not returning his calls, she decided not to question him further, and called up to Tony. "Tony, I'm taking a drive with Clay. Will you be alright for a little while?

Through the door they both heard Tony snort in disbelief, and yell down the stairs. "For crying out loud Mom, I'm not a baby. Go, I'll be fine."

With no further excuses, Vi suddenly felt a little frightened. Knowing she couldn't put this off, Vi called upstairs one more time to let Tony know she had her cell phone in case he needed to reach her. When Tony's muffled acknowledgement reached her through the closed bedroom door, she grabbed her cell phone and keys off the hall table then turned to go. When she turned around Vi saw that Clay was already outside, standing on the porch and holding the screen door open for her. Stepping outside she locked the door behind her then followed him to his police cruiser.

Silently, he held the passenger door open for Vi and waited while she slipped inside. Once inside Vi looked around at all the equipment the squad car held. She had no idea what all the lit-up gadgets were, but she did recognize the computer built into the dash. It took up most of the passenger side front dashboard and was angled toward the driver for easy access. She also noticed a shotgun mounted on the side of the console.

Clay got behind the wheel, backed out of her driveway and drove down the street without uttering one word. She watched him in the darkened interior of the car, his features seemed slightly strained and he appeared to definitely have something on his mind.

Beginning to feel uneasy with the tense silence filling the car, Vi took a deep breath to calm her nerves. Looking out the window, to take her mind off what was to come, she watched familiar scenery roll by wondering where they were headed. Absently, she asked him, "Where are we going?"

"Not far, just ……excuse me." Stopping in mid-sentence, Clay listened to the crackle coming from his radio. Vi didn't understand what the dispatcher was saying but sat quietly as he listened and responded to whatever call was coming through.

"Bravo, niner, two-three one, copy." He replaced the radio handset and turned down the volume. Although, they continued driving in silence a little while longer, to an unspecified location, Vi wasn't anxious to get there. She wasn't ready to discuss anything with anyone, let alone Clayton. Trying desperately to sort through everything over the past four days, she had to admit he'd never been far from her mind. Even so, the feelings he'd stirred up were too new, too confusing to discuss right now. And then there was the kiss they shared last Saturday.

Ohmigod! Whenever she thought about that kiss, which was quite often, she grew even more confused. Vi was totally embarrassed and more than a little shocked by the way she'd responded in his arms. At the time, it felt like she was searching out something in the warm recesses of his mouth, she hadn't known she was missing. No, she definitely wasn't ready to face him and talk about any of it. Thinking she might have a reprieve she turned to Clay and offered.

"Clayton, I think it would be better if we do this another time. I mean, if you're on duty we can talk tomorrow."

"It's fine," he said cutting her off. "I just had to check in, let dispatch know Pitt would be covering for me. Vi remembered that Craig did this also when he had an emergency and was on duty. The officers of the Amityville Police covered only the incorporated village of Amityville. Sometimes they helped Suffolk County, but mostly they worked their area and always worked as a team.

They drove in silence a little while longer before Vi noticed he was headed toward the village area, past the shopping mall and down toward the water. When Clayton turned his right signal on and pulled into the Amityville Beach parking lot, Vi was just a little curious.

The sound of the tide rushing to shore could be heard in the distance. The water beyond was dark and the beach stretched out gray and lonely beyond the lot they pulled into. He parked the car in the south lot and turned the engine off. For the longest time, neither of them spoke. Vi looked around at the deserted area in front of them. Tomorrow this area would be full of beach goers, sunbathers and children making sand castles.

"The beach closed hours ago, won't someone object to us being here so late?

"We're fine," was all he said.

Without saying another word Clay got out, walked around the front of the car and opened her passenger side door. The moment she was out of the car, he closed the door and faced her. Vi stared up at him and noted his firm lips were pulled into a straight and very tense line. His eyes were dark and brooding and she saw that a small muscle bunched in his chiseled jaw.

"Why haven't you returned my calls?" There was no mistaking the simmering anger behind his words.

"I... I was going to... really," Vi started on a feeble note. "I just wanted to try and sort through all of this on my own first."

"You could have picked up the phone to tell me that." The hurt tone in his voice was not lost on her.

"I would have eventually," she said a bit defensively.

"Now who's avoiding whom?" He accused.

"I wasn't..." she started then let out a long sigh, and tried again. "I wasn't trying to avoid you Clay, really. After last Saturday I just, I got a little scared and...."

"Scared? You've got to be kidding me," he said with a derisive snort.

That last statement made Vi's temper flare to life. Placing both hands on ample hips, she stared him down. She wasn't going to stand here and let him mock her without telling him a thing or two.

"Look, Clay if you're upset I apologize, but I won't be made fun of." She moved to open the passenger side door. With lightening speed, he closed the distance between them, his hand immediately covering hers on the door handle.

"No, don't leave," he said, his voice gentler now, but firm. "We're not done. I wasn't mocking you Vi. I'm just tired of playing games and I refuse to let you keep running away." He removed her hand from the door handle and brought it to his lips.

The tenderness of his lips caressing the back of her hand, struck a cord of longing in Vi, and her anger dissipated. When she raised her eyes to his this time, she saw longing in their depths. Suddenly, the powerful awareness between them raised several notches and the air around them began to crackle and snap, like it was the Fourth of July. And just like, that the fireworks they'd shared last Saturday came back to life.

She watched his eyes darken with desire and knew he would kiss her. She wanted him to, God help her. She also knew if they started in that direction, if things started heating up the way they had before, they would both probably go up in flames. With a tortured groan she leaned away from him and searched his face. Trying to make him understand, Vi told him with a pleading look in her eyes. "Clay, you make it seem so easy, it's not that easy for me."

"Why not?" His voice was a husky whisper close to her ear. "What are you afraid of—me? Don't be Vi, I would never do anything you didn't want me to do, and I would never hurt you." His tender words were practically her undoing. Vi closed her eyes as his nearness enveloped her and fought hard to ignore the feelings coursing through her, trying very hard to make him understand.

"I'm not scared of you...it's me. When I'm with you I feel alive. I have to admit, more alive than I've felt in years. When you kissed me last weekend I was lost, totally out of control, and that," she emphasized, "is what frightens me." Searching his eyes to ensure he understood, Vi continued to explain, "It's been a very long time, and even when I dated, I didn't have any wild flings. And besides that, how can I ignore the fact that I'm so much older than you."

Brushing off her paltry reasons for denying both of them what they obviously wanted most, he crocked his finger under her chin and brought her face very close to his for a very light, very tender kiss on her nose. "You're not that much older than me," he said gently, knowing in his gut the ten years that separated them in age couldn't be all that was bothering her. "In any event, I don't care about age."

Vi broke eye contact and, brushing past him, walked a short distance away. She folded her arms across her body and looked across the darkened beach and the even darker ocean beyond, and felt a bone deep chill. Feeling sand seep into the low sandals she's stepped into before leaving the house, Vi stood there thinking about what he'd just said, acknowledging he was speaking the truth, but there were still things he didn't understand. With her back to him, she tried again to share with him how she felt and what she would have to deal with. "I know you're right, but there are other things to think about. I mean, what will people say, my family, my friends? Oh God, Cynthia alone will have a cow." Vi shuddered at the thought of her sister's reaction.

Approaching her from behind, Clay placed both his hands on her shoulders and rested his chin on top of her head. He ran the pads of his thumbs leisurely, up and down her nape. Quietly they looked out at the turbulent sea, each lost in their own thoughts. She leaned into him as he settled his arms around her waist. Inhaling her sweet scent, Clayton tightened his forearms around her and leaned down to whisper close to her ear. "I don't care what people think and I don't think you should either. All I care about is you, about us."

His voice was like velvet sweeping across her sensitive skin. She felt the heat of his body surrounding her and reveled in how good it felt to be in his arms. Leaning closer, he buried his face in the crook of her neck and nuzzled that baby-soft area with his lips. When he lifted his head again, Clay slowly turned her around to face him. They stood facing one another, silently feeding off each other's needs and wants.

Clay watched the flames burning deep within her eyes and it caught at him, making him burn with need. He took a small step back from her, breaking the closeness they shared and, in the process, buying himself a little time to cool down. When he looked at her again, he glimpsed indecision mixed with wanting flickering deep within her eyes and knew he had to address her fears. Somehow, he had to get through to her and to do that he needed to watch his proximity.

He had to make her see they belonged together. Somehow, someway he would ensure they were together, but for now he needed to tread lightly. Trying a different tack, he spoke quietly.

"Vi, I think you're making too big a deal out of this. Last time I checked we were both consenting adults."

"But," before she could finish Clay raised a finger and placed it over her lips to still any further protest.

"Shhh. I think we're getting ahead of ourselves. I'm not sure what's happening between us, but I think we owe it to ourselves to find out, don't you?"

He sensed her wavering and knew he'd made the right decision. Clay knew she still had a lot of internal issues to work out concerning them, and taking the slow approach would help her work through those issues at her own pace. He, on the other hand, had worked out his issues long ago. Now the only thing he needed to work on was his desire to get her into his bed, and sink himself... He gave himself a mental shake. Keeping those desires hidden was going to be hard, but hide them he would. If she ever so much as guessed at his true feelings, he knew instinctively that she would probably go running for the hills.

Clay looked down into her captivating face, the eyes that were previously filled with indecision, were now hopeful. His gaze locked on her luscious lips. They were more alluring than any woman's lips had a right to be and definitely meant for kissing. As he'd hoped, she seemed to at least be open to the possibility of them being together. A wave of satisfaction filled Clay and his next words came out confident and assertive.

"Vi," he said, capturing her full attention. "Let's not jump off a building, okay? All I want to do is spend time with you, and I promise we'll take it slow, alright?

When she nodded her head in understanding, Clay let out a deep breath and took her gently in his arms.

"Good. Now, I've got to ask you something I've been dying to ask you for days."

"What? Her inquiry came out in a breathless whisper, totally unaware of his intent.

Then to her surprise, Vi heard him say the four words she hadn't realized she wanted him to say, since the first time she saw him tonight.

"Can I kiss you?"

"Oh, yes."

Instantly putting those four little words into action Clay captured her lips in a searing kiss. When she felt the intense heat of his tongue dart inside her mouth, Vi slid her arms around his neck. When it would have quickly retreated, she leaned into him, trapping his tongue lightly between her teeth, drawing it further into her mouth.

The eager way she reached for him went straight to his head. Struggling to calm his beating heart, Clay felt his control slip a notch. Her taste seduced him, making him wish for things he probably shouldn't wish for. But oh,

God, the feel of her pressed so close to him was enough to give a dying man hope. As their mouths continued to fuse, mate and explore one another, his hands began to run gently up and down her back, sliding lower now over the soft rise of her backside. Cupping her from behind, he pressed her as close as they could get. In turn, she tightened her arms around his neck and went up on tip toe, settling his arousal in the cradle of her hips. When Clay felt himself harden and strain painfully against his uniform trousers, his scrambled brains registered where they were and how he'd just promised her to go slow. Reluctantly he pulled back, breaking the kiss in a series of lingering sips to her bottom lip.

With her belly pressed so snug against him, it was hard to ignore his incredible hardness straining against her. It sent an answering ache between her thighs, reaching straight to the place that made her a woman. She felt his arm muscles bunch and tighten under her fingertips and the protective vest he wore made it feel like she was caressing a rock—a very solid rock.

When they finally parted, their arms were still twined around one another, neither of them knowing for sure who held up the other. For a brief moment, the intense heat coursing between them made it feel like they could have gone up in flames and been happy to make the trip. The strength of it rendered them speechless and for the longest time no one said a word, the act of breathing alone taking too much effort.

She smiled up at him, unaware this small action made his slowing heart beat race again. Poking him in the chest lightly, Vi told him in an amusing tone, "You feel so hard with all this on, it's like hugging a stone wall."

Picking up the teasing banter in her voice, he favored her with a sexy, lopsided grin. "Believe me, you have no idea how hard I really am," he replied with a wicked gleam in his eye.

"No silly, I meant your bullet-proof vest," she said, slapping his arm lightly.

"Oh, I thought you meant something else." Laughing out loud, Clay was glad when Vi joined in. When their laughter died down, he pinned her with a serious look, "Okay, I promise to take it slow, but you have to promise to talk to me if you feel things are moving too fast, okay."

"Okay," she said, still squirming with laughter.

Clay hadn't realized how much he missed her laugh, until he heard it tinkle from within her and seep into a little corner of his heart.

"Seriously, though," his sober tone captured her attention. "If you think we need to talk or anything moving forward, will you please call me?"

She placed her cool fingers against his strong jaw line and nodded. Satisfied, Clay hooked one arm around her waist and led her back to the cruiser. "Come on, let me take you home."

CHAPTER
TWENTY-THREE

When he pulled in front of her house, Clay kept the engine running. Reaching for Vi across the front seat, he pulled her toward his eager lips once more. Unaware that the street light, as well as a full moon, illuminated their movements inside the car, his fingers slipped under her tank top to cover her breast.

Tony was still on the phone up in his mother's bedroom when he heard the car pull in. He got up to see who it was and noticed that the street lamp a few feet away shone down on the police cruiser. Seeing it was just Clay dropping his mom off, he began to let the curtain fall back in place when he saw Clayton kiss his mom.

Oh, man!, he thought. Mesmerized, he held the curtain back and witnessed their passionate kiss, watched as Clay's searching fingers reached up under her shirt, and saw his mom's obvious response. *Wow! He knew they were friends, but this was no friendly kiss!*

"Tony...Tony?" Briana's raised voice came through the receiver, penetrating his thoughts.

"What...what did you say?"

"You weren't listening were you?"

He heard Briana's voice fill with annoyance and quickly tried to cover up. "No, I was listening, my mom just got home is all and it distracted me. Sorry." She seemed okay with this explanation and continued telling him about a girl on the cheerleading squad who dissed her earlier that day. Tony rarely paid attention to the female shenanigans Briana and her girlfriends seemed to thrive on. As he lay back on the bed pillows half listening to her talk, he thought about trying some of the moves he'd seen tonight on Briana when she got angry.

Clay reached across her lap and opened the car door to let Vi out. Leaning over her, he released the seatbelt and brushed his lips across hers once again. This time, however, Vi broke away quickly, in case the neighbors might be watching. These new feelings coursing through her veins was very new to her and Vi knew sleep would not come easy tonight thinking about all the possibilities that lay ahead. The way her body pulsed with awareness whenever he so much as looked at her was something Vi needed to decipher, preferably alone.

As an afterthought, Clay remembered he had to tell her about Casey and the information she gave that might lead to new clues in Craig's murder investigation.

"Vi, there's something else we have to discuss, but right now I need to get back to work."

"Okay, how about we meet for coffee tomorrow?," she suggested.

"I've got a better idea. I get off at 7:00 am and I'm not due back to work until late tomorrow night. How about I pick you up for breakfast and we spend the day together?"

"Oh, I was planning to go in tomorrow and work on supplies for a few hours."

The need to see her again as early as tomorrow was paramount to him. Clay decided he would make that happen, even if he had to go in to work with her and help with the supplies. Instead of pressing the issue, however, he replied simply, "Okay, call me."

They didn't hook up the next day. As it turned out, Vi finished the work on supplies early and eagerly answered the phone when he called early the next day. Unable to hide the disappointment in her voice, she listened quietly as he explained why he wouldn't be able to see her today.

Clay picked up on it and felt a tremendous hope rise up in him. The obvious disappointment in her voice almost made up for the fact he had to work a double shift for the next few days.

"Baby, I'm sorry."

Baby! Vi was overjoyed. Lately he'd begun to call her little things like that, and each time he did her heart went into immediate overdrive. *Silly woman!* She mentally admonished herself, feeling very much like a school girl with a crush.

Not seeing him over the next few days wasn't as bad as Vi thought it would be. Sure, she found herself distracted during the day thinking about Clay, and oh yeah, he regularly showed up in her dreams just about every night. But her days at the salon got pretty hectic. Besides having to look for a new shampoo girl, because the old one quit to attend school full time, somehow the supplier screwed up big time on her last order—again. By the time Wednesday rolled around Vi thought for sure she wouldn't get to see Clay until the weekend, if then. But, she was wrong. She was sitting in her office on Wednesday afternoon when she heard the phone ring. Waiting to see if someone would pick it up in the outer salon, Vi bent her head over the papers in front of her. She looked up when Nicole stuck her head in the doorway a few seconds later to say she had a call on line two. She put aside the invoices she'd been working on and picked up the phone.

"This is Vi."

"Hello pretty lady, what are you doing?

Pretty lady! Vi still couldn't get used to him calling her sweetheart, pretty lady and a host of other things that, to her frustration, made her blush like a sixteen-year-old girl. A huge smile lit up her entire face when she heard his voice and she laid her pen down, changed the receiver to her other hand and settled back in her chair. Lately, just the sound of his voice was enough to start a funny little fluttering low in her belly and send her heart racing out of control, and today was no exception. Trying to compose herself, Vi got more comfortable in her chair and responded brightly, "Hi, I thought you had to work a double shift all week."

"Yeah, I do…but…," Clay paused for a meaningfully long time, before continuing. "I was just thinking that I have a little time off today, between shifts, and…" his voice trailed off, teasingly low.

Vi noticed he had that – *I've got a proposition you just can't refuse* – tone in his voice. Eagerly listening as his words petered out, she waited for him to say what he had in mind.

"I'm sitting here at home," he continued, dragging out his words. "By myself, and wishing you were here." Her sweet laughter tinkled through the phone line, washing over him. Smiling, Clay settled more comfortably on his sofa and drank in the delightful sound. "So, can you get away for a few hours?" he asked, cutting right to the chase.

Vi stopped laughing and considered his proposal, "I don't know. I mean, shouldn't you be getting some sleep?" Just then, Cynthia walked in and sat down at her desk, right next to Vi's. Waving to her sister, Vi changed the phone back to her other ear, and lowered her voice before saying, "I'm not sure if I can, we're a little short-handed this week."

Although she was making excuses, he could hear in her voice that she wanted to see him just as much as he wanted to see her, so he continued to press. Clay didn't bother to analyze his overwhelming need to see her again, it was what it was. So, he countered every excuse she came up with and called on all the persuasive skills and reasonable deductions he possessed to get her over to his place today because he wasn't about to take "no" for an answer.

"Sweetheart, I need to see you." The underlying plea in this quiet statement was literally Vi's undoing. Feeling her resistance falter, Clay pushed his point home. "I'm talking lunch Vi, an hour or two tops. Come on," he implored. "You have to eat."

"Well, yes I do, but…" Vi watched Cynthia get up and walk over to the file cabinet near the back wall. She pulled out several files, then walked back to her desk and sat down. Lowering her voice a bit more, Vi said into the phone, "Listen, let me call you right back, okay?" After hanging up the phone, Vi turned toward her sister.

"Cyn, I need to go out for a while. Can you hang out for an hour or so, till I get back? Just in case Nikki or Andre need anything," she added.

"Sure, no problem," she told Vi, then bent her head over an open ledger.

"Thanks, I'll only be gone a little while," Vi told her sister as she grabbed up her purse and dashed out the door.

On her way over to his place, Vi thought about going home first to change, but in the end decided against it. She'd worn a powder blue, sleeveless, button-down shirt and lightweight khaki Capri pants to work that morning. A small, white Toyota blasted its horn as she accidentally cut that driver off. Anxious to see Clay, Vi slowed down a bit and raised her hand in apology to the driver as she got off the expressway. *Oh, God, she thought. I'm a total mess.*

Just thinking about Clay's last words and the low timbre of his voice on the phone when he encouraged her to get there right away, sent her imagination into overdrive. There was no mistaking his intent when she got there.

The coined phrase—*Afternoon Delight*—sprang up out of nowhere. She'd read about women who were married, single or otherwise sneaking off in the middle of the day to have sex with some handsome man, she'd even seen a few movies about it. At no time did she ever think she would be one of those women. Vi took a couple of shallow breaths to calm her nerves, however, thinking about the coined phrase sent some very X-rated thoughts rolling through her mind. They were very vivid, full-color images of her naked limbs entwined with Clay's muscular, young body. She started her breathing exercises again in earnest, desperately trying to cool down and get her mind off these wayward thoughts.

It didn't work. By the time she was standing at Clay's door preparing to knock, the wild thoughts she had rolling through her mind were now running a marathon. Trying to gather her wits about her, she raised her hand and knocked.

Clay answered the door on the first knock and reached for her hand, immediately sweeping her inside. When the door closed, he didn't waste any time covering her mouth in an earth-shattering kiss. She let herself be pressed against the wall, returning his kiss, matching the urgent need she felt in him with an answering need of her own. His insistent tongue traced the line where her lips joined, coaxing them open. When they parted, his tongue poured inside, filling her mouth and making her knees go weak. Finally he released her mouth, and they both came up for air, panting and breathing heavily, but still clinging to one another.

When she opened her eyes and glanced over his shoulder, Vi was pleasantly surprised to see lunch laid out on the table. Clay released her as she made her way over to the table, chuckling softly when her stomach made a very unladylike noise in reaction to all the food laid out before her. Embarrassed, Vi pushed at his chest gently, feeling the hard muscles under the T-shirt he wore.

"Wow, Clay. This looks wonderful. Why so much food?" she said as she reached out to taste a deliciously prepared seafood salad.

Clay watched her lick the tip of her finger, unaware how that simple action affected him. He stared down into her sweet face and bent his head to sip at her lips once more. When he raised his head, his eyes were lit with mischief when he said, "I figured you might actually be hungry for food. Me? I'm just hungry for you." He left her standing by the table and walked a short distance away. With a negligent flick of the wrist, he dimmed the lights.

A light lunch of club sandwiches, fruit and seafood salad was laid out on his dining room table. Although the simple fare looked very appetizing, it was the way it was displayed that took Vi's breath away. White linen covered the small table and matching napkins in gold rings complemented the setting. Black stoneware dishes, silverware and long-necked goblets also graced the table; while a single lit candle sat in the center, its warm glow flickering slightly.

How romantic, she thought, realizing he'd obviously gone to a great deal of trouble. As she turned toward him, some of the nervousness she'd felt earlier returned and Vi felt compelled to share some of those feelings with him.

"I don't know about all this, Clay. It's lovely, really. But, I feel like a teenager again, sneaking around in the afternoon, making out with the door against my back."

He walked up behind her and slipped his arms around her waist, as she stood looking down at the table setting. Nuzzling the soft skin of her neck, Clay inquired. "Oh, the door is not working for you? Maybe we can find a weigh bench to sit on," his voice was a whispered tease very close to her ear. *Ohmigod!* Turning slightly, she quickly shot him a mortified look then broke free of his arms and walked into the living room.

It was obvious from the way she sat down and covered her face with both hands that he'd said something wrong. Realizing his blunder, Clayton followed her into the living room and sat down on the coffee table in front of her. Gently, he pried her hands from her face and held them both lightly in his grasp.

"Vi, Baby, I'm sorry. I was kidding, really. I had no idea you'd be so sensitive about our little weight room rumble." Tightening his hold on her hands, Clayton searched her eyes to make sure she believed him, before saying. "Please, don't be embarrassed Baby," he urged. Holding her gaze, he felt the need to add, "I loved it and I just assumed that you did too." Keeping her hands gloved protectively in his larger ones, Clay got up off the coffee table and sat down next to her on the sofa.

Realizing he had to put her at ease about this immediately, Clay took a deep breath and attempted to explain how he felt. "I'm not sure you understand why it was so important to me. I mean, I was afraid the feelings I had for you would ruin our friendship, and if I dared to share them with you, you would probably shoot me down." Never letting his eyes leave hers, he held onto her hands a bit tighter than before as he continued. "I was scared to death you didn't feel anything for me. Then, last Saturday, I decided to hell with it. I couldn't go on pretending I wanted only friendship from you and decided to just lay it on the line. And then, after I kissed you I was certain you were going to send me packing."

"Clay, it's okay. I..."

"No, let me finish," he said, stopping her. "But then you walked over and surprised me. When you reached for me, swung your leg over me and sat on my lap! Well, I lost it completely. Having you in my arms, kissing you like that—it was almost too good to be true."

Vi watched him raise her hands to his lips and place a gentle kiss upon each knuckle. The intensity she glimpsed in his eyes while he did this made her breath catch in her throat.

"Vi when you came to me like that, I felt like a man in the desert, getting his first drink of water after a very long time."

His words reached a place in her heart that Vi didn't know was empty until he took up residence there. To think that this strong, virile, younger man wanted her—really wanted her—made her feel bold and a little reckless. Wanting to explore this feeling, Vi doubled her arms behind Clay's neck in a firm embrace and brought him closer. When she had him right where she wanted, she covered his mouth in a slow, moist, soul-searching kiss. Not missing a beat, his arms came around her waist, lifting her up from where she sat next to him. She felt his strong hands at the back of her knees as he guided her hips up and over him, and Vi found herself straddling his lap once again.

They sat face to face, her legs spread invitingly wide over him and bent at the knee. Clay felt the air leave his lungs in a rush, as a wave of desire such as he'd never known, held him in a vise-like grip. He released her lips and rested his cheek against the hollow of her neck. Taking a slow, measured breath, he whispered very close to her ear. "I want you to know this is officially my favorite position," he said, referring to the position she held across his lap.

Just before his lips descended on hers, Clay wound his arms around Vi in a strong embrace, and she felt the muscles in those arms contract and flex against the small of her back. While his tongue explored the soft inside of her mouth, his hands moved over her body, cupping her breasts through her shirt and then fumbling to undue the buttons of her blouse. Vi was so lost, so absorbed by his lips and his touch that she was hardly aware of his progress until her blouse lay completely open.

Clay released her lips and stared at the bounty before him. His fingertips traced lightly over the soft mocha mounds that sprang from the lacy garment she wore. Fingering the lacy edge of her bra, he whispered reverently, "So, beautiful."

She watched his eyes roam over her. The intensity of his heated stare made her breasts tighten and strain against the white lace cups encasing them. Cupping her gently, she watched him lift their weight in his hands and bury his face in her pillow softness.

Inhaling her scent, an intoxicating mixture of roses and woman made his head spin. Nuzzling her gently, he nibbled and inched his way to one straining nipple, making Vi cry out as he took it slowly between his teeth, suckling her through the thin lace.

As he tugged at her, she began to tremble, letting his name escape her lips again and again in a rasping plea. "*Ohmigod!*" she cried as his teeth slid swiftly across her sensitized crest. Although she felt like she was drowning, right now Vi couldn't think of a better way to go.

Reveling in her passionate response, Clay's hands moved possessively over her hips, pressing her more firmly in place. Filling his need to get closer, he sank those strong fingertips into her softness, but didn't stop there. Venturing lower, his anxious fingers quickly slid between their bodies, stopping when he reached the apex of her thighs. Branding his palm, the heat there immediately sent his already racing heartbeat into overdrive. Unprepared for the tremendous wave of desire that slammed into him, Clay shut his eyes tight, feeling his control begin to slip. It was almost his undoing, the feel of her opened over him, with only the material of her pants and the crotch of her panties separating the place he ached to be. In a rush, his lips released her breast, leaving it straining and wet against her lacy bra, to quickly trail moist kisses up her neck.

When he reached her ear, a tiny gasp escaped her throat and, involuntarily, Vi's body began to sway as his palm rubbed her below, slowly back and forth. The tiny sounds she made close to his ear and the deep shudder that ran through her body drove him closer and closer to the edge. Nuzzling the softness of her neck he whispered close to her ear, "Vi, I want you so badly."

Vi felt the muscular arms surrounding her tense and tighten for a split second right before he abruptly released her and, in a flash, he reached for the ends of his shirt, pulling it swiftly over his head. Once he was free of the shirt, he grabbed hold of her again and Vi felt her own desire strike with the force of a sledge hammer. Pressed so close against one another there was no mistaking the pulsing hardness she felt or the urgency of his movements. Although she welcomed the eager hands that circled her waist and slipped past the waistband of her pants, Vi struggled with the sensation his touch evoked, wanting it desperately, but overwhelmed and uncertain she could do this. However, when his nibble fingers crept over soft flesh, delving lower, she knew she knew she couldn't.

"Clay. Clay, I can't," she told him. "We can't. I..."

He felt her tense within his arms, but it still took a few seconds for his brain to register her words. When it did, he laid his forehead against hers and relaxed his arms around her. After a few moments, he raised his head and looked into her eyes. Their gold-flecked depths were filled with indecision and burning desire, which she quickly tried to hide by lowering her lashes. Staring at the top of her bowed head, Clayton expelled a lengthy sigh and told her very calmly,

"Sweetheart, I would never push you to do anything that you weren't ready to do—ever." Placing a finger under her chin, he raised her eyes to meet his and smiled. "Even if it kills me, we'll go as slow as you want. Okay?" With his index finger still cupping her chin, he continued holding her gaze, making sure she understood. When she returned his smile and nodded her head slightly, Clay felt the tension leave his body. Satisfied, he kissed the tip of her nose and pulled her into his warm embrace.

Nestled in his arms, Vi felt his steady breathing and the rumble of the words he drew out next. "You know, .I have a feeling that when we do come together, it's going to be incredible. But, we can wait and I'm completely okay with that. Baby, whatever happens between us, I need you to know you'll always be the one to set the pace."

And just like that she relaxed completely in his arms and the sexual tension in the air lessened. With that settled, Clayton smiled to himself, tucking her head under his chin. Resting his head there in the soft strands of her hair, he slipped a hand inside her open blouse and idly rubbed her back.

Lifting a tremendous weight from her shoulders, his words had a powerful effect on her, she acknowledged, thinking how intuitive he was to understand that no matter how much she desperately wanted him, she also needed to move very slowly. That he was willing to let her lead spoke volumes and her feelings for this man blossomed even more.

Vi felt his body shake slightly after a few minutes and she raised her head to see him smiling down at her. She noted the teasing quality in his voice was back, and Vi was glad to hear it. With a mischievous glint in his eye, he informed her in a very matter-of-fact manner, "Now that we've settled that, I want you to know, young lady, you're not getting off the hook that easily Sweetheart." His last words were said in classic Jimmy Cagney fashion, making Vi break out in peels of laughter.

When she sat up to face him, he gently cupped her breasts for emphasis and flashed a wicked grin before saying, "If I can't have you, my dear, I plan to at least sample your treats."

Vi laughed along with him until she felt his thumbs cover her hardened nipple, gasping as the pad of his thumb caressed it in a slow, enticing circle.

"Feel nice?" He whispered, nuzzling her ear.

Incapable of words, she swayed toward him, quickly getting caught up in the feel of his hands all over her body.

"So," he said very slowly. "Are you going to tell me?"

It was kind of hard to concentrate on what he was saying, when his hands were busy creating magic, but Vi pushed through one of the thick layers fogging up her brain. "Tell you what?" She asked a little breathlessly.

"Why we're not in my bed, right now, making love?"

His inquiry had a sobering effect on her. She sat up and struggled to focus on what he was asking and exactly how much she was willing to tell him. Although she wasn't cold, she shivered slightly and tried to pull the ends of blouse together with shaking fingers. Stopping her, Clay brushed Vi's hands away and continued to stroke her through the dainty lace of her undergarment. Taking a calming breath, she began slowly. "Okay," she said. "Do you remember the other night when you asked me about dating?" She pinned him with this question, then waited for him to incline his head before continuing. "Well, I didn't exactly tell you everything."

Continuing his torturous movements, Clayton softly implored, "So, tell me now."

Stopping him, she placed her hands firmly over his, covering the strong fingers kneading her flesh. She held onto his hands, clasping them together within her own, before continuing, "The last date I went on was with a friend my sister introduced me to. We went out to dinner with Cynthia and her husband and this man—who seemed like a nice guy—had a little too much to drink." She paused for such a long time Clay didn't think she would supply any further information. Watching her closely, it was clear to him the memory of whatever happened so long ago had badly affected her. Finally, she spoke again and all the hurt she must have felt back then poured into her next words.

"When dinner was over, my sister suggested this man see me home, and like a fool I let him into my house. Anyway, worrying about him driving home in that condition, I made some coffee. He drank one sip and laid the cup aside, then..." her voice lowered to a harsh whisper when she got to this part. "Then, he came on to me and wouldn't take no for an answer. Clay, I got so scared, he ripped my...." She broke off, hiding her face in the crook of his neck. He removed one of his hands from her tight grasp and laid it across the back of Vi's neck in comfort, waiting for her to continue.

"I'm sure he... he would have raped me, if it hadn't been for Craig waking up and trying to stop him. Thank God he was a little drunk. It was much easier for us to handle him and get him out of the house." Vi took a deep breath, hesitant to share what happened next, even with Clay. Remembering how bad she'd felt after that date and how she'd sworn she wouldn't go through it ever again, it was very hard to impart what came next.

Although every muscle in his body was tensed in anger, Clay did not let on how disturbed he was. She obviously had difficulty sharing this with him, and he wondered idly if she'd ever shared it with anyone else. Waiting patiently for her to tell it at her own pace, he stroked her hair softly with one hand.

"Before we kicked him out he...he said some pretty ugly things to me. He told me...he told me I was probably all dried up anyway and that...that no man would ever want me anyway." She sighed deeply before going on. "After that fiasco, I stopped dating altogether."

Trying to contain his anger, a tell-tale muscle worked in his jaw as he tried to clamp down his rising temper. Vi had no way of knowing the hand that stroked her hair so gently wanted to do bodily harm to this nameless, faceless piece of... Clay took a deep breath knowing if he had only one wish at that very moment, it would be an opportunity to get his hands on the jackass who had dared to manhandle and belittle her. He was certain that if he laid his hands on the creep, it would be the last time he touched any woman like that, much less Vi, again.

When she finished her story, Clay leaned down and touched her lips in a tender kiss. Tamping his anger down, he spoke very softly. "He was wrong, Vi. He was stupid and drunk and dead wrong. You are the most desirable woman I've ever known, and I don't know how any man could resist you. I know I certainly can't," he said intently. "In fact, I'm going to show you just how desirable you really are."

Her hands, which still held onto one of his, fell away when Clayton reached to cradle her face in his palms. As he kissed her, his hands slid slowly down the column of her neck and into the collar of her open shirt. His strong fingers pushed the ends of her sleeveless blouse off her shoulders and down her arms. Releasing her lips, he again studied in appreciation the bra she wore, then he announced in a husky warning his intentions, "If you don't help me find the catch on this thing, I'm afraid I'll be forced to rip it off you." Shaking her head, Vi stared at him, uncertain if he was kidding or not. Deciding on the latter, she quickly reached to release the hidden clasp, undoing the front of her bra. He quickly pushed the lacy cups aside and, free of restraint, she spilled before him, luscious and full. The sight of her, unclothed now from the waist up did horrible things to his control. His hands stilled on her as he took a moment to drink in her perfection, silently acknowledging what a sensuous angel she was. Her womanly curves spoke of experience and unlimited pleasure, mixed with a deep-rooted ignorance of just how perfect she really was. The fact she didn't realize how perfect she was somehow only added to her allure.

Clay closed his eyes and struggled for a measure of control. He'd just promised her they would take it slow, and dammit, he was going to keep that promise, even if it meant a million cold showers. Taking her breasts in each hand, he covered them completely, feeling the pert ends burn a hole in the center of his palms. Clay's long, strong fingers kneaded her pliant flesh and when his mouth replaced where his fingers had been, he heard a soft moan escape her lips. He laid tiny sipping kisses all around then placed his hands at her waist, raising her slightly, so one hardened peak was only inches from his lips, erect and begging for his caress. Without hesitation or introduction, he teased one milk chocolate bud with his tongue, then pulled it slowly inside his mouth.

In answer, she leaned closer to offer more of herself and swayed against him, giving in completely to the deep sensations. Every hungry pull he took sent liquid fire racing through her extremities, which pooled dangerously low between her thighs, causing a deep, throbbing ache. Taking what she offered without qualms, his eager lips latched onto her other nipple, making her whimper helplessly. When his teeth scraped swiftly across that sensitive nub, Vi cried out, hardly recognizing the tiny mewling sounds that erupted from her throat. Powerless against the onslaught, she began to shudder and shake as his tongue laved and sucked, drawing on her hard and fierce.

Her avid response and the feel of her body coming apart in his arms only fueled his movements. Caught up in the taste of her, Clay felt his control slip a notch and knew it was time to stop. Reluctantly, he released her breast and lifted his head. Feeling the abrupt loss, he watched her slowly open her eyes and let out a small sound of protest. Seeing she was clearly affected as much as him, Clay regarded her under heavy lids, before declaring. "I believe we could do this all day, but I do have to feed you before you go back to work."

Favoring her with his signature mega-watt smile, Vi couldn't help smiling back, as she reached for her discarded blouse. Trying to help her get dressed, Clayton reached for the ends of her bra. She had to help him, however, as his fingers fumbled to gather and re-close the lacy garment, and his blatant clumsiness and roaming fingers hindered their progress several times. After a time, relaxed and playful, Vi and Clay worked together to get her clothes back on. However, it was a very long time before she was fully dressed again.

Clay decided to wait until after lunch to tell Vi about Casey and her involvement with Craig. He broached the subject as he walked Vi to her car and, by the time they reached it, she was in shock. She sat in the car with Clay for a few moments, trying to digest the facts he'd just given her. Apparently, Craig had been involved with a woman who could be carrying his baby and there was also a possibility this woman knew the man who may have killed her son. Although Clay told her the woman was white, Vi could not wrap her brain around why Craig would keep such a secret from her. He had to know she wouldn't care. The knowledge that he hadn't trusted them enough hurt Vi deeply.

Watching her, Clay tried to gauge her reaction to all the information he'd just given her. Covering her hand, he rubbed his thumb gently across her palm several times before saying.

"I think Craig really cared for this girl Vi. He didn't want to keep it a secret, but…"

Deeply wounded, she cut him of, not bothering to hide the hurt in her voice. "Then why didn't he tell me?"

"She didn't want him to. Casey told me herself that she and Craig argued about it a lot. She was ashamed of her past and thought she didn't deserve Craig."

Clayton sat with Vi for several more minutes, stroking her hand in silence. She was silent for so long, he thought she was going to be okay. Then, suddenly her shoulders slumped slightly and he caught sight of one lone tear as it slipped down her cheek. He reached out to wipe it away and gently gather her in his arms.

When she calmed down, Vi asked him about the likelihood of Craig being the father of Casey's baby and if the man Casey knew could be Craig's killer. Clay saw the pain in her eyes when he explained Craig was not the father and the information they had on Raul, so far, was very minimal. "For what its worth, I told Casey she was wrong." When Vi gave him a questioning look, he explained in a gentle tone. "I told her she should have trusted Craig's judgment. After I told her how great your family is and that all of you would have welcomed her with open arms, Casey admitted she wished they had handled everything differently."

She gave him a gentle smile and reached up to touch his strong jaw, silently thanking him for his kind words. "Clay, will she be alright? I mean, with the baby coming and with Craig gone?"

"She'll be okay. I'm going to try and get her a job with a friend of mine so she can get the health benefits she needs."

They sat for a while longer talking, and when he was certain Vi was no longer upset and able to drive, Clay placed a gentle kiss on her forehead and got out of her car. He was still worried about her, though, as he watched her put the car in gear and drive away.

You gotta' be kiddin' me!

Clay rolled over and turned off the alarm in disbelief. Hoping this morning would be different, he pushed the covers aside to investigate. To his chagrin, the evidence of his embarrassing state protruded proudly, just like it had every morning for the past week. Swearing viciously, he pulled the cover back over himself and flopped back on his pillow. It didn't take a rocket scientist to figure out what type of dreams he'd had last night or, for that matter, who he'd been dreaming about.

He closed his eyes and propped one arm behind his head, and there she was again, her beautiful face popping up instantly behind his eyelids. In living color, his mind previewed all her luscious assets, cataloging them one by one. He felt himself harden when he got to….

Grunting in response to his bodies' frustrated condition, he searched his mind for the last time he'd had it this bad. It had to have been his freshman year in high school. He released a strangled groan, as his eyes snapped open. For some reason he couldn't seem to get Vi off his mind for more than a few minutes. She constantly entered his mind during odd hours of the day and filled up his nights starring in some very erotic dreams. This prolonged state of unrest in his body was new to him. It started right after the steamy afternoon they shared several days ago and, to his frustration, it had intensified each day thereafter. He shook his head to clear it and sat up in bed. He couldn't remember ever feeling so wired, so tense and hungry for any other woman. Realizing there was only one cure for the tension gripping him lately, he also acknowledged after their last encounter it might be a while before she was ready to make that move.

Clayton got out of bed and strode naked into his living room, flopping down unceremoniously on his sofa. Although he had plans to see Vi later tonight, later tonight began to feel like it was a billion years away. Needing to at least hear her voice, he picked up the phone and dialed her cell number. Although he had off the next two days, unfortunately, she had to work. While he waited for her to pick up, he toyed with the idea of getting her to take off early so they could spend some time together. A silly grin spread across his face, just thinking about the possibilities. His body began to twitch and stir to life again, until he heard her voice on the line. His smile quickly faded when he realized it wasn't Vi but her voice mail speaking. He hung up, not leaving a message, and thought about calling her at work. He even thought about getting dressed and going over there, but quickly squashed that idea, remembering the promise he'd made.

Somehow, in a weak moment, Vi had convinced him to keep their relationship discreet. He swore inwardly, wanting to kick himself for agreeing to such a thing. But then, he remembered how she'd coaxed that particular promise from him in the first place, and smiled. As he recalled, she'd been very persuasive when she covered his mouth and wrapped her arms tight around his neck, making it damn near impossible to think coherently. Shaking his head in shame, he admitted he was like putty in the woman's hands. All Vi had to do was touch him like that again and... Well, let's just say, she could probably get him to do just about anything.

Surprisingly, the fact she could distract him so easily didn't bother him like it might bother some brothers, he thought, reaching for the phone again. He dialed her work number, acknowledging the reason it didn't bother him was probably because she'd stolen his heart from the first time he'd laid eyes on her.

Just before he had a chance to punch in the last digit, his phone beeped. Glancing at the tiny screen, he saw he'd just missed a call. When he recognized it was her cell number on the caller I.D., Clay quickly redialed the missed call, and spoke without thinking.

"Hello beautiful."

A brief silence followed his greeting, then he heard a feminine voice say hello, but the voice wasn't Vi's.

"Clay?" The hesitant female voice coming through the receiver this time was loud and clear. Recognizing too late the voice he was hearing belonged to Janae, Clay silently swore a blue streak.

"Janae? I'm sorry, I didn't know it was you. I was on the phone with someone and," the lie slipped easily from his lips, "I thought they were calling me right back."

"Oh," was all she said, then fell silent.

Choosing his words very carefully, Clay asked about school and casually asked if she was on campus, knowing darn well he was speaking to her on Vi's cell phone.

"No, I'm home for a few days. I was in such a rush to get here though, I forgot my cell phone. Can you believe that? I mean, I'm home all weekend. How does a person survive without a cell phone? Anyway, I stopped by the salon this morning to borrow my mom's cell phone for the day."

"So, how are you?"

"I'm fine," she said, the nervous energy that spilled out moments ago suddenly dwindled away as Janae slowly broached the reason for calling him in the first place. "Clay, I've been meaning to call you. While I'm here I'd really like to see you to apologize for what happened the last time we were together."

Clay could only imagine how embarrassed Janae must have been after that fiasco. He smiled thinking about it, certain she hadn't planned to get drunk that night, throw herself at him and then vomit all over his passenger seat on purpose. Although….

"No need. There was no harm done and your apology is accepted." Sensing her distress, he tried to lighten the conversation with a little humor and told her in a amusing tone. "I sure you didn't intend to get drunk and throw up in my new truck." He heard her groan, loudly through the phone line.

"Oh, Clay I'm really sorry about that. Please, let me make it up to you."

"Stop apologizing, it was no big deal. Anyway, you're like family to me. But, you have to promise not to go around dressed like that anymore, or I might have to arrest some poor guy for getting the wrong idea." Hearing her soft laughter let him know he'd achieved his goal, eliminating any humiliation she might feel and shutting the door on what happened between them for good. Or so he thought.

"About getting together though?"

Not giving her time to ask again or leave any room for misunderstanding this time around, he told her plainly. "Janae, I don't think that's such a good idea. I'm kinda' seeing someone right now." Scrambling to fill the tense silence that followed his admission, Clay quickly apologized and told her. "Listen, I'm tied up this week, but when you're in town again have your mom call me. I'll take all of you out for dinner—my treat. Okay?"

"Oh, okay…sure. I'm sorry, I had no idea you were seeing someone."

Feeling bad about the disappointment he heard in her voice, he quickly supplied, "No need to apologize, really. There was no way you could have known. Listen, I'll talk with you soon," he told her, then hurriedly hung up the phone.

Wow. That had been close, he acknowledged, thinking about the huge bullet he'd just dodged, hopefully for good. Taking a chance, Clay picked up the telephone again and dialed the salon. When Nicole picked up and informed him Vi had just left work, he decided to leave a message for her at home. Punching in her home number, Clay waited for the answering machine to come on. On the third ring, Tony picked up.

"Tony, my man, what's up?"

"Nothin' much Clay."

"Say, is your mom at home?"

"Nope. She went to work this morning, but I think she said she was leaving early to go shopping."

Disheartened, Clay saw the delightful possibilities he'd imagined for this afternoon evaporate before his eyes. "Tony, do me a favor, have her call me when she gets home."

"Will do man."

Clay smiled, liking this kid more and more every day. He had the sneaking suspicion the boy knew he liked his mother and, miraculously, he seemed okay with it. Giving his head a slight shake, he thought about the possibility of everyone else in Vi's family reacting the same way. He knew, however, the only way to find out their reaction would be for him and Vi to stop sneaking around and come clean. He also knew that was something she was dead set against. Clay talked with the boy a few seconds longer and was just about to hang up when Tony stopped him.

"Oh, I almost forgot. While I got you on the line…"

"What's up?" Clay interrupted, certain he knew what Tony was about to say. Lately, every time he spoke with Tony, all his conversations revolved around either basketball or J.R. Clay thought it was great how the two boys had become friends so fast and shared the same enthusiasm for basketball.

"Grandpa was supposed to ask you, but I kept forgetting to give him your number."

"Ask me what?"

"Mom's birthday is next Sunday. After church we're having a little surprise party. Just the family though, Mom doesn't like to make a big fuss over her birthday. Anyway, Grandpa was supposed to call and invite you, but since I got you on the line—can you come?"

He quickly assured Tony he would be there, if he didn't have to work. After he hung up the phone, Clay turned over the information he'd just learned as his mind began to formulate an idea. Vi was always there for her family and friends. Always going out of her way to ensure everyone else's needs were met. In fact, he couldn't think of one single time when he'd seen her put herself first in any situation. He smiled, remembering the time he'd made the huge mistake of calling her Superwoman. Man, she'd gotten really mad. Her temper flared so fast it had taken him completely by surprise and excited him all at the same time. Clay recalled watching in fascination as she folded her arms tight across her bosom in anger and swiped her full bottom lip with the tip of her tongue, obviously gearing up for the tongue lashing she was about to give him. It had been the most sexually arousing experience he'd witnessed in a long time. Filing it away in his memory bank, he made a mental note to try and get her angry more often.

Clay realized now that his words had angered her because no one had ever said them before. The fact she'd taken it as a personal attack spoke volumes of how she cared for everyone else, when most often those people should have been taking care of themselves. She was unselfish and caring, and he acknowledged those qualities were just a few of the things he loved most about her.

Just once, though, it would be nice to see someone do something special for her. He picked up the phone and punched out a few numbers as the idea he was toying with formulated into a plan. Waiting for Skip to pick up the phone, Clay smiled thinking about some of the other things he liked about Vi—at least four of those other things were different parts of her body. Voice mail came on just then, snatching his attention back. "Skip. Hey man, it's Clay. Listen pal, I need a big favor. Call me as soon as you get this message."

CHAPTER
TWENTY-SIX

After turning thirty, Vi typically didn't like to make a big fuss about her birthday. Since that time, her family knowing how she felt, never planned big parties but they did insist on getting together for a small celebration. Besides that small get together, the only other thing Vi did on her birthday that made it different from any other day was to give thanks to God for letting her see another year right before drinking her morning coffee. With her birthday only two days away, she noticed Tony was making several hushed phone calls. Probably putting together a little celebration of some type, she figured. She figured she'd guessed right when Cynthia left earlier than usual today, to run some errands she didn't want to discuss.

Vi was in her office trying to clear up some paperwork on Friday afternoon when it arrived. A little after three o'clock, she heard the front door open and close, followed by some type of excitement in the outer salon. Trying to block out the commotion going on out front, she bent her head over the ledger she was trying to work on. Several seconds later Andre walked into her office. Working on some figures, Vi noticed after several moments Andre hadn't said anything when he came in. Before looking up to see what he needed, she finished making the last entry in her log. When she did, it wasn't his shiny shirt or the huge grin he wore that caught her off guard. It was what he was holding that took her completely by surprise. Andre stood in front of her desk, grinning like a Cheshire cat, all but hidden behind the largest arrangement of red roses Vi had ever seen.

With a knowing smile plastered across his face, Andre slowly drew out his words, as he pushed aside some pictures on her desk to make room for the flower vase he held. "Well, it sure looks like someone's been giving up something pretty special to somebody."

Ignoring his teasing remark, Vi sat back in her chair staring at the fragrant floral arrangement in the center of her desk, her mind overflowing with questions. Instinct immediately told her who the flowers had come from, but not why…

How had he known her birthday was coming? She surely hadn't told him. Wondering why he would send them today, with her birthday still two days away, Vi admired their beauty.

My God, she thought. *There's so many, this had to cost him a small fortune.*

Slowly shaking her head, Vi finally noticed the envelope taped to the side of the vase. Unaware of the huge grin that began to spread across her face, she reached for it and began to slit it open. Then, Vi looked up, suddenly realizing Andre was still standing there, watching her every move. The long suffering look she gave him made him leave her office in a hurry.

Worrying her bottom lip, Vi listened to the chatter in the next room when Andre rejoined the women in the outer salon. They were all having a grand ol' time, no doubt due to her little flower delivery. Finally alone, she looked at the flowers in the center of her desk. Thank God Cynthia decided to leave early today, she thought, as she opened the envelope.

Sweetheart, it read. The endearment sent up a gentle fluttering in the pit of her stomach. She leaned back in her chair a second time, propped her feet on top of her desk and began reading the letter again.

Sweetheart,

I should be mad at you for not telling me Sunday was your birthday, but I'm not. In any event, I'm way too crazy about you to stay mad for long. I don't mind coming over on Sunday to help you blow out your birthday candles. But, I'm a selfish man and I request that you spend a special birthday with only me. With that being said, I've made arrangements for an early birthday celebration for the two of us. The celebration will start tomorrow with a very special day I've planned for you, one that I hope you will enjoy and remember for many years to come. You go out of your way for everyone you care about and spend all day making your customers feel special. Now, it's your turn. You will not have to lift a finger to experience your special day. The only stipulation I have is that you read all the instructions I leave for you and follow them to the letter. Oh, and by the way, your first instruction is wake up early tomorrow morning. Your driver will be there at nine o'clock sharp. Dress casual and have fun.

Love,

Clay

Vi read the last line twice. *Her driver? What in the world?!*

When Vi tried to reach Clayton by phone to get some answers—and to thank him for the lovely flowers—she couldn't reach him at home or on his cell. By the time she left work, he still hadn't called her back.

She found out later that night why Clay hadn't returned her calls. Evidently, he'd been a very busy man. Somehow he and Tony convinced Nikki to give up her day off to cover for Vi at work tomorrow. Saturday was usually their busiest days and Vi was very surprised he'd been able to pull that off. In addition to working out her schedule for the day, he had apparently left her a little surprise at home.

Tony met Vi at the door and immediately started gushing over the huge floral arrangement she brought home with her. "Gee Mom, you must have cleared out the florist shop."

Barely able to see Tony through the foliage in her arms, she cast a suspicious eye at her son, noting the "cat that ate the canary" grin on his face. Something was definitely up and the look Tony was wearing meant he definitely knew more than he was letting on. Well, the night was young and she had all evening to grill him for information. Deciding there was no time like the present, she quickly asked him, "Why are you grinning from ear to ear? Out with it kid."

"I don't know anything. Well, nothing I can share anyway."

When Vi pinned him with a determined look Tony quickly raced down the hall and grabbed his back pack before she could question him further. "Gotta' go Mom. Mike's mom is taking us to the movies," he said, flying past her and added, as if it were an afterthought. "Oh, there was a delivery for you a while ago. I left it on your bed upstairs."

Vi watched Tony race out the front door wondering for the umpteenth time today. *What was going on?*

Checking the mail sitting on the hall table, Vi flipped through it, then slipped off her shoes and made her way upstairs. When she reached her bedroom she found a huge, white box sitting in the middle of her bed, taking up half the mattress. She sat down next to it and ran her hands under the large red ribbon covering the box. When she took the top off, another letter lay on top of the tissue paper inside, with her name on it.

Hello again, My Love,

Your mission, should you decide to take it, will be – wonderful. All you have to do is:

1) Follow all instructions

2) Keep your curiosity in check

3) Sit back and enjoy

4) Don't eat breakfast – I've taken care of that too.

5) Remember, your driver will pick you up at 9:00 am. Don't be late.

6) Do not open the overnight bag in this box until after breakfast tomorrow.

Oh, unlike the real Mission Impossible, this note will not self-destruct.

Sleep well, Darling. See you tomorrow afternoon.

He'd signed it again, simply, *Love Clay*. As she read this last part, Vi began to giggle. *Ohmigod!*. Rolling her eyes heavenward, Vi realized she was actually giggling like a teenager.   Getting totally caught up in the mystery she set the note aside and peeked inside the big box. A small gray overnight bag was under the tissue paper alongside another bouquet of flowers. She lifted the flowers out and found it was actually a plant of some type set in a white porcelain bowl.   Getting up, she walked over to her dressing table, sat the plant on top and then turned back to the box. She took the overnight bag out of the box and shook it. It appeared to be full inside, with God only knew what.   Vi put the bag down on her bed and sat down next to it again.   Its handle was made of smooth leather and a sturdy zipper ran its full length. It took a tremendous amount of willpower, but she didn't open the bag.

When Tony called later to ask if he could spend the night at Mike's, Vi agreed.   Once she'd done that, he quickly asked about going fishing with them tomorrow also.   After speaking with Mike's mom to ensure Tony would not be a burden, Vi hung up the phone.

Bubbling with anticipation, she decided to turn in early.   Unfortunately, sleep didn't come easily.   Too wired to sleep, she couldn't seem to shut down the zillion questions floating around in her brain.   She felt just like a child the night before Christmas, knowing Santa was coming with something special, but not knowing what that special something was. Finally, around two in the morning she started to get tired. Anxiously anticipating whatever was going to happen tomorrow, Vi fell asleep with a smile on her lips.

The next morning when Vi answered the door at exactly nine o'clock, she was expecting a taxi, or a car service of some type. She was not prepared for the long, black stretch limousine waiting in her driveway or the uniformed chauffeur who stood on her porch.   He smiled at Vi as he took her bag and asked her to follow him. Moving ahead of her, he held the door for her as she slid into the back of the sleek limousine. The plush interior had all the essentials, soft leather seating, television, stereo and a fully equipped mini bar. There was a note taped to the television screen with her name on it. Vi peeled it off and unfolded the note.

Good morning Darling,

I hope you like the limo. Wish I could be with you this morning. If I were, we could put up the privacy screen and steam up the windows before breakfast.   But, as much fun as that would be, I still have some details to take care of for your special day. As I said before, today you will not have to lift a finger. Where you'll be going this morning, everything will be done for you. So, please enjoy it and I'll see you later.

Clay

As she refolded the note, a nervous laugh escaped. *For goodness sake, she was doing it again!* Feeling a little foolish, Vi covered her mouth to catch the laughter bubbling in her throat.   Trying to compose herself, she helped herself to the orange juice laid out in the mini bar area, surprised to taste champagne mixed with it.

Oh, hell yeah!

Taking Clay's advice, she slipped off her shoes and swung her legs up on the seat across from her.   She was drinking mimosas in the back of one of the longest stretch limousines she'd ever seen and headed to God only knew where.   If the rest of the day was going to be anything like this, Vi thought—*bring it on.*

When her limo stopped in front of the most exclusive Day Spa on Long Island, Vi peered out the passenger side rear window in awe.   Staring up at the massive structure, she knew two things for certain.   It was very expensive and often frequented by wives of CEO's and the occasional celebrity.   When she walked up to the huge double glass doors, Vi was greeted by a petite, stylishly dressed woman who introduced herself as Cher.

Cher explained to Vi that she would be her personal attendant today, and then quickly ushered her inside.   Cher took Vi's overnight bag and led her through the posh lobby so quickly, Vi barely had time to glimpse the polished marble floors, pale peach décor and softly lit hanging chandeliers. Cher smiled and talked non-stop about the spa's numerous amenities while she whisked Vi up a flight of stairs and into a large, comfortable sitting room.   Done in muted shades of lavender and jade, it resembled a mini suite you might find at any five-star hotel, complete with wet bar, refrigerator and comfortable seating in front of a huge fireplace.

Vi stood watching Cher carry her overnight bag through a door she assumed led to the bathroom. Curious, she followed Cher and realized as she stepped across the threshold this was no ordinary bathroom. It was almost as large as the sitting room, lushly appointed with marble floors, quiet lighting, mirrored walls and an enormous sunken tub. Her eyes were drawn to the stairs leading down into the tub and the rose petals floating atop the steaming water.   There were plush towels, scented soaps and bath oils positioned all around the tub's perimeter.   Cher left her briefly to get refreshments, discreetly allowing Vi time to undress and sink into the scented bath water.

As soon as she left, Vi quickly undressed and stepped into the warm, scented water.   A short while later, Cher returned with a cushioned bath pillow and a tray laden with fresh fruit and juice. Vi had never felt more pampered in all her life. When she lay her head back against the soft bath pillow, the tub jets came on automatically, sending her straight to heaven.

After her bath, Vi received a vigorous massage and served a sumptuous breakfast fit for a queen.   The suite's dining area was set out on a private terrace that overlooked a huge atrium below, complete with flowing water running over several rock formations.   Looking across from her room, Vi saw that other private rooms also faced this beautiful oasis, filled with every tropical flower imaginable, palm trees and tall, green leafy plants.

Cher returned about an hour after breakfast and took Vi to yet another part of the spa.   This part resembled the Nu U hairstyling area, only it was three times larger and done entirely in white.   Cher styled her hair in an elegant swirl piled high on top of her head, leaving several loose curls hanging to softly caress Vi's neck and face.   Regrettably, her leisurely morning came to an end as she was led back to her suite to change out of the soft terry robe she'd worn all morning long.

When she walked over to the low table and picked up her overnight bag, another note was attached to the handle. Excitement coursed through her as she read the note. It stated that it was now okay to open the bag. When Vi laid the note aside and unzipped the bag to examine its contents, she found out Clayton wasn't just full of surprises, *the man was completely insane!*

CHAPTER
TWENTY-SEVEN

The yacht was docked in a private basin on the south side of the Long Island Sound. Its sheer size and gleaming surface made it stand out among the other large vessels docked alongside it. Across the water large, graceful beach houses stood in the background, lining the shore and making the scene look like something from a movie. Carrying her overnight bag, the chauffeur helped Vi from the limo and led her down the length of the pier. When he led her straight to the yacht that caught her eye just moments ago, Vi was speechless.

It was mid-September. After the hot, brutal months of June, July and August they had been experiencing a mildly refreshing Indian summer. Today was no exception; it was a beautiful late summer day, with a cloudless blue sky boasting a pleasant eighty-seven degrees.

Vi saw him standing on deck, dressed in khaki pants and a lightweight, unbuttoned white shirt that billowed out behind him in the afternoon breeze. When Clay turned around and saw her, his eyes lit up in a way that made her heart flip flop. He helped her come aboard and quickly gathered Vi in his arms as soon as her feet touched the deck. And, when she would have begun speaking, he silenced her with a brief kiss, knowing she had a million questions to ask he planned to answer later. Right now, it was enough that she was here.

Vi stood in his arms, feeling like a character in some romantic novel getting ready to sail away with the man of her dreams. The light breeze rustling his shirt also whipped through the chiffon dress she wore. How he knew she would love this dress was beyond Vi, but love it she did. The ultra feminine dress caressed her legs like a whisper when she walked. It was unlike anything Vi had ever owned, and although she had her doubts when she put it on earlier, they were quickly erased when she saw the look of appreciation in his eyes. She also had to admit its gold and peach floral design did complement her skin tone; but basically, the skirt that hugged her waist and flowed past her hips was the majority of the dress. When she'd pulled it out of the bag earlier at the Day spa, Vi had some serious doubts she could wear something so revealing. The top half of the dress consisted of two barely wide enough front panels that tied behind her neck, leaving her back exposed and a very deep neckline in front that almost reached her navel. Clay had left specific instructions in the bag for her to wear it when she left the spa. Alluringly feminine and elegantly soft, she had eagerly donned the dress and glanced in the full length mirror on a far wall. She smiled at her reflection there. Besides being very expensive and more daring than anything she'd ever worn, it made her feel like a glamour girl straight out of one of those fashion magazines.

Relaxing his hold on her Clay smiled down at her as he lifted her hand to his lips. With his eyes never leaving hers he gently brushed the center of her palm with a light kiss. "You are so beautiful," he whispered. When she felt the tip of his tongue swirl against the soft center of her hand, she closed her eyes, feeling the intimate gesture deep in the pit of her stomach.

"Ahem…"

Startled, Vi heard someone clear their throat. Realizing they were not alone, she and Clay quickly broke apart and she turned to look at the tall, blond teenage boy standing on deck behind them. Although he knew the young boy, Clay's obvious reaction indicated he'd clearly forgotten the boy was onboard.

"Eric, is everything ready?"

"Yes sir, Mr. Marshall. Everything's a go."

Clayton introduced the young man as the nephew of his close friend, Skip. Vi found out later that Skip had been Clay's partner when he first joined the force. Although he was retired now, Clayton still went sailing with him several times a year and it was no surprise, he told her, that Skip sank all his life savings into this yacht when he retired. In addition to living his dream, it seemed Skip made a comfortable living chartering the boat out on weekends.

Vi watched Clay walk into the wheelhouse with Eric to go over some last-minute details before the boy took his leave. From the way they talked the boy seemed to be very capable, although he appeared to be no more than sixteen or seventeen years old. Vi continued to stare in disbelief as the young man jumped from the deck to the pier in one quick, fluid motion and made his way toward a parking lot full of cars about a hundred yards away. While Vi watched the boy leave, Clay watched her from the wheelhouse. Although she had her back to him, he quickly sensed her apprehension as she nervously bit down on her lower lip, and continued watching Eric until he reached his car and drove away.

Seeing the worry evident on her lovely face, he spoke to her in a joking—and somewhat injured—tone. "Don't look so worried, I'm perfectly capable of handling this baby on my own."

When she slowly turned around to face him, Clay laughed out loud at the uncertainty plastered across her features. Deciding to show her a thing or two, he walked over and placed a possessive arm around her waist. "Since you seem to have so little faith in me, I guess I'll just have to show you." He grasped her hand and quickly retraced his steps, walking back toward the wheelhouse with Vi in tow.

She watched him sit down at the wheel. Then, to her surprise, he gently tugged on her arm and plunked her down on his lap, right in front of him. Twisting around slightly to face him, Vi shot him a questioning look. "Clay, what are you doing?" She squirmed in his lap, desperately trying to make her plea. "I can't drive this boat, or any boat for that matter," she protested and started to get up. "Now stop playing and let me go."

Clay held on tight and leaned close to whisper in her ear. "The term is pilot. You don't drive a boat, you pilot a boat," he said very patiently. "Now, I plan to show you how to turn the engine on and pilot this vessel out to sea, but...," he paused, purposely stretching out his next words. "If you keep wiggling your fanny like that I might decide to leave this boat docked right here all afternoon and do something else."

Heat rose in her cheeks and Vi wisely said no more and turned forward to study the gadgets before her with new-found interest. Staring at all the instruments in front of her, she immediately noted the wheelhouse was well equipped with state-of-the-art navigational devices, all of which held no meaning to her and looked more complex then the cockpit of a small airplane.

She listened as Clayton explained he was going to give her a crash course in sailing, and that all good teachers took the hands on approach. Right now, however, his hands were on a different kind of voyage. Reaching beneath the filmy hem of her dress, she felt his large hands start a slow uphill journey over her thighs, leaving a tingling sensation in their wake. She felt his hot breath fan against her neck as he chuckled softly when she shivered and her body began to sway under his gentle exploration. To her dismay he stopped only inches from the apex of her thighs and seemed content to rest his palms there, not initiating any further movement. She listened to him explain how to pilot the boat; his lips brushed her ear as he spoke and Vi felt a deep stirring low in her belly. It was sweet torture; his manner being as much playful and arousing as it was educational. While he teased her, he also continued to give her instructions and talk about Skip.

"Yeah, Skip charters her out for weekend parties most of the time, the other half he spends on this boat drinking beer and fishing. We go bass fishing sometimes when I get a couple of days off in a row."

"How did the two of you meet?" she asked.

"Skip was my first partner when I joined the force. He literally took me under his wing and taught me everything there was to know, including his favorite pastime – fishing and sailing."

It seemed that Skip had taken a quick liking to his new, much younger partner. In turn Clayton told her how much he respected the man like a father, learning so much from him on the job and in life. As they talked he continued to give her a crash course on sailing, explain each instrument's function on the boat and patiently answer all her questions as she pointed to certain dials and switches. After he'd answered all her questions, Clayton turned the key, started the motor and finally maneuvered the vessel away from the pier.

When he did this, Clay placed her hands on the wheel and covered them with his own to ensure she didn't hit anything. As they coasted further out in the water, he sped up a bit and let the vessel have her head. The boat surged forward, slicing decisively through the water. Gripping the wheel tighter, excitement rippled through Vi. Having never experienced anything like this before, she watched the shore fall behind them and the sea open up before them.

Vi was doing great, or so she thought, until she felt him gradually remove his hands, leaving her to pilot the boat alone in open water. She gripped the wheel tight, as his hands fell away and came to rest at her waist. It became extremely hard to concentrate on what she was doing, when she felt him casually lace his fingers together around her waist and press his face against her bare back. For several minutes he didn't do anything else, which allowed Vi a little time to gather her wits about her. For several minutes he seemed content to lie there and nuzzle the soft skin on her exposed back. Thinking that was all he would do, she began to relax her vise-like grip on the wheel. This was fun, she thought, and held onto the wheel, staring out at the sea as they sliced through the water, wave after wave. Just when she thought she was getting the hang of it, however, he suddenly moved again and ruined her fledging confidence. Clay unlaced his fingers from around her waist and ran them tentatively, sensuously down her back. Then she felt him place his lips to her nape, caressing that area lightly, while his nimble fingers slipped beneath the front panels of her dress.

It was a heady feeling, the wind at her back, the movement of the boat beneath her and the feel of Clay's hands boldly cupping her breasts. Each nipple tightened instantly against the palms covering them, making her tremble in response. His fingers gently kneaded her pliant flesh, testing its weight, and Vi closed her eyes when he swept his thumbs lightly across the straining tips several times. She couldn't be sure if it lasted an eternity or just a few minutes, whatever it was, it was over way too soon. Disappointed, her eyes fluttered open when she felt him sigh deeply and release his arms from around her waist.

After a while he retook the wheel, and they slowed down, apparently reaching their destination. The shore could no longer be seen in the distance, telling her they'd traveled pretty far out. Out in the middle of nowhere, with nothing but water surrounding them, Vi looked around curiously. Clay gave her a brilliant smile as he turned the engine off, lifted her from his lap and grabbed hold of her hand.

"Come on, let me show you around."

The yacht was an impressive sixty feet and had all the luxury and amenities you could imagine. Everywhere she looked, the wood was freshly varnished and the brass instruments sparkled in the afternoon sun. He led her to the rear of the vessel. Back here there was comfortable leather seating built into three sides of the boat. Downstairs, the galley below deck resembled a small apartment kitchen complete with a dinette table built into the wall with a sofa surrounding it on two sides.

He tucked her hand in his arm and led her further back, to the sleeping area. Vi noticed there was only one sleeping compartment. A comfortable, double bed sat directly under a small window at the prow and across the room an easy chair, foot stool and dresser made up the rest of room's furnishings.

Vi swallowed nervously when she saw the bed. Its cozy appeal was lit up by the recessed lighting made into the ceiling above. The lights were set on low and glittered invitingly off the mirrors covering all but one wall in the bedroom.

He watched her nervously survey the room. Wanting to reassure her, Clay placed both hands gently on her shoulders, squeezing them for emphasis. "Baby, relax. We won't use that bed unless you're ready to," he said earnestly. "There's no pressure on you to do anything you don't want to do, alright?"

Although her eyes were still pinned to the bed, she nodded her head slightly. Clay turned her around to face him and cradled her face in the palms of his hands. "This day is about you Vi. My only goal is to cater to your needs and make it special for you."

When she looked up at him and saw the sincerity in his eyes, Vi immediately felt at ease. Looking into his eyes, she saw desire flicker in their depths. But, when she thought he might kiss her again, he suddenly released her instead.

Trying to lighten the tension between them and soften up the serious mood of things, Clay smiled slightly and stepped away from her. "I've got some things to do on deck, why don't you go freshen up and join me up there in, say, five minutes?" After giving those instructions, he placed a chaste kiss on the tip of her nose and gave her backside a playful slap to get her moving. Signaling his departure, he climbed the stairs leading above deck and left her standing there. Vi heard his hearty laughter as he climbed the stairs. Watching him go, she shook her head ruefully and started laughing too.

Five minutes later, when she climbed the stairs to join him on deck, Vi came up short. Standing at the top of the stairwell, she stared in awe at the deck, which had been miraculously transformed into a scene from 'Lifestyles of the Rich and Famous' most romantic moments. A small table had been placed in the center of the deck, covered in white linen and flanked by two comfortable high-back, cushioned chairs. A floral centerpiece graced the table, its blossoms a profusion of wild colors and scented petals. The gold-trimmed bone china, gleaming silverware and long-neck champagne flutes complemented the exquisite candlelight setting.

After he pulled out her chair, Clayton made sure Vi was comfortably seated before he proceeded to serve her a delicious meal. Not until he was done serving her did he pull out a seat for himself. But instead of sitting across from her, he pulled his chair over so he could sit right beside her. All throughout the meal he never stopped touching her. Being this close to one another invited an exchange of lingering caresses, light laughter and significant eye contact. The romantic setting made it impossible to resist the urge to taunt and tease one another. Using her hands, Vi fed him shrimp. Tormenting her, Clay nibbled at the plump morsel then gently pulled her fingertip into his mouth, over and over again. When he would caress the curve of her neck, she would stroke the strong line of his jaw and let her hand run down his open shirt front. In return, he continuously ran his hands idly up and down her calf, while Vi leaned over several times, catching the shell of his ear with the tip of her tongue.

It was sweet torture, and when the two of them could stand no more Clay rose from the table. With the food lying cold and forgotten on their plates, he took her hand and led her below to a small sitting area build into the boat's stern. He then deposited Vi on the soft, oversized sofa and left briefly to turn the lights down low. She sat on the plush sofa watching him move about the small galley, filling a bowl with strawberries and turning on a CD player built into a hidden- wood grain cabinet. The sounds of smooth jazz filtered softly through overhead speakers, creating a cozy and relaxed atmosphere. When he finally emerged from the galley, Clay carried two glasses of chilled wine and fresh fruit. He handed one glass to Vi then sat down to propose a toast.

"Here's to us," he said, touching her glass to his, "and to our making new memories together." Slowly sipping the cool wine in her goblet, she met his gaze over the rim of her glass.   Watching her closely, Clay took one sip of wine, then took her glass and placed it with his on a nearby, low table. When he turned back to Vi, Clay quickly gathered her in his arms and, without hesitation, captured her lips in a tender kiss.   As he deepened the kiss his fingers pushed into her hair, releasing the pins there and allowing her curly auburn locks to fall free.   Grabbing a handful, he brought the strands to his nose and buried his face in its softness.   "I love your hair loose just like this," he whispered in a reverent sigh.   His words trailed off as he covered her mouth again and drew Vi back into his arms.   Her lips had an intoxicating effect on him and it didn't take long for the kiss to spin out of control.   Just like strong spirits, she went straight to his head, making him sink his teeth into the softness of her bottom lip, and then quickly soothe it with his tongue.   The sharp pain and quick pleasure made her gasp and he felt her body melt against him in response.

Light as a feather his strong fingers caressed her, grazing her cheek and sliding slowly down her neck to cover her breast possessively.   Through the thin material of her dress Clay felt her tighten against his hand and heard her breathing change when he slipped inside the deep neckline to cradle her fullness.   Relishing how incredibly soft and enticingly warm she felt, his skillful fingers scraped lightly over one pebbled crest, making her cry out his name in a strangled moan.

Needing to touch him in some way, Clay felt her soft hands trail down his chest and reach lower still, brushing lightly against his groin.   He sucked in a sharp breath and closed his fingers around her hand to stop her movements. Intoxicating, he thought plain and simple.   She was intoxicating and soft and sweet, oh so sweet.

Needing to see her, he shoved the material aside and replaced his hand with eager, moist lips.   She trembled in his arms as he tugged at her mercilessly, arching her back to give him better access.   Encouraged by her passionate response, Clay's hand slid over her hip and down her body.   With ease he reached under the hem of her dress and ran his fingers gradually along the inside of her thigh.   A sense of triumph washed over him when his journey led him to the damp silk covering what he desired most.   Vi's breathing turned shallow and rasping when he reached this barrier and they both waited in anticipation to see what he would do next.   They didn't have to wait long before he nudged her legs apart and slid one searching finger beneath the thin silk panel.   Dipping inside, the liquid heat scorched where he touched, making his head spin.

Giving herself up to his merciless caress, she teetered on the edge of pleasure that felt very close to pain.   As his fingers explored her feminine folds, his mouth continued to draw on her, eliciting tiny, mewling sounds from her throat that she did not recognize as her own.   It was too much, her mind registered right before she reached for him. Lifting his head from her breast she brought his mouth up to hers for a hungry kiss.

The hunger he tasted on her lips made Clay's gut clench and they both got caught up in the liquid dance. While his fingers continued working between her thighs, their tongues mingled, fused and mated over, and over again. When she came, the explosion rocked her entire body. Watching the passion sweep across her lovely face, he held her tight throughout the storm and whispered softly. "I know Baby…let go… let go."

Clay held her within his arms moments later, waiting for Vi to recover. As he held her, he struggled to find the right words to describe what was in his heart. Realizing there was no easy way to express himself, he took a deep breath and tried to explain. "Vi, I meant what I said earlier, I didn't bring you out here to pressure you," he stated plainly. "Today is about showing you how special you are to me, and even though everything in me wants to be buried deep inside you right now, I won't do anything you don't want me to do. But..."

Vi stared up at him, her eyes revealing her confusion. Seeing it, Clay blurted his next words out so quickly, he couldn't believe he'd actually said them.

"I know I promised to go slow, and I'll keep that promise if it kills me. But I never promised not to touch you…feel you. And, I want to do more, right now, to give you something to anticipate, because when we come together Vi, I want to know no other man is on your mind or in your heart but me."

Hoping to hell he hadn't scared her to death or set their relationship back to square one, he looked deep into her eyes trying to gauge her reaction, before continuing. "Baby, I want to erase from your mind the memory of any other man you've ever known, by feeling, touching and…tasting every inch of you," he said quietly.

When she would have opened her mouth to speak, he quickly covered her lips with his finger, stopping any further inquiry. Struggling to find the right word was too difficult, so he decided to show her instead. Quickly capturing her lips, plundering her mouth with an urgent kiss, he gently pressed her down on the sofa.

As soon as her back lay flat on the sofa it seemed his hands and lips were everywhere at once. Using his mouth, he leaned over her and deepened the kiss while his fingers slid over her hip and slipped possessively around the back of her thigh. Her breathing changed when she felt him lift her thigh and search out her warmth once more. Capitalizing on her reaction, Clayton released her mouth, and trailed his lips down the column of her neck and came to rest in the deep neckline of her dress.

"I've been so hungry for you all day," he said in a husky whisper, nudging the material aside to capture a sweet gumdrop between his lips. Suddenly, his lips released her, leaving her breast wet and aching for more to trail tiny kisses further down. She watched him lift her dress and dip his head, nuzzling her softness and trailing his tongue over her stomach and around her navel. Vi's breathe caught inside her chest as he dipped into that indentation several times in a leisurely fashion, then continued his torturous journey, trailing tiny kisses over the softness of her hip, her thigh and…lower still. When his questing fingers suddenly slipped out of her, Vi cried out. Then she forgot to breathe when he moved with blinding speed and lowered his mouth to replace where his fingers had been. The feel of his lips there made her gasp for air, as the initial shock faded and a delicious sensation took over.

The tiny tremors that shook her body urged him on and he buried his head deeper, increasing his pace and intensifying the intimate kiss. Cradling her hips, he brought her closer to his lips, using his skillful tongue to seek out all her buried treasures. He felt her fingernails dig into his shoulders when the first orgasm hit, gripping her with its sharp, piercing pleasure. Of their own volition, her hips rose in rhythm against him as wave after wave of ecstasy crashed over her. When it was over, he shifted to gather Vi in his arms, content to hold her until all the tremors passed.

Realizing she still held a generous amount of his shirt clutched in her fist, Vi released it.   Locked in his embrace she felt shell shocked, totally spent and completely amazed by the way she'd come apart in his arms. No man, not even her husband, had ever kissed her in such a way before.   It had been a mind-blowing meltdown, so new to her it still had her body humming. Trying to hold onto the delicious tingle still running through her, Vi snuggled closer to him. As soon as she did, however, it became painfully obvious to her how his efforts to please had cost him dearly.   She immediately sat up and searched his face. Although his eyes were closed, a telltale muscle bunched in his jaw and the evidence straining against his fly confirmed his need. A need he couldn't fulfill, she acknowledged, because he knew she wasn't ready.

When she reached for him, Clay's eyes shot open and he quickly sat up and brushed her hand away. "No, Baby…it's alright. This is not about me."

"But…you didn't…" she began to explain, right before he placed a finger to her lips, cutting off whatever she'd been about to say.

"Shhh," he whispered. "It's okay, I'm a big boy." Favoring Vi with one of his characteristic, achingly gorgeous lopsided grins, Clay placed a lingering, wet kiss on her lips, that stopped any further protest.

Watching the infectious grin that spread across his handsome face, Vi felt herself smile in response.   The words – *I love you* – lodged in her throat, but her heart would not let her release them. Unable to say the words, she went about showing him how she felt by wrapping her arms tight around his neck. With her arms locked around him, she brought his lips back to hers and poured all the feelings she held into one single kiss. She tasted her sex on his lips and all at once the kiss went from tender to explosive, gentle to combustible, and they both teetered dangerously close to going up in flames.

Reluctantly, it was Clayton who ended the kiss. Releasing her, he placed a chaste kiss on the bridge of her nose again and stood up. Although his smile was still intact, she noted that small muscle still bunched in his jaw.

"I'm going up to check on things and maybe grab a quick swim," he said distractedly. When he was halfway up the stairs, Clay thought to add.   "If you hurry, you can join me," then he was gone.

Above deck, Clay had his hands full trying to work out his own issues. The tension gripping his body had him so tightly strung that practically every muscle in his body ached. Planting his hands on lean hips, he recognized the most torturous ache rested just south of his belt buckle. He knew there was only one way to cure the sickness gripping his insides; the only problem was it entailed charging back downstairs and losing himself inside the woman he so desperately wanted.

Hell and damnation! He swore under his breath and began to pace the deck, trying to cool down his overheated body. Absently, he jammed one hand deep into his pants pocket and ran the other over his face in exasperation before realizing his error.

Big mistake! Her scent was still on his hand. It clung to his fingers and stayed on his tongue, reminding him of her taste and smell. She smelled like woman, sweet and…

Dammit! He began to pace the deck again, back and forth, back and forth, in an effort to gain some semblance of control. Recognizing his own stupidity, Clayton gave his head a rueful shake, realizing he had come very close to losing it just moments ago. What a fool he'd been to think he could be that close to her and touch her like that and not be affected by it. He had only intended to explore a bit and give her a sample of what to expect. Somewhere along the way, however, he'd gotten lost in her arms, lost in her softness and now his restraint lay in shreds. Clay knew for certain if he hadn't left her when he did, he wouldn't have been able to stay and just hold her any longer. The need to totally possess her had been so great just moments ago that he had, for the space of heartbeat, considered forcing the issue. He had a deep suspicion if he had, she might have welcomed it.

With a frustrated sigh, he removed his shirt with quick, jerky movements and unzipped his pants. When he stepped out of his trousers only the swim trunks he'd worn underneath, remained. Deciding there was only one way to cool down, he strode to the side of the boat and dove overboard.

Vi remembered coming above deck, feeling like she was half naked. Not normally a two piece kind of girl, she had to admit the swim suit Clay picked out did wonderful things to her figure. Her self-consciousness quickly vanished, however, when she searched the boat and checked the wheelhouse twice, but still couldn't find him. Just before panic set in, she heard a faint banging at the other end of the boat and rushed over to that side.

As she watched him emerge from the water, sloshing it everywhere, her normal fascination with Clay's powerful upper body took on a whole new meaning. Sleek lean muscles rippled with each movement he made, and her avid gaze swept over him while he toweled off his glistening wet, gorgeous body. In the midday sun it shined with a warm vibrancy, turning his skin to a golden chestnut. Vi stood there awestruck, feasting her eyes on his perfectly sculpted biceps, incredibly wide chest and flat dark nipples sheltered in a smattering of hair. She watched as droplets of water clung to that dark chest hair before running in crystal rivulets down his washboard abs to trickle in a single line into the waistband of the swim trunks he wore. Powerless to look away, her eyes drifted to the wet material clinging to his manhood; the outline leaving very little to the imagination.

The quick swim he took worked like a charm. That is, until he saw Vi standing there staring at him. And just like that, the heat that gripped his body before quickly consumed him again.

Unbelievable! Groaning inwardly, he felt himself harden all over again. On some level, his mind registered the bathing suit he'd bought for her looked sensational on her. Essentially, it was four tiny triangles held together by a network of strings and ties. However, actually seeing her in it made Clay's throat go dry. His Adam's apple bobbed up and down as his eyes traveled over the three triangles he could see. The two triangles barely covering her breasts were especially delightful, he decided, as he watched her nipples harden through the thin material with pure male satisfaction. Then there was the triangle covering...

Realizing it was going to be a very long afternoon, Clay quickly found a blanket below deck and after she went for a short swim, he promptly wrapped her in it. Luckily, she bought his story about afternoons at sea being chilly and kept the blanket around her for the rest of their trip.

They sat on deck after that, letting the afternoon drift away into early evening. Eventually Clay joined Vi under her blanket, and in between sipping champagne and eating fresh strawberries, they played under there, necking like teenagers at a drive-in movie. At one point, as they watched the sun set in a profusion of vibrant colors, washing the sky with magenta, orange and red, Vi turned to him and declared it was the most beautiful thing she'd ever seen. Looking at her animated expression, he had to disagree, as he drank in all her radiance.

Shortly afterwards, they sailed back to shore, anchored the boat and gathered their things to go home. As Clay drove her home and their evening came to an end, Vi felt an unexpected stab of disappointment that they hadn't taken their relationship to its logical conclusion.

He parked his truck in her driveway and cut the engine but made no move to get out. Tony was spending the night at a friend's, so the house was dark except for the porch light she always left on. Reluctant to end their time together, they sat on their respective sides of the truck's front seat in silence. When neither of them made a move to get out, Clayton reached across her lap and opened the glove compartment. She watched as he reached inside, then re-closed it and turn toward her holding a small box in his hand. He held it out to her and, like a child, Vi tore at the tiny white ribbon to get at what was inside. When she opened the box, her eyes instantly filled with tears. Inside laid the most exquisite diamond bracelet she'd ever seen.

He watched her, trying to gauge her reaction. When she pulled the bracelet out of the box and wrapped her arms around his neck he was, to say the least, pleased.

"Clay, thank you," she said, teary eyed. "I don't know what to say, its beautiful… the whole day was…wonderful."

Wiping a single tear with his finger, Clay shrugged off her words, before saying. "You deserved it and it was my extreme pleasure." Then he got out and walked around the front of the truck to open her door. In silence, he took her hand and walked Vi to her front door. Always a gentleman, he slipped the house keys from her hand and opened the door when they got there. With that done, he placed her keys back in the palm of her hand and stepped aside to let her go inside. When she turned to look at him, that sexy, lopsided grin of his fell into place and he politely informed her, "I don't get off work until eight o'clock tomorrow night, but don't you forget to save me a piece of birthday cake, okay?" After saying that, he leaned forward and placed a chaste kiss on her lips.

Vi felt cheated, after the day the two of them just shared, his polite kiss wasn't nearly enough. Standing on her front porch, one step above him, she reached out to stop him from leaving. As soon as he turned around and before she could lose her nerve, she quickly wrapped her arms around his neck and thrust her tongue deep into the warm, sweet recesses of his mouth. For an instant, he just stood there; then his arms snaked around her waist in a tight band. The kiss was long and deep, hot and wet and, when it was over, left them both shaken and breathing heavily.

When he slowly released her, Clay searched her eyes and read something there he found very hard to resist. Instinctively, he knew if he asked her anything at that very moment—*Can I come in for coffee? Can I come in for a drink? Can I come in, make love to you and stay the night?*—she would have said yes. He didn't ask. Instead, he placed a light kiss on the bridge of her nose, careful not to touch her again, then turned to leave.

Hours later Vi lay in bed remembering his touch and everything that he'd done for her today. A satisfied smile curved her lips as she fell into a deep, restful sleep.

CHAPTER
TWENTY-NINE

The piercing sound of the referee's whistle echoed in the gymnasium. The other team's point guard had just fouled Tony for the third time. The referee blew his whistle and waited for everyone to take their places, while Tony took his free throw. When he made it, Vi clapped the loudest, like any good parent would. She was sitting in the fourth row of bleachers with a dozen other parents, watching Tony and J.R.'s last tournament game. Watching her son play, Vi recognized how much better he'd become at basketball under Clayton's tutelage. Seeing how good Clay was with J.R., it was no surprise that Tony had began to worship the ground Clay walked on. She smiled to herself, thinking Tony wasn't the only one *who loved him,* she was...

Whoa! Now where had that come from, she thought. Vi shook her head, not wanting to examine that line of thinking too closely, but acknowledging deep down that loving Clay would be very, very easy to do.

When the coach called a time out, she stared past the empty court to the open doorway. It was a beautiful day, just like the afternoon she and Clay had spent together for her birthday. That had been over two weeks ago, but she remembered every detail of it just like it was yesterday. That day had been perfect and Vi couldn't remember the last time when she'd felt so special. Everyday it seemed Clay was slowly winding his way into her heart, like the other day...

Vi had been in the kitchen busy preparing Sunday dinner when he called yesterday. Tom was out of town again, so Vi invited Cynthia and Clarence to have dinner with her and Tony. She was at the sink when the phone rang. Quickly drying her hands, she left the water running and rushed to pick it up.

"Vi?"

Instantly her spirits soared and a tell-tale smile spread across her face from just hearing his voice. "I was just thinking about you!" she chimed.

"My God woman, it's bad enough you can't keep your hands off me when we're together," he said, gently teasing her. "Now, you can't control your lewd thoughts about me." As he'd anticipated, that statement made her laugh. He listened as her soft laugher tinkled through the phone line, its sweet sound piercing his heart and sending a tremor down his spine.

Pretending to be offended, he told her, "I'm glad to see you're taking me so seriously."

"You're nuts," she said in between giggles.

"See, there you go again…" he said, trailing off suggestively. "Now what were you saying about my nuts?"

Vi let out a snort so loud that she covered her mouth to smother the sound.

After laughing along with her for a little while, Clay quickly got down to his reason for calling.   "So, what are you doing?"

"Getting ready to make dinner, why?"

Instead of answering, he asked another question that took her completely off guard. "And what are you wearing?"

Vi looked down at herself and chuckled. "Mmmm, let's see, an old pair of jeans, a T-shirt and an apron."

"No, I meant underneath," he asked in a low, husky tone.

Vi looked up and quickly glanced into the living room. Clarence and Tony were watching ESPN, while Cynthia's eyes were closed in what she called one of her "power naps." Wiping her hands on a nearby towel, Vi turned the water off and leaned her hip against the counter top. Deciding to play with him a little it Vi told him a deliberate, little white lie, "Let me see…I'm braless and the only other thing I've got on is a black lace thong."

The image her words conjured up in his mind sent a wave of heat straight to his groin, making it hard for Clay to breathe, much less speak for several seconds.

Certain she'd just taken him off guard, Vi waited for his reply, silently reveling in the fact she'd been able to render him speechless. *Good*, she thought with a satisfied smile on her face. It was nice to know she was capable of shaking him up a bit, since he did it to her so often.

"So," she said very slowly. "What's up?"

At the time Clayton could probably have told her at least one thing that was definitely up, but he didn't comment on that. Instead he said, "I wanted to take you to dinner tonight, somewhere special."

"I thought you had to work."

"I do, but that's not until ten thirty tonight."

"I'd love to go Babe, but I already invited everyone to have dinner here."

"So, that's fine. Everyone can come, my treat."

"Clay, that's awfully nice of you, but you can come over here if you'd like."

"No, I'm always mooching dinner off you. It's my turn."

"But," she began before he cut her off.

"No 'buts,.' I bet everyone would love to go out and eat. Ask them."

Shaking her head, Vi put the phone down and yelled into the living room.

"Clay wants to take us all out for dinner. Who's game?"

He heard her family's resoundingly loud agreement to eat out before she picked up the phone again to tell him he'd been right.

"Well, I guess no one's interested in my meat loaf," she said, feigning an air of indignation. "So, where are we going?"

"That's a surprise," he told her. "I'll pick you all up in an hour."

To her surprise, instead of taking them to a family-type restaurant, Clay had taken her entire family to a new, upscale Italian restaurant. Everyone had a great time at dinner. Almost like second nature, interacting with her family was very easy for him. Lately, he'd become more and more wrapped up in her family. The more he interacted with them, the closer the two of them became. Remembering the way he sat at the table last night brushing her knee under the linen tablecloth and laughing and talking with her family, made Vi almost believe her family might just accept their relationship after all.

Lost in thought, she didn't see him come in. Startling Vi, he snuck up behind her and grabbed Vi around the waist. When she turned around in his arms, she was just as happy to see him as she was annoyed with him for sneaking up on her.

"You need to stop playing," she told him. However, the smile on her lips took the bite out of her words.

"But," he told her, a little too innocently, "I like playing with you." Right after he said this, Tony hit a three pointer and Vi raised her hands in the air. In her excitement, she nearly poked Clay in the eye.

"Ouch!" he said pretending to be in pain.

"Oh, Clay...I'm so sorry," she said, quickly turning to him. Her voice was full of concern and apology as she raised one hand to his eye and cradled his jaw with the other.

He shot her an irresistible grin, stopping her apology. "It's okay. I didn't need that eye anyway."

Realizing he was fine, she smiled back and gave him an elbow in the side for pulling her leg. As the game continued, Clay stood next to her on the bleachers, clapping and whistling as J.R. made a free throw that put their team ahead now, by eight. It was the last game of the season and J.R. and Tony were both having an awesome fourth quarter.

"Did you see that" she turned to Clay, still incredibly excited that Tony had gotten so much better at basketball in such a short time.

"Yeah…it's a good thing I didn't' lose an eye when you hit me, or I might've missed it. A huge grin spread across his face as he began to tease her again. "You know, in the future we may have to restrain you at these games."

Furrowing her brow in concern, Vi reached out to touch his face. "Baby, I'm so sorry. Are you okay?"

Smiling at her, Clayton covered the hand she laid on his cheek and felt a warm feeling settle over him. "I am now," he said hauling her closer to his side. They stood like that, hip to hip, for a few minutes watching the boys.

J.R. was the team's lead shooting guard while Tony was leading the team in assists. They were up by ten points in the last quarter and it looked like their team might win if they applied a strong defense. The excitement kept everyone on their feet, each person anticipating their team winning this very close game.

Clay stood very close to her with his arm still wrapped loosely around Vi's waist. Knowing she wasn't ready to let everyone know about their relationship he was usually careful how he touched her in public, especially around her family. But lately every time they were together, he couldn't seem to keep his hands off her and now was no exception. He glanced over at her as she watched the game with avid interest. She typically wore a lightweight sweater because the air conditioning in the gym was usually on full blast. Watching her now his eyes were instantly drawn to the pronounced state her nipples were in because of the cool temperature. The hand at her waist reached up under the sweater she wore and inched past the edge of the tee shirt she had on underneath. The feel of his warm hand against the soft skin at the small of her back made her tremble slightly. When the crowd around them sat down, Vi quickly took her seat leaving Clay to wonder if she'd been affected by his touch, or chilled from the cold. If she had been affected, he thought with a brooding frown creasing his brow, she chose to ignore it.

Keeping his hands to himself when they were together in public was getting harder everyday. And, the strain of keeping their relationship a secret was beginning to wear on him. As much as he wanted to respect her wishes, Clayton wasn't sure just how much more of this he could take.

While he sat beside her pondering their situation, Vi focused her attention on J.R. who had just scored another three pointer. Trying to ignore the intimate moment they'd just shared, she sat watching the game in silence. Looking around at all the parents in the crowd she thought about J.R. and his situation. Clayton told her very little when she asked him about it giving the impression he didn't want to talk about it; so she didn't press. Although he didn't look like he was in the mood right now to discuss anything, Vi turned to him desperately needing a distraction and asked, "So, tell me how did you meet J.R.?"

For the longest time, she thought he wasn't going to answer. When he did, she knew he was about to tell her something he didn't usually share with others.

"He was in trouble," he said slowly. "His parents are a lot like mine, only they snort their poison instead of drinking it. When they get high it gets pretty ugly. Sometimes they hit him, most times, they just ignore him."

"Did you report this to…," Vi searched her mind, "to family services?"

"Of course I did," the irritation in his voice was hard to ignore. "J.R. had to corroborate what I told them. He refused to do it then and he refuses to do it now."

Not sure what to say, she replied sadly, "that's too bad."

"Yeah, in my line of work it fails to amaze me how parents mistreat their kids, and the kids know it, but they don't want to tell anyone. They'd rather stay in the hell hole they're in instead of going into foster care."

Vi heard the deep-seated pain in his words, and knew that a lot of what J.R. was going through right now reminded Clay of how his childhood had been. As he watched the game lost in his thoughts, she studied his profile. She found amazingly new facets to this man every day, and they all seemed to make up the man she was quickly coming to love.

When she hooked her arm through his, Clayton turned to face her. "He's very lucky to have you, you know," she said very quietly.

"Yeah, well, he knows he can crash with me if things get too bad at home," he said with a dismissive shrug. "He also knows whatever he decides I'll be there for him." Uncomfortable with her praise he turned his attention back to the game and let the conversation drop.

On a brighter note, Vi added, "Clay, I know I've thanked you before, but I really appreciate the time you've taken with Tony too. You are so good with him."

Clayton latched onto her hand, lacing their fingers together and murmured close to her ear, "If you let me, I could be good for you too." Then he brought her fingers to his lips and kissed them softly.

Vi was never prepared when he turned the full force of his charm on her. When it happened, her heart-beat quickened and then her brain promptly shut down, making it hard to think straight. Thankfully, the clock buzzed signaling that the game had ended and effectively ended the spell. Vi blinked once, then twice, before her mind registered they were in the gym, at Tony's game!

Watching her under heavy lids, Clay felt her tense up and knew the exact moment she realized where they were. All these weeks he'd been priming her for the ultimate meltdown. He knew it was just a matter of time before they came together, and when they did it would be well worth the wait. Until then he intended to use everything he had in him to break down the barriers she tried to construct between them.

When it was only the two of them, he had the most success working her, plying her to help him break down those restraints. When they weren't alone, it was much harder. So he enjoyed little moments like this when he could catch her off guard in public. When she was off guard, he could assail all her senses at once, forcing her to focus on him and only him. He knew he should feel guilty, but he couldn't allow himself to care. No, he was way too busy fighting for their relationship to care what other people thought, and he was way too busy trying to get her to feel that way too.

Keeping her further off kilter, he held onto her hand when she would have pulled away, bringing her fingers to his lips once more. She raised her eyes to his and watched as he slowly ran the tip of his tongue lightly over each knuckle. Vi sucked in a sharp breath and looked around frantically, to see if anyone leaving the gym was watching.

As he left the gym with the rest of his team, Tony yelled up to his mother. "Hey, Mom did you see me make the final shot?"

Smiling, Vi waved to Tony with her free hand, while trying to wrestle the other out of Clayton's grasp. A few people leaving the stands gave the two of them a curious look as they walked by, but for the most part, the crowd ignored them, talking about the close game they'd just witnessed.

Suddenly, Clay was sick and tired. He was tired of sneaking around and whispering on the phone. He was sick of taking cold showers before bed and waking up so hard, it was painful. All morning he'd turned this impossible situation over in his mind and, for some reason, today he'd decided he couldn't do it anymore. Knowing they couldn't go on this way he formulated a plan to force her to choose what he knew she wanted, and in the process cure the ache that had taken up residence in his nether regions.

He knew if he gave her an ultimatum, she would probably get angry. He also acknowledged that while the prospect of her getting all fired up was very tempting, it might also backfire on him.

When she yanked the hand he held one last time, Clay quickly released it and gave her an Oscar-winning look of pure innocence. "What?"

"What? Is that all you have to say!" she shot back, glaring at him. "Clay, we've discussed this before, I'm not ready for Tony or anybody to know about us, and…" She didn't get a chance to say more before he raised his voice and cut her off.

"Why Vi? Why not? You keep saying in time, when is that going to be?"

Although she was at a loss for words, she definitely knew she didn't want to have this discussion here. "I…I don't know, I..," she started to say.

"I know you don't know," he said angrily. "You don't know squat."

Clay watched her chin raise a notch and her eyes widen. These were all indications that her temper was about to flair.

Good! He smothered a sudden urge to smile in satisfaction. Holding onto his anger, he said in an agitated whisper. "I'm sick and tired of sneaking around Vi. We're adults for Christ's sake! We should be able to do what we want to do."

Unable to argue with that, she said the only thing she could say, "I…I agree, but…"

"But nothing Vi," he continued to press her. "You and I are running around like children. Why?"

She wasn't quite sure what had gotten into him, but she realized there was no getting around this conversation, which he clearly wanted to have right here, right now. She took a deep breath and tried her best to appeal to him and make him understand, "Clay, you don't understand. Baby, as soon as I…"

"Vi, I'm not one of your children and I understand perfectly." The edge in his voice caused her to fall silent. "I've heard it all before. So what, you're older than me? I'm really tired of hearing about it."

In the face of his anger, Vi was rendered speechless and the confused, helpless look she gave him was almost his undoing. Stiffening his resolve, he chose to ignore her distress, knowing he couldn't back down this time. If he did, heaven only knew how long they would go on like this. "You don't get it, do you?" he asked pointedly. Realizing his question was completely rhetorical, Vi remained silent.

"If I kissed you right now Vi, none of these people would care. And, so what if they did? At the end of the day we're both adults," he said, trying to reason with her. "I think you're making way too big a deal about this."

By this time her anger had begun to flare. Shocked by his words, Vi tried to get a word in edgewise, realizing he was deliberately baiting her and she couldn't figure out why. It wasn't like they hadn't been over this a hundred times before. "I'm going home," she announced, picking up her purse from the bench in a huff.

"And another thing," Clay said challenging her and completely ignoring the fact she'd just told him she was leaving. "I've decided it's time we told your family about us."

That bold statement stopped her dead in her tracks. She turned around to face him but when she opened her mouth to say something, nothing came out. He waited, watching a series of emotions flit across her face—protest, denial, wanting, outright fear and finally resignation. Speechless, she heaved a weary sigh and he watched as all the fight fizzled out of her.

"Okay," she said hesitantly. "We'll tell them. Soon, I promise you we'll tell them very soon."

Feeling like he was finally making some headway, he pressed her further.

"When?"

The crowd had all but filed out of the gym and the two teams had already gone to the locker rooms, undoubtedly celebrating or having an after-game pep talk. When Vi lowered her head and didn't say anything, Clay took her hand in a firm grip and led her down the bleachers and into a deserted hallway outside the gym doors. As soon as the doors closed, he took her in his arms. Pleased when her arms went around his waist in return, Clay rested his chin on top of her head before asking her in soothing tone, "Tell me what you're afraid of."

He felt her spine stiffen defensively, before she said, "I'm not afraid of anything."

Clay rubbed her back in slow, sweeping circles to ease the tension he felt in her body. He bent his head very, very close to her ear and issued the ultimatum, "Prove it."

Still in his arms, Vi pushed away slightly and stared up at him. The challenge she saw in his eyes, however, gave her pause. Clay had always gone along with her desire to go slow and see each other discreetly. This new attitude left her feeling uncertain.

Wondering if he'd pressed her too hard, Clayton saw numerous emotions flit across her features. Again, the misery in her eyes caught at his heart and he thought about letting her off the hook. He heaved a long sigh preparing to do just that. Then she said, "I don't understand. 'Prove it,' how?" Her question came out a quiet whisper.

"You say you want this relationship; that you care about me. I want you to prove it."

"How?" she repeated.

"The annual law enforcement charity banquet is next Friday night. I'm taking you Vi. I'm coming to your door, no matter who's home or who knows, to pick you up and take you on a real date."

The conviction she heard in his voice was laced with steel resolve, as he continued to drive home his intentions. "I don't want there to be any mistakes about my intentions," he said firmly. "I won't be coming over to share a meal, or as your friend, or to take you and Tony to practice. I'm coming to get you, to take you on a real date in front of God and everybody and… I want you to be ready on time."

His piercing gaze latched onto hers and Vi saw there would be no arguing about this anymore, no more putting it off. A small part of her, the insecure part that questioned why a young, handsome man like him was even interested in her, was scared shitless. The other half of her was enormously relieved he'd taken the bull by the horns, because God knows, she probably wouldn't have done so herself. Unaware she had already subconsciously made her decision, she asked hesitantly, "But, what will I tell Tony and Janae?"

Inwardly, Clayton sent up a triumphant cheer. He'd done it! He'd taken a huge risk forcing her hand, but it had paid off. Keeping his voice firm, he told her, "I don't care what you tell them. Just tell them we're going out – that simple."

"It's not that simple," she said, still staring up at him.

He took her hand again in his and brushed his lips gently across her knuckles. "Baby, it is that simple. Only you make it difficult, only you. What it all boils down to is this." Making certain she was focusing all her attention on what he had to say, he held her gaze and watched her face. When he was sure she was listening, he continued, "I don't give a rat's fat ass what people say and who you tell. I do know we deserve to be together and life's too short Vi, too precious, to waste living it like someone else wants you to."

CHAPTER
THIRTY

"Wow! Mom, you look great."

Vi let Tony's compliment wash over her, glad that she'd bought a new dress for tonight. It had been years since she'd went out on a date and even longer since she'd bought something special for the occasion. The little black dress was form-fitting to the waist, and flared out from her hips in a multitude of chiffon triangles. It had spaghetti straps covered in sparkling sequins and a very low neckline, which exposed the slender column of her neck. The only jewelry she wore were shiny, dangling earrings with a matching comb, which held her hair up over one ear and left the rest of her auburn locks to caress her smooth shoulders.

Clarence looked up at his daughter-in-law and said unnecessarily, "Yes indeed, Tony, your Mom will be the prettiest woman there tonight, hands down."

"Those other women won't be able to hold a candle to you, Mom," Tony piped in. Glowing under their praise, Vi bounced down the stairs in her stocking feet, realizing she was already floating and she hadn't even hit the dance floor yet.

"Ya' think?" she asked Tony playfully, and gave him a swift hug when she reached him at the bottom of the stairs.

"Oh yeah, Clay better look out 'cause he may have to wait in line to dance with you tonight, Mom."

She gave her son another spontaneous hug, then turned to Clarence and gently kissed his cheek. Vi had labored for over a week about who to tell about tonight, and what she would say. Thinking about it, she determined Clayton was absolutely right, they were adults and there really wasn't that much difference in their ages. However, in the end she chickened out, telling Tony and Clarence because she had to ask him to stay with Tony for the night.

"Vi, Honey, you look amazing," Clarence told his daughter-in-law. "Now don't you worry a bit, I'll beat those two boys in Gin Rummy and then send them off to bed," he assured her. Clarence had volunteered to let Tony and his friend, Mike, sleep over at his place tonight. It seemed the boys planned to get their money back from the last time Clarence beat them both out of ten bucks each in the game. Vi didn't think either of them had a chance, since

Gin Rummy was clearly Clarence's game, but she didn't want to spoil their fun. Recalling Clarence's response when she told him she planned to go out with Clayton for the night, Vi had to smile. The older, much wiser man, had simply nodded his head in approval, and surprised her by stating it was about time. As a matter of fact, he'd taken it a step further by telling her he was glad she'd finally decided to come from underneath her rock and that Clay would be a fool to let her go back under it ever again.

The phone rang. From the way Tony raced upstairs to answer it, Vi assumed it had to be Briana. Clarence yelled after Tony to shake a leg, reminding him Mike was waiting to be picked up. Clarence grabbed up Tony's backpack by the front door and walked outside to put it in his car. As he was closing his car trunk, Clayton pulled into Vi's driveway. Clay walked over to the older man, greeting him with a strong handshake. Clay helped Clarence put some of Tony's video game equipment in the back seat then the two men walked side by side to the front door, talking congenially about the dance tonight.

"So, how's that knee feeling?" Clay asked the older man, remembering his arthritis had been acting up lately.

"As good as an old man my age can be, young fella," Clarence replied then cut right to the chase. "I understand your taking our Vi out tonight."

Nodding slowly, Clay noted the abrupt change in subject and waited patiently for the proverbial other shoe to drop. As it turned out, Clarence's next words totally banished all his worries.

"Well, I'm real glad you two finally got together," Clarence told him, with a broad smile creasing his weathered features and amusement dancing in his eyes. "When you're as old as I am my boy, you hate to see people wasting time, like the two of you were doing." Witnessing the pleasure Clarence had just derived from putting him in the hot seat, Clay visibly relaxed. He laughed along with the older man, clearly relieved Vi's father-in-law was okay with him taking her out.

Tony saw his granddad and Clay walking up the driveway as he came back downstairs. Stopping at the foot of the stair he held the door open for them. As Clarence came back inside, Vi heard him get in one last joke at her expense. Chuckling to himself, Clarence turned to the younger man and told him he couldn't let the two of them go out without giving Clayton ample warning.

"Now Clayton, my boy, I have to warn you, Vi can't stand being in high heels too long," he said with a touch of merriment in his voice. "So, watch out when she gets to kicking 'em off. You might lose an eye."

Vi was busy lacing up the new black, high-heel sandals she bought to go along with her dress, when she heard father-in-law's joke and Clayton's laughter, as the two men come through the front door. Instead of being embarrassed, she smiled in response to Clarence's outrageous remark, knowing deep down he was probably right. She finished putting her shoes on and stood up to check her appearance, feeling so happy tonight that nothing could spoil her good mood.

When Clay walked inside, he didn't see her right away. Thinking she might still be upstairs getting ready, he stopped to speak with Tony for a minute. It wasn't until he walked through the foyer and into the living room that he saw her talking to Clarence. Partially hidden from view, she stood with her back to him, giving her father-in-law some last-minute instructions. As if sensing his presence, she slowly turned around to face him and completely took his breath away.

If the low whistle Clay gave her wasn't enough to tell Vi he liked what he saw, she had only to look into his eyes. Walking toward him, she felt herself blushing as his appreciative eyes traveled slowly up and down her torso, causing a delicious tingle to race through her limbs.

When she reached him, Clay tamped down an uncontrollable urge to kiss her right there, on the spot. As much as he wanted to reach out and touch her, he knew he couldn't with Tony and Clarence nearby. Unable to do more than stand there and drink in her dark beauty, he grabbed hold of both her hands and softly whispered, "You look amazing."

Actually, amazing didn't actually describe the beautiful woman who stood before him, he thought. She was breathtaking, and her radiance seemed to warm him in places he didn't know were cold. The fact Tony and Clarence were in the same room didn't stop his smoldering gaze from traveling down every delectable inch of her, taking in the way her slinky black dress hugged her body to perfection. His eyes lingered at the teasingly short, flared hem then traveled lower over her long, shapely legs and the sexy, black sandals she wore. The sight of her made his gut clench in desire, and at that moment he wanted nothing more than to gather her up in his arms and spend the night exploring every inch of her body in great detail. Restraining himself because they weren't alone, he settled for a lingering kiss on her cheek. When his lips made contact with her smooth, satiny skin they lingered a little longer than necessary, savoring that tiny contact, before he stepped back and released her hands.

Exchanging a heated look, they parted and Clay walked into the dining room where Clarence and Tony were sitting. "So, what are you guys doing tonight?" he asked the two of them.

"Once I fill Tony and his buddy up on soda and cheese pizza, I plan to beat the pants off them in Gin Rummy and send them to bed," Clarence informed Clay in a joking manner, all the while winking at his grandson in jest.

Tony got up and walked over to where Clayton stood, shaking his head in denial. "We'll see, Grandpa," the boy said and turned his attention to Clayton. Slapping him on back, the boy smiled up at him, eyeballing his attire. "Hey man, you clean up real nice."

Warming up to Tony's compliment, Clay struck a G.Q. model pose and strode smoothly from the room. Watching him walk away, all Joe Cool like, Tony fell back on the sofa, laughing hysterically.

Overhearing her son's comment, Vi had to agree. His wide shoulders did fill out the European cut of the suit he wore to perfection. The peach shirt and matching tie he wore set off the dark Italian suit, giving him a definite G.Q. look if she ever saw one.

At that moment, Clarence announced to his grandson, "Tony, let's head out son. It's getting late and we still have to pick Mike up and the pizzas." He got up off the sofa and turned to Clay and Vi. "You two young people have a good time, ya' hear. Stay out as late as you want, and remember to have a dance or two for me."

Thanking him again for keeping Tony, Vi hugged her father-in-law and then went to hug her son goodbye. Tony quickly brushed off his mother's kiss, instantly rebelling, in true teenage fashion, against the implication that he needed a babysitter. "Mom, please...I'm fourteen. Nobody needs to watch me," he told his mom in an indignant tone. "Besides, as early as Grandpa goes to bed," he paused here before adding in his own rather matter-of-fact tone, "Mike and I will probably end up watching him."

Clarence came over and swung an arm across his grandson's shoulder, pretending to drag him from the room, then turned to wave goodbye. As Tony and his grandfather left, Clay moved up behind Vi as she closed the door behind them, wrapping his arms around her waist. He bent his head to nibble at her practically bare shoulder.

"Mmmm, you smell so good, I could kiss you all night," his voice was a husky whisper very close to her ear.

She leaned back against him, giving him better access to the silky column of her neck. When his strong forearms enveloped her, tightening around her like steel bands, Vi's eyes drifted close as she felt the tip of his tongue blaze a trail of fire over her sensitized skin.

When he touched her like this it set off a hungry, answering desire in her body that kept Vi feeling out of sorts. The lightest touch of his hand or brush of his lips never failed to make her body hum and send all her nerve endings sweeping to the surface. She was pliant, wanton and vulnerable under the spell he cast. Feeling guilty at first for having these feelings, she realized now that, in this man, her time had not past. He made her feel desirable, special, cherished, loved... How was that possible, she wondered?

Then, all thoughts vanished when he swiftly turned her around and captured her mouth in a hungry kiss. His hands sat low on her hips and slowly began to drift down much further, kneading her tender flesh through the black sheath she wore. Vi got lost in the onslaught his lips and hands created. Finally, he raised his head from hers and stared into her eyes. When he spoke, his voice was unsteady and filled with need. "Vi, if we...don't go now, I can't make you any promises this dress will stay on."

The radiant smile she flashed his way, Clay acknowledged, was enough to send a strong man to his knees. Then, in a manner he was coming to love, she slipped out of his arms with remarkable ease and planted a quick kiss on his lips in departure. Before she walked away, she turned slightly and politely informed him over her shoulder. "If you think you're going to sweet talk me out of this dress and a night on the town, you're sadly mistaken Mister." With that said, she sashayed over to the sofa, picked up her purse and grabbed his hand, literally dragging him out the door.

The Lexington Room at the Carlyle Hotel was swarming with people. Elegant furnishings and giant chandeliers cast a soft, golden light on the opulent marble surfaces and deep, plush carpeting. Huge, round tables boasted exquisite place settings and were scattered about the room around a large, parquet dance floor. Men in dark suits and women decked out in satin, silk and chiffon alternately took the dance floor or sat chatting at the many tables set up for the event. In a far corner, on a raised dais, a deejay played a nice blend of popular hits, slow jams and oldies.

When they arrived Vi's heart sped up to match the excitement she felt in the room. She did, however, feel a wee bit nervous about being here with Clay among his peers. Apparently not sharing her misgivings, Clayton took possession of her hand and led her into the ballroom. They made their way around the banquet tables and past the open bar, where he lifted two glasses from the tray of a passing waiter. Once they each had a flute champagne in hand, he proudly tucked her hand in the crook of his arm, led her around the room and started introducing her to his fellow officers and their wives or girlfriends. Piterrelli and his wife had commandeered a huge table in the back of the room, close to the second bar. When he spotted Clayton and Vi entering the room, he quickly waved them over to join their table. As they made their way over to Pitt's table, Clay stopped briefly to proudly introduce her to his Captain and Rev. Winters. When they finally reached Piterrelli's table, it was obvious to Vi, that almost everyone in their lively group seemed to have already had quite a bit to drink.

Vi was surprised what a great time she had mingling and sparking up conversations with people she hardly knew. The mouth-watering food and loud pulsing music combined with the laughter flowing very freely at their table and put her instantly at ease. Before long, at least four more tables had been pulled up next to their table, as other couples were drawn to the frivolity at the back of the room. All night they'd been practically inseparable, with Clay never straying very far from her side. Now, with so many people at their table, Clay and Vi suddenly found themselves separated for the first time that evening. Sometime during the night, the men in their group had commandeered one end of the three tables they'd pushed together. They sat a distance away talking about whatever guys talk about with one another, while the women took the other half of the table talking amongst themselves.

Clay sat at the far end of the table, in the midst of his group. Although he appeared to listening to the conversation around him and made the proper responses, Vi felt his eyes on her the whole time. His intense perusal made her nervous and several times when someone spoke to her she totally forgot her train of thought. Their gazes continued to collide all evening and as the hour grew late, the heat in his eyes only intensified, beginning to feel much like a caress. As Pitt's wife explained how yoga helped her previous back injury, Vi found herself only half listening. Her mind drifting to earlier in the evening and how Clay had managed to always keep contact with her somehow, holding her hand, touching her arm, pressing his fingers to the small of her back or around her slender waist. She realized he'd meant what he said earlier in the week. After tonight, if people here didn't know they were a couple, they had to be blind. She also realized no one here seemed to think there was anything wrong with them being together or cared about the difference in their ages.

Clay watched her stifle a yawn from across the room. Standing up, he excused himself from the group and made his way over to her. He'd taken off his suit jacket hours ago and it now lay draped over the back of Vi's chair.

She watched him walk across the floor in her direction and thought, my God, he was one magnificent man. His impossibly wide shoulders filled out the fitted dress shirt he wore to perfection. Loose, tailored slacks hugged narrow hips and shiny black shoes added a refined and sexy quality that she'd never seen before. She'd seen him in numerous situations in the past weeks and months. Dressed in shorts and cut-off jeans, he always looked young and fit. In uniform or a simple casual dinner jacket, he exemplified strength and maturity. However, tonight he had all these qualities and much more, exuding a sex appeal she was finding very hard to resist.

When he reached her side, Clay held out his hand. She looked up at him and placed her hand in his without hesitation. Grasping it lightly, he gave her hand a gentle tug, which brought Vi to her feet.

"Dance with me," was all he said before leading her onto the dance floor just as a slow, jazzy number started to play. The tune was mid-tempo and sultry. While most couples on the floor prepared to dance apart, Clayton, on the other hand, gathered Vi in his arms and set the pace for a very slow glide across the dance floor. She looped her arms around his neck and met his eyes in their hypnotizing spin around the room. He slid his hand gently down to the small of her back, splaying his fingers just slightly above her backside, and drew her very close to him.

The slow burn Vi saw in his eyes caused a light fluttering low in her belly. Were it not for a few subtle foot movements, one could hardly tell they were moving at all, so slow was their dance, so in tune they were with each other. So into each other that they both failed to notice their movements drew the attention of several people in the room. Pitterrelli's wife grabbed her husband's hand and pulled him onto the dance floor, while Captain Jackson and his spouse sat holding hands, watching Clay and Vi sway across the dance floor. As the music ended and couples began to leave the dance floor, Clay and Vi stayed.

Vi knew for a fact some of the most earth-shattering things happened when you least expected them, and tonight was no exception. Instead of releasing her, when the song ended, Clay's arms tightened around her waist. Then, in the next moment, he dipped his head and in front of God and the whole world, captured her mouth in a full-blown, no-holds-barred, heart-stopping kiss in the middle of that dance floor.

He plied her mouth in a desperate urgency that she eagerly returned with everything she had in her. They both got caught up in it and the mutual fire burning between them threatened to spin out of control right there, right on that dance floor. Finally, they broke apart and came up for air, vaguely registering that the song had changed. Clay dropped his hands from her waist, took her hand in his and led her from the dance floor. They made their way back to the table, where he grabbed up his jacket while she collected her purse. They said a hasty goodbye to Piterrelli, who sat alone at their table. Then, without another word, Clay led her across the room and out the door.

As they hurried outside, leaving the Hotel Carlyle's Lexington Room behind, neither of them said a word. Clay's hand went to his inside pocket to fish out their ticket, which he quickly handed to the valet. In silence, he felt for her hand at his side. Grasping it, he twined her fingers within his as they waited. When the truck pulled up, Clay tipped the valet and helped Vi into the passenger seat. A light rain began to fall as he made his way around to the driver's side.

Inside the luxurious cab, the dashboard lights cast a soft glow, illuminating the truck's dark interior. The air surrounding them in the intimacy of his vehicle was bursting with sexual awareness. When he glanced at her across the front seat, Clay saw her watching him and the super-charged air began to sizzle and pop with the tension straining between them. Although only inches separated them, it seemed like she was miles away on that bench seat. Trying to find something to do with his hands, he flipped on the defogger and turned on the radio. Smooth jazz spilled from the speakers but, instead of easing the tension, it heightened it as this song made them both think about what happened on the dance floor just a little while ago. Before Clay put the truck in gear, he reached for Vi.

"C'mere," he beckoned, helping her slide over closer to him in the driver's seat. When she was all cozy and close next to him Clay placed his hand possessively on her thigh, put the truck in gear and drove off. As he drove off, Vi snuggled even closer to him and draped one arm around his neck, while the other hand began to loosen the knot in his tie. When it was loose, she tossed the tie over her shoulder, where it hit the backseat in a silk whisper, then went to work on the buttons of his shirt.

Leaving the business district behind, Clay got onto the expressway heading home, but found it was increasingly hard to focus with her fingers moving over him. While handling the F150 on the highway or any other road was normally very easy, it became difficult to concentrate on his driving when every turn he took, and every movement she made, drove him just a little bit crazy. He felt her slender fingers reach inside his open shirt, sliding through dense chest hair. As if that wasn't enough to send him over the edge, Clay nearly drove off the road when one delicate finger searched out and found one very flat male nipple. He sucked in a harsh breath as she toyed with it, scraping her fingernail back and forth until it hardened into a very tight little nub.

"You're going to get us both killed if you don't stop that," he ground out and heard her small laugh tinkle near his ear. The hand that had been resting on her thigh the entire time now playfully squeezed her leg to get her to stop torturing him. Ignoring him, Vi ran the tip of her tongue along the inside shell of his ear and felt his body shudder. In response, he squeezed her leg again and then began inching higher, slipping his fingers beneath the hem of her dress.

Vi was on fire, as she felt his strong fingers trail up the soft inside of her thigh. Of their own volition, her legs parted to give him better access, that part of her that declared she was a woman, aching for his touch.

Ready to oblige, he flicked one finger across the lacy barrier and felt her tremble against his hand, thrilled that his slight touch could send such tiny tremors through her body. Continuing his search, he moved beyond that barrier and although she was incredibly warm and invitingly wet, his fingers stilled. Feeling a tremendous strain of longing grip his body like a vise he discovered the crotch of her panties was extremely narrow.

Was she wearing a thong?

His mind screamed, *Sweet Jesus!* He had to get her home – or somewhere – in a hurry! Clay knew he wasn't going to make it if he didn't do something to calm his racing heartbeat. Breathing deeply he fought for control and tried to keep his mind on his driving. But, what she said next could have gave a weaker man a stroke.

"I bought these for you, you know," she whispered into his ear. He listened intently as she recalled a phone conversation she had with him not so long ago. She recounted how she's teased him into thinking she was wearing a thong; when in reality she had really been wearing serviceable white cotton briefs. On a whim, she told him with a wicked gleam in her eyes, that she'd brought this expensive little, almost there, scrap of lace just to see the look on his face. In the quiet interior of his truck her teasing laughter died, when Clay asked, "Can I have them?"

He spoke softly for a second, Vi wasn't sure if she'd heard him correctly. Quite sure he was joking, she smiled at him and said, "I don't think these will fit you."

For the space of a heartbeat, he turned his head from the road to look at her. His gaze was intent and dead serious when he replied.

"No. I want to keep them, take them off."

If she had any misgivings about what would happen tonight, they completely vanished when he uttered those words. With those few, simple words he expertly conveyed the level of his desire and started a total meltdown within her. The pulsing desire Vi felt coursing through her was a new feeling for her and she was left speechless in the face of it. There was nothing in her past to draw upon, no experience she'd ever had could compare to this moment, so she drew on her own intuition. Slowly, she removed her arm from around his neck and reached under her dress. With her eyes on him, she quickly hooked her fingers into the elastic waistband and pulled the panties from under her bottom, over her knees and down her legs.

Sweet Mother of God! Clay couldn't believe his own eyes. Every time in the past when he'd kissed or touched her, she had come apart in his arms giving him a small glimpse of her very sensuous nature. He believed that it was so well hidden, she probably didn't even know how incredibly sexy she was. What she was doing right now only proved he'd been right. As the panties cleared her ankles, he grabbed them from her hand. With her scent still clinging to them, he brought the tiny scrap of lace to his face, inhaling deeply.

Just then, the slight rain coming down got heavy and within seconds turned into a blinding downpour. Swearing under his breath, Clay shoved the lacy garment into his pocket and tightened his grip on the steering wheel. When the heavens opened up, he had to slow down to a crawl, as visibility lessened and the pouring rain beat heavily on the truck's roof. It hit the windshield so hard and fast, the wiper blades were barely able to keep up.

Suddenly, a white car in front of them jammed on its brakes. To avoid plowing into the rear of this car, Clay immediately applied his brakes and swerved into the next lane. As he gained control of the vehicle, he heard a tiny gasp. Glancing over at her, he saw that she was clutching the door handle with trembling fingers, obviously shaken by their near miss. He made the decision then to pull over, knowing the rain would make it more dangerous to drive any further. As much as he wanted to keep going, he knew he couldn't and reluctantly slowed down to look for a place to stop.

"I'm going to pull over until it slacks off," he told her calmly. Problem was, there was no shoulder on this road to pull off onto. He took the next exit and turned off onto a dark and desolate country road. The only light came from the full moon above and the scattered street lights along this rural road. Clay saw a small gas station ahead on the right and pulled into the deserted parking lot to wait out the storm.

Vi had been scared by how close they came to having an accident. At some point, she had scooted back to her side of the truck's front seat. Clay let the engine run and kept the defogger on as they settled in to wait. The only sound in the cab was the rain pelting on the hood and roof of his truck and their shallow breathing.

For the space of thirty seconds, they both sat on their respective sides of the front seat, staring out the windshield at the falling rain. Then like the lightening streaking the sky, in a flash they met in the middle of that front seat. Simultaneously, they reached for one another in a mix of searching lips, groping hands and impatient fingers. Clay's open mouth settled hungrily over hers, his tongue pouring into her like hot honey filling her mouth. When it did, Vi welcomed it eagerly and avidly returned his kiss.

He felt lightheaded and completely lost as she aggressively claimed his mouth, swirling her tongue around his, running the tip across his front teeth. Apparently, it wasn't enough for her and she drove her tongue deeper, wanting more. She rose up on her knees beside him; bending over and above him slightly, but never breaking contact with his mouth.

Not missing a beat, Clay leaned his head back against the headrest to allow her better access. With strong hands he circled her waist and held on tight as she leaned over him, deepening their kiss further than he thought was possible.

He let out a strangled moan, or was that her? Vi couldn't be sure and knew it didn't matter. The only thing that mattered was this man, and she knew she couldn't wait any longer. To hell with the rain, she had to have him—now. Wanton thoughts permeated her mind as she tried to get even closer to him, trying to press her body nearer but it still wasn't near enough.

In response, his chest expanded and Clay heaved a shuddering breath when her full, sensuous mouth left his to run moist lips across his eyelids, nose and neck. The feel of her moving against him was almost too much. He sent up a plea she wouldn't stop and loosened the arms surrounding her to run his hands down her back and over the soft rise of her sweet backside, massaging the soft flesh of her derriere.

His unhurried caress was lighter than a feather as he laid back passively, seemingly content to let her have her way with him. The heady feeling of control went straight to her head and Vi's movements became more insistent. Clay relaxed his arms around her to revel in her sweet assault until...

Ohmigod! Until she crept closer to him and...moved her right leg over to straddle his lap, settling down into... *His favorite position!*

Without hesitation his arms came back around her, pressing her close as he sought out her mouth with his. For a split second his head swam and Clay broke the kiss to take in a fortifying breath, fighting for the control he felt slipping away. But being this close to her, it was impossible to not keep touching her and he bent his head to run the tip of his tongue down the side of her neck. His lips worked magic down the column of her throat as his hands brushed aside the skinny strap on her dress and peeled down one side of the soft material, he exposed one perfect, pouting breast. He let out a penned up breathe and captured the straining tip between his lips.

Moaning her pleasure she arched into him, giving him better access to that sensitive area. Taking what she offered without qualms, his eager lips latched on pulling it deep into his warm mouth.

From where she sat Vi could feel his arousal and, without thought, she swiveled her hips over him. His hands clenched around the softness of her thighs, spread so invitingly over him. He dug strong fingers into the pliant flesh of her buttocks, kneading and squeezing while she continued her torturous rotation.

Clay released her breast and swore under his breath, desperately trying to control the pulsing need coursing through his body. Wanting to slow down the pace, he inhaled sharply and tightened his hold on Vi, to still her movements. Content to obey for the moment, she sat very still and allowed him to just hold her. Vi lay her head in the warm spot where his shoulder and neck joined, nuzzling him where his shirt lay open, inhaling his male scent.

Clay held her tight against him, as his breathing returned to normal. While they'd been in this position before, it suddenly occurred to him that this time was somewhat different. This time she was wearing a slinky black dress and nothing else underneath. He could actually feel the heat between her thighs sear him through the material of his slacks. This knowledge suddenly galvanized him into action, causing the hands cradling her sweet bottom to move again as he captured her lips in a deep kiss.

Joining the foray, Vi drove her tongue deep into his mouth, moaning her pleasure as his mouth and hands roamed over her. Encouraged, his fingers slid slowly down the back of her shapely thighs, just as she involuntarily began rotating her hips again.

Learning the shape and contour of her soft limbs, his fingers continued moving slowly down the back of her legs. When he reached the back of her knees his downward journey ended and then his knowing fingers trailed upward again, across the front of her soft thighs and slipped under the hem of her dress. Teasing her, he prolonged the caress she longed for in that secret place that became instantly wet and fairly screamed for his touch. Then he was there. Like heat-seeking missiles, his fingers crept through her damp curls and found her moist center. One finger, then two dipped inside moving in and out, in and out. As he kissed her, his expert tongue darted in and out imitating the movement of his deft fingers below.

She whimpered at the pleasure he elicited as he explored, stroked and loved her with his fingers. She spread her legs wider over him and bore down to meet his sweet torture, giving herself up to the magic only he could create. She broke the kiss and, as the fever racing through her took over, Vi threw her head back and closed her eyes against the feel of his fingers inside her.

"Claaaaaay," she cried out, as her breathing quickened to small, shallow pants and her body quivered and shook. "Oh, God…"

He watched her, his own excitement mounting in response to her reckless abandon. And, when he felt her tighten around his fingers, signaling her release, he quickly covered her mouth as she cried out in shattering release.

Moments later he wrapped his arms around her trembling body. Lightly kissing the softness of her exposed neck, Clay settled in staring out the window, idly watching the rain come down. To his disappointment the rain seemed to be coming down now, even harder than before. Wondering how much longer the downpour would last, he held Vi close and mentally calculated how fast he could go when it stopped, without getting a ticket.

While Clay was busy thinking about the two of them rolling around on his king size bed, Vi's train of thought was running in the same direction, only her plans didn't include waiting, or a bed. Although she lay spent in his arms, Vi was not totally immune to the man who held her. Nestled this close to where her body still throbbed, the long, hard ridge of his masculinity created a deep longing within her. It was too much…just the thought of feeling him there started an unbearable ache between her thighs. By silent agreement, sometime during the night the two of them had acknowledged tonight would be the night. When Vi thought about all the weeks and months they'd shared, she began to wonder if the two of them had waited too long. Suddenly, a loud bolt of thunder crackled in the sky overhead, making her eyes fly open. Growing impatient with the rain and unable to wait any longer, she sat up and prepared to take matters in her own hands.

Eyeing the saucy grin she gave him, Clay witnessed the gleam in her eyes but it did not allow him to guess at what she would do next. Surprising him again for the second time that night, he watched her fingers deftly unbuckle his belt. With that done, she boldly slid her hands between his briefs and skin and began unfastening his trousers. Knowing what would happen if she touched him, his brain slowly registered—*I have to stop her….but…but not yet…*

The quiet hiss of his zipper, as it came down, matched his rasping breathe when he felt her cool fingers delve into the dense hair surrounding his sex.

Taking matters in her own hands, Vi reached for him, wrapping her slender fingers around his shaft. He was soft and hard at the same time—like silk and steel she thought—while running her hand down the length of him and then back up again.

Leaning forward, he kissed her quickly, running his tongue over her full bottom lip. Then, just as quickly, he released her mouth to sit back and enjoy the feel her fingers working on him. Vaguely recalling her confession that she'd not been intimate with anyone in quite a while, Clay thought the way she was handling him now showed she knew how to make up for lost time. Who was he to argue if she wanted to do all her catching up in one night? Unable to stand it, he slowly closed his eyes and laid his head back against the headrest, letting her toy with him a little longer. After a while though, his restraint started to fade. Gritting his teeth against the feel of her cool fingers on him he knew he had to make her stop. When he did finally move to stop her, however, Clay came up short, totally unprepared for Vi's third and final surprise of the night.

When it came, his eyes shot open and he sucked in a sharp breath as he felt her unceremoniously reach down and lift his erection totally out of his pants. Then, in slow motion, he watched as she wrapped her small hand firmly around him and deftly maneuver herself down over him. Clay's breath caught in his chest as she placed the tip of his shaft at her moist opening and slid her warm treasure, ever so slowly, down his arousal. Wanting to make sure she would have no regrets, he immediately stiffened and grabbed hold of her hips. "Vi…are…you sure..?" The strangled question came out in a hoarse whisper.

"I can't wait…," she said breathlessly, then chased his lips and covered his mouth in a passionate kiss, giving him all the answer he needed. And then she was there. "Mmmmm…" he heard himself groan as she took all of him inside of her. Squeezing his eyes shut against the feeling of complete enclosure, his mind screamed,

Sweet Jesus!

When she rose slightly and rotated her hips quickly, a moment of clarity returned. He'd waited for this moment for so long, Clay could hardly believe he had to put on the brakes, even for a second, but….

"Baby… baby," his voice came out a rasping whisper. "Wait, wait!"

The intense longing he saw in her searching gaze mirrored his own, as she raised her eyes to his in question. He fumbled in his pants pocket, his hands suddenly clumsy and thick, and nearly shouted in triumph when his fingers felt the sharp edge of the condom package.

Realizing what he needed to do, Vi raised up a bit to allow him to place it on. She watched him, resting her forehead against his and loving him more for remembering something so important, in the heat of the moment. Ironically, she thought, between the two of them he was the one acting like the older, more responsible, adult now.

Then all thoughts vanished, as she felt Clay's strong hands at her hips guiding her back onto him. Simultaneously, they let out a collective sigh when their bodies were joined once again as an enormous feeling of completeness washed over the two of them. Then, they started to move in unison. After waiting so long, their coupling was like an explosive substance ignited by too much heat threatening to send them both, collectively, up in flames.

Sliding his hands up and down her spinal cord, Clay frantically shoved her dress down further, exposing both her shoulders. Yanking down the remaining thin strap on her dress, he pushed it aside, exposing all of her. As she rose up over him again he held her by the waist and latched onto her breast. He sucked and drew on her hungrily as her hips came down repeatedly to meet his upward thrust, matching him stroke for stroke.

He was liquid heat, pulsing and hard, while she was slick, tight and all-consuming. As she rocked her hips over him setting a slow, sliding pace, he rose up to take as much as he gave and all the wanting and yearning they'd played at for weeks and months came to this one cataclysmic moment.

Under heavy lids Clay opened his eyes a fraction, locking his gaze with hers as they strained against one another, broaching the point of no return. When she threw back her head, exposing the elegant column of her neck, he couldn't resist tasting her quickening pulse with his tongue. She moved over him in smooth, feline grace, rocking and rotating with an urgency that threatened to snap what little control he had left. Gritting his teeth, Clay's fingers dug into her flesh as he tried to hold back, waiting for her to catch up. He didn't have long to wait before he felt her inner muscles contract around him, signaling her release. She cried his name as her body began to quake and she toppled over the edge. Her instant release triggered his. Unlike anything he'd ever felt before, it sent him catapulting head first, over the top, right after her.

Still embedded inside her, they came back to earth breathless and gasping for air. Clay latched onto her mouth, slowly imprisoning her lips in a tender, heart-stopping kiss. Several heated seconds later they slowly disengaged, each feeling the loss and realizing that sometime during the maelstrom the rainstorm had turned into a light sprinkle. Clay grabbed her trembling hand and brought it to his lips then gently squeezed it in anticipation. As Vi settled back into the passenger seat, he put the truck in gear and punched the accelerator. Anxious to get there, he sped up knowing he would commit several moving violations on the way to his place.

CHAPTER
THIRTY-TWO

Vi sat in the middle of his bed, watching him shed his clothes like a bad habit. Although she'd seen him bare-chested before, nothing could have prepared her for this moment. He was truly magnificent. As he moved, she watched the powerful play of muscles in his arms and legs while he worked off the last of his clothing. Completely fascinated by the fine, dark hair covering those muscular limbs and the even darker, dense fur surrounding his manhood, her eyes were glued to him. He stood proud, erect and more than ready and suddenly her throat went dry as her eyes latched onto that part of him... the size of him. *Lord above!*

Uncertain how much time had passed, she became aware he was watching her watching him when her gaze traveled up the length of his body and their eyes met.

Clay walked over, placed one knee on the bed and reached for her. Placing his hands on both her shoulders, he whispered in a teasing tone. "Babe, you have on way too many clothes." His fingers grabbed hold of the thin straps of her dress, as he said this, and began deftly brush aside. When she felt him begin to tug her dress further down, Vi experienced a moment of panic. Suddenly, very conscious of her body she began to wonder what Clay would think when he saw her fully nude. Her body was, after all, the body of a forty-four year-old woman; one who had given birth to three children. She drew in a sharp breath and quickly covered the loving hands that tugged at her dress. "Can we turn off the light first?" she inquired, while pulling the straps of her dress back over her shoulders.

Uncertain he'd heard her correctly, Clay's hand stilled as he looked down at her. With a note of teasing disbelief in his voice, he asked, "What's this? You can't possibly be shy, not after the *ride* we just took in my truck." After saying this, however, he noticed her teeth nervously worrying her bottom lip and quickly changed his tone. Realizing there really was something bothering her, Clay spoke softly to try and get to the bottom of her discomfort. "Vi, honey, I'm sorry. Tell me what's wrong."

"Nothing's wrong, it's just that I'm not..."

"Not what? Leave the light on, baby. I want to see you," he stated simply.

"No," she said her voiced edged with panic. "Clay, I'm not twenty or thirty years old anymore," she said plainly. "I've had three kids and," she hesitated here. "I don't want you to see me."

The real anxiety he heard in her voice, surprised him. He searched her face for a time, trying to ascertain if she was truly serious. Clearly, the woman had no idea how she appealed to him, how she would appeal to any man. He took a lengthy breath and searched his mind for a way to get through to her.

"You don't get it, do you?" Not waiting for a response to his rhetorical question, he continued. "You can't see how exquisite you are, can you? Vi, you're beautiful, naturally perfect in a way most women try hard to be but never achieve." He held both her hands in a tight grip before reminding her, "I've told you before, I'm not looking for some young, skinny thing. I want someone I can hold onto, softness I can sink into."

Wanting to ensure she understood this time and never doubted her appeal ever again, he declared earnestly. "Vi, I'm crazy about you. I love your body and I want you so bad right now. I can't believe you don't know it." Thinking quickly, he suddenly stood up, pulling her up with him off the bed. "C'mere," he said and led her across the room.

When they arrived at his place earlier, the two of them had gotten out of his truck and scampered up the stairs to his apartment both breathless and anxious to be in each others arms. When they'd made their way to his bedroom her attention had been focused on Clay and not the room itself. As he pulled her up and led her from the bed now, she had a chance to look around the room. It was clean, orderly and no nonsense, just like the man. Its white walls were relieved by the vibrant hues in the soft comforter covering his bed and the matching curtains and sheets. The room had a masculine feel to it, like the rest of his apartment, and the earth tone bedding fit in well, complementing the dark furnishings. The four-poster, king size bed was the most prominent piece of furniture in the room and in the corner sat a handsome cherry wood, matching bureau. The bureau had a wide mirror on top with playful angels engraved in the dark wood frame surrounding it. It was this bureau that he led her to now, standing behind her as he stood her in front of the mirror. He placed both his hands on her shoulders and softly stroked her bare arms as his intense gaze held hers in their combined reflection in the mirror.

"Vi, I want you so much. Touching you, learning what makes you tremble has made me love your body and anticipate this moment for so long." As he spoke these words his fingers lightly traced the line of her collar bone before dipping lower to cover her breasts. Her breath hissed between her teeth when he pressed a kiss behind her ear, then nipped at the lobe playfully as his hands unfastened the back of her dress. A brush of his hand slipped it off her shoulders and a second later it lay in a soft, black pool around her hips.

Vi stood there trembling with need and the terrible fear that he wouldn't be pleased by what he had unveiled. But, he didn't look, so she needn't have worried. Instead he let his hands discover her. His hands moved lightly, almost casually, brushing very gentle fingertips across the hard, sensitive pinpoints of her nipples before moving lower to glide over her rib cage. A shiver ran through her as he placed a soft kiss to the sensitive area just below her ear and whispered, "I felt it for the first time that day in my bathroom. When you put your arms around me and laid your hands on me I almost lost it. When you touched me that day Vi, you branded me forever and the way I feel about you now is unlike anything I've ever felt for any other woman I've ever known."

His lips nuzzled her ear as his hands idly traced the angles of her shoulder blades. Then he filled his hands with her breasts, kneading them and savoring their weight, while his tongue tested her quickening pulse. She moaned in response and felt the pads of his thumbs brush across the swollen crests.

Pausing, he dipped his head to kiss her neck, before raising his eyes to meet hers in their reflection once again. "Do you have any idea how much I want you now?"

Breathing heavily, she shook her head, unable to formulate any verbal response.

"Well, I do, desperately," he assured her. "I fought it at first. Hell, at first I felt like a pervert wanting you the way I did. And then I thought I was experiencing some type of misplaced grief. Trying to fight the way I felt about you nearly drove me insane."

Kneading her softness, his hands stilled and held her breasts for a moment, cupped in the palms of his hands. He swept a fingernail idly across the tips, thinking back on the time leading up to this moment. "Do you remember the night I took you to the movies?" he paused, waiting until she nodded her head. "That night was pure torture. Remember those loose, khaki shorts you wore?"

Again she nodded. Talk about torture, she thought he was doing a pretty good job as his fingertips slowly circled her aureoles, making the tips harden and ache. His touch rendered her speechless and made it very difficult to concentrate on what he was saying.

In the mirror he watched the effect his touch was having on her and it buoyed his confidence. Starting to feel like he was getting through to her, Clayton continued to talk softly near her ear. "You have no idea what a distraction your legs were in those shorts. I sat through that entire movie but I couldn't tell you one detail about it because I spent half the night wanting to run my hands up those loose shorts."

She watched him in the mirror as his fingers stroked her, over and over again, circling the hard, chocolate centers. Vi closed her eyes as he continued to toy with her, the sensation his hands created made her body sway against him. Continuing his verbal seduction, he said in a hoarse murmur, "You're so damn beautiful." Speaking softly and very close to her ear he watched her eyes close and when he felt her body sway slightly under his ministrations, it encouraged him further.

Vi's eyes flew open when the hands cupping her breasts slide lower, pushing her dress further down around her hips. He paused, watching along with her their combined reflection in the mirror as his hands slid over her ribs and dipped inside her navel. "Vi....I've made love to you a thousand times in my mind," his voice was almost inaudible near her ear. Then, in one swift move, he hooked his fingers inside the dress bunched at her waist and pushed it over her hips. It swept down her legs and dropped to the floor at her feet. Having discarded her panties hours ago in the truck, Vi now stood before the mirror, completely naked.

She felt his arousal nestled in between the natural curve of her backside, and a burning desire pooled low in her belly as she watched his wide hand inch lower toward her aching center.

Clay's next words were not planned, but they slipped past his lips nonetheless. "I love you Vi, I do," he whispered and immediately caught the outer shell of her ear lightly in his teeth, licking his way around its delicate edge before continuing. "I don't know if you're ready to hear that, but it is what it is." She felt him nip lightly at the soft, sensitive skin below her earlobe. "You're everything I could ever want and more than I thought I could ever have."

His words tore at her heart and Vi found herself struggling to respond. "Clay, I..."

"Shhh....I don't want you to say anything you're not ready to say." His lips drew on the slender curve of her neck, his tongue leaving a wet path down to her shoulder. When he felt her tremble in his arms, he used one hand to lightly caress her breast, while the other rested casually low on her belly.

Her knees wouldn't hold her, and Vi leaned back against him for support. "Clay, please..."

"Please what, baby?" he muttered against her throat, but knew exactly what she wanted because his hand moved lower, down her abdomen, until his fingers were sliding through soft, damp curls, then deeper still into the very center of the fiery ache burning inside her.

She gasped his name when his fingers began to move in her, nestling in her dampness and slipping past her gentle folds. Arching her back, Vi instinctively ground her buttocks against the hard ridge of his arousal. When she did this, his other hand left her breast and pinned her to him as his fingers danced inside her, urging her to a higher plane of arousal. He watched her rock against his hand, straining toward the pleasure that was building.

"Clay, please…please…Clay…oh yes…" She cried out his name again and again as the heat of her climax coursed wildly through her.

Clay watched her sensual climb and felt her shattering release in every fiber of his being. When her knees buckled from her violent meltdown, he caught her limp body and carried her across the room. He swept away the covers, then quickly tumbled down with her to the mattress.

Vi was overwhelmed. It felt like his hands were everywhere at once, around her, inside her. He left her briefly to sheath himself in a condom, then returned quickly and slid one knee between her legs. Vi's legs rose and she opened to him, feeling his hand skim her thighs, encouraging her to fold her legs around torso. She closed her eyes and arched upward, but he only hovered above her, withholding the pleasure she wanted now more than anything in her life. Overcome with need, she cried out his name as he settled between her thighs, still holding back. "Now Clay…now…please…"

"Look at me Vi," he commanded. "Look at me." His voice was a harsh rumble near her ear, husky with desire but firm. "I want to see your face, your eyes…" She slowly opened her eyes and when she did, the heated invitation Clay saw there trapped the air in his lungs.

"Baby, please…" she cried breathlessly. Taking matters into her own hands, she ran her hand impatiently down his body, seeking his manhood. Finding it, she wrapped her fingers around him and guided him to her, into her. Although she knew it was coming, her breath came in a long, hoarse moan as he filled her slowly and fully.

He held very still within her for what seemed like an eternity, drinking in the expression of ecstasy on her face, and then, mercifully, he began to move. Slowly at first, then he picked up speed, in there, using powerful thrusts. He moved inside, her almost pulling out, and then his thrusts came faster and harder and oh so demanding. She couldn't breathe, couldn't think. She could only feel, and the feelings were exquisite, overwhelming.

"Ohhh, Clay…Clay" she cried as the walls of her body tightened around him, wanting him there. Caught up in the urgency of their coupling, she raised her legs higher to encircle his hips and caught his rhythm, matching each stroke. The pleasure was so intense it bordered on pain, pulling at them catching them both unaware. It built to a crescendo with every thrust he took until the pleasure exploded inside her. Vi soared, up and over the peak she climbed and then slowly, very slowly, they slid down the other side.

Clay swallowed her hoarse cry of ecstasy with a deep, wet kiss as his own climax rocked him, sending him over the brink directly behind her. Regaining his sanity and gasping for air, he slipped out of her and rolled onto his back, taking her with him. He gathered her in his arms and they lay spent, breathing heavily with their limbs still entwined. When he was capable of speaking again, he raised his head and captured her lips in a lingeringly tender kiss. "Baby, stay with me tonight."

The hushed urgency in his plea made something blossom within her. "I, I can't…" she started. But before she could make any excuses, he said, "Yes you can. You said Tony was spending the night with Clarence, right?" He hesitated then added, "Stay…please."

When she looked at him, the undisguised love she saw swimming in the depths of his chocolate brown eyes made it impossible to say no. "Okay, but I have to call Tony and tell him good night."

He placed a quick kiss on her lips, unable to hide the visible relief that washed over him. "Okay, but hurry back," he said, playfully swatting her naked backside as she left the bed.

Vi found her purse on the sofa and pulled out her cell phone. As she punched in Clarence's number, she realized she'd forgotten to charge her cell phone. As an afterthought, she yelled to Clay in the next room, "Is it okay to leave your number with Clarence in case of an emergency?"

"Do whatever you need to do, sweet cheeks, just hurry back," he called to her from the bedroom. He listened to her in the next room, talking faintly to Clarence on the phone. Satisfied, he folded his arms behind his head. A smile played across his lips as he stared up at the ceiling, waiting for her and feeling like a million bucks.

Janae sat in Renee's car looking out the passenger side window, feeling like death warmed over and served up cold. Somehow she'd caught the virus sweeping her campus for the past few weeks. When she didn't catch it the first week like everyone else, Janae had started to feel like she was immune. Then it hit her—at the worst possible time. Mid–term exams were scheduled this week and the next, and Janae and her friend Renee had already made plans to drive home right after their last exam on Monday. However, when Professor Connor came down with the virus and moved his biology test to this Friday, instead of the following Monday, Janae saw this as a perfect opportunity to go home early and get some rest. After she and Renee finished their test late Friday afternoon, both girls hit their dorm room to pack a few things. By six o'clock they were in the car and on the road, just in time to catch the tail end of Friday rush hour traffic, which made their four-hour drive a whole lot longer.

Although she called home a couple of times to let her mom know they'd be getting in a few days early, Janae got the answering machine each time. Not bothering to leave a message, she tucked her cell phone back into her purse, laid her head against the passenger door window, and fell asleep. The house was dark when Renee pulled into the driveway, but Janae still didn't think that was unusual. She opened the car door and got out, thinking her mom and Tony were probably already asleep.

"Are you sure your Mom's home," Renee asked peering out the front windshield at the darkened house.

"Yeah, it's after one in the morning. They're probably asleep."

Renee called out to her as she backed slowly out of the driveway. "Okay, feel better. And, don't forget to call me on Monday so we can do something." Janae stood watching her friend drive away. Then with her suitcase in hand, she turned around to face the dark house. Using her key, she let herself in and placed her bag on the floor in the foyer. Not wanting to wake anyone, she quietly made her way to the kitchen to find some aspirin and get a cup of juice.

An hour later, she was still sitting at the kitchen table. After searching the house and finding no one home, Janae sat a while debating if she should call anyone at this hour. Finally, she decided to call Tony's cell phone. The grogginess in her brother's voice made it hard to understand him at first and it was obvious to her she'd waken him up from a sound sleep.

"Where are you?"

"Janae? Do you know what time it is?"

"Yes, I do butthead. I got home a little while ago and no one is home," she said to him, a bit annoyed. "So, where are you?"   '

"I'm at Grandpa's."

Relieved to know that everyone was okay, Janae asked him, "Is Mom there too?"

"No."

"No?"

"No."

"Well, where is she? Is she okay?"

Tony had just about gotten the cobwebs out of his eyes and thought to ask a question of his own. "Janae, why aren't you at school, is everything alright?"

"I'm fine, everything's okay. I just came home early because I caught some kind of bug at school."

"Oh," was all he said.

"So!" She said to Tony in exasperation. "Where's Mom?"

"Oh…umm..…she and Clay went out tonight."

After he told her Grandpa would be dropping him off tomorrow afternoon, Janae hung up and dialed her mother's cell phone. She repeated that action at least ten times over the next hour and each time the only thing she received was Vi's voice mail. Finally she gave up, deciding one of two things had happened. If she were hurt, Clay would know to call someone so either her battery was dead or she just wasn't answering the phone. Suddenly very tired, Janae left the kitchen and walked into the living room to lie down on the sofa.

Sunlight peeked through the closed bedroom blinds, brightening the walls and causing Vi to stir. She stretched in her sleep like a satisfied kitten languishing in the warm afternoon sun. She opened her eyes a fraction, squinting against the bright light, and felt a bone-deep satiation, acknowledging the fact she hadn't felt this rested or this relaxed in years.

Glancing around the room briefly, she was momentarily confused about where she was. When she opened her eyes a bit wider and scanned the room again, she instantly realized where she was and whose bed she'd slept in.

The previous night came rushing back to her as she recalled all the sensuous memories and the countless times and ways in which she and Clay had made love. Recollecting it made Vi's body start to tingle from head to toe. She shifted slightly and felt his warm body close behind her, solid and strong and seemingly wrapped all around her. One muscular forearm was draped under her raised arm, cupping one breast possessively, while the other held her tight around the waist. She felt him cradle her softness within his large palm, while his nimble fingers busily stroked the hardened crest of her nipple. The sensation created a sharp tingle, where he touched, that shot straight to the very core of her. Vi turned over to face him, suddenly realizing it was probably his fondling fingers that woke her up in the first place.

When she turned to face him, Clay rose up and leaned on one elbow to watch her head turn on the pillow. From this position he could look down on her, and so he did, searching her eyes from his higher vantage point. A radiant smile lit her face as she turned to face him, and he couldn't help smiling back feeling the simplicity of her beauty embed itself deep within his heart. He drank in her lovely face, flushed from sleep and satiated from the workout he'd given her body late into the night. In her sleep, the sheet had slipped a notch and left her perfect breasts exposed for his eyes only. Gazing down at her, Clay sent up a silent prayer, wishing he could wake up like this every day for the rest of his life.

When she turned toward him, Vi saw that he lay on his side with the sheet riding low on his torso. His arm was bent at the elbow and his head was propped up on one hand, as he looked down on her. Her happy, sated eyes met his and instantly the intensity she saw there turned brooding in a matter of seconds. Vi's smile slipped a notch in the face of this sudden mood change and his very serious demeanor.

Clay saw her smile fade and confusion fill her eyes. There was no way for her to know that he'd been awake for hours, watching her sleep with his mind full of troubling thoughts. There was no way for her to guess at the overwhelming amount of new feelings rushing through him. He had plenty of time this morning to think long and hard about the two of them, and shortly before sunrise he'd come up with the only plausible solution. Trying to erase the apprehension and confusion in her eyes, Clay silently held her gaze and bent his head before capturing her lips in a bittersweet kiss. When he lifted his head, Vi saw that the serious intent was gone from his eyes, replaced with a tenderness that took her breath away and instantly made her feel better.

She was even more beautiful in the light of day, he thought. Her curly, auburn locks lay tousled against the whiteness of his pillowcase and her kiss-swollen lips beckoned him, but he tamped down the urge to devour them again. Although he had definite plans to sink himself deep into her sleep-warmed body before he let her leave this bed, Clay fought the desire coursing through him. Just thinking about that made him harden, and he shook himself slightly, knowing first that they needed to talk.

"Good morning, Gorgeous," he murmured softly, with a sexy grin tilting the side of his mouth. He bent his head and lightly brushed her lips, then pulled her close and slowly gathered her in his arms.

Beneath her ear, his heartbeat was strong and sure and his hard body felt solid and warm. Vi snuggled against him and spread her fingers through the dense hair covering his chest. After a time, she felt his fingers snake into her hair and closed her eyes as his long fingers massaged her scalp, lulling her back to sleep. Suddenly, those fingers stilled and Vi became aware of the tension in the gentle arms surrounding her. Although he didn't say anything right away, she could sense there was something on his mind. She waited, idly running her fingers across his chest, silently encouraging him to share what was troubling him.

While Vi patiently waited for him to open up to her, she suffered a brief moment of panic. What if he had regrets about last night? What if she had been lacking in some way, she thought in despair? Being out of the loop for so long, she thought it was a definite possibility that she may not have matched up to the other women he'd been with. What if, her mind wandered frantically, he decided all those heated encounters they'd shared didn't quite live up to the real thing. Worrying her bottom lip, she turned it over and over in her mind. Last night she'd been certain he shared the mutual explosion that erupted each time they came together. But, in the light of day she started to have serious doubts.

Clay sighed heavily, the movement expanding his chest and interrupting her troubled thoughts. With her head lying near his heart, Vi felt his anxiety and raised her eyes to look at him. She propped her chin on his furry chest and stared at him, waiting for him to say whatever it was and having the distinct feeling it couldn't be anything good. Clayton returned her gaze, searching her eyes with such intensity that Vi's fears mounted with every second that ticked by. Finally, he spoke into the tense silence surrounding them, and miraculously banished all her doubts and fears.

"I don't know how to say this Vi, except to just say it," he started tentatively, letting her hang by a thread as several seconds ticked by before he continued. "Vi, I want you here every day."

Visibly relieved the other shoe hadn't dropped, she smiled up at him in agreement. "I know, Baby, I understand how you feel. After last night I couldn't imagine not being with you again either."

"No," he said a bit harsher than he'd intended. "You don't understand. I want you here….in this bed every day." His fingers dug into the pillow under her head for emphasize. "I want to wake up beside you every morning and sleep near you every night."

Her eyes widened, huge as saucers and bore into him as she struggled to comprehend what he was saying. Clay reached out to cradle her face in both his hands and laid his heart bare. "Marry me Vi." With a sense of urgency, he added in a rush, "Not today, not tomorrow, but someday soon I want to marry you."

Clay watched her face as the meaning of what he'd just said finally sunk in. The intensity in her eyes, as his gaze locked with hers, touched something deep within him. Inwardly he was glad to clear his mind and plainly state what it was he wanted. He only hoped he hadn't scared her away by saying too much. The most he could hope for, he reasoned, was that she would at least think about it. God, he hoped she would. Guessing he'd said enough for one morning, Clay placed a chaste kiss on her lips and released her. Hoping to break the tense silence in the room, he tossed her a sexy, lopsided grin, before adding, "I'm not asking you to say 'Yes' right now. I just wanted you to marinate on that for a while. Okay?"

He lifted his left brow a fraction, indicating he sought some type of acknowledgement. Unsure what to say and shocked to her toes, Vi was totally speechless. She did the only thing she was capable of and gave a slight nod of her head.

"Good," he said, apparently satisfied with that response. "Now, why don't you hit the shower while I fix breakfast?" The teasing light was back in his eyes and Vi, coward that she was, was eternally grateful to see it. She was definitely not ready to discuss the things he'd just laid on her this morning.

On impulse, Clayton gave her exposed rump a playful slap to get her moving. His idea of a joke instantly grabbed her attention and made her shriek, "Ouch."

Thinking about getting up to take a shower made her suddenly conscious of the fact she lay practically on top of him, completely naked. Rubbing her rump, Vi suffered a moment's embarrassment, which was totally ridiculous considering what they'd done last night. Even so, she quickly rolled off him, simultaneously grabbing the bed cover to wrap around herself.

Vi soon found out she was the only one in the room concerned about modesty. Apparently very comfortable with his nudity, Clayton rose from the bed with fluid, panther-like grace. Hell, he should be comfortable she thought—with the physique he possessed, why not run around naked? He was built like a strong, ancient warrior prince and his café-mocha colored body was dusted lightly with much darker hair over a multitude of rippling muscles and sinew.

When he picked up a pair of jeans lying on a chair and bent over to pull them on, Clayton glanced up and caught Vi staring at him. Holding the sheet around her body like that, he knew she was totally unaware of how sensuous she looked standing there. She was utterly breathtaking, and the heat embedded in her gaze as she watched him was almost his undoing. The sudden urge to walk over and whip that sheet off and jump back into bed with her was extremely tempting. He fought the urge; as much as he relished making love to her all day long, he realized they needed to get moving. Remember Vi promising Tony she'd be home by noon last night, Clay wanted to make sure she was there when he got home.

Although they did need to get moving to get her home in time, Clay decided to toy with her a bit, and dropped the pants he was about to put on to the floor. Turning his back to her, he strode naked across the room and laughingly tossed over his shoulder as he left the room. "If you don't stop gawking at my assets, I'm gonna' cancel breakfast and come over there, throw your legs up and seek sustenance elsewhere."

On that note, he strutted out of the room giving her a birds-eye-view of his saucy backside. Behind him, he heard her shriek and ducked just in time as a pillow sailed past his head.

Breakfast turned into a sensuous affair. The melon slices she fed him, dripped juice all over the place. Luckily, Vi's quick tongue and deft fingers did an excellent job of cleaning up the mess. In turn Clay latched onto her mouth, while piling jelly on a piece of toast. Somehow, jelly accidentally found its way onto certain parts of her anatomy. Always the obliging host, he cleaned all those areas spic and spotless, without lifting a finger. An hour later they came together again in the shower. Taking her under the warm spray, Vi experienced a blinding release with all her limbs wrapped tightly around him. Afterwards they showered again—separately this time—and got dressed so Clay could take her home.

It was a little after eleven thirty when they pulled into Vi's driveway. Reluctant to bring their time together to an end, they didn't get out of his truck right away. Clay reached across the front seat, drawing Vi closer and kissed her sweet and long before getting out. She watched him quickly walk around the front of the truck and open her door. Taking her hand as she got out, he wrapped his arm around her and the two of them walked arm in arm up the driveway. Clay had graciously loaned Vi one of his oversized shirts and an old pair of running shorts that, thank God for elastic waistbands, managed to fit her tiny waist. Immensely happy, Vi carried her black dress over one arm and the black, high heels in her hand.

CHAPTER

THIRTY-FOUR

Janae was waiting as they came through the front door. "Mom, where have you been all night?"

Frozen into silence, Vi stared at her daughter in shock and said the first thing that came to mind. "Janae, honey... I... I thought you weren't coming home until next week."

"Obviously," she shot back at Vi with a sneer. "Otherwise, you wouldn't have spent the night with him."   Janae's chin came up defiantly as she bit out this last part, indicating Clayton. Suffused with anger, she chose not to look at him or address him directly. All her fury and indignation was focused totally on her mother.

Still holding Vi's hand, Clayton felt her begin to tremble under Janae's admonishing glare.

"Janae, I can explain."

Janae raised her voice, cutting Vi off, the anger boiling over within her, coming quickly to a head. "I came home last night because I got sick at school. It's a good thing I did, too." The reproach in her tone cut Vi like a knife.   On a roll, her voice rose even higher, dripping with censure, as she continued to spit out accusations.   "If I hadn't come home now, I wouldn't have caught you sneaking around with this man, making a fool of yourself."

Although Janae's hurtful words hit Vi like a slap in the face, she withstood the verbal assault without comment.   Surprisingly, it was her motherly instincts that prompted the next words she uttered.   "Hon, are you sick? Let me call the doctor's emergency number," Vi said, moving to touch her daughter, checking for fever.

When Vi tried to place her hand on Janae's forehead in an age-old nurturing action of mothers everywhere, Janae evaded her touch.

Silent up until now, Clayton saw tears pool in Vi's eyes when Janae shrank away from her.   Stepping in between Vi and her daughter, Clayton turned to address Janae directly. "Look Janae, I know you're upset, but you shouldn't talk to your mother like that."

The tentative hold Janae had on her temper snapped entirely when he dared to speak to her about what was right and wrong.   For the first time since they'd both came in the door, Janae turned all her anger toward him. "You," she shouted, "don't say anything to me. I don't want to talk to you. You don't even belong here."

Clay stood strong and silent in the face of her rage. Unfortunately, his calm demeanor only seemed to anger Janae further.

Ignoring Clayton, Janae looked over his shoulder and cast a critical eye at her mother, pinning her down before accusing, "I can't believe this, Mom….you're old enough to be this…this man's mother for Christ sake!"

Clay glanced over his shoulder at Vi and saw how each demeaning remark Janae threw at her, made Vi flinch like she'd been struck by a whip. Inwardly, his own temper rose and bubbled dangerously close to the surface. Trying very hard to deal calmly with this and control his temper, Clay turned to Janae and tried to reason with her again. "Janae, what your mother and I do is our business, it doesn't concern anyone else."

Refusing to meet his eyes or listen to anything he had to say, Janae turned a deaf ear on his opinion and told him emphatically, "I told you, I'm not talking to you." Suddenly, Janae remembered how she'd thrown herself at this man, and how humiliated she'd felt when he rejected her. The rage coursing through her mixed with this simmering humiliation made her lash out at him. "So," she started in on him. "I get it now; this is who you've been seeing. You must be hopelessly desperate or completely blind…"

She didn't get any further before Clay reached out and grabbed her arm, startling her into silence. Janae struggled to free her arm from his strong, unyielding grip. Although his hold was not painful, just the thought of his hands on her was unbearable. Janae screamed at the top of her lungs, "Get your hands off me you… you…"

Vi watched Clay grab hold of Janae, and then just as quickly release her. She also saw a muscle in his jaw begin to bunch, as he clenched his jaw tight, trying to tamp down his anger.

Clay shook himself and counted to ten to clear his head. Obviously not thinking, he had lightly grabbed Janae's arm to get her to calm down. His good intentions only seemed to infuriate her more. Fortunately, he'd come to his senses and released her just as quickly. He did experience for the briefest of seconds an uncontrollable urge to take the girl across his knee, and spank her like a five year old, which was exactly how she was acting.

Realizing his presence here was only making matters worse, Vi turned to Clayton and pleaded with him. "Clay, I think you should leave."

"No, I won't leave you like this."

"I can handle this, really. Please, go," she pleaded.

Janae, sickened by this tender exchange, stared at the two of them in disbelief. Finally, she announced to them both, "Don't bother leaving on my account. I'm leaving."

Vi looked from Clayton to her daughter, staring at her wide-eyed in disbelief. Suddenly, she found herself now pleading with her daughter. "Janae, Honey where are you going? This is your home. Let me take care of you."

"I can't stay here. I'm going to Aunt Cynthia's for the remainder of my time off." As if on cue, a taxi pulled up out front and beeped its horn.

Clayton and Vi glanced out the open front door and saw the cab waiting outside in front of the house. Janae took this opportunity to collect her bag and brush past them both, making her way quickly out the front door.

Vi watched her pick up the bag and walk out, having no idea the bag had sat by the front door all night, while Janae waited for her to come home. "Janae, don't go," she called after her daughter, to no avail. Feeling helpless, Vi stood at the screen door, watching the taxi take Janae away. Clay came up behind her and placed his hands on her shoulders and gently turned her around. She went willingly into his open arms and began to cry. "Ohmigod, Clay what have I done? What have I done?" she sobbed into his chest.

The despair in her voice clutched at his heart. Unsure what to do, he held her tight and stroked her hair trying to comfort her. "Vi, it's going to be okay. She'll calm down, you'll see."

After an unknown amount of time, he started to feel a mounting panic, when nothing he said or did seemed to comfort her. After her tears dried up, she pushed at his chest lightly and said very quietly, "I'm going to lie down for a while." The solemn eyes she turned up to him were red and swollen from crying and small hiccups racked her slender frame. "Can you call Clarence for me and tell him I'll pick Tony up later tonight."

"Sure," he said, watching her go silently up the stairs. When the door closed upstairs, he immediately went to the downstairs bathroom, opened the medicine cabinet and found a bottle of aspirin. Leaving the bathroom, he retraced his steps and walked into the kitchen. Clay turned on the faucet and filled a glass with water as he punched in the speed dial number for Clarence. After he hung up with Clarence, Clayton went up to her bedroom, taking the stairs two at a time.

It was a very feminine room, its peach-colored walls blended nicely with the floral comforter and matching curtains. Her vanity and night tables had lace coverings on top and the smell of roses permeated the air. He saw all this from the half-open door, not bothering to knock he pushed the door all the way open and came inside the room.

She lay on her side, curled in a protective fetal position. Helpless didn't begin to explain the way he felt, as he sat down on the edge of the bed beside her. Clay reached out and smoothed her hair from her face and helped Vi sit up. She looked drained and completely exhausted, but she took the aspirin he offered and drank the water. When he kissed her lightly on the forehead, she smiled faintly and lay back down, instantly closing her eyes. He sat there a while on the edge of her bed, watching her and idly rubbing her back feeling deeply troubled by all this. Besides the obvious worries over their situation, he was much more disturbed for a reason he couldn't quite discern. She covered his hand where it rested on her bed, which was the only movement she made to let him know she hadn't fallen asleep, and asked quietly. "Did you reach Clarence for me?"

"Yes," he said, watching her still form, the only other movement she made was her slow and rhythmic breathing. She looked bone tired and although he knew she needed rest, he thought it might be best to stay and keep an eye on her. "Vi, I can stay here with you Baby. Just say the word."

She lifted her eyes to his and said with a weary look. "No, you go on. Go to work. I'll be fine, really. Suddenly I've got a huge headache and all I want to do right now is sleep, okay?"

Not sure what to say, he repeated, "I called Clarence for you, okay?

"Thanks," she told him. "Why don't you go ahead and go. I'll pick Tony up later and call you afterwards," she told him reassuringly.

Clay made her promise to call him if she needed him. With nothing left to say, he got up to leave, taking one final look at her before closing the bedroom door. He came downstairs slowly, making sure to lock up, and reluctantly left her house. He couldn't explain it, but he had a bad feeling in the pit of his stomach about all this. His worst fears grew on the drive home and continued to mount while he was on duty later that evening. He'd tried to call her at the station when he arrived at work and continued to try and reach her while he was on duty. Each time, her voice mail picked up.

After Clay left, the phone kept ringing. Vi tried to get some sleep, but the constant ringing made that all but impossible. She lay there for a while trying to sleep, dozing off only to wake up again and again. Finally, she swung her legs over the side of the bed, got up and went downstairs. Fast forwarding through her messages, Vi saw Clayton had called five times, and Cynthia had called three. She caught bits and pieces of her sister's messages before erasing each one. Cynthia's voice came through loud and clear as she listened to the first one.

"Vi, Janae's beside herself. I'm coming over there. Call me."

Vi hit the erase button then the second message came on.

"Vi, have you lost your mind? That man is half your age."

When she got to the third one, Vi instantly deleted it, refusing to listen to any more. Then she picked up the phone and dialed Clarence.

"Vi, are you okay?" Clarence's voice was filled with concern but, to Vi's relief, there was no trace of judgment or reprimand in his tone. Hearing the concern in her father-in-law's voice made Vi feel somewhat better. Her spirits soared when Clarence told her, "Your sister called me all in a snit about something. But, I told her she'd have to deal with me if she came over there harassing you."

Vi's heart felt lighter, hearing Clarence take up for her without fully knowing the details, and it did wonders for her frame of mind. "I love you Clarence Simpson, you are my lifesaver. I'm supposed to pick Tony up later, but would you be a dear and bring him home for me later tonight?"

Clarence assured her bringing his grandson home later would not be a problem and offered to keep him another night if she needed him to. She thanked him but told him later tonight would be fine.

"Of course, Dear. You know you don't even have to ask. Do you need me to come over?"

"No," she said interrupting him. "That's not necessary. I've just developed a killer migraine that won't go away."

She stayed on the phone a few more minutes, assuring Clarence she would be alright and setting a time for him to bring Tony home later. After she hung up, Vi grabbed up her car keys and left the house.

Much later that night, Tony called his grandfather. "Grandpa, something is wrong with Mom. She got home twenty minutes after you dropped me off and she's been up in her room ever since. She's been crying the whole time, Grandpa."

Clarence shifted in his recliner and pointed the remote at the television to lower the volume. "Son, I don't know everything that's going on, but your Aunt Cynthia's on the rampage about your mom going out with Clayton."

"I don't understand Grandpa," Tony told his Grandfather. "Clay is cool. I mean, since he's been around, Mom's smiling more. Why would Aunt Cynthia be upset?"

"I don't know son. Your aunt is always in others people's business and she doesn't believe they should be dating at all." Changing the subject Clarence asked Tony why he thought something was wrong with Vi.

"She told me to order us a pizza with anything I wanted on it."

"So?" Clarence prompted.

"So, she gave me money and said to let the driver keep the change," he explained to Clarence. "Mom hates pizza, Grandpa, and when I pulled out the money she gave me to pay the pizza guy, it was a fifty dollar bill. Grandpa, the pizza cost eleven dollars and Mom told me to give him a thirty-nine dollar tip!"

"Is she sleeping now?" Clarence asked the boy.

"Yeah, I checked on her a little while ago." Worry was evident in his grandson's voice when he asked Clarence, "What should I do?"

"Let her sleep Son. I'll be over in the morning. Okay?"

"Okay Grandpa." Before Clarence hung up Tony asked him one more question. "Grandpa, do you think I ought to' call Clay?"

"Tony my boy, that's a good idea."

When Clarence hung up, Tony dialed the Amityville Police Station. He had to leave a message because Clay was on duty, but less than five minutes later the phone rang and he picked it up.

"Hello."

"Tony, it's Clay, I got your message. I've been trying to call and check on your mom all evening. Is she alright? Is everything okay?"

"Yeah, I mean, no….I don't know Clay. Something's wrong and nobody tells me anything." Tony voice cracked a little before he said, "Mom's losing it Clay. She's been upstairs crying hysterically all night. What happened?"

Clay was silent for a moment trying to decide what to tell the boy. In the end, he decided to tell him the truth. "Tony, I like your mom. You know that don't you?"

"Yeah," he responded, surprising Clay. "I think she likes you too, so what's the big deal?"

That one, simple statement had the power to mend all the hurt that went on earlier in the day. Clay was happy to know at least one person in the Simpson family was on his side.

"Tony, unfortunately, your aunt and your sister don't feel the way you do."

"Janae? What's Janae got to do with this?"

He didn't want to go into the details regarding Janae and what went on this afternoon, and changed the subject. "Tony, where's your mom been all day? I called her at least ten times."

"I dunno," Tony told him. "She told Grandpa not to bring me home until ten tonight, but when I got home she wasn't here. She came home a few minutes afterward, went upstairs to her room and hasn't come out since."

Clay was worried about Vi. He suspected she wouldn't take his call, since she hadn't returned any of his messages yet. He asked Tony to take the cordless phone up to her.

Tony knocked several times before he opened her bedroom door. He made out his mother's still form lying across her bed and walked over to give her a light shake. "Mom? Mom? Mom?."

Vi turned over, squinting at the bright hall light shining in the darkened room. "Oh, hey Baby. Mom is very tired, okay? Why don't you go to bed too?"

"But Mom…I got a call for you," he said extending the phone to her.

"I don't want to talk to anybody Honey. Could you take a message?"

"Mom, I think you should take this call."

Somewhere in the fog invading her brain, Vi surfaced long enough to think it could be an emergency. Maybe Janae was really sick or, mom or dad, or…

Tony held the phone out to her and watched her sit up. Her hair was mussed up and her eyes were puffy and swollen, but she calmly took the phone from his hands and spoke tentatively into the receiver. "Hello."

"Vi?" The sound of his voice, which had always filled her with unexplainable joy, now caused a piercingly sharp pain near Vi's heart.

"Clay…" Watching Tony leave the room, Vi whispered his name softly.

"Baby, are you okay?" The worry she heard in his voice made her feel ashamed she hadn't returned his calls. It was just that she hadn't felt like talking to anyone.

"I've been calling you all day. Where have you been?"

"Out. I just needed to get out and just think, be by myself."

"I also stopped by twice on duty tonight but…."

Whatever he'd been about to say, was interrupted as she told him. "Clayton, about us…"

That uneasy feeling he'd had all day returned full force and Clayton hesitated, before inquiring. "What about us?"

"I think we need some time, maybe we shouldn't…"

"Vi, don't say it, please. Vi don't tell me what you think. Baby, tell me what you feel." The desperate plea in his voice fell on deaf ears.

"I…It doesn't matter what I feel…"

"You're wrong…you're…"

"No." She stopped him in mid-sentence. "I don't think we should see each other anymore." He couldn't stop the words that rushed out of her, words that would change their lives, words that would ultimately cut him to shreds.

"Vi, no, don't do this Baby."

She went on as if he hadn't said a word, as if what they had together meant nothing to her.

"I was foolish to think it could work. Clay, I'm very sorry."

"Sorry? I can't believe this," all the desperation and fear he was feeling surfaced and he tried one last time to reason with her. Devastated that they might lose what they had even before it got started, the forceful tone of his voice surprised even him. "Vi, please...please. Don't buckle under the pressure. Baby, give it some time. Give us a chance."

The weight of his words sliced into her. Didn't he know how hard this was for her? Overcome with emotion, his plea tugged at her heart and she wavered for just a moment. Then sanity returned and Vi recognized what they'd shared had been a dream, a wonderful dream. They made magic together, a magic she'd never experienced before in her life. But everyone knows magic isn't real. It's nice, it's spectacular, but it's not real.

"I'm sorry, I can't." Forcing the painful words past her lips, she told him. "It's not you, this is all me. I just can't do this." Then she hung up, not giving him a chance to say more. When she placed the phone on her nearby night table, she lay back down and cried herself to sleep in the dark.

Clay was numb. There wasn't any other word for this vicious assault on his nervous system. He stayed on patrol for several hours, and then decided to call dispatch and tell them he had an emergency. He waited for the dispatcher to contact his captain, who would work out coverage before he could go off duty. As boggled as his mind was tonight, he knew from years of training that on patrol is not where he should be. It was much too dangerous to be this distracted in his line of work.

The need to race over there and talk with her face to face was overwhelming, but he fought the urge. It was late and the finality in her voice, when she hung up on him earlier stayed with him. Clay decided to give her some time to come around. She had to see they belonged together, that he loved her and no one or nothing could or should come between them.

As it turned out Clay was dead wrong.

After waiting several days he tried calling her countless times, always getting her machine. When Vi finally picked up the phone more than a week later, he was surprised to reach her. Premature hope rose up in him, until she told him without greeting or feelings. "Clay, I can't see you anymore. Please don't call here anymore."

He lay on his bed with an arm folded behind his head, listening to the phone click and the dial tone come on as she hung up on him yet again. Stunned, he replaced the receiver, covered his eyes with his other arm, and felt a gut-wrenching pain of loss; such as he'd never experienced before.

The town of Amityville was a pretty close community. Although, Clayton didn't bother her anymore, he still saw Vi on occasion. During the day when he was on duty, he went past Nu U several times. As painful as it was, he strained his eyes to see into her shop window, knowing if he did catch a glimpse of her it would feel like salt applied to an open wound. By chance he sometimes saw her from afar, shopping around town and, like an addiction, he'd also taken to driving by her house several times each night when he was on patrol. Only when he was certain she'd definitely be asleep would he cruise slowly by her house. Just like a junkie, he knew he shouldn't partake of the substance that hurt him, but he was powerless to resist it. And so, each time he caught sight of her—by accident or design— his heart would race then splinter again, into a million tiny pieces.

Vi saw him around town too many times for her peace of mind. He was there sometimes when she was shopping or walking down the street. Usually he was doing his job when she saw him, writing a ticket or on a call somewhere in town. A sharp pain settled in her heart whenever he was near. From a distance, she could feel his eyes on her and for the life of her she couldn't help staring back. When this happened, he was the first to look away, causing the sharp pain lodged in her chest to deepen.

One night she got home late from work and fell asleep in front of the television downstairs. As she got up to turn it off and check the front door locks, she saw a squad car slowly cruising down her street. It was him, she was certain of it. She wondered how many times he'd done this that she was unaware of. Tears fell unchecked as she closed the blinds and went upstairs where she promptly fell into a troubled sleep.

In the weeks following their family fallout, the tension between Vi and Cynthia at work was so thick even a knife couldn't cut through it. Vi was working in her office one morning remembering her first confrontation with Cynthia, two days after Janae left home, and two days after she'd pushed Clayton out of her life.

Cynthia had finally tracked her down at home that evening, clearly annoyed with Vi for avoiding her phone calls. Her sister didn't waste any time getting right down to the facts, laying the guilt on heavily and demanding answers from Vi.

"Vi, how could you do this to Janae, to your family?"

"Cynthia, Janae is my daughter and we'll work this out without your involvement," she shot back at her sister and sat down at the kitchen table, shuffling through paperwork she'd brought home from the salon.

Clearly just getting warmed up, Cynthia propped her hands on her hips and said in a tone dripping with reproach, "Well, it's too late for that, I'm already involved. Mother is beside herself with shock over all this too, you know."

Watching her sister's defiant stance Vi counted to ten very, very slowly, feeling her anger rise dangerously close to a head. Oblivious to Vi's growing annoyance, Cynthia continued her tirade.

"Really Vi, a woman your age has no business cavorting with a young boy like that. It's downright disgraceful," she informed Vi in a tone dripping with distaste. "To go after a man your daughter was interested is just so beneath you..." she suddenly stopped in mid-sentence. From Vi's reaction Cynthia suspected she had no idea Janae was interested in Clay and drove home the final screws in a very smug manner. "You didn't know poor Janae had feelings for that man too?"

Vi had taken all she could take. This news shocked her, but she gave her sister a pointed look and said in her own defense, "I had no idea, but I'm certain Janae's feelings were one-sided."

"You should be with men your own age Vi," Cynthia said in her usual high-handed manner. "Tom and I have tried countless times to introduce you to some of his friends, but...."

Vi didn't give her a chance to finish, pouncing on her sister in anger. "I can do without your introductions, thank you very much. Just for the record,

I'll have you know, the last blind date you set me up with almost raped me!" It was obvious her words had shocked her sister, but for the life of her Vi couldn't bring herself to care. "That so-called nice, respectful friend of yours would have raped me if Craig hadn't helped me beat him off."

Cynthia fell silent, for the space of a minute, and then turned to leave. Before she did, she looked Vi straight in the eye and said, "You're a fool to think a man that young wants you. If you don't break it off, you're going to lose your family and your daughter, if you haven't already."

Knowing her sister's threats were groundless didn't stop the hurt they inflicted. Feeling bone weary, Vi looked at her sister and said, in sad resignation, "Well, then I guess I broke it off just in time so the only one losing out will be me." Vi said this under her breath, mostly for herself than for Cynthia's ears.

"What did you say?"

"Nothing. Look Cynthia, I'll handle this my way. As for Clay and I, we're not seeing each other anymore, not that it's any of your concern."

"Well, that's good. That's a step in the right direction." Vi wasn't sure if she heard a sense of triumph in Cynthia's voice when she added, "So, maybe you can come to dinner this weekend, sit down and talk this out with Janae."

"I can't come to dinner, I'm busy this weekend," she'd stated plainly and bent her head back over the paperwork laid out on the kitchen table. She didn't look up until she heard the door close, signaling Cynthia's retreat.

That had been three weeks ago, and during that time Vi had grown distant from virtually everyone in the family except Tony and Clarence. They were, unknowingly, her support system and Vi wasn't sure how she would have gotten through any of this without them.

Nicole's grandmother was in the hospital, so with her gone, Vi spent most of her time with Tony eating out or going to the movies. Although, she made sure Clay would not be at any of Tony's practice games she attended, Vi continued to miss him desperately. During her waking hours everything she did reminded her of him, but the nights were far worse. Clay plagued her thoughts constantly, making it impossible to sleep without dreaming about him and difficult to wake up without feeling so much yearning, the pain was almost unbearable.

In the weeks following the fallout, Vi spent a lot of time catching up on work that needed to be done at the salon. She was in her office doing some of that work when the noise in the outer salon interrupted her thoughts. Vi looked up as Cynthia entered the room and slammed the door shut behind her. Just that morning Vi had announced Nicole would be her new assistant manager. While everyone else went over to congratulate Nikki, Cynthia had immediately grabbed her purse and walked out in a huff. Now, almost an hour later, she had apparently decided to come back to the work. Obviously still fuming, she shot Vi a scathing look as she walked over to her desk and said, "I know you promoted that girl just to annoy me."

Ignoring the accusation, Vi didn't look up from the ledger she was working on when she responded, "I own this business and make all my decisions based on business needs."

In the last few weeks Vi and Cynthia had barely tolerated one another on the few days when Cynthia was scheduled to work. The chill in the air between the two of them was not lost on Andre or Nicole and, although they both asked on several occasions what was going on, Vi simply replied it was a personal family matter that would work itself out over time.

"Well, just don't let her mess with the general accounts. It took a lot of work to put those in order." After issuing that warning, Cynthia sat down at her desk.

Sighing heavily, Vi stood up and walked over to stand in front of Cynthia's desk. "About those general accounts," she began. "I have something…"

Cynthia's phone rang interrupting what Vi was about to say. Excusing herself, Cynthia spoke quietly to whoever it was. When she hung up, she turned to Vi and said, "That was Janae. She said she's been trying to call you and you haven't returned any of her phone calls."

Retracing her steps, Vi sat back down at her own desk and said in a cool tone, "I've been terribly busy. If Janae needs to see me, she knows how to find me."

Clearly taken aback by Vi's lack of interest, Cynthia wasted no time telling her so. "I know you've been mad at me for weeks Vi. But I really think your breakup with Clayton was for the best."

Giving her sister a pointed look, Vi asked her, "Do you Cynthia? Do you really?"

"Well, yes." Cynthia answered with a touch of alarm. Where was Vi going with this she wondered?

"You know what Cynthia? Since everyone is so determined to tell me what's best for me, let me tell you what's best for you." Vi stood up again and, with determination in her voice, she addressed Cynthia like she'd never done before. Feet planted firmly apart, she folded her arms across her chest and gave her sister a piece of her mind. "I am sick and tired of you acting like my children are your children. If you wanted children so badly Cynthia, I think you and Tom should have had some."

Totally speechless, Cynthia stared up at Vi with a horrified look in her eyes. "I've done nothing with your children but love them, you know that Vi," she cried defensively. "Tom and I decided long ago..."

Vi didn't let her finish. Cynthia was famous for using high-handed tactics and monopolizing every conversation with her opinionated views. It felt good to finally get the things she'd been holding in for so long off her chest. "Oh, and another thing. I'm sick and tired of you telling me what to do. You did it when we were children Cynthia, and for some reason you think you can still do it."

Cynthia felt like she was being attacked. She stood up to face her sister and raised her chin in defiance. "Vi, that's so unfair. I've simply tried to tell you when I felt you needed..."

Vi's temper spilled over and she raised her voice, not caring if anyone could hear them in the outer salon area. "I'm a grown woman Cynthia, and you would do well to remember that in future. I don't intend to let you dictate what goes on in my life ever again."

Through all of this, Cynthia wore a dumbfounded look. She sank back into her chair, speechless. After a few moments, she spoke in a quiet, bewildered voice. "Vi, I never knew you felt this way. We're family, we're sisters. Anything I ever tried to do was for your own good."

"You're right, but the only thing between us now is blood Cynthia. And I'm not so sure how strong that tie is anymore."

When Cynthia started to say more, Vi held up a hand forestalling anything further conversation. "Cynthia, do you remember I told you earlier, that I've been busy this week? Well I have. I've been interviewing."

Unsure why they were discussing this now or what this had to do with her, Cynthia had to admit she was glad Vi had finally decided to replace Andre—it was long overdue as far as she was concerned. "Oh, well that's good. It shouldn't be too hard to replace Andre, but I don't see how that has anything to do with me."

"I'm not replacing Andre, Cynthia. I hired a new bookkeeper." She waited for her words to sink in, before continuing. "There's been too much tension between us Cynthia and I think it would be best if you don't work here anymore." As she said this, Vi began walking toward the door.

The dismissive gesture was not lost on her sister. "What? Vi, are you serious?" Cynthia's voice rose in alarm.

"I believe what I said was pretty clear. Please clear out your desk by Friday," she said as she opened the door to leave. "The new girl starts on Monday."

Tony was really worried about his mom. She wasn't speaking to Aunt Cynthia or Janae. The few weekends she was home from school, Janae stayed with Aunt Cynthia and the only time Tony spoke with her was over the phone. Whenever Janae asked to speak with her, Vi always told Tony to tell Janae she would call her back later. As far as Tony could tell, his mother never called Janae back any of those times.

Although she appeared to be taking everything in stride and started spending more time with him and his grandfather on the weekends, Tony knew the person she missed the most was Clayton. He didn't call or come by anymore and, in the weeks since they broke up, Tony noticed that his mom seemed to sink into a depression. When she was with him in the evenings or on the weekends, Vi was constantly distracted. But on a couple of nights when he was up late talking to Briana on the phone, he'd overheard her crying softly in her room.

Tony turned to the one person he knew could help him. He went to his grandfather with his concerns, hoping Clarence could come up with a plan to help Vi get back to her usual self and, ultimately, get the family back together.

The two of them decided to schedule Sunday dinner at his grandfather's house. Tony spent Saturday night at his grandfather's to help prepare Sunday dinner. When Clarence invited Vi over for dinner, however, he neglected to tell her the rest of the family would also be there. He also had her arriving an hour after everyone else, so they could all talk prior to Vi's arrival.

Sunday came and the entire family, excluding Vi, was assembled in Clarence's living room. Tony made sure everyone had something to drink before Grandpa started to speak with everyone. Vi's parents lived about an hour away, but they had driven down yesterday and arrived with Cynthia and her husband, Tom. Janae arrived right after her grandparents and aunt and uncle. After everyone had something to drink in their hands, Clarence addressed the room.

"My grandson here called me last week and asked for my help." He put an arm around Tony's shoulders. "So, I called us all here because Tony is closest to his mom and he's very worried about her. She's in a great deal of pain, and I don't believe any of you truly know the effect all this is having on her or the family as a whole." Clarence paused, making eye contact with everyone assembled. "She hasn't been herself for quite some time and I believe everyone in this room knows the cause."

Clarence turned his attention to his granddaughter Janae, and said in a kind voice. "Janae, Honey, you owe your mom an apology. She's raised you, loved you and supported you in everything, and this is the thanks you give her? You should be ashamed."

"But Granddad, she's old enough to be his mother, and..."

Clarence held up a hand to stop whatever his granddaughter was about to say. "Now you know that's not true. Clayton is quite a bit older than your brother was, don't forget that. As for the difference in their ages, that doesn't matter when two people love each other." Clarence let the group collectively think on that one for a moment, feeling certain they had no idea just how much Vi and Clayton were hurting over all this.

Cynthia sat straighter in her chair, waiting for Clarence to finish. It was clear by her body language that she wasn't about to apologize to anyone and didn't appreciate Clarence meddling in things that didn't concern him. After all, he was Vi's father-in-law. It wasn't like he was flesh and blood. She sat stewing in her own juices, holding her tongue for the moment.

"Granddad, Mom had to know I liked him." Guilt over her own actions surfacing, Janae took a different tack and asked, "Why would she deliberately go after him?"

Clarence eyed her, considering what she had to say, before responding. "You say you liked him. I'm curious, did Clayton ever return your feelings? Did he in any way encourage you, Child?"

Janae's silence answered his question better than anything she could have said. "Well, there you have it. Now stop being selfish, whatever designs you might have had on that man, it's time to get over it." Clarence went over to give his granddaughter's shoulders an affectionate squeeze to go along with his harsh words. Above all he wanted to ensure Janae knew he loved her, but it was also time for her to act like the adult he knew she could be.

Finally Clarence turned to Vi's parents. "Thank you both for coming. I know you both love Vi very much. But I must say, with all due respect, the two of you tend to bend toward Cynthia's way of thinking. This matter is no exception."

Vi's mother stood up, clearly offended. "That's not true, how dare you..." Vi's father grabbed hold of his wife's hand and pulled her back down into her seat. He told her, "Dear, Clarence may be speaking the truth here. Let the man talk. I've tried to talk with Vi myself recently and I noticed she was very distant, not her usual self. I do believe we have to do something, Hon."

"My thoughts exactly," Clarence said and then turned his attention to Cynthia, who sat near her husband. Clarence noted she'd been unusually quiet during all this, probably stewing in her own juices and biding her time.

Not waiting for Clarence to attack her, Cynthia stood up and faced him head on. "I don't care what you say, or how you try to dress it up. It's a disgrace," Cynthia spat out.   Aiming her words directly at Clarence, she lashed out. "Vi's acting like a lonely, pathetic older woman."

From past experience, Clarence knew Cynthia was just getting started on one of her tantrums. In the face of the storm she was stirring up, he told her calmly. "We all know how you feel Cynthia.   God knows you've forced more than one of your opinions down our throats before."

Clarence watched her jaw drop open and decided it was time he told Cynthia everything that was on his mind. "You know darn well you shouldn't have encouraged Janae to practically move in with you. When she gets home from school, she knows she's got a perfectly good home to go to." He could clearly see his admonishing tone only made Cynthia bristle more. Undaunted, Clarence pushed ahead.   "When she and her mother had to work things out, you should have sent her home right away. But, you didn't, did you?"

Tony watched his grandfather, saying all that he—as a kid—couldn't say about what had been going on in this family. He smiled at his grandfather, giving him silent support. Lowering his voice, Clarence tried to get Cynthia to see reason and told her, calmly, "Cynthia, she's your niece. I know you love her, but she's not your child."

Cynthia glared at Clarence, feeling his words cut deeply. She turned to her husband Tom, but found no support there. When Cynthia turned back to Clarence, her fury was in full force and she didn't make any effort to restrain herself.   "Clarence, you are Vi's father-in-law! Her dead husband's father! You have no right to speak to me or any of us this way. You've gone too far."

"The hell I do," Clarence shot back at her. "I have every right. Janae, Tony and Vi are my family too. Even though my son's been dead many years, they are as close to me now as if he were still alive." Clearly Clarence had no intention of backing down in the face of Cynthia's ranting and raving. "I love the three of them and I can't stand by and let you orchestrate this family's ruin."

Quick to grab hold of any insecurity she could find, Cynthia threw back at him.   "I don't care what you say Clarence, wrong is wrong. Vi has to realize she's not a child anymore, she has a family to think about."   Straight as a board, Cynthia stiffened her spine and threw back at him, "If anyone's ruining this family, it's Vi."

"If anyone should have an objection to Vi seeing or loving another man, it should be me," Clarence told her, not missing a beat.   "But, I don't and I don't think my son would want Vi to live out the rest of her life alone." Clarence's next words said all that he felt in his heart. "I'd like to think my son would have wanted Vi to find happiness with him gone."

Clearly frustrated that he didn't seem to be getting through to her, Clarence stated in a calmer tone. "Vi's a good girl. She has gone out of her way for everyone in this family, always putting everyone's needs before her own. She doesn't deserve this."

Cynthia let out a derisive snort and glared at the older, much wiser man. Totally unaffected by his plea, Cynthia didn't care if her next words came out condescending. "Well, Clarence that was a nice speech, but…"

"No but's Cynthia!" Clarence's voice rose again when he said, "I'm through talking and I think you should butt out."

When Cynthia started to say more, her husband, Tom, got up and led her off to a private corner of the room. From where they stood, no one in the room could hear what Tom told his wife, but it seemed to calm her down. Tom folded Cynthia in his arms and held her tight when she struggled to be released. Finally, she wilted in his arms and silently began to cry.

Janae watched her aunt and uncle from a distance. She'd heard everything her grandfather said and knew he spoke the truth. Walking over to Clarence, she placed a hand on her grandfather's arm, and Clarence immediately took this sweet child in his arms. Janae wept silently in her grandfather's embrace and whispered very low, so only he could hear.

"You're right Granddad. I've been meaning to go to Mom and talk with her, but she won't return my calls. I'm afraid now what to say to her. I mean, she fired Aunt Cynthia from doing the books at Nu U and every time I go over or call, she's out or locked up in her room." A note of desperation crept into her voice as she finally admitted. "I don't know what to do."

Clarence released his hold on Janae and looked her straight in the eye. "Have you tried just going to her and asking her forgiveness?"

Janae hung her head in shame, knowing she hadn't tried hard enough to reach her mother because she hadn't really known what to say. She made a decision to try again and this time she would find the right words.

"She's coming," Tony shouted from his position at the front window as he watched his mother get out of her car and walk slowly up the driveway to Clarence's door. Surely she recognized Aunt Cynthia's car outside, but she rang the bell anyway.

Vi recognized two family cars in Clarence's driveway and became instantly annoyed. She had been looking forward to dinner with Tony and Clarence, but knowing that Cynthia was here suddenly made Vi lose her appetite. As she walked in the front door, Vi quickly surveyed the room. Walking over to Clarence first, she gave him a hug to thank him for inviting her to dinner. Then she walked over to Tony. "Hi Pal, did you plan all this?" she asked him, giving Tony a reassuring hug.

"Yeah, I did Mom. But…"

"It's okay, Honey. I love you, but this is all unnecessary."

She gave Cynthia a cool nod, then smiled faintly at Janae and her parents, but kept her distance.   Instantly realizing what dear Clarence and her wonderful son had been trying to do, she sighed heavily and said, "I'm not sure why you are all here. I can only think that Tony and Clarence, whom I love to death, are trying to patch up our big, happy family."

Vi hugged Tony tightly at her side then walked over to touch Clarence lightly on the arm to show him she wasn't angry with him.   "Well," Vi continued, "there's really no need. You see, you all got what you wanted. I'm not seeing Clayton anymore."

"Mom," Janae stepped forward to speak to her mother.

Vi held out her hand, stopping her daughter from coming any further. "Janae, there's really nothing to say." Her words came out like those of a close acquaintance, rather than words spoken from a mother to her daughter. "I hope you're feeling better, and oh, there'll be more money on your student Visa card next week for the new textbooks you need."

The impersonal statement made Janae want to cry. She didn't care about the money or anything else. She just wanted to get close to her mother again, like they'd been close before. But she didn't know how to fix it.

Vi surprised everyone when she suddenly kissed Tony on the cheek, hugged Clarence quickly, then turned to go back out the front door. Over her shoulder she told Clarence, "Thanks for inviting me to dinner Clarence, but suddenly I'm not very hungry." And, then she was gone.

CHAPTER
THIRTY-SIX

Casey left the doctor's office with specific instructions to stay off her feet.

Fat chance! She knew she couldn't possibly do that and keep her new job. The loose clothing she wore when she'd gotten the job hid her pregnancy very well, however, she was certain her new boss would flip if he knew he'd hired a pregnant woman who had to go out on bed rest right after being hired.

Besides, Casey was determined to keep this job for her baby. The pay wasn't that great but it had excellent health benefits. An unpleasant thought crept into her thoughts, and she quickly dismissed it. Unfortunately, it kept coming back. What if she kept the job and lost the baby?! Since Craig was gone, everything Casey did was for the baby. Getting a job, getting enough sleep at night and eating better even when she was sick to her stomach were just some of the things she was determined to do to help her unborn child. Craig used to nag her about taking good care of herself and the baby and, over time, she'd come to rely on him to remind her to eat and sleep. Now she had to depend on herself, and she needed to be strong so her baby would be able to depend on his mother. Casey fingered the crumpled disability note in her pocket as she walked the few blocks to her apartment.

She stopped at the corner delicatessen and ordered a turkey sandwich and milk. When it was ready, she paid the cashier and went outside to sit at one of the curbside tables. As she ate, her mind began to wander. Somewhere along the line she'd developed a craving for turkey and pastrami, it was Craig's favorite sandwich—correction, it used to be Craig's favorite sandwich. Lately she thought about him at odd hours of the day, and missed him desperately every hour in between. Casey took another bite from her sandwich and heaved a small sigh. She knew she needed to focus on the problems facing her today, not the past. God knows, there was absolutely nothing she could do about the past. As she contemplated what to do about her doctor's advice and her new job, Casey caught sight of him in her peripheral vision.

Pretending she hadn't seen him, Casey continued to sip her drink and look off into space. All the while, she sat there stealing glances over her shoulder at the man across the street. When the lunch crowd started packing into the deli and swarming around the tables outside, Casey decided to get up and leave. Acting like she wasn't aware she was being followed home was a bit of strain on her already frazzled nerves. She entered her building, still feigning ignorance, checked the mail and went upstairs. Casey quickly unlocked her door and went inside. Breathing heavily, with the door at her back, she fought to calm her nerves. It wasn't good for the baby to get this worked up. Casey pushed away from the door and began searching in her purse frantically. She knew for certain now exactly who was following her. She also knew for certain who she needed to call. Breathing a sigh of relief, Casey fingered the card she'd found in one hand as she dialed Clayton's number with her other hand.

The phone rang six times before he picked up.

"Hello," his voice was raspy and deep, as if he'd been sleeping.

"Officer Marshall? It's Casey." She remembered too late that Craig and Clay often worked the graveyard shift.

"I'm so sorry," she apologized. "Did I wake you?" Casey glanced at her clock. It was after eleven o'clock in the morning.

"Yeah, I just got off four hours ago; it's okay. What's up?"

"I saw him again," she waited for him to remember.

Clay rubbed his tired eyes and sat up when she said this.

"Who? The guy following you?"

"Yeah, it's him, I'm sure it's Raul." Clay thought he heard a trace of fear in her voice. "What should I do?" she asked him.

"Stay inside and lock your door," he instructed. "I'll get in touch with J.R. and have him come over to stay with you until I can make other arrangements."

"Okay," she said in agreement, clearly relieved to have someone, besides herself, deal with Raul.

Fully awake now, Clay placed a call to J.R. then dialed the station. He wanted to see if the information Casey had given homicide on Raul matched any of the evidence in Craig's case. The homicide detective working Craig's case wasn't available, so the dispatcher put him on hold. After a few seconds voicemail came on. Opting not to leave a message, he swung his legs over the side of the bed, grabbed a pair of jeans and a shirt from a nearby chair, and hit the shower. Within fifteen minutes Clayton was in his truck, heading back to the station. It was time he had a face to face with Detective Sloan.

Several hours later, when he left the station for the second time that day, Clayton was more than a little disappointed about his meeting. Sloan was a nice enough guy; graying, in his sixties and very close to retirement. He had a lot of experience and time on the job. Although Clay had confidence in his ability, he found his laid-back attitude a bit annoying. He'd been nonchalant about the information Casey had given him, and completely against any possibility Raul's presence might be a clue in Craig's murder case.

Clay had been a trained police officer for many years. When you were out there everyday in the trenches, over time you listened to your hunches. Sometimes those hunches saved your life in dangerous situations. Clay had a very strong hunch that somehow Raul was involved in the case. He pressed Sloan before he left to look further into Raul's past and get back with him. With nothing else to do, Clay drove away from the station feeling helpless. He made a mental note to check back with Sloan in two days time. If the detective balked at being pressured to move on this case, Clay decided he would take his concerns to Captain Jackson personally.

Six weeks to the day they broke up, Vi bumped into him. Prior to today, they'd only glimpsed each other from a great distance. It was bound to happen, she realized, in a small community like the one they lived in. Perhaps it took so long, Vi thought, because of their different work schedules. But this particular Monday morning when she decided to stop at the market proved to be her downfall. Vi used to shop only on the weekends, but hadn't been doing so for the past several weeks. Lately, the simple tasks—cooking, cleaning and shopping—all felt like a chore and the weight of her obligations dragged her down mentally and physically. The only two people she saw and whose company she enjoyed the most was her son and Clarence.

Blessedly, everyone else in her family—her mother, Cynthia and Janae—stopped calling. Vi had nothing to say to them, not that she planned to answer their calls in the first place. The only misgivings she had in all this was the strain on her relationship with Janae. In the beginning Vi went over to Cynthia's to try and speak with Janae countless times and left her endless messages, begging her to talk. The first few weeks after her break up with Clayton, Janae had avoided Vi like the plague. Now it was almost time for final exams and the end of the fall term. She knew they needed to talk, but right now Vi just couldn't dredge up enough strength to deal with Janae's anger at the moment. She'd also been working longer hours at the shop, not because she had to, but because she needed to keep her mind busy. Tony was back in school and life, it seemed, went on.

It's funny, she thought, just when you feel like you've gotten over someone you run into that person and realize how much you've been fooling yourself. She was down the meat aisle picking up chicken cutlets for dinner when the hair on the back of her neck stood on end. Vi knew before she picked her head up that he was nearby. Although she knew she shouldn't look up, Vi was unable to resist and did it anyway. And, there he was, standing just fifty feet away in the same store, standing at the same meat counter she stood at. Her heart sped up and the longing she felt well up inside her was so fierce, it nearly choked her.

Clayton was pissed off. At work lately, he alternated between being testy to downright intolerable. Piterrelli, who knew him better than anyone else on the force, sensed there was something wrong but he couldn't get Clay to talk about it. When all his badgering failed, Clay found out Pitt had enlisted the help of his wife to help bring him around. When Pitt's tiny powerhouse of a wife called him earlier today to invite him over for an impromptu barbeque at their place tonight, he'd tried to refuse. He'd spent ten minutes trying to tell her "No," before realizing "No" was not a word in her vocabulary. After reluctantly accepting her invite he made the mistake of asking politely what he should bring. To his surprise the woman actually had a list to give him. Clay shook his head as he wrote down what she ordered him to bring, making a mental note at the same time to talk with Piterrelli about his sweet little wife as he hung up the phone.

When his shift ended Clay stopped at the local supermarket. After his little get together at the Piterrelli's later tonight, he had to get home and pack a few things. It had taken some doing, but his captain had finally gotten Detective Sloan on board with their plan. The details of that plan ran through his mind as he pulled into the parking lot and got out of his truck. Anxious to put those plans into action, he walked inside the brightly lit store to pick up the items on his list.

So, here he was in the market, buying country ribs for a barbeque he didn't feel like going to in the first place. Clay checked his watch and then consulted his shopping list again. He'd just gotten off work and was still in uniform, so several folks easily recognized him and stopped to chat as he walked into the store.

Clayton saw her first and instead of high tailing it out of there he walked closer to where she stood. An uncontrollable force made it impossible for him to turn away. So he stood there, rooted in place, drinking in the sight of her standing less than thirty feet away. She wore a pretty, yellow sundress with one of those long, flowing skirts that reached her ankles. The spaghetti straps left her shoulders bare and his fingers itched to touch the softness he remembered so well. Her naturally curly hair was pulled up into a loose knot on top of her head and delicate tendrils fell away from this bun and caressed the nape of her neck. Swallowing audibly, Clayton knew he was in deep trouble. This woman had turned him inside out; had unknowingly worked herself deep inside his heart, then dropped him like a hot potato at the first sign of trouble.

She was totally to blame for the growing number of sleepless nights he'd had since their break up. The feel of her body wrapped around him, her smile, the softness of her skin, and the tinkle of her laughter filled his dreams every night. His days were no better, because he could not erase from his mind the sense of contentment he felt embedded deep inside her body. Thinking about it, made him wake up most mornings in a cold sweat, aching with longing and fully aroused.

Just as he gathered his wits about him and turned to leave, she picked her head up and their gazes collided. Both of them were oblivious to how long they stood staring at one another. It could have been ten seconds, ten minutes or ten hours. However long it was, it wasn't long enough. The pull between them was a tangible thing. He met the wanting in her eyes with an equal need of his own. Time slipped by. A mother with a crying baby in her arms stepped in between them at the meat counter, momentarily blocking their view of one another. It was enough to break the spell. When mother and baby moved out of the way, Clay lowered his eyes, turning away and walked down another aisle.

Vi was too shaken to go into work after seeing him like that. She left the market and took out her cell phone as she walked toward her car. "Andre, hi it's Vi. Listen, I won't be in this morning. I'm not feeling well."

"Not a problem Vi, we can handle it. I hope you feel better," he said before hanging up.

Thankfully Tony was at school when she got home. It was only ten thirty when she walked into her bedroom and laid down. Like an alcoholic falling off the wagon, she felt the stabbing pain of withdrawal. Curling up in a ball, she let out a gut-wrenching cry, which was followed by uncontrollable tears.

Oh, God it hurt. It hurt. This man had loved her and she realized now, like a fool, she'd thrown that love back in his face. Vi sat up and reached for a tissue box on her night table. Rocking back and forth she continued to cry, seeking a consolation she knew would not come. The reasons for breaking up with him tumbled around and around in her mind. They'd seemed so real, so overwhelming at the time. Now, when she mentally added them all up, the reasons she'd had didn't amount to very much at all.

She felt angry and hurt. And resentment washed over her that she'd been a good mother, sister and daughter all her life. Yet when she had this chance for happiness, her entire family—except Tony and Clarence—had all tried to take it away. She lay down again and squeezed her eyes shut and immediately a steady flow of tears streamed from her closed eyes, wetting the pillow under her head.

No, she was to blame, she thought, giving herself a mental kick. No one made her make this decision, only her, she thought in all honesty. While her family had done their best to tear them apart, it was she who folded so easily under the pressure. It had been her decision to break it off, and Vi wept harder for the loss she had imposed on herself. When she saw him today, it made her realize just how much she missed him, how much she loved him. She also realized that she never told him how she felt, when he had always been open and honest with her. She could admit it now that she'd probably been in love with him all along and had selfishly held back those three, simple words. How she wished now that she'd had the courage to tell him before.

Was it too late? Vi sat up again, this time her mind was racing just as fast as her heart. Maybe it wasn't too late. For the first time in well over a month, she felt a surge of hope fill her. Hoping against hope that it wasn't too late, she decided to go to him. Go to him, beg his forgiveness and tell him how much she loved him.

Vi dried her eyes and went downstairs to call him. After trying his apartment, the station and his cell phone, Vi felt some of the hope blossoming a minute ago begin to wilt. She hung up in frustration when she found out his cell phone number had been changed, voice mail picked up at home and dispatch told her he'd be off for a few days. Straightening her spine, Vi determined she would wait, however long it took. She would get in touch with him eventually and, when she did, she'd make the best of it and hope it wasn't too late.

Four days later, Vi still hadn't reached him and he hadn't returned any of the messages she left at his work or home. Unsure what to do, she reasoned he must be out of town.

CHAPTER
THIRTY-SEVEN

Tony got off the school bus and started walking the four blocks home. As he rounded the corner of Richard Court, he heard someone call out his name. When he looked back, he saw it was J.R. running toward him and yelling his name.

Out of breath, J.R. slapped Tony's hand when he reached him. "Hey Man," Tony said in greeting. "It's been a while," Tony said. "Where you been, Man?"

"Around, you know. Listen," he paused, trying to catch his breath. "I know Clay don't hang around you guys no more, but I thought you should know about this."

"Know about what?" Tony asked with a puzzled look on his face.

J.R. sat down on a nearby bus stop bench, and motioned for Tony to join him. J.R. liked Tony; the two of them became good friends during basketball season. Although their backgrounds were very different—really like day and night—Tony had accepted J.R. for what he was. He'd just found out the two people he cared about the most were about to do something pretty crazy, in J.R.'s opinion. And the more he thought about it, the more he thought Tony's family should know about it, just in case something went wrong.

When Tony sat down on the bench next to him, J.R. gave him the short version. When J.R. finished, Tony knew about a girl named Casey, who could possibly be carrying Craig's baby, and that she was in trouble with a man who they thought had something to do with Craig's murder. Tony sat very still for a full minute, trying to let it all sink in, then J.R. laid another bombshell on him.

"Tony, Casey is gonna' bait this guy to get him to make a move."

When Tony didn't say anything, J.R. rushed on to explain that Casey wouldn't agree to do it unless Clay was involved. J.R. explained that Clayton was the only officer Casey trusted. The alarmed look on Tony's face urged J.R. to quickly explain exactly how Clayton was involved. "The police figure this guy may have killed your brother, Craig, in a jealous fit or something, so Clay's gone undercover to pose as Casey's new boyfriend."

Before he could say another word, Tony jumped off the bench and started running down the block. J.R. jumped up and started running too, following close on his heels. Out of breath again, J.R. asked Tony's retreating back, "Why are we running?"

"I gotta' get home fast. Mom needs to hear this."

Vi's first thought, when she saw the two boys come rushing inside, was they must be in some kind of trouble. Then the two of them started talking at once and at first it was hard to understand what they were trying to say.

"Mom, Clay is going to try and catch the guy that killed Craig by going undercover or something." When what J.R. and Tony were trying to tell her finally sank in, tremendous fear slammed into Vi. If this man they were after was responsible for Craig's death, then Clay was placing himself in grave danger. Why would he put himself in that kind of danger, he was a patrolman, not a detective?

Clayton didn't have to volunteer for this, but he had. Through her fear she acknowledged that not only was he the bravest man she'd ever met, he was also the craziest man she knew. Beyond being scared for him, she knew he'd probably made this decision clearly and it spoke of his true character and strength. His fearless courage, obligation to his duties and loyalty to his best friend were all the qualities that made Clayton Marshall who he was. They were also just a few of the qualities she loved most about him.

Vi plied J.R. with question after question. Unfortunately, J.R. didn't have many details. Casey told J.R. what was going on so he wouldn't worry if he couldn't reach her or Clay for a few days.

For several days afterwards, Vi was frantic with worry. Captain Jackson couldn't or wouldn't give out any details and Officer Piterrelli was either very good at feigning ignorance or Clayton hadn't told him a thing either. Over the next few days Piterrelli became Vi's eyes and ears in the precinct. It wasn't hard for Piterrelli to see that Vi cared for Clayton and that they had been much more than just friends. The only information Piterrelli could gather for her was that Clay and Casey were at an undisclosed location, trying to draw this guy out. With no further information being given the only thing they could do now, it seemed, was worry and wait.

Over the next few days Vi stopped screening her calls, thinking it might be Piterrelli with some news. It was one of those days when her phone rang that she picked it up on the first ring, not bothering to check the caller ID. Thinking it might be Piterrelli, she answered in a rush, "What's up?"

Janae was surprised to hear her mother's voice instead of the answering machine. "Mom....?" She paused. "Hi. I thought I was going to get your machine again."

"Janae? Do you need something? I put money on your Visa last week."

Her mother's words stung. The fact that the two of them had been reduced to small talk about school and money was a travesty. "Mom, I didn't call about school, or money, I...I want to see you, Mom."

"Oh," was all she could manage, surprised that Janae would want to be in the same room with her.

"Mom, I don't know how to say this. I'm so sorry for what I said that day..." her voice took on an urgent plea. "Mom, can I come over?"

Vi didn't want to put off seeing Janae, but now was such a bad time. Answering very carefully, she told her daughter. "Janae, Honey I would love to see you, but..."

Janae cut her off, misunderstanding her hesitation. "Mom, I'm really, really sorry. Please don't be mad at me any longer."

"No baby, no. I'm not. It's just that...listen can you come over now? I really could use a hand to hold right now."

"Mom, you sound strange. What's wrong? Is Tony alright?"

"Tony's fine. This is something else. Listen I can't tie up the phone line. Come on over and I'll tell you everything."

Later that night, Janae was settled back in her own room and sitting in their living room with her mother on the sofa. While she was glad they'd worked out their differences, her homecoming wasn't as joyful as it could have been. Janae got up to make a sandwich for Tony and J.R., allowing her mother and Officer Piterrelli to speak privately. He'd stopped by a little while ago and Vi immediately fixed him some food and sat down to find out what he might know. Janae left the two of them with their heads bent close together, discussing in hushed tones the information he'd been able to find out.

As she poured milk for the boys, Janae thought back on the uncertainty she'd felt earlier today when she got out of Renee's car. She stood on the front porch for a minute, feeling apprehensive and unsure how she would be received. Before she had a chance to knock, the warmth she experienced when her mother came outside and pulled her into a fierce hug, banished all her fears and insecurities. Now all her worries were centered on Clayton, as it was for everyone else in the house.

Although she did her best to console her mother, the worry she saw in her eyes was intensified by the love she also saw there. It was plain to see her mother was in love with Clay. She wondered if Clayton knew it. The next time she saw him, she planned to let him know, just in case he didn't. It was the least she could do, since she was partly responsible for their breakup in the first place.

Then there was the mystery woman Craig had never told anyone about. Janae was a little shocked when Vi told her Casey was pregnant but the baby wasn't Craig's. Knowing her brother as she had, Janae knew this woman must have been very special to Craig for him to love her while she carried another man's child.

CHAPTER
THIRTY-EIGHT

At least two thousand concert goers filled the row of seats and the grassy areas beyond, at the Jones Beach Smooth Jazz Concert Series. The Concert Series ran all summer and fall, catering to Long Islanders and tourists visiting New York. The various restaurants and gift shops lining the boardwalk drew people like flies. And after a long day of sun and fun on the beach, the local residents gathered to relax and enjoy jazz music in the evenings. Although the beach was closed, the surrounding park-like area was pleasant enough this time of year. A huge full moon and the bright lights surrounding the stage area were the only illumination besides the stars in the night sky.

Clayton had finally convinced Detective Sloan tonight was probably their best shot at drawing Raul out. With his Captain's blessing, Clay had volunteered for this two-to-three week assignment. It had taken some convincing on his part and Casey's to convince Detective Sloan that Raul was somehow involved in Craig's murder. However, after so many months with no new leads, the detective finally gave in. He didn't want Clayton involved, though, thinking a more experienced plain clothes detective could handle this assignment better. The only problem was Casey refused to go through with this undercover business unless Clay was right there by her side.

A plan had been laid out for Clayton to pose as Casey's new love interest, and for the past week the two of them had been virtually inseparable. Prior to setting this up, Casey told them as much as she could about Raul; most of what she knew had come from her dead boyfriend, Troy. It turned out that Raul had a long list of bad relationships, and some of them ended with the women pressing assault charges or filing restraining orders. She related to Detective Sloan what she'd told Clayton earlier, how she considered Raul a friend because Troy knew him. She told him how Raul's twisted mind made him believe there was something more than friendship between them, and how he became violent when she rejected his advances.

Over the last few days Clayton and Casey had given some Oscar-winning performances. Anyone who had seen the two of them together this past week would be hard pressed not to believe they were a couple. He made quite a show of kissing Casey over dinner in a crowded restaurant and touching her constantly as they strolled hand in hand around the city. He brought her trinkets and flowers in public and followed her upstairs to her new place, every night, to give the impression they were sleeping together. After five days of play acting and last nights steamy display of affection over dinner, Clayton was about ready for this whole thing to be over. They always ended the night going up to her apartment where Clay had to stay all night, sleeping on Casey's small sofa. Although both he and Casey caught glimpses of Raul watching them in the past week, it seemed what they were doing wasn't enough. They were going to have to do something more severe to push Raul over the edge. But what?

On their fifth night together, Casey revealed something by accident, something that she hadn't thought to tell Clayton before. Although they were sharing a tub of popcorn and watching television, the blinds were drawn to make it seem like the two of them had gone to bed together.

"I remember one night when Troy was alive I stayed the night at his place," she said, trying to recall the practically forgotten incident. "Raul came over and he was too drunk to drive, so Troy let him crash in the next room. The next morning, after I left, Troy told me he drove Raul home. As they were driving, Troy noticed a bunch of tiny cuts all over Raul's forearms and asked him about it."

Clay was only half listening as Casey related her story. He was bone tired and sorry he'd gotten himself involved in this charade in the first place. Idly sipping a beer and watching the TV screen, he pretended interest in her story, and prompted her to continue. "Go on."

"Well, that's the thing. When Troy asked about the cuts, he said Raul looked him dead in the eye and..." she hesitated, before continuing, looking at Clayton over the top of her soda can. "He told Troy he heard us the night before making love and that he cut himself each time he heard me...you know."

Clay's head swiveled quickly around to look at her. Uncertain he'd heard correctly, he asked her to repeat what she'd just said.

"He told Troy he cut himself when he heard us making love the night before."

"What the hell?" Clay fell silent, waiting for Casey to finish her story, although personally, he didn't need any further elaboration. The rest of her story faded as his mind worked over this new information.

"So, you know Troy sat there looking at Raul, trying to figure out if he was serious or not."

"And, was he?" Clay asked.

"At the time Troy thought so. But, then after Raul made that insane remark with such a serious face, he quickly laughed it off and told Troy he was only joking."

In the line of work he did Clay had learned a long time ago that sometimes you had to follow your gut instinct. When Casey finished her story and went to bed, Clay stayed awake into the wee hours of the morning, thinking. His gut was telling him this new information Casey revealed about Raul was probably the key to breaking this case.

Early the next morning Clayton arranged to meet with Detective Sloan. He had a difficult time getting him to buy into the plan he'd formulated late last night, however in the end the detective had agreed. He went over his plan again and again to ensure they had all the bases covered. He had to drive his point home so the detective could see what they'd been doing all week wasn't going to work. Every night this week Clay and Casey went into her apartment to give the illusion they were sleeping together, but Raul couldn't actually hear or see them. Clayton believed if they could actually give Raul a visual, some type of encounter to make him think he and Casey were having sex—or were about to—it just might push him over the edge.

When he was finally able to convince Detective Sloan to give his plan a try, Clayton came up with the concert series idea. It was public enough and held at night, and he knew from past experience from working this venue that everyone didn't come out just to hear the music. Sometimes couples retreated behind the cover of the large oak trees at these events, drank a bit too much and did some things they didn't remember doing the next morning. They both decided tonight would be the right time to put their plan into action.

Saturday night Vi was lying on the living room sofa staring at the television. Tony was sprawled on the floor along with J.R. playing a hand held video game and eating popcorn. Janae had decided to go out with friends, but promised to be home early. Vi reflected on the past week, thinking about how much had happened in such a short time. The fact that she and Janae were no longer at odds made her mother's heart leap for joy. That joy, however, was not as bright as it should have been because her mind was constantly on Clayton and the unknown danger he might be in. The fear of not knowing what was happening had begun to eat away at her. Every time the phone rang she jumped, and the few days she did go in to work were a total waste of time. She was so terribly distracted there that she always ended up leaving early. Thank God Nikki was there to handle things. Her frazzled nerves felt like a rubber band straining to hold something together and ready to pop at any minute.

The evening news came on and Vi watched the screen with little interest, closing her eyes when a commercial came on touting work-at-home riches. When the news returned, Vi's eyes fluttered open as a breaking news story caught her attention.

"Tonight's breaking news just in," the announcer's booming voice began. "Summer Jazz Fest concert goers were given a scare tonight, as police shot an armed man. The gunman and two Amityville police officers were injured, one person was fatally wounded. Witness accounts tell us the dispute involved a local woman, Casey Taylor, who was also taken to Brunswick Hospital and is listed in stable condition."

Casey Taylor? Alarmed, Vi threw her legs over the edge of the sofa, sitting up so quickly that she knocked over the popcorn bowl. She immediately grabbed the remote and began flicking through the channels to catch more details on the other news stations. Tony looked up from his hand-held game as his mom threw the remote down, picked up the cordless phone and rushed into the kitchen. He got up and followed her into the kitchen. Sensing something was wrong, J.R. was close on his heels. From the kitchen doorway, Tony watched her flip through the pad by the phone, find the Amityville Police Department's entry and punch in the number.

"Mom, what's wrong? Is everything alright?"

With the phone to her ear, Vi raised her hand, silently asking him to give her a minute. As it turned out he didn't have to wait that long. He and J.R. listened to her ask the person on the other end of the phone if Captain Jackson was there. In a panic, she ripped the page with Piterrelli's number on it from the pad and crumpled it nervously in her hands. After a second or two, Captain Jackson came on the line.

"Captain Jackson, this is Vi Simpson. I just heard Casey Taylor's name on the news. They said there were officers shot."

She paused, listening to what Captain Jackson had to say. Whatever he said didn't appease her because she literally shouted into the receiver. "I want to know if Clayton was involved. I know you know something. Please, please tell me. I need to know if he's hurt!" she pleaded. Tony heard Jackson's muffled voice on the other end of the phone line, and watched his mother pick up a pen and write down what the Captain was telling her.

"Yes, Brunswick Hospital. Is that all you can tell me?" Vi listened to his response and then hung up the phone. She ripped the page she'd just written on from the pad and turned to Tony and J.R.

"I've got to go out. Before you guys go to bed, leave a note for Janae to call my cell phone as soon as she gets home," Vi told Tony as she flew past the two boys and dashed down the hall.

"Where are you going Mom?" Tony called after her.

"Clay's been shot, they took him to Brunswick Hospital," she said as she slipped into her shoes and picked up her keys from the hall table.

J.R. and Tony said in unison, "We're going with you."

She stopped, looked at them and saw the determination in their young faces. "Okay," she told them. "J.R. put your sneakers back on and Tony, leave Janae that note...and hurry."

The music could still be heard in the distance as they sat on a blanket under the cover of a huge oak tree. The stars overhead let in filtered light through the heavy tree branches. They chose a secluded spot, atop a small rise and set several hundred yards from the crowd.

It was a picture-perfect, romantic setting, Clayton thought. Tonight was probably their best shot to catch this guy and if they didn't draw him out tonight, he acknowledged, they might never have another opportunity. Clay decided it was time they turned up the heat a notch with this little charade they had going. Pouring it on thick, he gathered Casey in his arms and captured her mouth in a very slow, very wet kiss. She warmed up to his tongue sliding in and out of her mouth and clutched at his lightweight sport shirt, bunching it in her fingers. They broke the kiss just long enough for her to pull the shirt he wore over his head. She discarded his cotton pullover shirt and turned her attention to his wide shoulders, running her slender fingers across his sculpted chest. Clay's hand tangled in her long, honey gold curls, holding her head to receive his avid kiss. Releasing Casey's hair, he caressed her neck and ran his hand down her shoulders. She wore a knee-length, floral summer skirt and gauzy peasant top that left her shoulders exposed. It was an ultra-feminine outfit and well suited for a hot, sultry night. His hand rested for a time at her waist, kneading the flesh exposed there, then slid over the rise of her hips and down her shapely legs. She clung to him as he deepened their kiss, as if the two of them could not get enough of one another. Getting into it, Casey let out a deep moan when his questing fingers slid up and under the hem of her skirt to boldly caress her thigh, as their tongues dueled in sensuous unison.

During all this, Clay's mind drifted to another night when he needed to pretend the women he was kissing was someone else. He remembered that night, so long ago, when he'd kissed Lisa Lopez, the friend Piterrelli's wife had set him up with. He remembered having to call on all the male instincts he possessed that night on how to pleasure a woman this way and, luckily, he did all the right things, made all the right moves. The blind date Pitt set him up with had absolutely no idea he was thinking about Vi the entire time he was kissing her. While Ms. Lopez wrapped her arms around him, Clay's mind was busy playing out how Vi's lips would taste, and pretending the arms surrounding him belonged to someone else. Not having actually experienced kissing Vi helped him that night to get through the motions. Of course, he had no way of knowing then just how sweet kissing Vi would be. Now that he knew, it was much, much harder to pretend.

Clayton tried desperately to call on those same male instincts now to make kissing Casey more believable, but it was no use.   Thoughts of Vi, her sweet, full bottom lip and the luscious softness of her breast cradled in his palm, almost made him push Casey away in distaste.   This time, when he kissed another woman, he knew exactly how Vi would respond to his touch and how she could simultaneously light an answering fire within him. The knowledge was bittersweet because he knew he would never kiss Vi again. He was certain she had no idea, but on some level Vi had come into his life and branded him as hers forever.   And, he was dead certain, no matter whom he met in the future, no other woman would be able to compare with her.

Raul watched from behind a tall arborvitae. His anger simmered and grew like a living thing, threatening to boil over. His fingers tightened around the gun concealed in his pocket when he saw that bastard's hand cover Casey's breast.   Spewing profanities in a violent whisper, he watched them groping one another and remembered another night when that slut had opened her legs for Troy. Not just once but three times, she'd given herself to Troy knowing he was in the next room!   Raul stepped out from behind the bushes just as Clay's hand disappeared under her skirt.   He moved toward them while they were caught up in the moment and too busy to see him approach.

"You filthy whore," Raul spit out as he loomed over them.   Casey and Clay broke apart breathless and shocked, and he knew the exact moment when the two of them finally noticed the gun in his hand. The alarm he saw in their eyes aroused Raul. It was always like this.   The threat of violence always excited him.

"Raul…don't do this," Casey pleaded.

Raul turned on her then, releasing all his rage and delusional grievances upon her. "Shut up, you bitch!" His voice took on a hysterically harsh tone as he shouted, "You make me do it, you slut. You made me kill Troy and the black guy too."   They witnessed Raul's eyes glaze over as he continued to berate Casey for betraying him.   "I tried to love you, but you're just a stinking whore," he shouted and aimed the gun at her chest.

As Raul stood over them, Clayton eyed him wearily, noting every movement he made, biding his time. However, when he aimed the gun at Casey, Clay rose with lightening speed.   Galvanized into action when he heard the trigger engage, Clay pushed Casey to the ground and threw himself at Raul. The gun went off and suddenly undercover cops swarmed from the trees beyond the clearing.   Several more shots were fired, reaching the concert-going crowd.

"A man's been shot," someone yelled out from the crowd farthest from the stage. For the space of a second everyone in the crowd sat staring at one another, then in the next instant, panic set in and people began running in all directions.

CHAPTER
THIRTY-NINE

The hospital emergency room was packed. There were so many people clogging the small waiting area that the less injured stood outside smoking cigarettes or talking. Impatient to get inside, Vi parked her car in a spot designated for doctors only. Only the threat of being towed by hospital security made her get back in the car and find another spot. The only spots left were far from the entrance. Having no other choice, she parked there, got out and made her way swiftly to the emergency room doors. Tony and J.R. had to run to keep up with her.

Vi burst through the doors and made her way to the in take desk. The woman behind the glass had short brown hair and wore thick, bifocal glasses and an air of indifference. Switching the phone she held near her left ear to her right, she glared with disapproval as Vi barged through the emergency room doors. Her already frowning countenance became even more pinched as she watched Vi make her way to the front desk where she sat.

Vi approached the woman and spoke to her through the thick glass divider. "Excuse me."

The nurse quickly held up her hand, indicating Vi had to wait, while she finished her conversation on the phone. Pasting a false smile on her face, she finally hung up the phone and turned her attention to Vi.

"A police officer was shot at the amphitheatre an hour ago. Is he here?" Vi asked, breathlessly.

Pushing her glasses up on the bridge of her nose, the in take nurse patiently asked, "And you are?"

In her present state of mind, Vi was suddenly glad a glass partition separated her from this woman. She knew enough to spot a difficult person when she ran up against one. Thinking fast, she blurted out. "I'm his wife."

The nurse looked down, studying the papers in front of her. After reviewing the in take sheets on her desk, she looked up again. Studying Vi closely, she adjusted her glasses on her nose again and said, "Please have a seat Ma'am. The doctor will be out shortly."

Vi eyed the nurse a moment longer, her gaze slamming into the challenging look she received from this woman. Deciding she wasn't going to get anything out of this nurse, Vi turned to Tony and J.R. and explained, "It looks like we'll have to wait for the doctor."

She put an arm around each of the boys as they stood on either side of her, and led them back down the short hall. It was still pretty crowded in the small sitting area, but they managed to find three seats together next to a man with a deep laceration on his forearm. He held a blood soaked towel to the open wound and stared off into space. Not sure what his story was, Vi sat down closest to him, putting herself between the injured man and the boys. Turned out it was an unnecessary protective measure because the whole time they sat there, the man never so much as looked their way.

While they sat waiting for the doctor, Vi pulled out her cell phone to check for any messages from Captain Jackson, Piterrelli or Janae. Seeing that no one had called, she put the cell phone away. About twenty minutes later, Janae and Clarence walked into the emergency room. To her chagrin, she saw Cynthia walk in directly behind them. Janae spotted Vi first and rushed over to her mother.

"Mom, is there any word? How bad was Clay hurt?"

"There's no word yet," she said returning her daughter's hug, and then reached for Clarence's outstretched hand.

Clarence squeezed her hand tight in reassurance, lending her the moral support she desperately needed right now and told Vi. "You hang in there Kiddo. Don't fret too much 'til we know we have to."

His words didn't do anything to alleviate the knots forming in her stomach. While Vi was glad he was here, she couldn't share in his bright philosophy right now. Not wanting to appear ungrateful, she issued a neutral response. "Thanks for being here, Clarence. I'm trying not to go insane, but we've been sitting here for what seems like forever," she said, indicating Tony and J.R. who were seated next to her.

Clarence hugged Tony and cuffed J.R. affectionately around the neck before turning back to Vi. "I can take these boys home with me if you want. There's no telling when you'll hear anything," he suggested.

Vi thought this was a good idea and quickly agreed until Tony stood up in protest. She gave her son a reassuring hug and tried to explain it didn't make sense for all of them to have to wait. He only agreed to leave after she promised to call the minute she heard anything.

Cynthia stood in the background. She didn't approach Vi until Clarence left with the boys and Janae went in search of coffee for her mother. She was silent so long Vi had forgotten she was even standing there. As Cynthia approached her, Vi sat down quietly, too distracted and too tired to be cordial. She watched Cynthia take the seat next to her, trying desperately to fortify herself against whatever her sister was about to say.

"Vi, I know we've been at odds for sometime. I just…I just want you to know I'm very sorry."

Vi experienced a moment's panic, and began to wonder frantically - *What was she sorry about? Was this about their disagreement or did she know something the doctors hadn't told anyone else yet?* Her next words mirrored her distress. "Is this about Clayton? Did you hear something more from the police?" she asked Cynthia in alarm.

Cynthia was quick to assure her she didn't have any more information than Clarence or Janae had given her. Cynthia took a deep breath, and tried again to clarify why she was here. "I'm here for you, if you need me, is all. I just felt so bad when Janae called me. Actually I've been feeling badly for quite a while, I just didn't know how to face you." Vi heard the tremor in Cynthia's voice when she made this confession.

On the drive to the hospital, Cynthia had a little time to think about what she would say to Vi. Afraid she might lose the courage to say what needed to be said now that Vi was in front of her, she let the words tumble from her lips. "Vi, I hate how things have been between us. I know I'm to blame and realize now how wrong I was. I'm sorry for sticking my nose where it didn't belong, thinking I had all the answers when I really didn't. I said some pretty terrible things to you Vi and I'm sorry. Very, very sorry."

Vi was speechless. The honesty and desperation she heard in Cynthia's voice was completely genuine. She had never seen Cynthia so shaken up, or for that matter, apologize for anything she said. While she was glad to have Cynthia here, it was a lot to process right now.

"Cynthia, can we talk about this later when…." Vi started to say.

Seeing her window of opportunity fading fast, Cynthia grabbed her sister's hand, speaking from the heart. "I know you're preoccupied with worry about Clayton's condition, but I knew I had to come here and say this before I lost my nerve. I came here to tell you I don't know everything. I thought I did, but as it turns out, I don't. Vi, I was wrong about you and Clay and a lot of things. I was jealous of how happy he seemed to make you."

Studying Cynthia closely, Vi got the distinct impression she was trying to tell her something more—more than how wrong she'd been for meddling.

"Cyn, are you alright? What's really going on?" Her assumption had been dead on, Vi realized, as she watched her sister's face crumple and she let out a wrenching sob, and swiped at the tears she'd been unable to hold back. Cynthia broke down completely. She'd been so awful to Vi in the past weeks, but here she was, showing concern for her at a time when so much was going wrong in her own life.

"Oh Vi, all this time I thought I had it all. The perfect marriage, perfect house, the perfect life."

Seeing how upset Cynthia was, Vi stood up and pulled Cynthia up with her and led her out of the waiting room area. They walked out the sliding glass doors and found a private spot a short distance away from the people milling outside.

Thankful for the distraction, Vi stood in front of Cynthia with worry written all over her face. She searched Cynthia's eyes, but when she didn't open up to her, Vi took the initiative and quietly asked her. "Cynthia, you're obviously upset, please tell me what's wrong."

"Ohmigod!" She said, on a shudder. "Vi,…I found out Tom's been having an affair." Seeing she'd managed to shock her sister, Cynthia didn't dare stop. She had to tell all of it, she had to tell someone. "I've been suspicious for a while. So, like a fool I started trying to be a better wife. You know, so he would stop seeing this other woman."

When she didn't continue, Vi had to ask, "So, did you confront him?"

For some reason, that question made Cynthia cry even harder. The anguish she witnessed on Cynthia's face was painful to watch. While uselessly drying her eyes for a second time, Cynthia looked at Vi and reluctantly told her everything. "I did… oh God, I did. He got so angry Vi. He told me he was trying to spare me and that I couldn't possibly compete."

This surprised Vi. She'd known Tom for many years, but she'd never known her brother-in-law to be cruel. Angry now, on her sister's behalf, Vi asked in disbelief. "Why would he say such a thing to you?"

"Because…be...because the person Tom's sleeping with is…is another …man," Cynthia cried.

Vi was stunned into silence, the only thing she could think to do was gather Cynthia in her arms. She sobbed quietly in her embrace, and Vi held her tight, not sure if the soothing words she spoke would ever be able to ease her sister's pain. It was quite a while before Cynthia was able to compose herself. But after a time, she looked at her sister with tear-stained, bleak eyes and appealed to Vi. "If…I mean…when Clay makes it through this, you two should be together. What the two of you share is very rare, don't let anyone ever take away your happiness again."

The sincerity in Cynthia's voice was touchingly humble. It struck a resonant cord in Vi, realizing her sister's admission spoke volumes of the pain she must be experiencing. Vi still couldn't actually believe her own ears, Cynthia apologizing, Cynthia so broke down was not the normal course of things. She thought about that as she hugged her sister tighter, silently letting her know she appreciated everything she'd just said.

Reflecting on how she'd conducted herself lately, Cynthia sighed heavily. She straightened up and pulled a dainty handkerchief from her pocket to dab at her eyes. "I've always envied you, you know? Your strength, your independence, and the way you've raised your children. You've been able to find a man to love you twice in your lifetime. I once thought I had that kind of love, but it turns out I never really did."

When Cynthia fell silent again, Vi hooked her by the arm and the two women walked back into the emergency room waiting area. They found two vacant seats in the corner. Vi put a reassuring arm around her sister's shoulder and sat back down to wait for the doctor.

The small waiting room started emptying out as patient after patient went in to receive treatment. After sitting for close to an hour, Vi got up and stalked back to the in take desk. She peered at the women through the glass divider. Her obvious distress over not getting any information for close to an hour came to a head, and when she spoke to the nurse, her anger swelled out of control.

"I demand to see the doctor right now."

The in-take nurse peered back at Vi through the thick glass window. Obviously used to being yelled at by obnoxious people, she quickly gave Vi a standard, but firm, reply. "The doctor is seeing other patients, Ma'am. He will be out shortly."

"But, you said that over an hour ago," Vi reminded her unnecessarily.

"Ma'am, please lower your voice. It is not necessary to yell at me."

Vi took a calming breath and immediately apologized.

"I'm sorry Miss, really. I didn't...." Just then a young intern appeared at her side. His green scrubs and white name tag identified him as Dr. Green. He smiled at Vi then quickly unhooked a pager that had been clipped to his side. After checking his messages, he looked at Vi again in inquiry.

"I'm Dr. Green. I understand you're here to see the officer shot earlier tonight."

"Yes doctor, I am. Please can I see him? Is he going to be okay?"

The doctor favored Vi with a friendly, bedside-manner smile, and then took her aside into a small alcove by the nurse's station. When they both stood in this private area, he looked her over curiously, before saying. "It's against hospital policy to share patient information with anyone except family members."

Way to go Vi! Silently berating herself for claiming to be Clay's wife earlier, her mind raced now for an explanation. She wasn't sure what she would do if they asked her for some type identification or proof, never mind the fact she couldn't possibly produce something she didn't have. Frantically searching her mind for something to say, she stammered, "I...umm..."

Dr. Green held up one hand, forestalling the potential lie she was about to tell him. He studied the woman standing in front of him. Whoever she was, she was obviously beside herself with worry. Not totally immune to her distress, he offered what little information he could. "I can tell you that the policeman brought in earlier had immediate surgery. He's out now and should be okay. But I can't let you see him," Dr. Green informed her, pinning Vi with a meaningful look. "You see, Officer Piterrelli's wife arrived hours ago, and she's been with her husband the entire time."

CHAPTER
FORTY

The prospect of being out of work for the next several days annoyed Clayton. Although he would have welcomed getting right back on the job, his boss and the doctor made sure that was not going to happen. Anxious to get out of this hospital, Clay lay on an extremely uncomfortable hospital bed thinking about the events of today and the past week. Casey was busy making plans to leave town. She'd been able to save up a little money and, thanks to Clayton, she would have a job when she moved to Florida. An old girlfriend of his that moved to Florida several years ago had opened up a trendy health food store. The success of the first shop had allowed her to open up two other locations. When Casey found out Clayton had managed to get her a job in one of the new stores, she had been thrilled. The job and the move would be good for her, and they'd discussed the possibility of it leading to assistant manager, if she did well.

For the past three hours he'd been poked and prodded, and now his patience was wearing thin. Besides Casey, the only other people he'd seen in the last few hours had been his nurse and Dr. Green. Clay smiled thinking about Casey's refusal to leave his side, even after he'd told her repeatedly to go home and get some sleep. He had to admit, though, working this undercover assignment had allowed him to get to know her better, and after spending so much time with her he could see now why Craig had cared about her. Besides her kind nature, Casey was funny and surprisingly, very smart. He liked her and had started to feel bad that she and Craig had lost their chance at happiness.

It made him think a lot about his own happiness and his life in general. Like her, Clay knew he had to get on with his life, but every which way he looked, he couldn't picture moving forward without Vi in it. She was on his mind every waking moment, as well as, constantly traipsing through his dreams at night. Listening to the monitors hooked up to him, silently reading his vital signs, Clay closed his eyes, recalling the last time he'd seen her. When he'd seen Vi at the market last week, all the hurt and rejection he'd experienced at her hands fell away in those few seconds, leaving him raw, vulnerable and so much in love that he momentarily forgot to breathe.

After seeing her, though, he couldn't seem to get a moment's peace. All last week at Casey's place, Clay had lain awake at night thinking about her. His sleepless nights left him a lot of time to think about a lot of things. He thought about Vi, his life without her and J.R. Before taking the undercover assignment, Clayton and J.R. had talked several times about his situation.

He'd finally gotten the boy to talk with social services about his problems at home, and the end result had been very promising. Apparently, there was a state law that allowed a kid his age to emancipate himself from his parents—with cause—and this, Clayton believed, might allow him to become J.R.'s temporary guardian. Discussing the possibility of temporary guardianship and assuring J.R. his parents would not be jailed for neglect, had seemed to put the boy at ease. While finding a solution to J.R.'s troubles had been fairly easy, unfortunately, the answer to the situation between himself and Vi still eluded him.

Thinking about the past week, Clay recalled a conversation he had with Casey one night while they sat watching a late night movie. Out of nowhere, she began to ask him about Craig's mom. Without thinking, Clay started talking about Vi and didn't stop until the movie had ended.

When he finished, Clay finally notice how closely she was watching him. Searching his eyes, Casey placed a hand lightly over his and spoke earnestly. "Clay, if you love her, go get her. Don't waste precious time like I did. I can't ever get the time I had with Craig back. If you want her as much as I think you do, don't let anything stand in your way."

"It's not that simple," he stated blandly, surprised that his feelings had been so transparent.

"It is that simple, if you want it to be," Casey replied, squeezing his hand for emphasize.

Casey's words came back to him now, as he waited for the doctor's return. The reality was a night like tonight, or any night on patrol, could be an officer's last. While he was thankful Piterrelli was going to pull through, he couldn't help feeling responsible for him getting shot in the first place. Clay didn't find out until it was too late that his friend had forced Sloan to let him tag along tonight. Feeling like he needed to be there to watch Clay's back, Pitt had shown up without Clay knowing about it until the very last minute. Thinking about how badly this assignment could have gone, he sent a silent prayer of thanks heavenward that Pitt would be okay.

Using the remote control, Clay adjusted the bed so he was able to sit up. He flicked channels on the TV overhead, but kept the volume down. For the umpteenth time he glanced at the doorway, impatient for the doctor's arrival. Lying here, he came to the conclusion that Casey had been right. He had to give this thing with Vi one more shot. He'd been through hell and back since they'd broken up. But, the other morning, when he saw her in the market, he'd felt a glimmer of hope. The way she looked at him that morning had mirrored all the pain and longing he'd endured over the past several weeks.

Casey walked back in the room just as a nurse strode in to check his vital signs. Stoically refusing to leave his side, Casey continued to sit by his hospital bed, even though she was clearly exhausted. While the nurse took his temperature, Casey took her seat by the window and went over the plans she had for herself and the baby. "I'm looking forward to making a fresh start, Clay. It'll be good for the baby and me. I only wish I didn't have to leave J.R."

"I don't want you worrying about that, I'll take good care of J.R. Besides, I think we've come up with a solution to his situation."

Smiling in relief, Casey squeezed his hand right before the doctor came in. Dr. Green examined him and went over Clay's x-ray results. He'd suffered a few cracked ribs, but luckily, no internal bleeding or serious injury. The doctor made a few notes on Clay's chart and suggested he stay overnight for observation. Clearly unprepared for Clayton's stubborn refusal, Dr. Green quickly pointed out the number of complications he could have by leaving the hospital in his condition. He listened to all the doctor's warnings, then promptly swung his legs over the side of the bed and informed the good doctor that he was leaving. Although the movement caused him pain, Clay sat up anyway and, against doctor's orders, asked for the papers to sign himself out.

Without assistance he got out of bed and slowly stood up, holding tight to the back end of his hospital gown for modesty's sake. Dr. Green and Casey were both talking to him at once, voicing their concerns over his decision when Clay calmly told them both he had no intention of staying overnight in anyone's hospital. Dr. Green gave him one last admonishing lecture. Seeing he wasn't getting anywhere, he finally gave up and left the room. Once the doctor left, Clayton turned to Casey and pointed a finger in her direction, twirling it in a wide arching circle. Confused at first by the long, suffering look he shot her way, it quickly dawned on her what that finger meant. She got up from her seat and silently turned around, so he could get dressed.

On her way to Clay's apartment, Vi silently thanked God in heaven at least a hundred times that he was going to be okay. Before she left the hospital, Dr. Green told her Clay signed himself out against doctor's orders. The doctor also told her Clayton was a very lucky man. Apparently after tackling the gunman, his only injuries consisted of a concussion and a few cracked ribs he received in the tousle. Piterrelli hadn't been so lucky, catching a bullet near his lung that required surgery. Shot by officers staking out the park, the gunman had been brought to the emergency room, dead on arrival.

Unaware that she was speeding, Vi took a curve way too fast. Forcing herself to slow down, she eased up on the gas and took a few deep breaths to calm her racing heartbeat. Earlier tonight she'd been so scared, not knowing if Clay was alive or dead. The agony she'd gone through tonight realizing she might have taken too long to tell him she loved him, and now, might never get the chance to tell him, had literally torn her apart. Although she wanted to be mad at him for leaving against doctor's orders, she couldn't. It was exactly what she would have expected. He was, after all, a very stubborn man. He was also strong and courageous and a host of other things that made her love him all the more. By the time she got to his place, Vi was an emotional wreck, thinking about what to say to him. Whatever it was, she hoped like hell it would be good enough to win him back.

She pulled into the parking lot, got out of her car and walked up to his front door. Now that she was here, all her insecurities returned as she stood on his threshold. *What if he rejected her?* Her mind screamed. *What If—no matter how hard she tried—he still didn't want her back.*

Although her brain commanded her feet to flee, her heart refused to give up without a fight. Standing her ground, she gathered her courage and knocked.

CHAPTER
FORTY-ONE

It was late when Clay got home. His ribs hurt like hell, even with the bandage wrapped around his mid-section that was intended to minimize the pain. He'd felt the excruciating pain as soon as he maneuvered himself out of his truck and made his way upstairs. He got on the elevator and leaned against one wall for support. Although the doctor had given him a prescription for pain, he didn't dare take it until he'd driven himself home.

When he opened his apartment door and walked in, he saw that everything was just as he'd left it. He kicked off his shoes and, very carefully, unbuttoned the loose shirt he'd worn home from the hospital. Throwing it on a nearby chair, Clay strode into the kitchen, barefoot and shirtless, to get a glass of water. The adrenaline rush inherent in dangerous situations was wearing off, leaving in its wake a bone-weary exhaustion now that the whole ordeal was over. Fishing in his pocket for the pain pills the doctor gave him, Clay felt the weight of the day crash in on him.

He was in the kitchen getting a glass of water when he heard a faint knock on the door. Popping the pain pill in his mouth, he swallowed some water to chase it down and went to answer it.

The insistent knocking grew louder as he walked toward the door, making Clay wonder who would be here this late. Deciding it must be one of the guys checking on him, he reached the door and opened it, totally unprepared for the person he found standing there.

He stood in the open doorway unable to do more than stare at Vi. It was as if thinking about her just now, had somehow conjured her up. Her presence began to do a number on him, instantly making his heart race out of control and rendering him speechless at the same time. Inwardly, he swore in frustration that his tongue would pick right now to go on vacation. Fortunate for him, his inability to speak had no affect on his vision. Standing this close to her, his eyes had a veritable feast, as they slowly drank in the sight of her.

Just as hungry for the sight of him, Vi didn't bother with words either. Her greedy eyes traveled over him as he stood all loose limbed in the doorway, clad in jeans and nothing else. When he placed one strong forearm against the door jam, her wandering eyes took in the bandage wrapped tight around his mid-section, noting how its stark whiteness was in direct contrast with his café mocha skin tone.

Vi cleared her throat when she realized she was staring, and slowly raised her eyes to meet his gaze head on. A deep scowl marred his familiar, handsome features and the anguish she saw there caused her a great deal of pain. Along with the hurt she saw reflected in his eyes, there was something else there that did give her a small glimmer of hope. It was banked low in the inky depths, but she saw it. Staring into his eyes, she recognized, if she'd looked away for a split second, she might have missed it. As he stared back at her, his gaze caressing her from head to toe, she glimpsed a magnitude of barely suppressed longing. It burned brightly for several brief moments then, just as quickly, the flicker was gone. Her own desperation and longing resurfaced, making it difficult to speak. When she did, her voice came out so weak that Vi hardly recognized it as her own.

"Clay, I'm so glad you're alright," she said, stalling for time. "I was so worried when I heard about the shooting."

"It was no big deal. Piterrelli was the one who got shot." His harsh tone of voice surprised Vi and she fell silent, feeling her insecurities escalate all over again.

Although his detached manner and clipped words left Vi momentarily speechless, she acknowledged on a subconscious level, just hearing it made her heart leap for joy. After being away from him for so long, the sound of it had an intoxicating effect on her. It also made it very hard to focus on what he was saying. She watched his lips move, realizing he was actually saying something, but darned if she knew what it was.

Get a grip! Her mind screamed. Clamping down on the drugging effect of his voice, Vi tried hard to concentrate on what he was saying. "...Oh, yes...I just left the hospital..." she said faintly. "They told me Officer Piterrelli is going to be fine."

The shock of seeing Vi on his doorstep floored him. Clay gave her an odd look and shifted his stance a little, trying to cover up the nervous tension creeping up his spine. Although he outwardly appeared calm and detached, inside he was anything but. He quickly found out that—her proximity alone presented a challenge. The urge to touch her was strong making it damn near impossible stand here and waste time, exchanging foolish small talk with her.

Instead, using all the willpower he possessed, Clay stood his ground and listened to her make idle chatter when all he wanted to do was yank her inside and.... He leaned one hand on the door frame and rammed the other into his pocket to keep from reaching for her. If she was here to say something, he was not going to make it easy. If he had to stand here all night and listen to her ramble on and on, he would do it. For the past several weeks he'd nearly gone out of his mind and knew deep down he couldn't put himself out there like that again. As much as he wanted her—and he definitely wanted her—Clay knew he couldn't go through that anguish again. She had to be the one to overcome all her hang-ups about the two of them, she had to realize the obstacles facing them didn't amount to anything.

Vi faltered, unsure how to say what she had planned to say. "Well, I just came by to see if you were alright." Nervously twisting her purse strap, she studied him, struggling with what to say next. His cool nonchalance fooled her at first, until she saw a small tell tale muscle bunch in his jaw and a flicker of heat in his eyes. Although brief, these little signs gave her courage.

Sensing his restraint, she silently acknowledged how badly she must have hurt him, realizing now, while her heartbreak had been voluntary, his had been just the opposite. She'd been the one to break it off, hardly giving him a chance to say anything.

This was killing her! Vi thought in frustration when it became obvious he wasn't going to make this easy for her and knowing she didn't deserve anything more than she was getting didn't make it any easier. His short answers and her inability to find the right words to get through to him frustrated her and before Vi knew what happened, she blurted angrily, "I can't believe you left the hospital. I mean, what if there were complications or something?"

Clay caught the spark of anger in her voice and was momentarily distracted. Immediately, he remembered how he used to love it when she got mad, and how much it turned him on. Unfortunately, today was no exception. Clay straightened to his full height, determined to ignore his body's treacherous reaction to her and ground out in a dismissive tone. "As you can see Vi, I'm fine. So…now that you've seen I'm okay, I guess we're done."

If the words he'd spoken were intended to hurt her, Vi thought, he'd succeeded.

Okay, she thought. He really wasn't going to make this easy. For one fleeting moment she thought about leaving, just forgetting about the whole thing. Frantically searching her mind, Vi knew deep down she couldn't just walk away. Straightening her spine, she asked tentatively. "Clay, may I come in for a moment… to talk?"

His eyes bore into her, and for several seconds she saw indecision flicker there before he took Vi's arm and pulled her inside. His hand shot out and quickly closed the door then pressed her back against the wall. Vi stood very close to him, basically toe to toe with the wall at her back, while Clay stared down at her. Then, suddenly realizing he still held onto her, Clay quickly released her arm and said, "Talk."

His one word command made her afraid to move, afraid to ask if they could sit down, but mostly it made her afraid he wouldn't give her enough time to say what she came here to say.   Struggling with the uncontrollable fear lodged in her throat, Vi finally found her voice. When she did speak, however, her voice came out in a near whisper. "I…I don't know quite how to say this."

She watched him place a hand on his hip and plant the other firmly against the wall, right above her shoulder and very close to her head. His penetrating gaze pinned her to the wall as he looked down at her and issued a husky command. "Just say it."

When she opened her mouth, and nothing came out, Vi took a calming breath and quickly decided on a different approach. Swallowing slowly, she started again. "I…I have this problem that I was hoping you could help me with."

Although the deep chocolate center of his eyes bore into her, Clay said nothing.

"You see, I have this friend, and she's made a terrible mistake," Vi continued, not sure if this tactic would work, but hoping to God it would. "And, you see, she's lost someone she loves very much because of it."

The intensity in his eyes pierced her heart and, when he spoke in a slow whisper, Vi felt hopeful. "So, what's the problem?" He asked in a husky voice.

"Well, she knows she's given up the best thing that's happened to her in a very, very long time…"

"Go on." His words gave her pause and Vi nervously licked her bottom lip with the tip of her tongue.

Clay caught the movement. Powerless, his eyes involuntarily watched her tiny pink tongue swipe over very wet lips and instantly, a wave of longing slammed into him like a sucker punch, making his gut clench painfully. Through the fog, he registered she was speaking again and, thankfully, hadn't noticed the turmoil afflicting him.

"The problem is… she's not sure how to tell him she was a fool… that she's so sorry and…." Vi trailed off and at this point in her story he noticed tears begin to pool in her eyes. A runaway tear spilled over her bottom lash and started a slow descent down her smooth cheek.   "And…that she wants him back. If…he'll take her back."

Vi's words hung in the air between them and the tense silence that followed nearly drove her insane.   As the silence dragged on, she slowly became convinced she had, indeed, waited too long. Evidently he'd gotten over her and that, unfortunately, was that.   Pushing lightly against his chest, she moved away from the wall and reached for the doorknob.

Moving with panther-like grace, Clay used the palm still resting against the wall near her head to grab her shoulder and plaster her back against that wall. Holding her breath, Vi watched him place his free hand on her hip and bring his face close to hers. With his warm, solid strength surrounding her, she stared up at him as he came even closer.

Filling her senses, his unique, robust scent enveloped her. After a very long day, the cologne still lingered on his body, smelling very masculine and incredibly sexy. Vi's heart beat a wild cadence against her ribs, as she watched his head slowly descend toward hers. His hot breath fanned her face and, as he leaned forward, Clay caught the tear sliding down her cheek with the tip of his tongue. His feather light touch initiated a serious meltdown, making it terribly hard to breath. She inhaled sharply and felt the air in her lungs get painfully trapped inside.

When she felt the air surrounding them heat up and begin a slow sizzle, Vi witnessed the look in his eyes, making it clear she wasn't alone. Her heart suddenly jumped for joy. They were both powerless, right now, to do more than simply stand there staring at one another. After an eternity, he finally spoke and the words he said were pure music to her ears. "I have two things to say. First off, I hope you realize you owe me big time for the hell you've put me through. Secondly, I'm not sure if you realize it or not, but you had me at—'Can I come in'?"

Too happy to speak, Vi smiled up at him and threw her arms around his neck. She held her breath as he moved a fraction of an inch and covered her mouth with his, kissing her strong and fierce, like a dying man. This meeting of lips was altogether hungry and giving, loving and healing and filled with a desire and longing, so deep, so strong it threatened to drown them both.

CHAPTER
FORTY-TWO

As his mouth laid claim to every inch of hers, Vi welcomed it eagerly. Returning the kiss, her head swam under the onslaught as his arms tightened and his persuasive tongue investigated the warm recesses of her mouth. Feeling like her whole life depended on never letting him go, Vi clung to him fiercely and heard him wince in pain. The sound was so faint, she almost missed it. When she suddenly realized her actions had caused him pain, however, she immediately let go. "Oh God...Baby. I'm so sorry. Did I hurt ...."

She didn't get any further before his lips descended on hers again, in a demanding, urgent and bone-melting kiss. Her lips trembled beneath his, making Clay feel weak and strong, all at the same time, as he got lost in her. In her arms again, he reveled in her sweetness and her softness and he poured all the lonely nights he'd spent into this moment. By his actions he tried to show her just how much he loved her, how much they both belonged together. Giving her everything he had, his heart swelled when his efforts were instantly rewarded. He was elated when her arms tightened around him and she became an active participant, kissing him strong and sure, and very much like a woman desperately in love.

The hands circling her waist slid lower and pulled her closer to him. Feeling the edge of her shirt brush against the back of his hands, Clay gave in to the temptation and reached under there. As his nimble fingertips slipped beneath the soft cotton, the feel of her supple flesh against his hands sent a wave of longing straight to his groin. He kissed her everywhere before grabbing the edge of it. Then, with lightening speed, he pulled it up and over her head, looking at her just as the shirt hit the floor. Blazing with desire, his eyes worshiped her and his throat worked around a strangled whisper. *"Oh God, I've missed you."*

He tugged at her bra, pushing the straps off her shoulders. Struggling with the inconvenience of the garment, Clay finally gave up trying to unfasten it and reached in to lift one soft mound from its lacy nest. The mangled condition of her bra only served to push her breast upward, its tip tight and exposed. Without hesitation, he ducked his head and took the erect bud between his lips.

The light swirl of his tongue started a sweet tingle from that pleasure point and branched out to all her extremities. Vi was just starting to warm up to the delightful play when his sucking turned seriously intense. Tugging at her sensitive flesh, he made her drag in a sharp breath as he drew her deeper into his mouth.   Arching against him in a silent plea, Vi simultaneously begged him to continue and threatened him not to stop.   A strangled moan escaped her throat when he suddenly released her to trail tiny kisses along her neck before recapturing her lips once more.

She felt his hands tighten at her waist as they journeyed lower, sliding past her hips and over the rise of her backside.   As he deepened the kiss, his palms spread over that soft expanse and lifted her, high up against him. Apparently, it wasn't enough so he raised her even higher and coaxed her legs around his waist.   Then, in a blatantly sexual move, Clay braced her back against the wall and planted himself with authority between her legs. Vi felt his arousal, hot and hard, where their bodies were pressed together so intimately.   Like wildfire, his need burned so hot against her it scorched through the thin material of the pants she wore, and she felt herself go up in flames.

Suddenly he released her mouth and they broke apart, breathing heavily and panting for dear life.   She watched his nostrils flare like a stallion scenting its mate as his heated gaze bore into hers, acknowledging it had to mirror the pulsing desire in her own.   She closed her eyes and tightened her hold around his neck. Bringing him back, she lifted her face and brought his lips back to hers.   Taking matters in her own hands, Vi assaulted his mouth, kissing him deeply using her tongue and teeth to gently nibble on his lower lip.

In response, his gut clenched painfully and an answering desire pooled into every part of his body.   Holding her close against him, her hips to his, Clay suddenly tightened his hold on her backside and pulled her back away from the wall.   Supporting her weight in the palm of his hands, he quickly spun around in one fluid motion and carried her swiftly down the hall toward his bedroom.

She twined her legs around his waist and held on tight, kissing him senseless all the way to his bed.   Unfortunately, the way she clung to him, her soft flesh pressed against his bare chest, was nearly his undoing. They'd just about made it to his bed when she ran the tip of her tongue inside his ear, and…

Sweet Jesus, Mary and Joseph!   Clay suddenly felt his knees give way. Fortunately, they made it to the bed, but it was a near thing. He fell with her to the mattress, quickly tumbling down together and taking all the weight of their fall.

Somewhere in the passionate storm, Vi heard him groan softly. Her eyes flew to his face and she caught the flash of pain there before he had time to hide it.   "Oh Baby, I'm sorry…"

He tried to stop her apology with another kiss, but she avoided his lips. Her soft, delicate voice beseeched him in the semi dark room. "I don't want to hurt you," she quietly whispered, moving beneath him. Then, before Clay knew what was happening, she slipped from beneath him, and deftly rolled with him until he lay flat on his back. Her next movement was a pleasant surprise, when he felt her wiggle and scoot over his legs, straddling his hips and settling into *his favorite position.*

Vi smiled down at him from her higher vantage point, and said very slowly, "Now...see...." As she drew out her words, he watched her reach behind and unclasp her bra then let it dangle before his eyes, before letting it fall to the floor. "Isn't this much better?" she said sweetly.

He couldn't argue with her there, this position did provide a great view of her luscious breasts right above him, within easy reach. No sooner had the thought entered his mind, Clay reached up to test the weight of each one in his palms. Then, slowly, he drew her down to take first one and then the other between his lips. He circled each peak, rolling the tender crest between his teeth and tongue in an action that held Vi on the brink.

Trying to hold herself up, inches away from the bandage around his torso, Vi was afraid of causing him further pain, and braced both her arms on either side of his shoulders. As she leaned over him, her entire body began to tremble in response to the tug and pull of his tongue on her and, when she could stand no more of his sweet torture, she leaned over him further and latched onto his lips in a fierce kiss. The time they'd spent apart from each other caught up with her and somehow she couldn't seem to get enough. She placed fiery kisses on his eyes, his nose, his strong jaw; then trailed tiny kisses down his neck and chin.

His large hands rested loosely at her hips. Content to let her set the pace, Clay submitted to her lips on him and lay back passively for the time being. But, when he felt her tongue taste the texture of his skin, tracing a wet path down his chest, he sucked in a sharp breath as she swirled it briefly over one very flat male aureole. His hands tightened at her waist as she nipped at him, sending a fierce excitement ripping through him. A strangled moan escaped his throat as his hands found their way into her hair, holding her mouth to the spot she worked on so feverishly. The hand tangled in her hair became anything but gentle, as she continued to work at her task, licking and laving his tiny nipple into a hardened pebble.

When Vi heard his tortured groan, she raised her head and met his gaze. The fire burning there empowered her to reach for his waistband, and very slowly she began to lower his zipper.

Clay watched her reach inside, wrap her gentle fingers around him and lift his straining manhood free. He felt himself lengthen and swell within her small hands, and he squeezed his eyes shut against the extreme pleasure as her cool fingers encircled him. She ran her hands up and down his length, stroking the smooth skin with featherlike strokes, tracing the tip with her finger and making his heartbeat quicken. As soon as he closed his eyes against this sweet torture, they immediately flew open again when she replaced her fingers with her eager mouth, stroking his length with her tongue. The hands in her hair tightened again, when he felt her hot mouth close over him, and Clay felt his control begin to snap completely. Grasping her waist, he let out a fierce growl and in one deft move, rolled Vi onto her back.

Vi's world spun wildly as his strong arms circled her waist and swiftly rolled her onto her back. She shrieked in surprise and began to protest as he landed on top of her and quickly covered her lips in a passionate kiss. With his mouth laying claim to hers he reached between their bodies and unzipped the pants she wore. Lifting away slightly, he hooked his fingers inside the waistband and she helped him slide them off. He gave an appreciative glance to the lace panties she wore, before he hooked a finger in the elastic waistband and tossed them over his shoulder to join her pants already on the floor. Then, without ceremony or delay, Clay settled between her thighs and covered her body completely.

Concerned with his rib injury, Vi began to protest again but quickly placed a gentle finger over her mouth to cut off her words. With his lips only inches away from hers, he ground out. "No, please don't say it. I've missed you and I need you. You...you feel like home baby and I feel like a man who's been away for far too long and...I'm not about to let a few busted ribs stop me from coming home."

With those words spoken, he sank into her with one powerful thrust, filling her and stretching her with glorious power. She was ready, taking all of him and relishing this thing between them that she had never thought to feel again. Every muscle in his body tensed as he bore down and felt her body expand and fit to him. Her throbbing response was instant, explosive as he drove into her and pulled out; then rushed back in like the tide. She gorged herself on him, having been hungry for so long and pulled his head down for a scorching kiss, pouring all her pain and loneliness into it.

Clay was engulfed so suddenly, experiencing a desire so great that he was having trouble breathing. When he felt her long, silky legs slid up his torso and wrap around his waist, he struggled for control. But, after so very long without her, he lost the battle and himself in her slick, hot depths.

Their coupling this time was so intense it burned out of control, threatening to consume them both. As he drove home again and again, she met him, taking all he had and giving back things he hadn't known he needed. The cold, empty place inside him was gone. In her arms she was able to banish it and make him feel whole in a way he'd never felt before.

They strained and flowed against one another as his thrusts brought her closer to the brink, making her cry out breathlessly. Sensing she was close his intense gaze bore into hers, willing Vi to open her eyes he quietly demanded, "Look at me." He'd made the same request every other time they'd made love before, needing to see her face at the moment of her release.

Under heavy lids Vi opened her eyes and looked up at him. She was almost there. He could tell by the way she dug her fingernails into his back as he quickened his strokes. This time, however, he needed to see more than desire in her eyes. This time he wanted much more.

"Tell me you love me." The command in his voice came out harsh with the tension of holding back his own release. Gritting his teeth, he held back, "Tell me, Vi."

"Clay…" her voice was no more than a whisper.

"Say it," he moved again, making her body shudder. "I need to hear it," he urged. "Vi —stay with me baby…say it."

"I love you," she whispered, almost too soft to hear.

"Again,"

"I love you."

"Again…."

"I love you."

They repeated the litany over and over as their pleasure mounted. Then it hit her. Reaching the top, she cried out his name on a strangled breath as her body came apart in an explosive climax.

Watching her peak was the most beautiful thing Clay had ever seen. Then, he could watch no more as the storm caught hold of him. Shutting his eyes tight against the feel her surrounding him, feeling his own eminent release was near, he had only a moment to think about how much he loved this woman right before his body stiffened and an enormous wave of pleasure slammed into him. That was the last coherent thought he able to manage right before he threw his head back, and his body erupted in a blinding release, as he spilled his essence deep within her. Bearing his weight with his arms, he collapsed on top of her as she continued to tighten around him, pulling every drop of his body possessed.

When they recovered, Clay placed a tender kiss on the tip of her nose and raised his head to look into her eyes. Her tousled hair and kiss-swollen lips beckoned him as he stared down at her, knowing without a doubt she was the most beautiful creature he'd ever seen. A slow, cocky smile curved his lips as grinned down at her and politely advised,

"I hope you realize, you're not leaving this bed until you've agreed to marry me, set a date for the wedding and promise to never leave me again." Although his voice carried a teasing note, Vi noted the look in his eyes was anything but. Unable to put into words how happy she felt at this very moment, she smiled up at him and said, "Okay."

Lifting one brow in confusion, Clay gave her a questioning look. "Okay? Okay to what—marrying me, setting the date, or never leaving me again?"

"All three!" Vi announced sweetly and turned in his arms, stretching with feline grace. She watched a huge grin spread across his handsome features as he planted a sound kiss on her lip's. When he released her mouth, though, she saw that he wore a serious expression again.

"What about your family? What are we going to do about them?"

"It seems they're okay with us. In any event, I'd already made my decision to come to you anyway." She gave his shoulder a playful punch, before explaining, "I just couldn't find you to tell you, because somebody had to foolishly go off on a dangerous undercover assignment and worry me half to death."

He smiled faintly, catching her meaning, then spoke again earnestly. "Vi, there's something I need to tell you."

The tone of his voice and his choice of words gave her pause. "What is it?" she asked anxiously.

"Well...about two months ago Janae came to my place and..."

Instantly relieved, Vi spoke up to put him out of his misery. "Clay, I know all about what Janae did. She and I talked about everything, including that dress she put on my Visa without permission."

It was Clay's turn to look relieved. "She told you about that night?" he asked, in disbelief.

"Yes, she did. Janae and I settled our differences when she came home. We had a lot of time to work things out sitting around waiting to get word about where you were. She helped me through all this and I think we have a better understanding now."

Then it was Vi's turn to ask him a question that had been troubling her. "Now...I have something I need to ask you."

"Ask me anything," he replied, as he lifted her hand and brought it to his lips.

"Do you…do you want children? I mean, I think I can still have a child, if we start…"

"Shhh…" he said, stopping her. "Vi, if you want to give me babies, I will be eternally grateful. But, if we don't have children, that's fine too. All I really want is you."

His words filled her with more joy then she thought was possible. "I love you Clayton Marshall. I was foolish not to tell you sooner, but I do love you with all my heart."

Kissing her deeply, he gathered her close and they talked for a while about how life would be for the two of them and their family. Naturally, their plans included Tony and Janae and, to Clay's surprise, J.R. The fact Vi was willing to include J.R. in their new family warmed him in ways that were hard to describe.

After a while they dozed for a short time. Playful when she woke up, Vi brushed a finger against him and he woke up made a soft growl then tossed her to her back. Covering her body with his, he looked down at her with amusement dancing in his eyes. "Okay, so now that we've settled all our family issues, I believe there's still one small item left that we need to clear up."

Vi looked up at him, catching the amusement dancing in his eyes.

"Oh, this sounds serious," she said in a teasing tone.

"Yes it is," he said, trying to keep a straight face. "Now, as I recall there's the small matter of how much hell you put me through in the past few weeks. I believe we need to talk about your punishment." As he said this, his lips brushed across hers in a bruising kiss, then trailed slowly down the slope of her soft shoulder.

"I can't believe your doling out punishment when I haven't even been arrested, handcuffed, or formally charged."

"Let's see, I believe I'm holding you in custody right now," he said nudging his hips meaningfully against her. "I also believe you know exactly what the charges are against you," he said with a suggestive hint in his eyes. "As for the handcuffs, I hadn't thought about using those, but that's not such a bad idea."

Trying not to laugh she played along with him and tried to buy herself some time. Very cautiously, she said, "Baby…maybe we can talk about this and discuss some type of arrangement. I mean, what if I did this…" she suggested and lifted her hands to either side of his face to bring his mouth down for a persuasively, hungry kiss.

With a wicked grin on his face, Clay broke the kiss and quickly positioned himself between her thighs, and before Vi could utter one word he twisted his hips and embedded himself deep inside her, before saying," don't think you can just waltz in here, jump my bones and think I'll forget to punish you."

She let out a breathless sigh as she felt him swell and surge within her. "Mmmmm…. I thought you law enforcement types were supposed to aide helpless women…not punish them. Whatever happened to your oath to— protect and serve?" Although her breathless inquiry was heavily laced with sweet innocence, Clay felt her two very experienced hands run feverishly over his torso.

Clay slid out of her slick passage in a torturously slow fashion and gave her an astonished look. "Woman, please! We both know you don't have a helpless bone in your body!"

"Even so, all women need to feel loved and protected," she said in a mockingly innocent tone.

Not missing a beat he placed a chaste kiss on the tip of her nose. Then he looked at her, suddenly serious again and spoke from the heart, "For the rest of my life I promise to always love and protect you."

His solemn words touched her heart, and just when she felt close to tears he smiled down on her, jumping back into their playful banter, "Okay…now that we have an understanding…I think its time to get back to our little unfinished business…" With a slow, sexy grin full of hidden meaning, he drew out his next words very carefully. "So…I'm still gonna' need you to lie still…and take your punishment," he whispered gently, right before capturing her lips in a tender kiss.